ADAM'S DIARY

Adam's Diary

KNUT FALDBAKKEN

Translated from the Norwegian
and with an Afterword by
Sverre Lyngstad

PETER OWEN · LONDON

ISBN 0 7206 0729 9

Translated from the Norwegian *Adams dagbok*

All Rights Reserved. No part of this publication
may be reproduced in any form or by any means
without the prior permission of the publishers.

Peter Owen Limited gratefully
acknowledge the assistance of the Arts
Council of Great Britain in the
publication of this book.

PETER OWEN PUBLISHERS
73 Kenway Road London SW5 0RE

First published in Great Britain 1989
Originally published as *Adams dagbok* © Gyldenal Norsk
Forlag A/S 1978
Translation © 1988 by the University of Nebraska Press

Printed in Great Britain by Billings of Worcester

CONTENTS

ACKNOWLEDGMENTS

The translator would like to
thank the following persons:
Michael Hurd and Eléonore
Zimmermann for reading the
entire manuscript and making
helpful suggestions on style;
my brother, Ingvar Lyngstad,
for advice on contemporary
Norwegian neologisms and
slang; and Knut Faldbakken
for the clarification of a few
special usages.

THE THIEF

1 I'm a thief. I live by stealing. It may sound brash, but it's true. Theft is quite a lucrative profession today, and not at all uncommon. There's less risk involved than you'd think. The percentage of crimes that get solved is small. Very few criminals are caught and sentenced. And thieves, especially petty, common thieves who only steal what they need to get by from day to day, hardly even count as criminals. They are a nuisance to the police, a bit of sand in the machinery of justice, a fluctuating statistic figured into the price lists of department stores and the rates of insurance companies. Thieves are an accepted thing. They don't scare anybody. Most people hardly know they exist, the way they hardly notice the rest of their fellow men. That's why it's so easy to decide to be a thief. Our society makes the thief's game an easy one. And so, thieves have become part of the community. We are not a group of outcasts, as so many believe. Our operations interlock with the complexity and vitality of social life. Most of us are very ordinary people. Some you wouldn't hesitate calling good solid citizens, even pillars of society. There's not much difference between an able thief and his surroundings, as long as the rules of the game are observed. And—like everywhere else in our society—these rules concern things like form and style.

What *thief* means to most people is probably the derelict who, sorely pressed, throws a stone through the plate-glass front of a gaudy shop-window and is caught with his head and shoulders inside, his hands buried in the floodlit abundance; but this is bad style, not theft. A thief is not violent but quiet. An able thief chooses to ply his trade where it's least noticed. An able thief works in such a way that you can hardly tell he's been there.

The thought of the derelict who's dragged away, lacerated and covered with blood, his fingers perhaps clenched in a convulsive grip around some article that stirred his fancy or greed among the displayed merchandise—a striped sweater, a transistor radio, a bottle of beer—evokes no less fear and disgust in me than it does, no doubt, in the gentleman sitting next to me in the streetcar with turned-up coat collar and an open newspaper. He's on his way to work, just like me. "How revolting!" we both think (I read, on the sly, the small item at the bottom of page 6 in his paper). "And there's more and more of it. What times we live in!" We need no words to communicate, we're in tune. We agree. He on the way to his job, I to mine. And the elegant young lady on the cross seat opposite us also seems to agree, judging by her remote, knowing smile, half-mournful that anybody can sink that low.

As for myself, what I find most shocking is the vulgarity, the lack of discipline, I almost said professional ethics, as I inspect the young lady's hands, fingers, and the ring that gleams at me the moment she opens the top buttons of her expensive coat (I have a sense for such things). It amuses me to appraise the stone, fifteen hundred kroner, maybe two thousand—I've gradually become good at this—no fortune, surely, but not bad for an ordinary day. And I reflect how simple it would be, losing myself in dreams for a moment . . . In Istanbul, the thieves' paradise, a street vendor could have slipped the ring off her slender finger while brushing her eyes with a peacock feather . . . My dream, Istanbul, with heat, crowds, narrow covered sidewalks, noise of people and animals: Istanbul, where I've never been.

Thieves are dreamers.

I look at the purse she holds on her lap. It's a soft bag without zipper or buckle; the tip of her wallet is visible, her checkbook exposed for all to see, and it amuses me to imagine how easy it would be, at a jam-packed stop during the morning rush hour . . . But, needless to say, I don't operate that way. I'm neither a pickpocket nor a purse snatcher. Instead, I concentrate on a necklace that peeps out from the opening of her low-cut blouse: a stone in a genuine setting, the chain made of interwoven threads, gleaming gold. How lovely! It goes with the ring. Altogether, it's worth at least six to eight thousand. She has fair skin, with a rosy tint. It's October and warm in the trolley, from so many people jammed together. But she appears cool. I ask myself how her bedroom looks. What articles of value may be lying around in it. There's more than one way of getting an address . . . But no. I seldom operate that way. Besides, she looks self-confident; her jewelry is certain to be insured, with the policy number engraved on it, perhaps. Too dangerous. I know my place. A woman like her is beyond my circuit. But I can sit in the streetcar on my way to work and watch the bright gold against her skin, dream, and steal a caress where the rhythmical undulation of the gold jewel betrays a beating heart.

A thief must have self-discipline; he must know his limitations or he'll overreach himself. But he can dream.

2 I haven't always been a thief—not in a systematic or deliberate way anyhow. And it's only recently that I've become what can be called a professional. Previously I had other occupations, very ordinary ones. I'm a very ordinary man. My story is quickly told. Jobs as a salesclerk after business school. Then office work. Finally bookkeeping with a large insurance company. Secure but underpaid; an ever so long wait between promotions. I'm married. That is, separated. After four years of marriage. The separation period will soon be over, and I expect the case will run its course without a hitch. In February the divorce should be a fact. Living alone suits me fine. Most people consider it unfortunate that a man has to move out of his home under such circumstances. To me it was a relief. Not that my life with *her* was particularly trying; we probably lived about the same as any other married couple, with ups and downs, sunshine and rain. But I still longed to go, a fact she couldn't understand. When I proposed we should part (it was obvious that we'd been mistaken in each other, had disappointed each other's expectations, did nothing to enrich each other's lives, and were less and less attracted to each other as time went on), she asked again and again in her hysterical way if there was "someone else." "What do you mean?" I asked. "Someone else," she said. "Another woman." She refused to believe I didn't want some other woman. That, on the contrary, after living with her at such close quarters for four years, I wanted *no one*. But apparently I failed to make her understand. She couldn't possibly believe me, she said. She cried. We were getting along so nicely. Though *she* was the one who always complained, about one thing or another, especially money and our not having children. I thought we could afford to wait. We wouldn't be "too old," as she put it, for quite a while yet. She was twenty-eight. The thought of children made me uneasy—I feared the commotion they would bring, the financial consequences, moving (our apartment would get too small), the uncertainty of the situation. I like to have an overview. I like to be in control. I wouldn't have minded moving as such (though it's true I was worried about the expense), I had never liked our apartment very much. On the other hand, I'm not the sort to make a fuss about details in my surroundings. No place can make me feel entirely happy or unhappy. I don't expect my surroundings to reflect my heart's desire. In all honesty, if my circumstances permitted me to arrange my existence the way I wanted, I would probably find it difficult to formulate any precise wishes. What do I really want? Wealth? Comfort? Career? No doubt, I'm like everybody else in that respect too—only, things like that seem so irrelevant, almost abstract, and to associate them with my own person and my ordinary life seems immodest. *I* wealthy? *I* at the top?

My doctor found I had a low level of ambition, said it was due to my negative attitude toward myself. Self-hatred. Neurotic fear of love, or god knows what. He spoke as if the separation was something I didn't really want. He talked a lot; it's his job, after all. There was nothing wrong with me, so I listened with half an ear. But the pills helped. I was able to sleep.

Incidentally, it was there, at the doctor's, that it happened—my becoming a thief, that is, a conscious and deliberate thief. A forgotten scarf in the waiting room: I noticed its lovely colors, the good quality (I've always had a sense for beautiful things as long as they are beyond my reach); I touched it, couldn't help myself—it felt like cool skin against my fingers. I stuffed it in my inside pocket. Of course it was madness, risky; there was nobody else in the waiting room. If the person who'd left it behind were to . . . But I was overcome by a burning desire I couldn't resist, the texture of the light scarf was so fine that no words can describe it: like a caress. The cold silk against my warm skin! Desire made me act quickly and surely, though as a rule I hesitate, embarrassed, afraid of being clumsy or doing the wrong thing. In the empty, depressing waiting room I felt the excitement contract my middle, burn my skin—yet I was in full control. Afterwards I hardly heard a word the doctor said, just sat feeling the little bundle under my jacket. I think he was talking about inhibitions, about surrogates for actual needs. He had had (against my will) a conference with my wife and proposed family therapy, perhaps the tangles could be unraveled if we both . . . ? It might possibly remedy my amputated ability to love (as he called it). But I hardly listened. I didn't want to be "consolidated." I didn't want to move back. My only problem (after he decided to start me on the pills) was that I sat there with a fervent longing to be alone with my desire.

I had stolen things before, of course, like everybody else, in stores, from my acquaintances, when opportunity offered and the chances of being detected were minimal. But this was something else, a suspense, a satisfaction so profound that it stayed with me for many days, long after the scarf had lost its power over my senses.

My spell of insomnia after the separation provided me with sick leave, first one month, then one more. I decided not to go back to my job with the insurance company. In a brief conversation with the section manager, I explained that I had other plans. It went off without complications of any sort. He accepted my resignation and gave me a so-called reference, faultlessly typed on the firm's best stationery. In reality, it merely confirmed that I'd worked there for the last four years without in any way distinguishing myself, either positively or negatively. Before I left, he wished me good luck. He couldn't know my decision had been made: that I would make theft my livelihood and had already started to learn the trade.

3 It seems I've forgotten to describe myself, but on reflection it strikes me as quite superfluous. I look like any other man in the morning streetcar on his way to work. Medium height; in my mid-thirties (I look a bit older); in slacks, jacket and tie (amazing how many wear a tie even these days!), poplin coat when it rains, checked, single-breasted winter coat when it's cold. A hat when needed. Umbrella, this time of year anyway. I said I was of medium height, it's not true; I'm a little under, but compensate by buying (or naturally stealing) shoes with slightly raised heels. A thief who operates the way I do must take care not to stand out. My briefcase is in place, of course. Where else should I deposit the day's catch or the bunch of false keys? The piece of hard plastic? A couple of books and a few papers to fake it in a pinch complete the picture. I'm a quite ordinary man on my way to work. The briefcase is a necessity, not a disguise.

I step off the trolley at Kirkeristen with ten or fifteen other people. Five or six tag along across Railway Square, down the stairs to the subway stop. How many of them are thieves? The thought amuses me as I take care not to hurry or lag behind the others. Moderately long, goal-conscious steps. As a rule, keep within the marked areas when crossing the street. If you pay attention to things like that you'll never stand out—never be recognized in case your portrait should be reproduced on the front pages of the afternoon papers (the big nightmare!).

I've chosen the Grorud train today. Already on the stairs I meet the stream of men and women it carries downtown to work every morning, leaving hundreds, even thousands, of empty dwellings in the city's residential sections and in satellite towns. Residences that are easy to find, where I can proceed to carry out *my* work.

Apartment houses are the best. Row houses are a bit too conspicuous, even if the financial situation of most row-house dwellers is such that both spouses are forced to work. I carefully avoid single-family houses. They're for amateurs and desperadoes. Alarm systems. Insurance on valuables. Uproar. I shun it all, though the profit *can* be tempting, of course. Two or three weeks' worth of ordinary takes in a single blow, perhaps more. But no—such exploits are not in my line. Best of all are apartment houses of three, maybe four floors with no elevator. There no one will notice if someone takes the stairs.

The procedure itself is the simplest imaginable. You step into an entrance hall, decide on a door after first listening for a moment (it's also helpful to check which mailboxes have been emptied, there you can be sure the owner is up at least and perhaps out; a newspaper on the doormat is another sure sign), and give a short ring on the doorbell when you're not sure (camouflaged by stamping or a cough in order not to alert the neighbors)—this way you can also spot those damn dogs that are becoming more and more common. If, unexpectedly, someone is home anyway and opens the door, you just politely inquire after some name or other, protectively raising the briefcase to demonstrate that you are a salesman or perhaps from the income tax bureau, apologize for the inconvenience, and leave. If experienced, you might venture to ask the names of others on the same stairway. That way you also usually learn if they're home . . .

But if the coast is clear, two or three minutes' work with the piece of plastic should do the trick. The thin, hard, yet flexible disk is easy to insert into the smallest crack in the door. Then, it takes just a little practice to ease and push the latch aside. If the crack is narrow or if the owner has installed a burglar-proof lock—they've begun to appear on the scene, though not as many as you'd expect, considering the number of thieves and thefts—you must fall back on the false keys; no lock is *completely* safe, though there's obviously a limit to how long you can stand at a door. Still, it's my experience that it gets progressively easier, not more difficult, to break into people's homes. I believe this is due to the fact that building methods and materials grow increasingly mediocre as pressure increases on the contractors to build more and more within a shorter period, while keeping the prices as low as possible. Another trend in the wrong direction: poorer housing in a wealthier country. There's also the fact that I've gradually become more capable, but that has mostly to do with things like selecting the correct apartments in the proper buildings, appraising the value of what I can take with me, and quickly locating items of value that may be stashed away; experience shows more in things like that than in the technical aspects of the break-in.

When the door of an apartment slowly glides open and it's quiet on the stairs, no voices or steps, perhaps just the soft hum of the nine or ten o'clock tunes from a kitchen radio on the floor above, then a thief is happy as can be. Not a sound in the abandoned apartment, which is so enticing, so full of promise that it seems the perfect product of his creative imagination, his dream. First enter quickly, closing the door noiselessly behind you. Then off with your shoes—steps can easily be heard on the lower floors, though most people nowadays put in wall-to-wall carpeting, thereby making the thief's work easier. The first few moments' exploration: What kind of home is this? What kind of people live here? How many? What occupation, or occupations, do they have? The entry already reveals a great deal, by its order or disorder, its display of hanging clothes, shoes. A quick search through all the pockets and on the telephone shelf. First of all for cash, naturally, the simplest, most direct, least risky thing—and the least personal. Money is absolutely neutral. There's never any trouble with it. And if the sums you take are relatively small (always leave *a little* in pocketbooks and wallets), nobody will suspect they've been the victim of a theft (I can almost hear their words, "Gosh, have I really spent that much . . . ?!").

As a rule it takes only minutes to locate the money people have put aside, hidden or forgotten. It's strange how similarly people think—or fail to think—when they have to choose a place for money or valuables. And I'm always amazed at how few possibilities there are for hiding something so well that a fairly experienced thief won't find it immediately. You ordinarily concentrate your search on two rooms, the kitchen (especially if it's apparent the owners of the apartment are elderly or middle-aged) and the bedroom. The living room is interesting only if it's evident that someone works there, if there is a writing desk or worktable in a corner, for example. But those who do some work at home tend to have their own workrooms, where the thief can reap treasure like ripe apples in an orchard; just imagine all those precious books! ("Where *did* I put that book?") Second-hand dealers don't care where a book came from or ask for a receipt. And if there is a safe or a strongbox in such a workroom or private office, which is often the case (chiefly to protect securities against fire, not theft!), you can bet it's open, or at least unlocked.

In practically every kitchen there is a shelf, a cupboard, or a drawer where letters, bills, tax deduction cards, and petty cash accumulate; perhaps it's also where the housekeeping money is kept, as well as the checkbook, along with warranties, money orders, receipts, maybe also the wife's rings that she takes off when doing the dishes—in other words, a gold mine for a thief. Forging a check is risky, but writing a check to yourself (naturally, after you've made sure there's enough money in the account to cover it) using a false name (I have half a dozen stolen IDs for such purposes—most photos on such cards are fairly good likenesses of me), and imitating the signature (which you can always find in a letter, a copy or some document, or in the passport, always conspicuously hidden in the drawer of the night table, the desk or the secretary, or in a pinch in one of the drawers of the wall unit, together with birth and marriage certificates, diplomas, and wedding pictures)—all this entails no great risk. Anyway, people don't check their bank statements. In the bedroom you find keys (those for all locked cabinets in the apartment included), money (forgotten in pockets and on the night table), and intimate items like jewelry.

Jewelry is a dangerous temptation for thieves. It's beautiful (thieves are aesthetes) and valuable, takes little space, and is easy to take along: condensed money. But it's not so easy to market, unless you're willing to take the risk of establishing contacts with professional receivers, something I want to avoid as long as possible. Still I get tempted, though never by the elegant, really expensive things; nor do I run into very many of those at the level where I prefer to operate. But if I see a nice ring, a wristwatch, a necklace, a pair of cuff links, I do occasionally get tempted. If you're experienced enough to appraise the risky elements, you really don't risk very much. The trouble with amateurs is that their patience runs out so quickly and that they take undue chances and commit the worst stupidities because they are scared. I'm often scared myself, but I keep my head and don't act rashly. Some time ago I even went back to an apartment to collect the reward for a wristwatch I'd stolen the week before (the owner made the most extravagant promises in his ad). In my haste I'd overlooked an inscription. It's sheer madness to try to sell an article of value with an inscription. I realized, of course, that the ad could be a trap or, more innocently, an invitation to the thief to return the merchandise against payment; but I'd picked up the watch from under a pair of black socks and a bow tie on the bathroom floor (Monday morning!) and assumed that the owner really thought he'd lost it. If you have your wits about you and keep your mind on what you're doing, it takes a lot to be fooled. If anything brings a thief down, it's his own weakness. True, I'm partial to jewelry, but I restrain myself. I stick to the simple, ordinary things—necklaces and bracelets in precious metals but conventional design; ornaments and clips with semiprecious stones that are so "in" at the moment; I may risk going for an amethyst, a small emerald, a brooch or a ring with little diamonds (which seem to have become popular presents at confirmations and weddings . . .) ranging in price from ca. five or six hundred to a couple of thousand. Never more than that. Never larger or more expensive. Such things are also easier to sell. A jeweler always listens sympathetically to the story about a deceased mother or aunt, an anniversary present you'd like to get rid of, and makes his bid. Which you don't always have to accept, making your inquiry appear even more genuine.

Other articles—more conventional stolen goods like radios, TVs, phonographs, cameras, cassettes, and so forth—I never touch. Once in a while, maybe, when I come across something brand-new and find the receipt (on the kitchen shelf or in the drawer of the writing desk), then go back to the store, return the things and get the money refunded, or at least the difference if they insist that the merchandise be exchanged. If the new purchase is something I have no use for, it can be pawned. But the store must be large enough to minimize the chance of being caught by a salesman with a good memory for faces. A couple of times I've actually been "recognized" and have engaged in a long, pleasant conversation with the salesman who sold "me" the item. Such things can happen when you don't stand out. For a thief to be successful he must be like the rest, at any rate in externals.

It takes fifteen or twenty minutes to half an hour to go through an apartment in this thorough fashion after you have some practice. The proceeds are often meager, of course, but to make up for it I can "do" two, three, maybe four apartments in a good day. It depends on the house and the neighborhood, all the external circumstances that come into play—quiet or noise in the hallway, the layout of the entrances, the chances of alerting a neighbor; now and then it takes no more than an hour to "cover" three to four apartments on the same stairway. The proceeds vary, but I seldom gross less than two or three hundred kroner per day. As a rule I do considerably better. Though I only work a four-day week (Fridays have become so uncertain, being taken as an "extra Saturday" by many; the few times I've gotten into trouble have always been on a Friday), the returns are still quite nice. I make a good living by what I do, no complaints.

4 With the doctor's help I got myself registered as occupationally handicapped. This means that I receive a small benefit while waiting for appropriate employment. I'm careful to consult the employment office from time to time and to show up where I've been assigned a job, but it's easy to use insomnia as an excuse after a week or two. Sometimes I even get it, along with a headache. And the doctor is full of understanding and puts me on sick leave again, though there's nothing wrong with me. I've pondered this, since I'm told some people have a hard time getting the benefits they're entitled to, that both doctors and employers ignore them and their troubles. Whereas I was practically forced into my present situation. (Thus, it was *she* who put me up to taking medical advice during the last period we lived together, when I was unable to sleep; I'd never done anything like that myself . . .) And now the doctor is willing and ready to honor my slightest complaint with a prescription or a medical certificate. I've concluded it must be due to my manner: I'm never pushy. I never ask anything for myself. I'm modest. I give the impression, I believe, that I can straighten out my own problems without bothering other people. I never complain. And this, I think, creates a good impression, makes people want to help me, even in situations where it would never occur to me to ask for help. To be reserved, polite, and considerate is also a way of gaining control, a method of achieving what you want, often at the expense of others.

When the loot (I always call it "the goods") has been safely put away in my briefcase, and drawers and shelves have been carefully tidied, lamps put out (or left lighted if they were when I came), doors closed or left partially open as when I came, I sometimes sit down for a few minutes in a good chair or on a sofa. At such times, when the technical part of the theft is over, I'm able to give myself up to the intoxicating sense of power, of total control, that a thief feels in the empty apartment he's taken possession of. In such moments I can get caught up in an excitement that's purely sensual; the intimacy of the situation is overwhelming. During the preceding half hour I've scrutinized the apartment for "goods," things to steal, valuables or money. My power of concentration has been focused on this, my senses have been sharpened, my imagination strained to the utmost in the search for hiding places and in dreaming up safe ways of selling what I find. But now, when the business aspect is over (I have to live from this, after all!), my attention is drawn to entirely different things. Cool, professional observation gives way to a new experience of the atmosphere in the apartment, and my imagination begins to ask questions about the kind of people who live there. What do they do? How do they look? The latter is quickly answered, thanks to the many photographs people frame and display everywhere. You can get a good general idea of the occupants' family situation in this way. And if you have the time and the nerves for it, you can amuse yourself by comparing the impression received from the photographs with the climate that otherwise prevails in the apartment. Photographs always lie (all my six stolen IDs look like me!); besides they were always taken some time back, maybe years ago. What has time done to the people in the photographs? What connection is there between a face, a half- or full-length portrait in a frame on the TV set, and the articles of clothing lying around in the bedroom? The handwriting on an envelope? The comb on the night table? The assortment of cold cuts in the refrigerator? (Incidentally, I sometimes help myself to a thing or two from a well-stocked freezer, wrap it in a newspaper, and put the whole thing in the shopping bag from Oluf Lorentzen's I always carry with me; a theft from a freezer won't be discovered for months, if ever. People in today's society haven't the foggiest notion what they own, certainly not what they have in the freezer.)

In this way the occupants' innermost being is laid bare to the thief, who treats it as his needs and his temperament, his knowledge and his experience dictate. Nothing shocks me more than to hear about thieves who wrecked a house or an apartment they visited, or even simply wreaked havoc perhaps, without taking anything. Such things are outrageous! You can read the most awful stories—orgies, excrement, filth . . . It's enough to make you blush with shame! Though it probably springs from exactly the same kind of longing and sensitivity that compels me to touch the objects these people, now at the mercy of my desires and whims, surround themselves with. And I admit it without shame: occasionally I've masturbated into the sink or a washbasin when my longing and tenderness have become too overwhelming, my delight at the intoxicating power I've acquired over these people who, while not here, have nonetheless left their essence behind so I can touch it, feel close to it. When an emotion I can only call my "love" for them surges up in me so strongly that it's impossible to resist, so distracting that my face would betray it if I were to meet someone in the corridor or on the stairs. Nicely attuned colors in the bedroom, a couple of stockings lying around on the shaggy white rug before the bed, the soft texture of the bath towel—this may be all it takes. A few loose hairs in a hairbrush, or a rolled-up handkerchief between two sofa cushions, can set my "love" throbbing! A thief must see and touch everything, he's tactile and visual. When something catches his eye, he cannot resist his desire to touch it, have it, and own it. To the thief, objects are at the center of life. If he owns them he has conquered the world, people, love. For things give away their secrets more directly and truthfully than a human being gives away his. And the secrets of objects deal with people.

An apartment is about the people who live there. I know immediately what relationship I'll have to them: sympathetic or disdainful, patronizing, timid, or perhaps even humble. Good, expensive taste instills respect, while the cheap mass-produced articles that are mostly seen on my circuit give away those who've surrounded their lives with them. Strangely enough, though, in the homes of people who always choose the inexpensive, modern, practical and simple solution, you're apt to find money, even large sums, scattered about in pockets, drawers, purses, and on the telephone shelf. You'd think that people with money to throw around would use it to brighten up their surroundings with suitable things, nice and solid. But no. The mail-order catalogs rule supreme and the whims of fashion determine their selections: kitchens and bathrooms with tawdry tile panels, bits of rug in modern patterns and textures (synthetic material), wall units (with locks and fittings of stamped brass) filled with cheap ceramics and souvenirs from package tours to southern Europe (daggers, dolls, bottles in odd forms and shapes that once contained an ordinary red wine). Almost no books, except for reference works (unopened) and series in identical bindings (reluctantly purchased from the traveling salesman of a large publisher at a special price). In the place of honor a lamp with multicolored blinking lights, perhaps. Then, next to it, the framed photographs: the people living in these surroundings as they wish to see themselves, successful and contented. Things like that put the thief in a strange mood. The connection between the evidence of helter-skelter, insecurity, poor sense of economy and bad taste betrayed by the apartment, and the pride and longing in the faces within those frames, makes the thief soft-hearted. "That's the way they are," he thinks. "Look, how they expose themselves!" "How much I know about you!" he tells the pictures of men and women, youths and children in their Sunday best, well-groomed and with freshly cut hair, and happy, yes, happy (though

I, the thief, know how little they really have to be happy about). They look self-satisfied and expectant in their poverty (perhaps expensive poverty, but poverty nonetheless). Who can help being touched by such a contrast? By people who give themselves away so artlessly?

You're tempted for a moment to reappraise everything—the interior, the objects, the personal belongings—in the light of their obvious pride and contentment. "It's not their fault, after all," I think out loud as I turn on the light in the liquor cabinet, perhaps, its nearly empty shelves gleaming in the middle of the wall unit. Red fluorescent lights may betoken a love of beauty and a longing for happiness just as truly and effectively as period furniture and original art.

In any case, I'm most at ease precisely where I feel a bit superior and can bask in my patronizing benevolence toward those I thus engage in silent conversation. With the well-to-do it's different. When I run across expensive, solid luxury—the uninhibited appetite for exclusiveness in everything that characterizes wealth, from doormats to bathroom fixtures—I become insecure. I feel that my own flair, my own good taste, falls short. A wealthy home immediately gives me the impression that there are many things in it whose value even I, a thief, don't know how to assess, that what really means something, the style, the culture, the very atmosphere, cannot be caught, taken away, or sold. This makes me restless and frustrated; in apartments like that I sometimes steal articles I know I can sell only for a fraction of their value and even then, possibly, at a certain risk. I do it out of spite, as if wanting to attain the unattainable, the *class* that would still characterize these places even if I removed *everything* from them . . . But it would be a pure accident if I found myself in a wealthy home, and fortunately it doesn't happen very often. I don't seek them out, quite the contrary. There's obviously a good chance of profit for the person who steals from the rich, but always a greater risk as well. For example, you hardly ever find money left where it's easy to spot. Bankbooks, yes. And keys to safe-deposit boxes. But no cash. For the rich take good care of their money. There are plenty of articles of value, but they're dangerous to sell. Art, for example, requires quite special connections. And how do you transport art in a modest briefcase? Besides, you have to assume that the police will be informed of the theft. The wealthy know exactly what they own. It's different with the newly rich and those who aren't rich at all, those who work the hardest, thinking prosperity means abundance and waste.

No, on the whole I stick to my own level, with people for whom I can make allowances and therefore also have some real sympathy for. It's the safest way. There I am in control. They hardly notice I've been visiting. I seem to hear them: "Where was it I put this or that . . . ? Who has mislaid this or that . . . ?"

Such things warm my heart. It's almost tempting to go back and tell them: "It was me, here I am—the thing you're looking for, there it is!" But this is obviously nonsense. I establish contact with people through the things, a better, truer contact than I would have meeting them face to face, less tiresome and binding. That has always been my experience.

5 Usually I have lunch in the restaurant Bel Ami, a quite reasonable but nondescript place near Majorstua. It's far enough removed from my most common hunting grounds and about the right distance from the section where I live (Skøyen, in a fairly old five-story apartment house—ideal as far as that goes, if I didn't live there myself—two rooms and kitchen acquired through the company I used to work for). I lay stress on this—the importance of maintaining certain steady habits, producing an impression of solidity outwardly as well as inwardly— but at the same time I must take care to limit my regular comings and goings to places where there's a minimum of probability that people I meet elsewhere will see me and recognize me; I have in mind those I meet in the morning trolley and on my scouting rounds, neighbors in the apartment house, and so on.

It suits me to lead a double life in this manner, a multiple life, you could say. To the neighbors I'm only a quiet single man who goes to work every morning and returns home at the usual time every afternoon. To my rush-hour colleagues (if they notice me at all) I'm one of many who change from the trolley to the subway at Kirkeristen, assumed to be working in the commercial-industrial sections at Økern or Alnabru. And to the waitresses at Bel Ami and the three or four regular clients I see there nearly every day, I am an official, a salesman, or a clerical worker with a steady job in the bustle around Kirkeveien/Bogstadveien, a faceless person who drops in for lunch around one o'clock.

visiting. I seem to hear them: "Where was it I put this or that . . . ? Who has mislaid this or that . . . ?"

I would obviously choose a better restaurant than Bel Ami if I were free to (I can certainly afford it). It's one of those newly opened restaurants with insufficient space and poor lighting, a fake, "atmosphere-creating" interior and inane canned music. God knows how long it will stay in business, most likely only till the owner finds a more promising opportunity to invest his money elsewhere and sells the premises to the express dry-cleaning firm next door, or to an importer of fashionable clothes who'll soon open yet another boutique. But it's precisely its semivulgar anonymity, its lack of tradition, the impression it gives of being unreal and temporary, that I find attractive about Bel Ami. This atmosphere also rubs off on the customers, who look unsettled, stereotyped and faceless—exactly the kind of surroundings and climate where a thief feels safe.

At the end of the working day, with a more or less favorable outcome in my briefcase, it feels good to step into the dim interior of the restaurant, take a seat at one of the tables (against the wall, as far as possible from the window), order a filet of fried flounder with rémoulade, a paprika schnitzel *garni,* or the day's special, which usually consists of bouillon cube broth and meat stew (goulash, dark hash, Indonesian pot) with ice cream or fruit compote for dessert, and let my fork play with the checked pattern of the tablecloth while my order is being filled. While I wait for *her* to bring me the food.

It never takes long at Bel Ami. The place is small and run in such a way that you eat and leave; everything, including the menu, is geared to a quick turnover: the courses are based on precooked items, deep-frozen delicacies, with french fries as the only really fresh ingredient (if you disregard the frying oil, which carries the taste of yesterday's dinner over to next day's specials).

She serves me with a friendly, "Here you are, hope y'enjoy it." I nod for thanks; I always do enjoy it. I've never been particular about food.

There are only two waitresses and I have, without really meaning to, established a kind of contact with one of them. I guess it's just the sort of contact you always make with the personnel in places you often go to, but I must admit that the smile she gives me across the checked tablecloth as she asks if I want anything else seems both sincere and pleasant. She's quick, efficient, with brisk movements and a trim figure (I despise overweight people, especially young ones who let their bodies deteriorate . . .). She wears the uniform of Bel Ami: blouse, short skirt, a broad belt over a mini-apron, without personal ornaments of any kind, no rings, necklaces or bracelets. Not even a watch. Nothing that can tell me something about her, which naturally makes me curious. Quite apart from the fact that I notice I've stayed away from women too long. There's been only one since the separation, a dismally unsuccessful pickup from an equally dismal nightclub. It happened during a spell of insomnia when I'd walk around aimlessly in the evenings—this much by way of excuse. Anyway, I discovered I couldn't do anything when I had to pay for it. Compensate with cash for what I'd "taken." I'd always thought till then it must be simple with a prostitute. No courting, no lies or pretenses: give and take. But it didn't turn out that way. The thought that one kind of product was equal in value to another in such matters also nearly paralyzed me. The fact that she could turn what we did into money, almost like a taximeter—an extra hundred for this, two hundred for that—made *me* a victim, gave *her* the control. Even so, the performance didn't come off as quickly as I'd hoped, the glands brooked no denial, and she labored a long, dreary hour to get it "hearty," as she put it (that kind of exercise also had its established tariff). And when her tricks were still unsuccessful, she didn't storm out the door with her meager profit as I'd gradually begun to hope, humiliated as I was. Oh no, she offered to come see me again! I mustn't take it too hard, she said. She knew many with such problems.

Problems! The problem was that her bold language, her deliberately businesslike attitude, her immunity to my obscure ideas of "conquest" hindered me from functioning naturally. It was as if my helpless advances got tacked on a diagram for exact reading and evaluation!

Yet, afterwards, there she stood, a package of cool programmed sex, claiming that she liked me because I was "nice" and "considerate." I know I give women this impression now and then, and I ask myself why. Is it perhaps simply because I'm a bit reserved, refuse to let them get close to me? At least at first . . . ?

Today "Consommé," "Chicken Marengo," and "Peach Melba" are on the menu. The fine names cannot camouflage the mediocre preparation. Second-rate ingredients. Haste. Greed. But it's all right. I like the food, and there's no reason to drag out the meal longer than it takes to put it away. Bel Ami isn't a place where you sit and relax. That's precisely one of the reasons why I like to eat there. The chances of personal contact with other clients are small, and the tawdry yet pretentious vulgarity of the place gives me a satisfying feeling of superiority, of not "really" belonging. Which again warms my heart with a sort of sympathy. Like now, when I see her bringing my "Chicken Marengo," a bottle of beer and a glass on a tray, dressed in her blouse, short skirt and broad belt—an outfit which doesn't really suit her, which appears affectedly youthful and makes her anonymous and perhaps a trifle cheap, though she's probably quite the opposite: I'm filled with a kind of tenderness for her as she bends forward to place the food on the table, pours half a glass of beer and asks, smiling, if I would like anything else. Thank you, no, everything's fine, and she leaves, while I'm slowly realizing that what I really want right then is for her to just stand there and watch me eating. And suddenly—what a strange day—there she is beside me again, asking with a smile if I'd please pay right away because she's through for the day. And so we reach the exit the same moment, after I've finished, and after she no doubt has had her serving in the back room, her plate on her knees and her back against a curtain of coats the personnel have left on the hooks by the telephone shelf.

At first I can't place her, of course, and just open the door automatically, but when she smiles in return I see who she is, and I can tell she must be my own age, if not older, married most likely, with a child or two, and with fairly good, slightly eccentric taste and limited means (molded shoes, worn gloves, poplin coat of good quality but spotted, a batik scarf around her neck, a bright-colored crocheted cap on her head, glasses—which she never uses on the job—a pin with a green emblem and a brief motto on her coat collar).

"Hi," she says on the sidewalk as I'm digesting all this information in silence. "Going that way?" She nods in the direction I'm about to go, so it would be too silly to say no and turn around. We walk side by side in a silent, half-hearted way, each movement betraying so much embarrassment that I feel the situation might blow up and fall apart any moment. Though, actually, the embarrassment seems to be all mine. A quick sideways glance reveals that she's smiling contentedly to herself, humming a snatch of song, in fact.

"I kind of like the fall, you know," she exclaims when a gust of wind sprinkles a handful of leaves over us. "It's sad to see everything die, but then things become clearer; summer is too damn lush, gives you all kinds of ideas . . ."

I manage an answer of sorts; needless to say, I can talk normally with people who address me, but as a rule I avoid engaging in casual conversation. What's the point of exchanging a few platitudes and then goodbye? To me, too, fall seems the best season. Fall makes people turn a bit inward, reflect, take a breather after their summer excesses. People live regularly in the fall, as if afraid to challenge fate and winter after the provocations and frivolity of summer. Rain gives relief. Sleet and then snow seal off everything, cover it up. People are full of good intentions, work harder (come home unexpectedly in the middle of the day less often!), borrow money they haven't been able to save, and buy things they've wanted—most people can't bear to wait till Christmas, as if the purchase of new clothes, furniture, or equipment for the house were an act of exorcism against the menace of darkness and cold, a deeply engrained ritual for holding on to the abundance of summer, for filling the silence of winter . . .

Yes, fall is good. Spring is worse with the many absurd hopes it inspires, with all its mildness and light to no purpose. And in the summer the thief must watch out, or else he'll run amuck just as nature does when proportion is left behind, when gifts are heaped on top of gifts, exaggeration on exaggeration. Fall is the season for thieves.

But I can't say this to the woman walking beside me, almost taller than I despite her "sensible" shoes and my built-up heels. Instead I comment on the weather, making her laugh. What a gift for laughter she must have, being able to laugh at a little remark about the weather! "It's not so bad when you have a place to go," she smiles. Then she suddenly doesn't smile anymore, as if the thought of the place where she lives made her uneasy. "Where do you work?" she asks, somewhat hurriedly, as if interrupting a train of thought. I make a vague gesture toward Sørkedalsveien. We stand at the crowded corner of Kirkeveien/Valkyriegaten. I dimly hope that my indefinite but forever binding indication of place will be shattered, annihilated in the noisy afternoon confusion of traffic directions, but she has caught it, holds on to it:

"That building over there?" She's making a special effort, really trying to make contact.

I nod; I've let myself in for it now!

"In the publishing house?" With enthusiasm.

Another nod. I know it's dangerous, yet notice that this bit of information impresses her, as if working for a publisher were something special. And I'm pleased at her being impressed. I have walked a few hundred feet down the sidewalk with her one busy afternoon and she's already attacking my anonymity, its essential quality—the very *will* to remain anonymous!

"What's your name?" she asks, but seems to realize at once that the question makes me confused and ill at ease, so she interrupts: "No, that's really none of my business! A person should hang on to his name, if he wants to. I don't give my name to strangers either, not right away anyhow." A light touch on my arm as if to soothe a potential runaway, one moment, no more, but it gives me a strange desire to reciprocate.

"I call you Bel Ami," I say. "Just for fun, to myself. Since you work there . . ."

Laughter once more; how she laughs!

"Then it has to be Belle Amie," she says, "with two *e*'s in French. Or else I'd be a man, a kind of comrade. And that couldn't be what you meant?"

And again she laughs, to spare me mumbling my embarrassed answer.

6 Back in my apartment in the house directly across from the Thune trolley stop (up a narrow, bumpy little street under the birch trees, now sticky with dead leaves underfoot, the third row of apartment houses to the left), I think about this business with the name, that she respected my reluctance to tell her my name, that she didn't try to force herself on me by revealing her own name . . . In the midst of the uneasiness this incident has brought on, the thought of this business with the name gives me a strange sense of security. As if in some curious way she were in agreement, almost an accomplice . . .

I'm sitting, as usual, at the kitchen table surveying the day's catch, which is well above average. No reason for complaint: over three hundred kroner in pure cash, a brand-new portable radio (I found the receipt!), two old Ibsen editions (stashed away in a secretary among warranties and insurance policies), a genuine cameo (from the same place), a shirt (unopened), a heavy silk tie and a bottle of aftershave lotion for myself—I know what I want, I'm well dressed and well groomed, if I do say so myself, though not in any conspicuous or sensational way.

The radio will be an easy job. The receipt is from one of the many discount stores that are popping up like mushrooms these days. Nobody can make personal contacts in such places. Small risk of being recognized—that is, *not* being recognized. A jeweler will be glad to take the cameo. The old fashion still holds its own with some people, a nostalgia for the days before plastic, traffic jams, and TV became universal, though nobody can imagine life without them . . .

But "the goods" can't occupy me very long tonight. For the first time in several weeks I'm thinking of my wife. She is my wife still, though by February it will be over. As far as I know, it's over for her already; she told me straight out she had a friend last time we met. She said she hoped I wouldn't use it to complicate the winding-up of the divorce (neither of us is interested in assuming the expense and the humiliation of a divorce suit). As far as she knew, she said, I was just as determined to get it over with as she was. And abstinence during the separation period was a fiction, as everybody knew. If it were to serve any purpose at all, it must be to force unwilling separated couples into each other's arms again through sheer need; as a matter of fact, that seemed to be what society was interested in.

I said yes, that I agreed, in a tone I hoped would convey that I, too, had "made arrangements" (though I still had the humiliating experience with my nightclub friend fresh in mind and shuddered at the thought of it). I wasn't really surprised by her radical statement, or by the forthright way she handled her privations. It agreed well with her abrupt, impulsive and rather selfish character, which I haven't missed a single day during these several months' absence.

Still, I'm now thinking about her, and I realize why of course: Bel Ami, her pressure on my arm, her laughter (though her face isn't really carefree but rather pensive, full of problems), her tact, her sympathetic "complicity," which gives her the edge on me, appeals to me, though her openness also has a meddlesome and aggressive streak I know I ought to avoid. That I let myself unawares be trapped into disclosing my "place of work" was a slip-up, no, worse: a grave mistake. The logical conclusion to such an incident would be to avoid all further association with her, find another restaurant, stay away for a few weeks anyway. And during the afternoon I've played with such thoughts. But, on the other hand, why dramatize the situation? As a matter of fact, I *did* work in that publishing house for four weeks before the vacation, substituting as a stock clerk, a position I was offered through my contact in the employment office. It was really quite convenient. Anyhow, spring and summer are tough periods for a determined, cautious thief. Full of possibilities and promise of quick and big profit, granted, but hazardous and unpredictable. The job was easy but terribly boring. I missed my free, independent life as a thief, hunting for opportunities among fields of row houses and apartment buildings on the immediate outskirts of Oslo. Your chances are good even in the very newest bedroom-town areas, where nothing is yet established, where large numbers of people have recently moved in from all over and sit in newly fabricated surroundings watching one another in fear and jealousy, where you cannot walk past a kitchen window without being noticed. But in such places, where concern over identity turns everybody into a judge of what's supposed to be normal, insecurity runs so deep that nobody dares decide what's irregular. And a man with a briefcase, barely medium height, handsomely and conventionally dressed, can hardly be said to be irregular where people still don't know one another's habits and circles of acquaintance. Also, buying mania easily becomes an obsession in such newly developed neighborhoods, since the sole common denominator, the only perceptible, measurable signs of a convention or connection, of solidarity between people, are things. Where the communication between people isn't developed, things take over the role of language: glass pearls, bits of a mirror . . .

Anyway, with time heavy on my hands, I sat daydreaming in the business office of the publishing house from one end of June to the other, while truckloads of pocket books were unloaded from the printers and delivery trucks full of weekly magazines were signed out. And on July 9, the Friday before the general holidays, I walked out the gate in Sørkedalsveien, a free man and disposed for adventure. The sultry vapor from the newly mown lawns around Marienlyst seemed to be drifting toward me as I stood waiting for the Røa line at the Majorstua trolley stop, full of daring plans and with the paycheck in my pocket (so I could really have allowed myself a vacation!). And then to Røa, a semifashionable, quasi-rural section I'd wisely stayed away from. People at Røa have order in their things, keep their securities and jewelry locked up, pay by check. People at Røa have a certain elusive good taste even when they put on their rags to take a walk, an assurance of quality that no thief can capture. Yet, on July 9 this year, at the Majorstua trolley stop, with a warm sun at the back of my head and a sharp, stupefying fragrance of greenery everywhere, even in the dust, I decided that today Røa would get its comeuppance!

It was madness, of course, as I knew the moment I got off the trolley. The houses sat there as if encapsulated in a sort of impenetrable peace that no outsider would ever be able, or even dare try, to break through, as if the insertion of a false key into the lock (equipped with wrought-iron fittings) on one of those wide brown-stained doors would immediately set off an alarm—through the treetops, through the sprinkler systems, through flocks of sparrows from ornamental shrub to ornamental shrub, from veranda door to veranda door sparkling with icily transparent windowpanes in the cozy shadows of the terraces: Away with the intruder! Out with the uninvited guests! Stop thief!

But I chanced it anyway, walked with firm steps down the narrow paved roads (always walk as if you know where you're going when out cruising), my eyes peeled, on the lookout, on the lookout! Children on bikes were sweeping past. Portable radios could be heard from patches of lawn behind protective hedges, the carefree notes of afternoon, an insane time of day for a thief to work, but I chanced it. I chanced it! Actually, it went off almost too easily. The entrance was three steps from the road, protected by bushes and gateposts. Rolled-down awnings in front of the windows where the sun was no longer beating down. Everything tightly shut up in the heat. And the door sprang open at once, as if someone were expecting a visit . . .

The family had obviously gone on vacation. Everything was clean and tidy, valuables removed, locked up or deposited, cords unplugged, not much for a thief to take notice of. Once I was safely inside, the recklessness of the expedition seemed finally to dawn on me. What was I doing here in the middle of the afternoon? Why was I taking such a chance? My first impulse was to sneak out again, unseen as when I walked in. But I didn't. I fought my common sense. I sat right down in the nearest chair, contrary to all routine, laying myself open to the afternoon light that streamed in under the flower awnings, letting myself be filled by the freedom of the Friday afternoon. I quite simply enjoyed life! Meanwhile, everything in this comfortable two-family house at Røa had put me in a peculiar mood: the pictures on the walls were paintings, authentic! A couple of them even with a dedication, to and from. On a shelf stood two ceramic vases, together with stones and potsherds, of no value whatsoever but strangely refined anyway. The furniture was not ritzy but inviting, in some odd, unattainable way just right, as if made to be placed exactly there . . . (I've never sat in a better chair than the one I tried that afternoon in the living room at Røa, a simple but ingenious construction of canvas and unpainted wood. Even if I hunted for the rest of my life, I'd never find one to match it for simplicity and comfort.) Enclosed, aromatic heat. Potted plants removed from the scorching desert plains of the windowsill. Even potted plants grew and did well here, being greener and more lush than elsewhere. It was maddening! I wasn't sitting down any longer but wandered around, doing things a burglar shouldn't do, while telling myself every minute that time was precious, that I had to get away before it was too late . . .

But a wild ambition had put it into my head that I wasn't to have made this trip for nothing. I noticed a TV set, quite new, and it gave me an idea. In the basement, sure enough, I found the carton in which the set had been delivered. Hanging there (among garden hoses, carpentry tools, and bundles of steel wire) was also a smock, which I slipped on. In a closet I found an old hat, which I put on my head. Then I called the nearest taxi stand, gave the address and waited ten minutes for the car, which suddenly stood humming outside the gate, half hidden behind the dense thicket of flowering bushes. I got the driver to help me ease the carton with the TV into the trunk and gave the address of a large electronics store downtown. To be on the safe side, I threw in a remark to the effect that "they wanted to have the set fixed while they were on vacation." The driver agreed: "Christ, yes, some people are completely nuts, can't miss a single program!" He backed out of the narrow side road, and hey presto . . . Farewell to Røa!

I installed the set at home and spent the remaining summer afternoons and the long sultry evenings in its cool, passivity-inducing company. To watch TV is also a form of theft. To watch TV is theft of a reality, the reality of other people, with no risk, no gamble. Through TV you can be a part of the rich and the mighty, the stars, those you admire or envy, while nothing is changed, while the thief is disarmed and kept in his place.

Summer is the most dangerous time for thieves, it's good to have something to cool off with. I watch a lot of TV. I know my place.

7 Going to the city today I saw her again in the trolley, that young, fair-haired lady with the expensive taste in jewelry and clothes. She's been away for a while—that is, I haven't seen her for some time. For I've gotten into the habit of looking for her in the trolley, I take a seat fairly close to her, keep alert, and make my observations. We both seem to be creatures of habit, prefer to use the same seats day after day. I have no scruples about this subtle form of overture. Catching the trolley at Thune two minutes before half-past eight has become part of my "image" as an ordinary citizen, working, dutiful, with regular habits. And even if I have an instinctive aversion to being recognized, I realize that—in this situation—it must be an implicit part of my purpose. Still, I'm not the type that ladies like her will recognize: I'm average, one of the many, that's my strategy and my great advantage. My ability, my freedom of movement, and my success as a thief depend precisely on this.

So I feel safe as I sit directly opposite her today, noting that she's become tanned during her absence. Her face positively glows among all the others, October-gray. And her tinted blond hair has been streaked with something vividly bright, like silver or ashes . . . A week in the South, of course—fall vacation with the family. The Mediterranean, some island—perhaps something exotic, a dream about the mystery of a thousand and one nights? Istanbul?

It's chillier; she has a heavier coat today, expensive tweed (that elusive difference between the expensive and the commonplace!), a high-necked sweater in light green pastel (goes with her eye shadow), and therefore no necklace (but I have a good memory, I can see the gold chain twisting and turning against the golden skin on her neck!). And the silk scarf is fastened with the gold pin I've noticed once before, ordinary enough, shaped like an insect but large and beautifully made, no doubt valuable; these are quite popular, easy to sell . . . And around her wrist I glimpse (when she raises her hand and opens the top button of her coat, as she's in the habit of doing when the car fills up, the temperature and stuffiness rise, and the windowpanes become misted) a bracelet I haven't seen before, wide, beaten, seems to be genuine, surely not made in this country. Once more my imagination takes off. Is she the type who takes a chance on purchasing gold on vacation trips to the South? Sitting there at her ease with her (no doubt) precious gold bracelet nonchalantly hanging over the glove she hasn't taken off, she appears to be totally defenseless. In Istanbul, the thieves' capital, where theft has been perfected to the highest form of intimacy between people, a master would at this moment have bent forward and relieved her of this burden, a superfluous demonstration of affluence that merely seems to bother her and to inhibit her movements. Istanbul, where the men cluster around the coffee tables in the streets and in alleyways during the cool, windy winter afternoons to steal a little bodily heat from one another . . .

She plays with her purse. The glittering, scented purse, soft as a glove, containing a wallet, an address book, key chain, a handkerchief, a pen (fountain pen), some loose papers, a few cosmetic articles—that's all I've been able to make out. Opens it, takes out a letter, plays with it absentmindedly until it falls out of her hand and glides to the floor, ending up in the slush at my feet. I bend down quick as lightning to pick it up and return it to the gloved hand: a grateful glance. Grateful? Hardly more than polite attention. Then the letter is put away in the purse again. But I've had time to note the addressee: Attorneys Krogh & Matiassen, Øvre Vollgate, Oslo 1. And the sender's name is marked in elegant blue on the back of the letter: Ada Dahl, Bekkelifaret 14 C, Oslo 3.

My memory for names and addresses is like that of a magician for the combinations, sequences, symbols, and numbers in a deck of cards.

Grorud—the valley of valleys for a thief!

I've ventured into a top apartment in one of the buildings at the summit of Ravnkollen. In the row houses down below there's a swarm of baby-sitters, kids and older people, an eternal procession to and from the supermarket. But in these high-rise buildings the apartments are smaller and more expensive, intended for single professionals or working couples without children. Such apartments become intermediate stops in their owners' (or tenants') development, marriage or career: a step ahead while waiting for something better—a salary raise, transfer, completion of continued education, a building loan, or an addition to the family. The furnishings, too, often have a provisional character,

meager and economical, limited to the most essential while they wait
for a breakthrough of one kind or another; fortunately, I seldom come
across such places (where the thief usually finds only bankbooks and
materials for self-study or evening school). Much more often these
luxury apartments of two small rooms, kitchen, and a tiny entry are
lavishly equipped, a projection of the occupants' ambitions and hopes,
a surrogate wish fulfillment here and now. And in such places the thief
doesn't need to feel embarrassed; here everything has been supplied
with a furious consumer's appetite, to be replaced according to whim
and fashion. Temporary comfort is itself temporary, created and installed to be removed, discarded, or stolen after a brief period.

Today I do something I don't usually do very often; standing in the
bathroom I study my face in the mirror, the face of a thief at the scene of
the crime. It seems unnaturally pale even for October, framed by the
dark modern bathroom interior (glossy formica with rosewood finish);
its expression seems tense, as if he were poised for flight (or on the verge
of bursting into a peal of laughter?), eyes wide open (larger pupils than
usual?), mouth small and thin-lipped, never at rest. The pulse throb is
visible on the side of the neck. Pearls of sweat along the hair line—or is
this something I imagine? I must admit I've seldom felt in such a good
mood; in fact, I'd almost forgotten how *suspenseful* it is to steal!

And there's plenty to take. It's a typical bachelor's apartment I've
entered, with the imprint of masculine affectation everywhere. Smart
pinups and pop art décor. A wide (unmade) bed with lovely brown and
beige bedclothes. Masses of clothes, light suits, tapered shirts, jeans and
khaki trousers. Shoes with high heels (there's my chance!). T-shirts
with prints. Minibriefs in sparkling colors. A bull-worker at the back of
the closet, together with an extra set of dumbbells. A faithful model of a
Formula I racing car on the writing table, which only contains some
stationery and envelopes with the name of the firm (car import),
besides degree and course diplomas, and discharge papers from the Air
Force Academy. A drawer half-filled with stained restaurant menus,
matches from large hotels in Germany and Switzerland, postcards with
hastily scribbled greetings in English and German. Some porno magazines. A lovely portable typewriter looks completely unused. And so
does the kitchen, apart from the kettle, a jar of instant coffee, and a few
unwashed glasses. The ashtrays haven't been emptied. A wall unit with
stereo and liquor cabinet dominates one side of the living room. Low

lounge chairs of steel tubing and leather. White shaggy rugs full of wine spots, ashes, and food crumbs. On the full-length mirror in the hallway numerous visitors, male as well as female, have signed their autographs with lipstick. The place is a wilderness of typical male wish-fulfillment, indiscriminately cut straight out of the magazines: here lives Tarzan, king of the apes! Which isn't contradicted by the pictures he's hung around the apartment, shots of himself on different occasions, in his uniform at the military academy, with friends in a restaurant, on an excursion in drunken company, in his car with sunglasses. And so on. But I find over two hundred kroner in his pockets, besides a couple of expensive cigarette lighters, an admission ticket to a popular disco club (I can't resist!), a pair of heavy cuff links (gold!) left negligently in an unlaundered shirt. The portable typewriter (with guarantee and invoice in the writing-desk drawer) is a real bonus, and among his countless pairs of shoes, flung helter-skelter on the closet floor and under the shelf in the entry, I find some that I like, change on the spot and stick another pair in a plastic bag from a men's shop. From the bathroom a bottle of expensive eau de cologne, an electric razor in a lovely soft leather case, and—on a sudden impulse—a silk scarf in a gaudy, colorful pattern. Finally an unopened bottle of cognac from the well-stocked liquor cabinet (though I hardly ever touch the stuff!).

All this is quickly done; I can hear my own tense breath as my diligent fingers probe and search. It's suspenseful, exciting! I feel in tiptop form. As a final gesture I snap up an object from his bookcase, a bright dainty "Executive toy" sculptured in steel and sparkling plexiglass; the gleaming ball rolling in its frictionless bubbles of nothing makes me feel happy as a child in a toy shop!

In the corridor I take yet another chance, leaving the door to the apartment open while I drop my old shoes in the garbage shaft and rush back with the key. While waiting for the elevator, I glance through a section of the tall window on the stairway and catch a dizzying glimpse of the narrow valley below, its stony ridges and crags—covered with tiny houses—surrounded by lines of row houses in the shadow of towering high-rise constructions; a multitude of roofs and sparse, October-black vegetation, shopping centers and poky little streets, small islands of homeless suburban architecture falling, or tumbling, down toward the flatter industrial areas of Alnabru; and farther west, the highway constructions of Økern, the recreational area around

Tøyen and Ensjø—the lawns are still green, luminous islets in all the gray—encircling Old Kampen like a protective rampart; then down to the bottom of the hazy Oslo bowl, the Old City and the port, Loenga and the Harbor Basin, which, from the fumes of the big city, weaves pastel veils that enfold the dead gray water. The islands! The ships! My quickened senses have never seen anything so beautiful, and I have to lean against the granite-gray wall to overcome a consuming longing, which fuses with my urge to plunge into the half-light of October as it changes to that of a milk-gray afternoon, down into the whispering stairwell that opens before my feet. Then the elevator is waiting.

"You have new shoes?" she asks. "How smart! And a typewriter? Do you have to work overtime at home?"

Since her hours were changed we've often left the restaurant together. I have a feeling she waits for me, and I am amused. Our walk to the corner of Valkyriegaten and Kirkeveien has almost become routine. She talks and asks questions. I try to answer, surprised by her obvious need for contact. A woman like her must have lots of acquaintances and friends. I've gathered she lives with some fellow who's not her husband, but I haven't felt like pursuing the subject. Knowing too much about a person can also become an obligation.

Her good but inconsistent and often slightly careless taste tells me she's an extrovert verging on the eccentric, but changeable and unsure of herself. And that she has the courage to admit it to herself, even make a point of it. This makes her strong in my eyes, yet she's easily astonished, easily put at disadvantage. And that appeals to me. A pair of new shoes—how little it takes to impress her! And the "job" at the publishers'; I've already taken precautions by defining myself as a "freelance." It can mean all or nothing. Her eyes have an elusive, flickering look, individualistic perhaps, freedom-loving, near-heroic, who knows?

"You're not married . . . ?" she says, as if stating a fact. She wears a woollen coat with a wrap belt today and a cottage-industry scarf on her head. The glasses make her face look more serious than it actually is. Tall boots that must have been expensive, they have worn well. I've gotten used to her asking about all sorts of things. But not about my name. Not again. Nor has she told me her own. She's satisfied with Bel Ami. This strange mutual anonymity increases the suspense between us as we slowly get to know each other better. For this chit-chatty association for a couple of hundred yards along the congested sidewalk three or four days a week has acquired a definite, almost planned character. As if we were stepping into a pattern, a development neither of us will be able to turn around, not now. "People meet and sweet music . . . ," I'm thinking. The title of a book I once snapped up by mistake, mostly because of these strange words. But I don't like to think this way. If there's anything that repels me and puts me in a wretched mood, it's precisely people's helpless rituals for making overtures, their pitiful and always abortive attempts to reach one another, with words, with small actions . . . Ever since school this has struck me as degrading. Then it all had to do with physical closeness, edging toward those you wished to achieve intimacy with, stealing glances, words and movements, stealing a touch, a little warmth . . .

Yet I do nothing to stop what's going on between her and me. I admit it: I look forward to these short walks. And to our conversations.

So I answer, it's true I'm not married. "Separated since last winter," I add when I see she's about to ask another question.

She's silent for a moment.

"Is that so . . . ? I really thought you'd *never* . . . You seem so independent, not tied down somehow. As though nobody had ever owned you. And then I thought that a man who can stand the food at Bel Ami for months, day after day, can never really have discovered what it means to eat well at home." She laughs, then becomes serious again. "Don't you feel lonely? I mean, in the separation period . . . ?"

How like her to ask so thoughtlessly, fearlessly, at such a big risk to herself. What if I answered, Yes, terribly! And: Only a woman like you . . . ! But I don't answer that, of course. I say: "Well—no, not really. I enjoy being alone."

I can see she's both displeased and a little pleased by this answer, as though it confirmed hunches she's had, and I'm therefore forced to make a move that has haunted me since this morning, since my visit to the apartment of Tarzan, king of the apes: "But we could perhaps go out sometime . . . That is, if you can make it. The two of you . . ." Mostly to astonish her, not because I really have such a tremendous desire to.

"Of course I can!" She's surprised and glad. "We're both free that way. It's part of our arrangement: not to own but to trust each other, as they say so prettily."

Her sarcastic expression contradicts her words.

"Tomorrow maybe . . . ?" I suggest.

Tomorrow is Friday. Holiday. I'll have plenty of time to get ready, map it out.

"Tomorrow? Fine! Where shall we go?"

I haven't been prepared for her hungry response, must think of something quick; but where in the world . . . ? Then I remember the admission ticket to the popular club that I found in Tarzan's place. I propose we go there.

"Gosh, there?" She's obviously impressed. "Do you go to such places?"

"Not very often." I try to sound sophisticated, notice she's flattered, that she's considering the same possibilities I have thought about.

"I love to dance!"

She's already taking a turn on the dance floor.

I might have guessed it. She loves to dance. I hate dancing!

8 Friday evening we are tripping the light fantastic on the tiny dance floor of the club, with flushed cheeks and both of us excited after our drinks. I'm really rigged out, in a dark suit, discreetly striped white shirt of the most crisp, newly ironed cotton, my heavy shipowner's tie with the club design, and Tarzan's high-heeled demi-boots. She in a tasteful long cotton print, modern Scandinavian, with bare neck, bare shoulders, silver earrings and a simple silver chain around her neck. The glasses make her face look more serious than it actually is, for I can see she's happy and in high spirits tonight.

And she loves to dance. Soft and supple, she almost makes me like it too. At the start, early in the evening, there's plenty of space, we have the floor to ourselves. Usually such a situation would have made me embarrassed. But not now, not with her. She enjoys it so openly. Almost makes me enjoy it too. She makes me wish I knew more anyway. So I compensate by drinking. Two or three rounds. More than usual. She doesn't turn them down either and says again and again: "This is real nice!"

Later more people turn up and space is scarce; there are opportunities to get close to each other on the dance floor, embrace, steal a little closeness, the imprint of a body against your own. Such self-surrender under cover of something else, like dancing, is a joy to thieves. She obviously enjoys it too, doesn't hold back at any rate. *I* do, feeling I run the risk of losing control because the situation is developing so rapidly, because I've taken a few drinks and can't help noticing how long it's been since I was so close to a woman. And it gives an edge to it, for both of us, to think of her friend who sits alone at home; a dropped remark about "him," a glance—I understand it so well and feel myself moving closer to her.

But then there are all those around us. The dance floor is full now, mostly young people; we're among the oldest. On the whole they look like us, though the majority are perhaps a bit less starchily dressed. Generally they're out to play the same game as we are, while the music of the band boils around us and over us like a foaming ocean. They seem to be occupied with their own things, but in reality they are all occupied with ours, with stealing a little intimacy from one another. And I must admit it's distracting, because it feels unnatural to operate with so many people around. Despite the fact that the subdued lighting and the music—which gets distorted in its passage through the ear canals, kills thought and impairs the senses—along with the drinks and everybody's self-absorption, make the place into a paradise for a thief. The involuntary comparison with all the others here disturbs me all the same.

So many thieves, perhaps even unsuspecting thieves, out cruising at the same time frighten me and make me withdraw into myself again, adopt a critical, patronizing attitude. I watch the young men maneuver their dates more or less graciously to and from the dance floor, the lounge, or the tempting bar, gleaming like a festively decorated spaceship in the darkness. I see their childish excitement, observe their banal hopes of conquest and glory. I decipher their backgrounds and circumstances from the details of their dress (shoes, cuff links, ties, wristwatches—especially the bands—rings, arm chains and medallions, if any, things like the cut of their suits, the stitchings on the lapels, haircut, shave . . .). I register their suppressed brutality from the working of their mouths and the movements of their hands; nothing escapes a thief's attention. I see that two or three could easily be Mr. Tarzan himself, to whom I paid a visit yesterday morning; he looks exactly like that as far as I can recall from the photographs—though everything gets to look the same in such a place—and I think with satisfaction that I do, after all, have the edge on them: *I* steal from the thieves! And it gives me pleasure to feel that my soft demiboots fit me like a pair of gloves. Still I pull back as we dance like two mourners, letting her come while I pull back—I have to be in control, can't forget myself in the presence of witnesses. Can't let *them* get a hold on *me*.

We dance. We sit in deep chairs in the lounge, where the air is poisonous with smoke. We hang over the bar. We look at the others in the club.

"Do you know," she confides, "I've actually been here once before. With my husband—when I was married. It's many years ago now. The place was different then. It's more fun now, more lively." Her arm never lets go of mine. After another dance and another drink, she whispers:

"I could come to your place if you like."

I give a start.

"No."

I'm not prepared for it, not like this, so suddenly. Though I knew of course it would come, it was in the cards. In fact, I have already played with the possibility of spending the night in a hotel. We have reached that point, lacking only a place and the opportunity. The fact that she wants it, wants to go someplace with me, sleep with me and leave "him" to his own fate, wants to team up with me to steal from him—because that's what I feel we're doing, stealing from her friend—this fills me with a kind of tenderness for her, so strong that I place my arm around her and pull her close as we stand at the end of the overcrowded bar, whispering near her face, loudly in order to be heard:

"It won't work, you see, Bel Ami. It's impossible!" in a tone meant to explain everything. And it has the intended effect; she understands at once, assumes I'm thinking of my separated wife.

"Do you think she'll make trouble?"

I give a shrug. She understands again, thinks I ought to do my utmost to avoid legal complications, a divorce suit, strokes my chin compassionately, empties her glass and says, with an almost devil-may-care gleam in her eye:

"Then we'll go to my place!"

I hesitate, though my heart leaps in my breast at this offer. What a unique situation for a thief!

"But is it possible . . . ?"

"Possible, sure it is! Why shouldn't it be? We haven't done anything wrong, have we? Besides, he's always telling me he'd be glad to meet my friends. Not that I really have any friends who aren't *his* friends too; for that matter he doesn't have so many either. Anyway, it's something he keeps telling me. So now we'll go home and take him at his word! Come on!"

In the taxi up to Grefsen she holds my hand between both of hers and presses her cheek hard against my coat sleeve. I breathe down into her hair, which smells of shampoo. Suddenly she bites my knuckles and I bore my face into the nape of her neck; we sit like this till we arrive.

We stand at the end of the driveway till the car has left; my knees are weak from excitement after the drive, her unreserved advances, and the many drinks. Her face is flushed with complicity even here in the sallow light of the street. She has taken off her glasses. We draw a deep breath, as if hoping the air up here will clear the heavy mist of compromising thoughts that envelop us in a pact, an unshakable solidarity. Our faces are grave as we stand there, wide-eyed, staring at each other but ready to start laughing at any moment. She holds on to my arm as we walk slowly up the gravel path toward the two-family house, lying behind an uneven hedge and a row of crooked apple trees that cast spectral shadows on the board fence beneath the glaring neon lamp at the gate.

She quickly takes out her key while explaining that the apartment they've rented is half of one unit of the two-family house. There are lights in two windows on the ground floor. Inside the little entry she calls:

"Hi, here we are!" (Are we going to be respectable now?)

Nobody answers. She takes my coat, puts it on a hanger on top of her own, opens the door beside the closet, and repeats in a tone of voice that suddenly sounds inappropriately gay:

"Hi, here we are!"

She crosses the threshold. I stay behind in the unfamiliar entry, fighting the steadily increasing sensation that I'm here on my usual errand. Automatically, I register the surroundings with a thief's glance. Pretty poor; scattered glimpses of her artistic taste (a couple of re-produced etchings and a poster from an arts and crafts exhibit), but all the same a dominant impression of masculine disorder and indifference (newspapers and unopened letters in an untidy pile on the table under a little unframed mirror, an Icelandic sweater rolled up and thrown onto the hat rack, dirty shoes with a pair of socks in them, two plastic bags in a corner by the exit, building material—I recognize the name of the firm—a handsaw hanging on a hook under the shelf in the closet . . .).

Then she turns around and calls:

"Why don't you come in. Say hello to Payk."

Payk? What a name.

"Actually Per Kristian," he says, embarrassed and forbearing at once as he gets up from a low, wide studio couch full of pillows in all colors.

"Pee-Kay. Pay-K. See? It has stuck to me all my life."

"Well, not *quite* all your life," she corrects him as we shake hands. If he checks he'll notice the marks from her teeth. He's taller than I, but thin and stooped.

"He *too* has a quite remarkable name . . ." Without glasses her face seems to open up, to blush—any fool would see and understand . . .

"Bel Ami!" she says with a laugh. "What d'you think of that? I call him Bel Ami because he comes to eat there several times a week. It was there we got to know each other." The floor literally rocks under me. I've underestimated her! She is as experienced a thief as any; steals the pet name I use for her in order to outmaneuver her friend! And at the same time she ties an unbreakable bond of complicity between us by "betraying" an intimacy that only she and I can understand, to him, who believes he's getting informed and is thereby definitively excluded. The indecency of the situation makes it hard for me to control my voice. I almost feel like that summer afternoon at Røa, free after four weeks in stockrooms where I stole pocket books to obtain a cheap erotic flame and masturbated in the basement john, where the pipes roared and water was always trickling into the bowl.

"Did you have a good time?" he asks as he drops onto the untidy sofa again.

"Should I get something to drink for us?" she says without answering. "I may have a bottle of beer or two . . ." She walks toward a door that I assume leads to the kitchen.

"Are you doing carpentry?" I ask, just to say something, pointing vaguely in the direction of the hallway, the saw and the bags with building materials. Then, realizing we haven't answered his question, I add:

"Places like that are damn noisy."

"Oh, you mean the saw and those things in the hallway?" He spreads his hands with a dreary look.

"Yes, as a matter of fact I'm putting together a bed . . ."

Per Kristian—Payk—is obviously younger than she, barely in his middle twenties, tall and thin. His long nose and his longish blond hair that falls in waves from a part in the middle to form a symmetrical frame around his face, give him a mournful expression. A sprouting beard lends his face a woollen, childish appearance, like a puppy. He seems uncertain and nervous, observant, follows her with his eyes as she walks and stands, talks little, preferably about things that concern them, barely mentions a friend who has called, the plans for the refurnishing, a job he has applied for but not been offered (I understand he's unemployed)—on the whole, things I can't have any knowledge of, as if trying in this way to break through the wall of indifference that she bluntly demonstrates by letting all her warmth and openness flow in my direction. I'm myself painfully affected by this dissymmetry and try to correct it by bringing up subjects of general interest, so that he too can be included in the conversation. But nothing doing. He seems wrapped up in something he's pondering, some sorrow that's beyond us. All the same, he follows her slightest movement with an imploring look in his brown eyes, as if a smile, a glance, a touch could rescue him from his sullen, introspective, almost despairing mood. Of me he takes no notice. The contrast between my white shirt and dark suit and his shabby cotton sweater and faded jeans is too great. My soft, shiny demiboot nearly touches his naked foot under the coffee table.

Something else that strikes me as I sit there, awkwardly trying to start a three-way conversation, is the fact that she and I actually know each other very poorly, that our sporadic conversations during a few short walks a couple of blocks to the corner where we have to part have given us little common ground to stand on. Except, of course, for what's "happening" between us, our "complicity," which both of us must try to hide in every way. But, in all honesty, she doesn't seem to take great pains to hide it before him: her interest and initiative are obviously directed toward me. She strokes my shoulder as she passes behind my chair. She honors my strained conversation (that also stolen goods: newspaper articles, radio debates, cheap opinions and conventional wisdom) with remarks, laughter, enthusiasm. She makes it almost too easy for the thief she's invited home for a visit. I would have been made of stone if I didn't react to her little invitations, especially after an evening like tonight! And the beer on top of the many drinks doesn't make the situation any less murky. Mutual laughter lurks in our eyes as his melancholy expression makes him look more and more like a mournful dog.

Finally he yawns, stretches, gets up, and says:

"It's getting late . . ."

"Oh, already?" she says quickly.

"Must you go too? Not quite yet, Bel Ami, eh? Are you working tomorrow?"

"I probably ought to . . . ," I have the sense to say. The alarm clock is ringing at the back of my head; it's dangerous to compromise yourself. And here I am getting compromised. But she interrupts:

"It isn't *that* late. Just a moment or two. Here, a little more beer . . ."

I sink back in my chair. Still standing, he must see he has lost, that this is the sign for him to pull out; I can tell from his hands, which make a weak, resigned gesture, exposing the palms in a hopeless appeal.

"Anyway, I'm tired," he mutters and walks toward the kitchen door. "Good night. Nice meeting you."

He looks at her. He closes the door resolutely behind him.

And now it's she and I, as in the taxi, only more dangerous, more unavoidable.

"It doesn't matter, he won't come out," she whispers when she notices I hold back.

"He doesn't dare . . . !"

She laughs noiselessly against my cheek. We're on the sofa now, and she clears away the pillows so we can lie down comfortably. She's quick and impatient, as if set on getting somewhere before the time is up.

"He can't hear anything either. The kitchen is between." She's taking the lead now, is in full control. I ought to get up and straighten my clothes, thank her for a pleasant evening and say good-bye. Make a date for later, order a hotel room. Get the relationship into a clearly defined, orderly framework. But she's taken the lead, I can't deny it. We're collaborating on this, but she has the command now. She's out on her big thief's errand, and nobody is going to prevent her from seeing it through. This thought makes me even hotter than the eager hands that have started to undo my buttons. For a moment I regret not taking a few pairs of Tarzan's maroon minibriefs. But soon that's no longer of any importance. We both struggle to make a go of it, to get rid of our clothes and lie down properly. I've become just as eager as she, for I know that at some point I'll have to regain the initiative, recover the lead and the control, if things are going to be right, and I yearn for this with increasing intensity: I've got to arrive first and have done with it, carry out *my* thief's errand, then I'll have arrived. Then it's I who decide!

Afterwards, calm and in control of everything, I give out and go for more. Now it's I who control the tempo and the distribution of what's left after the race, she has to wait for my signal. And she waits gratefully, gratefully gathers up all she gets.

"You're strange," she says. "Sometimes it seems as if you weren't *there,* as if I had to bring you back from some faraway place. But once you come, then . . . !"

I let her suck and bite pretty much the way she wants. It isn't over for her, she's searching, she wants more. It's never over for women.

"You're kind," she says. "You're calm. It makes me so calm to be with you. It's as if you radiated confidence. It doesn't seem necessary for you to talk very much, to rush in with information about yourself and questions about me, to insist on *communicating* about everything. I'm so tired of these men I run into who chatter on and on about their problems, what they believe are my problems, and about what they call "our" problems . . . Do you notice how unnecessary it is to talk when we're together? I noticed the contact between us in the restaurant, didn't *you?* I was so happy you didn't try to check up on me. I thought: "Here at last is someone who knows more than just shooting off his mouth. I've been trying—"

I nod. She licks my ear. I dislike it but don't let on. She's getting all sorts of fancies about me and I don't stop her. *I* have felt the pauses between us as embarrassing, as a pressure on me to say or come up with something; I've felt inadequate.

"And I'm glad I tried. You're dependable. You're kind. You're strong without having to be brutal . . ."

I'm thinking: How can a woman like her be so easy to fool? Perhaps the answer is that women like her are the very ones who are easy to fool—those who seek and are so eager to find. It's not hard for me to be "kind" to her: I simply use the prudence of the thief, guess her wishes and fulfill them before she has time to formulate them. To be "kind" can also be a way of stealing. It doesn't cost me much to be "kind" as long as I can decide myself how "kind" I am to be.

"Time for me to leave soon," I say. My body begins to feel the same alert restlessness that replaces the sense of well-being I often experience after I've stripped an apartment, until I get out into the hallway and down the stairs again.

"Yes, perhaps." She hesitates. She doesn't want me to go, holds on to her feeling of happiness. She's still an amateur:

"It was so good with you . . ." And then:

"You mustn't get the idea that I run after *every* steady customer."

"Of course not—you chose me because I was the only one who didn't try to check up on you."

"Not bad!" She's invulnerable.

"It's getting late. I really must be on my way."

"Perhaps you'd better. Poor Payk might be awake. He's jealous as a dog . . ."

"Maybe he has reason to be?"

"Not till now. On my word! Though it would've served him right. These so-called liberated types aren't always what they seem to be. Perhaps I'm treating him badly, ugh. Last summer he was my lush green island. But now it's fall . . ."

"Summer makes you do strange things. Fall, too, now and then."

It occurs to me that having sex with her in the living room, with her friend eavesdropping behind the unlocked door, was at least as rash as stealing that TV at Røa and driving off in a taxi.

"We're not married," she says when we have dressed. I reply that I've understood this much.

"I was married once but it went to hell. After nine years I just ran away, couldn't take it anymore. He was a brute. This happened last summer. Couldn't stand it anymore, so I just left without telling him. I probably ought to take care of the formalities . . . I have a daughter of eight, she's living with him. If I arranged it through a lawyer, perhaps . . . But I don't dare, I don't dare meet him. He's so strong. He's an active sportsman. He can be so violent . . ."

She too seems to be fond of talking when the chips are down.

I tell her I must leave. I hold her close, pressing myself against this body from which I won't be able to steal any more until a few hours have gone by. On the sidewalk I feel like shouting and laughing aloud!

9 A remarkably clear and calm day. Sunny and warm, like May.

A single plaited band of red Mediterranean gold around her tanned neck (her coat unbuttoned, shirt wide open and collar turned up, in a soft beige lamb's wool pullover with a low-cut V neck). Ada Dahl, with that calm, almost absentminded face and those nervous hands around the nonchalantly open handbag, on the seat directly opposite me. Doesn't see me. On her way to a conference with her lawyers, perhaps? The subdued light coming from the fjord fills the trolley as we pass Skarpsno. Her hair like ashes of birch, with a cool glow, Nordic. The red gold trickles from under her shirt, hesitating in the hollow of her neck before it falls softly across her collarbone, as if it were still liquid, melting and at the same time cool, like caresses on the skin directly after a bath before the sun has warmed the body again . . . God!

Her face, in profile, is as delicately etched as the facades of the prestigious villas along venerable Drammensveien. Just as impenetrable. Unattainable.

"But *her* breasts are bigger," I think vindictively.

All Saturday and Sunday I was tossed from one mood to another like an old chestnut tree in changing winds. The incident on Friday never left my thoughts; I reconstructed, memorized, and interpreted the details; I alternated between finding the whole thing ridiculous, dangerous, and strangely exciting. A challenge and a victory. Victory? Oh, well. The victory must have been just as much on her side; *at least* as much, judging by her satisfaction when our joint efforts were successful. Even if *I* was in full control at the end. Even if, in the end, *I* could pay out, give and take as I pleased.

I've put on my silk scarf and my high demiboots today, but she doesn't notice me. Looking as though carved from cold, luminous Nordic amber, she lets me feed on her golden, Mediterranean neck, protected by clinging gold of a weight and karat I'd never dare touch. As she sits there, ignoring the rest of the world and letting the October sky dim her bright blue eyes, she becomes a challenge to my instinct for conquest. I think of Bel Ami, of her sweaty forehead against mine, our warm bodies intertwined on the sofa, crumpled-up garments we didn't bother to kick off, the clumsy indelicacies of love in action, and I feel almost disgusted.

As I stand up to get off at the National Theater—the stop before hers—and, following some wild impulse, intentionally bump her knees, mumbling "sorry" so that I can get a glance at least, maybe catch the sound of her voice, she looks, not at me, but at the hem of her skirt, adjusts an invisible crease and then, for a brief second, lets her eyes sail around the overcrowded car, where people are struggling to get off and on, with a faint, frosty smile as if to say she'll still forgive us all for being there, creating a jam around her.

I tumble out. My mind is set on a vague plan I really don't like a bit, but the voice of reason is muted on an October day like today. I cross the trolley track and walk fifty yards in the direction of the National Theater to the stop on the opposite side, getting there just in time to catch the trolley to Jar.

Outbound the same route. It's madness but inevitable. Bekkelifaret, must be the Ullern stop. Perhaps Bestum. Neighborhoods where I've never set foot professionally, if that's the right word for it. Not that I plan to *take* anything . . . In that kind of neighborhood? I haven't gone completely crazy! But I must get out there all the same, it's as if my self-respect depended on it.

Bekkelifaret is easy to find. Luxury row houses. Millionaires' bunkers along the hillside with a panoramic view toward Frogner and Filipstad and, far out, the Ekeberg Hill, dark, clear, and sharply etched like the shape of a capsized boat in the morning back-light. Farther up the road some smug older wooden villas. A few newer ones, flatter, more newly rich. *Her* house, no. 23, somewhere in between, is a spacious, low one-and-a-half-story affair, but not conspicuously modern. Withdrawn from the road in a manner that shows it was built at a time with different views on zoning. The well-planned garden is overgrown, its age evident to all as it surrounds the house in protective harmony—in supreme contrast, for example, to the adjacent garden, whose straggly cotoneaster saplings can't even disguise the owner's poor taste in the choice of slabs for his garden paths and stones for his barbecue. (I know a lot about furnishings and comfort, outdoors as well as indoors; it belongs to my profession. I read *Housing News* and architectural journals, noting any details that may be of use, such as the way lock mechanisms function on veranda doors and pivot windows.)

Her house. Just as I had expected it to be. Even so, it looks abandoned, empty in a way that makes me wonder. Naturally because it *is* empty, I tell myself, because they're working, he in his director's or manager's job, she in conference with her lawyer, perhaps concerning the purchase or sale of a piece of property, details in the administration of her private capital, an inheritance . . . ?

Still I can't get rid of the feeling that I'm overlooking something important. A feeling so strong that I stop at the driveway, although I know I shouldn't attract anyone's attention. I hitch the briefcase up to my armpit like a determined salesman, throw all caution to the wind, and open the low wrought-iron gate beside the entrance to the garage. Then I see it in a flash, the most obvious thing in the world: the driveway! Its entire surface, broad and asphalted and extending to the brown-stained roll-up garage door, is covered by a thick layer of autumnal leaves, golden yellow on top, decaying brown underneath. No car has been driving in or out of here for a month! And as if to underscore the indisputable nature of this observation, a pile of cardboard boxes sits outside the garage door, carelessly placed beside and on top of one another as though left there in anticipation of the daily sanitation truck. But they've been there a while, perhaps for weeks, that's obvious: soaked with moisture, their bulging sides have sagged and collapsed. I take in the whole situation while covering the few feet up to the house. Overcome by curiosity, I walk over to the cartons to see what they contain. Three of them, with rotting sides and bulging contents, have been carelessly wound with rope or string, clumsily tied, but the two topmost ones have given way to the pressure. Here the side has torn and part of the contents have fallen out: a stack of magazines (*National Geographic*), a pair of slippers, a binoculars case, two pipes, bundles of receipts with rubber bands around them, a green parka, a pair of khaki trousers with paint spots . . . I take it in with a glance and understand: there are things here one doesn't just throw out after cleaning the attic. Here, a while ago, the man of the house, the car owner, must have moved out. These are his property and effects!

I've seen enough. I walk resolutely up to the main entrance, pretend to ring the bell in case I'm observed (I don't ring, someone *could* be there after all, a cleaning woman or the like!), wait a couple of minutes with the briefcase squeezed firmly under my arm. Turn around and stride resolutely down the driveway, into the street, and down to the trolley stop again. A ten minutes' wait for the Avløs line; it's a quarter of ten. I can still manage a job or two around Økern today.

After I've eaten and she's off duty, we walk together over to Majorstua as we always do. It is a sort of morning after, which makes it difficult for both of us. The restaurant was exceptionally crowded, so she had to run more than usual. Not that we ordinarily engage in any special contact in the restaurant (I'm grateful for her discretion), but today she's been busier than usual, has whisked past me innumerable times with an apologetic glance in my direction. I refused dessert today, just stayed a little while after the main course (beef stroganoff with gooey rice), paid and left at once. I don't feel comfortable with so many people in the restaurant.

She came scurrying after me and caught up with me at the corner.

"There was so much to do, I couldn't get away." She feels she has to explain and excuse herself, though the fact was I left earlier than usual. She could just as well have said: "Why didn't you stay a little longer?" Or, "Why didn't you wait?" But she says:

"It's almost impossible to get people to pay. They sit on and on . . ."

Their fault, that is, not mine. Her fault, not mine. I'm the one in control.

She has taken off her glasses. I must have said I liked her face better without them. I must have said many strange things there on the sofa. We're standing at a crowded corner, waiting to cross the street while the cars zoom past in a steady stream.

"Wasn't it nice the other night . . . ?"

She almost has to shout for me to hear her. I answer yes, think of something I've wondered about, feel like asking her, hesitate (is it too intimate, too binding?), but ask all the same:

"How did your friend take the situation? Was he awake when you came in?"

We almost run across the intersection. It's quieter on the other sidewalk.

"Payk? Yes, he was awake but pretended to be asleep. He's the most jealous man I know, but he doesn't dare admit it. He says he wants an open relationship, but I think this is only because he's afraid of the consequences and the obligations of a regular union. I know I'm treating him badly, but he's really asking for it!"

We laugh together. When she mentions Payk, her face flushes and I want her again. She notices and finally dares to touch my arm.

"It's impossible to talk here, couldn't we go someplace? For a cup of coffee?"

Just as I'd thought! I've been afraid of this, that our affair would deteriorate. It's obviously a logical consequence of what occurred Friday. It has obviously deteriorated already. But I hold back. Would prefer not to let it go any further; it suits me as it is. All the same, I've put on my high-heeled boots and my silk scarf today, and I didn't go to the barber as I'd planned because she'd remarked I would look good with longer hair. And when I caught sight of her in the restaurant, I saw more clearly than ever how Bel Ami's drab uniform actually accentuates her good figure, slender legs, and opulent bosom (but she's not really pretty), and I couldn't bear sitting in the cramped, smoke-filled room full of strange people, mostly men, eating "Pineapple Melba."

"A cup of coffee . . . ?"

I gasp for a postponement like a stranded fish.

"Yes, why not? You skipped dessert today, remember? We can go over there, to 'The Major.'"

We walk in. I fear the worst, that she'll talk about our relationship, make all sorts of proposals, that she'll cry and tell me she needs me. But she has something else in mind:

"I've been thinking so much about Eli the last few days," she says. Eli is the name of her daughter.

"I've failed her so terribly. Just imagine, I simply ran away and left the child with the man I myself couldn't stand the sight of anymore. I was so depressed and scared. That's the only explanation I can offer. But now . . ." I ask if she intends to go to court and bring her daughter home.

"No, not with Payk, that'll never work. He could never handle that situation. It would be like having two children . . . It's just that I haven't been able to take my mind off her. I don't know what to do . . ."

I gather that what she really wants to say is that she has already visualized a possibility with me. It turns me cold, like ice. But at the same time I'm aware with my whole body how my foot in its trim leather boot rests against her leg under the table, and I can hear my words take shape almost without my participation: "We'll have to try and get together again," although the alarm signals are buzzing in my head. What is it actually I'm embarking upon? Do I really want to jump in at the deep end of the pool, commit myself by giving her expecta- tions? But when I see how delighted she is, it rubs off on me too. And when she leans across the table and presses my arm, it makes me think how unproblematic it is with her, how straightforward, how easy and direct the contact between us has been. And I do feel a sort of gratitude toward her, wondering once more as I look at her face how little it takes to make her happy, at least more happy than she has been.

"Yes," she says, "we have to meet again. Can't you drop by on Thursday?"

Drop by?

"To see both of you? But is that possible? What about *him,* how do you think he'll take it?"

"Payk, you mean? That doesn't matter. You and I are established now, whether we want to or not. He always imagines the worst in any case. I'm sure he thinks you take me in the back room at the restaurant while I gulp down a bratwurst for lunch!"

She snickers and makes a face at her own bizarre humor, but such thoughts naturally make me hot for her again, so hot that it seems hard to have to wait till Thursday.

"And then he's so well-trained, does anything I tell him. Besides, I think he has a meeting on Thursday. So you see it's quite convenient."

"Do you want me to come after he's left then?" (An ideal situation for a lovesick thief.)

"No, why? I'll tell him about it anyway." Exposed! To be exposed is my biggest fear. To her it seems to be the greatest joy. She's not the kind of thief I thought she was. Perhaps she's even told him about us? How we were stretched out on the sofa while he lay writhing in his bed in the other room, alone and unable to sleep. Perhaps she provoked him to get inquisitive and ask questions? Perhaps she gave him details . . . ? I find the idea shocking, but at the same time it's almost unbearably exciting.

"On Thursday then, Bel Ami?"

I ought to pull out while there's still time. I don't really want to get involved in anything, and she's the type who gets involved; her clothes, her face, her whole person testify to spontaneity, warmth, commitment. Apart from the things she tells me about herself. But the word has been said. I've said it. I see how satisfied she is, how happy she gets when I squeeze her hand lying on the table near my own (holding hands in a restaurant—good Lord, is this really me?), and I feel uncomfortable, wishing I were somewhere else while wondering once more how little it takes to make her happy.

"On Thursday, Karl Jansen!"

That name!

I must have looked utterly dumbfounded, for she goes into a peal of laughter.

"Just take it easy, James Bond. I won't betray your big secret. I just think it's about time we got introduced to each other!"

She has such an advantage over me that she can joke about it. I've been exposed and feel sweat oozing from every pore. That name! Of course, my name's not Karl Jansen. It's a name on an ID I've used occasionally when it was convenient, but how has she . . . ?

"How I got hold of your name? Exposed your "secret identity"? Very simple, my dear Jansen—I took a peek that time when you forgot your wallet in the restaurant. I've had an eye on you for quite a while, you see . . ."

She laughs again, radiant, fired up, with her strong teeth, as if she'd like to take a bite out of me then and there. It looks as if my confusion over this business with the name only makes me more interesting in her eyes. At length I too manage to force a gasp of laughter or two, so she won't notice that something is really wrong.

"You must forgive my spying on you. That wasn't nice. But I was so curious. Honestly, I'm glad I did, because it didn't take me long to realize it would be more than 'a stab in the dark' with you . . ."

More than "a stab in the dark." I'd been afraid it would end like that. And we're there already.

10 Thursday evening I steal up the graveled path under the apple trees in the darkness. It has frozen over and the hoarfrost crackles under my shoes. I ought to have stayed home, been careful, but I'm excited as I approach the quiet house, where a faint light is shining from the ground-floor windows. The cold air nips my nostrils, but my face is warm behind the clouds of frozen breath and Tarzan's aftershave. I ring the bell, feeling my knees tremble. This is worse than standing with a piece of hard plastic, briefcase, and false keys on the smug wide stairs of a villa. She opens the door—thank God!—and looks at me as if she hadn't quite expected I would come. Or perhaps it's the way she's dressed: checked shirt, faded blue jeans, toes naked in her leather sandals. She says:

"Hi, come in! We're just rearranging things a bit, so pardon the mess."

"Who is it?"

The barking voice of Per Kristian, Payk, from inside. Then he doesn't know I was to come. Then she isn't *that* damn sure of the two of us!

"Oh, it's Bel Ami."

She squeezes my hand, then lets it go as she opens the living-room door and walks in.

"I asked him to drop by—"

"Today?"

He comes from the kitchen dressed like her, with dust in his hair and on his hands. They are evidently engaged in refurnishing the place, though there are no signs of it in the living room. It's the same as the first time I was here, untidy in a happy-go-lucky, lighthearted way, which strikes me as purely sensual. Or perhaps it's only the sofa, where the pillows are piled up at one end and the lap rug is rolled up in the other, after she or he—or both?—have taken an afternoon nap there.

"But we're going to a meeting."

He hasn't yet said hello, but I can see he's almost painfully aware of my presence. His nostrils quiver as if my person radiated an odor he can't stand.

"You can go to your meeting. I'm not up to it. Sit down, Bel Ami, I'll get some beer."

She goes and we just stand there. He taller than I but bent and crestfallen. I tell him I didn't know they were going out, that I'm sorry to interrupt their work, that of course I'll leave if—

"No, just do as the lady says and sit down."

He smiles maliciously, as if it gave him pleasure to get us both settled in the same boat, subject to her will. He sits down straight across from me in a safari chair of steel and canvas, uncertainly, as though wondering if he's permitted to. But the look he gives me is watchful, more sly and aggressive than last time.

"What, honestly, do you think about environmental protection? For or against nuclear power?"

The question gets drawn out to something resembling a snarl, as if he already foresaw my answer—that I don't take any position on the matter at all, have no idea what it is about—and showed his contempt in advance. I don't care what he thinks or believes. His long unwashed hair, faded checked shirt, patched jeans, naked feet with dust between the toes, turn him into a pitiful, barely human existence in my eyes; groping, without contours, scarcely worth stealing anything from . . .

"Stop that recruiting, won't you!"

She comes in with beer and glasses.

"He's so committed to 'causes,' crusading from morning till night. Cheers!" She fills the glasses and drinks. The beer tastes bitter. Payk hasn't touched his glass. He sits with bowed head, as if waiting. I ask how the carpentry is going, if they're refurnishing the apartment. She laughs with abandon, as if I'd touched on a particularly funny subject, but dismisses it by saying that "we're sprucing up the bedroom a bit."

"It's ten of," he says suddenly, looking so imploringly at her that I could swear there were tears sparkling in his melancholy brown eyes.

"You just go—I'm not up to it, I already told you!"

Annoyed, she simply waves aside his intense entreaty. He sits for another moment, his eyes intent on her, then sighs, gets up and slinks out through the kitchen. He returns in heavy boots and duffel coat, with a long scarf. Pinned to the duffel coat is a small round emblem matching the one I saw on her coat earlier this fall—she must have removed it by now. He stops by the hall door for a moment, as if expecting to be followed.

"So long, tell me what happened when you get home."

She barely looks at him as she sends him out into the cold.

We can't make a go of it right away this evening. That is, I can't, for lack of alcohol to give me a lift. I don't have a thief's inciting flush of victory to ride on. He has exposed us, after all, and isn't worth stealing from anymore. And she? She makes no resistance, opens up, simply opens up and seems satisfied despite everything, despite my feeble performance. Takes advantage of my difficulty to propose other things we can do, equally good things. She uses me and enjoys it, while I can only torment myself by wondering if, in the end, I'll get there anyway.

During the scuffle she wants beer, walks naked to the kitchen, gets two bottles and opens them, and while she pours it she perches nonchalantly on the smooth glass table. We drink greedily, I in hope of getting a bit drunk at least, she to quench her thirst. Drops of beer and perspiration form beads on her wintry-pale skin, and she looks down at me, loving and expectant, as if I were the prize in a lottery.

"Hey, look here!" she exclaims, laughing, as she gets up from a sitting position astride the corner of the table.

"An imprint of my hot love!"

On the glass slab the steam from her warm skin has drawn a large juicy flower, with the outline of her bottom and her broad thighs as four petals around a big, messy scar.

"Etched into the glass slab forever!" I have to gasp for air; her outspokenness makes me helpless and wild at the same time. Uncontrollable. Even when I've taken control again, driving her where I want her, maneuvering according to her moans and groans but as I please, and racing her toward the point where I know that I become supreme, invulnerable, unapproachable, even then I can't get rid of the thought that I'll *never* be able to overtake her, pass her or rule over her, quite simply because she can't be found where I am, doesn't take part in the same race, doesn't focus her rapture on the genitals and on technique, as I do, but flows everywhere in her sensuality, in every touch, every fond utterance and every look. And this makes me furious, makes me want to hit her, scratch, bite, hurt her, tear her out of this perpetual state of bliss, ride her till she bleeds and foams . . . Till I finally come and slide away, limp and indifferent. I lie there remote and cool like a castle with its drawbridge up (and with the insides burnt out), feeling her sweaty skin against mine and hearing her thank me because I waited and let it take its time, gave her time to enjoy it completely, because I know by a kind of intuition exactly how she wants to be loved . . .

I lie still as a statue, longing to be home in my apartment, in my own living room where, sure enough, there's a bit of dust in the corners but where, nonetheless, everything is well arranged and orderly—home to my own sofa of smooth cool hide, without clammy colorful pillows. And I think vindictively that *my* woman shall have a fragrance of mild eau de cologne and precious, cool gold, not of sweat and sickly-sweet lust.

11 Bekkelifaret next morning. Friday.

She was in the trolley as usual, cool and self-assured. The light sprinkling of snow, which makes everything else clammy and wet in the warmth of the car, sparkles on her like a last precious shower from her morning toilet. Her skin is golden, she's retaining her tan from the South remarkably well. I imagine her in Istanbul, the thieves' paradise, just stepping out of the Turkish bath, where the middle-aged attendant in her worn silk panties stealthily removes heavy coins from her purse, while the skilled hands hold out one garment after another in a large, airy room filled with the sound of running water and a yellow filtered sunlight under the tall vaulted ceiling with the inscribed characters. Light garments, stockings and underwear of top quality, cool against her skin from lying on the stone bench . . .

Utterly confused by these dreams and by yesterday's caresses suddenly burning under my skin, I got up as the car stopped at the National Theater, all but pushed the briefcase (with keys, hard plastic, and shopping bags!) onto her lap in pressing forward, called out an excuse to her and everybody in the car (I who hate to attract attention!) and tumbled out without daring to turn around to check if she was looking at me. Without daring to meet the glance of the indifferent blue, covered with a dusting of early winter snow.

And now Bekkelifaret.

A wild plan. No, not even a plan, an obsession, a hunger I have to satisfy. I feel strong after yesterday, strong and grateful in a patronizing way—now that I have her at a safe distance. Strong enough to approach Ada Dahl.

A messy track from the garage entrance to the porch. Fine. I was afraid that perhaps the fresh snow . . . No, I'm exaggerating. I hitch the briefcase under my arm and walk up to the front steps. Stop to kick the snow off my boots. Press the button. The doorbell rings far back in the house somewhere. Otherwise nothing. Not a sound. Not even a car. Behind some pine trees I see the blank back wall of the nearest house and can make out the roof of the next one. What happy times they must have been when people had enough space, and the means, to protect themselves from the noise of the road! Ready to start.

The entrance door is easy—not even a burglarproof lock. Perhaps I've exaggerated the risk of operating in neighborhoods with single-family houses? Or is it simply that today is a good day? In this business, as in most, there are good and bad days. Today I'm invincible!

Even so, the door, the way it opens, its thickness, width, the dark wood, the subdued click as the lock snaps shut after me, makes me stop for a moment. The weight of the door can tell you so much.

The large entrance hall seems half-empty despite expensive paneling, solid furniture, and the mirror with a frame in pure Empire style. All the doors are open. In the kitchen (ultramodern with furnishings in imitation mahogany and all appliances in brown), the dishes are soaking. A glance into the bedroom ascertains that the double bed is unmade and the floor strewn with clothes. The living room hasn't been aired and smells pungently of tobacco smoke. So this is the way Ada Dahl lives!

I'm stunned and stirred up at the same time. I don't know what I'd expected, but this . . . I'm not really disappointed, excited rather. She has her secrets, my good Ada. Involved in some shady business on the sly! The entire double bed has been used. A man's pajamas (the top) lies on the floor. His toothbrush and electric razor are in the bathroom. The kitchen displays remainders of breakfast for two. There are cocktail glasses on the coffee table in the living room. The cigarette butts are of different brands. But otherwise no traces can be found of a man living here. The drawers of the night table and the cabinets are empty. In the closet hang only the wraps I know so well.

A quick look at a bundle of letters, some unopened, others opened and with papers and documents carelessly stuffed back in the envelope or quite simply left in a messy pile, makes it clear that she's negotiating a divorce with her husband, as I thought. But there are also other letters, from other men, several different men, ardent letters full of platitudes about love, quite helpless, the way men write when they are in a hurry and, being quite unprepared, try to express their feelings. And in some of the letters are checks for 700, 900, 1200 kroner, with the warmest, saddest regards "to my golden dream at a difficult time." I understand . . .

I understand, and feel dizzy. So this is the manner in which my cool, unattainable Ada, my November queen with hoarfrost crystals in her eyelashes, supplements her alimony! Though as for alimony . . . I can tell by the documents among the rest of her mail that her lawyers are filing a damage suit against her husband: cruelty, adultery, and so forth. Interesting. Very interesting.

Back to the bedroom. The dressing table is a chaos of jewels and expensive cosmetics. This is where the morning mask is created. This is where her streetcar facade is painstakingly sketched. What deception! What a double life! My own masking of the thief as office clerk, salesman, municipal employee is a mere puppet show by comparison. I let my fingers play with bottles and tubes, smooth and shiny, giving off a pleasant scent. She too is a thief, knows all the dodges and how to hide behind the tricks of the profession. The thought makes me feel hot all over. My fingers play with the gold chain that has lain around her neck, which I've seen countless times on her golden skin. The cool gold ripples between my fingers. Ada! Ada! A thief to a thief. Tarzan's briefs are swelling, this is his element! No trouble with the potency now!

In the bathroom I make myself comfortable with one of her expensive creams before the wide mirror above the double washstand. The thief stares back at me with wide-open eyes and an inward glance, an uncontrollable smile on his lips while he works with a methodical obsession to gain control of his distraction, the only unreserved devotion he knows: Tarzan's ornament. (It's bigger than you'd expect it to be on a man of barely medium height.) I just manage to reflect that time may be getting perilously short—that she'll certainly soon be on her way home after her morning excursion to the city, home to tidy up (she's too discreet to hire a loose-tongued maid, imagine her ex-husband learning about all this with the lawsuit approaching!), home to take a good rest, fix herself up, make everything ready for her upcoming (lucrative!) rendezvous—before I come in her fragrant honey-colored towel. Goodbye, Ada, and thanks for a pleasant day. But I'll be back!

We sit once again in The Major, holding hands while two pairs of feet in winter shoes grope to make contact. Everything becomes a habit once it's done, and there seems to be no way back.

I can see she's glad to be sitting here with me, more glad than she would be if it were merely the excitement of doing something illegal that fired her. And again I think how little she knows me, how little it takes for women to think they love a man, how much they give in return for so little.

She relates the scene they had when Payk came back from the meeting with his suspicions, which she obviously does nothing at all to soften, quite the contrary! It amazes, troubles, and stirs me; it links me to her in a kind of reluctant fascination—her openness, her delight in being unmasked.

Again she says:

"I know it's extremely mean of me, but he asks for it. He has followed me like a dog since early fall. He saved me last summer when I was on the rocks and desperate, that's true. And we had a good time. I had a lovely time with him, after *the other one,* my husband. That brute. It was fantastic to be with someone who was always kind. But he's so kind, there's no end to it! He's so considerate he can't do anything. I'm ten years older than him. We're tremendously different. And then he wants me to be his mother kind of and to pet him till everything is all right, and that I can't do, not in the long run." Then:

"We won't be able to use our place anymore. I think he's going to make scenes. He was quite beside himself yesterday, almost violent. Actually, he showed more spunk than he has for a long time." To my shock, I catch myself thinking she may have gone to bed with him last night after I left. And although common sense tells me, Why shouldn't she? She's his partner. There's no agreement between her and you. It just shows she hasn't become completely dependent on you. It will only give you a little freedom a while longer—still, my heart beats somewhere between despair and elation, and I squeeze her hand hard while my other hand rummages in my pocket:

"Look, here's something for you . . ." Ada Dahl's gold chain illuminates the semidark recess where our table is located with its cool, yellowish brilliance.

"Gee, for me?"

She fingers the metal, cautiously.

"So heavy, is it really genuine?"

I ask her to put it on. Ada Dahl's gold against Bel Ami's skin makes her *mine* in the same way Ada Dahl was this morning. I have thought of that, hoped for it.

"Here? Now? Under this shabby blouse?"

But she does as I say, and the gold gives her neck and face a remote, almost lofty dignity that calms me.

"But Bel Ami, what a lovely present! How could you afford it . . .

Or perhaps you've stolen it?" Engrossed by the piece of jewelry, she laughs at her own joke, not fully aware of what she's saying.

"Yes, perhaps," I answer with a smile. "I'm prepared to do anything for your sake, you know."

A little later we arrange where to meet.

"It must be at your place," she says. "We won't be able to use mine anymore, with Payk there. He won't budge from the sofa as long as you're in the house. You should've heard him yesterday . . ."

"At my place?" I say. "Well, all right . . ." The supreme risk! The unthinkable! But I know I must humor her, the logic of the situation dictates it: there's only one direction I can take. Trying to turn back now will mean losing her, to Payk or someone else.

She plays with my fingers.

"I miss it so much," she says. "Sometimes I miss it so badly I think I'd have to walk the streets if I didn't know we'd soon be together again."

"Me too," I feel obliged to say. And I really mean it, for Ada Dahl's gold around Bel Ami's neck stirs my feelings.

"Tomorrow is Saturday, maybe we could meet here when you quit work?"

Somehow I don't like the thought of having to show up at the restaurant every single day. I don't usually go there on Saturday.

"Okay," she says, intertwining her fingers with mine, while her eyes wander contentedly around the room—until they become aware of something and change their expression.

"What is it?"

"Oh, nothing. *He . . .*"

Looking around, at first I see nobody I know, then I notice him on the sidewalk outside the window. He walks slowly past, peering boldly through the plate-glass window. Turns and retraces his steps. He's spying on us. He has tracked us down like a bloodhound.

"Oh well," she sighs as he disappears from view. "I guess it's time to get home to my baby-sitting again."

"Good God," I say to myself, but I can hear I'm saying it aloud. "You can't go on that way with a type like him . . ." She looks at me, waiting for the continuation.

"Come along to my place," I tell her, knowing I've lost, while I tremble in fear and delight at the thought that I'm going to be unmasked. That I'll unmask myself to her.

12 "How many nice things you have!" is her first remark as she walks about, wondering and looking at my apartment as if she had to touch and smell everything, view it from all angles.

"Still it's a regular bachelor's quarters. Strange how difficult it is for men to arrange things comfortably. Look at that sofa, for example . . ." She's already refurnishing my existence, while I stand as if nailed to the floor by the entrance, thinking I've been unmasked. Oh, well, unmasked—it doesn't show on the furniture or the interior decoration, the paint or the wallpaper, that I'm a thief. Presumably, my apartment looks like those of a great many other people—it has gotten its furnishings from a good many others, at any rate! Gradually, I've developed fairly good taste. It sharpens the senses to be a thief. It sharpens one's awareness of quality. I'm really quite proud of my apartment. Viewed soberly, it testifies to an owner with a certain culture, one who's tolerably well-off and considers quality before judging the price. When I look around me here I can say to myself that I've made good, in spite of everything. It's not everybody who can live like this. I've often wished I could invite my ex-wife here to show her. She always complained I had no drive or ambition. *She* was the climber of us two.

Bel Ami has already pushed my sofa of cool, fragrant oxhide to the wall, moved the table and made a cozy corner with two armchairs (picked up in a bold moment on the strength of a credit slip I came across).

"We can roll out the TV, you know, when there's something worth watching." We. She has already moved in.

I'd expected she would comment on the set, my expensive color TV from Røa, but she's not interested. Turning to the wall unit (whitewashed oak), she says:

"I can't believe it!" She looks at me with a teasing smile:

"Working in publishing and not a book on your shelves!"

I just delivered the whole stack to the second-hand bookstore. Damn it, now she suspects me!

But she suspects no one, just walks around taking possession of the apartment. And I stand rooted to the spot and let it happen.

But at night, in the bedroom, we're doing poorly, although we have dined out, with wine, and are moderately intoxicated. I'm apprehensive, tense, worried about my things, wondering if they can speak, if they can unmask me; I feel naked, in a far more costly, more merciless and revealing way than what concerns the physical. She has to guide me, gently, lovingly and patiently, until I bring her to a climax, while I feel the pressure of the things and see their silhouettes in the darkened room (it didn't even help much to turn out the light). Panting and sweating, she becomes a foreign body in *my* narrow bed. It seems to me that the objects around us, the furniture, the lamps, even Tarzan's chocolate-colored sheets (I've bought identical ones!) must speak to her, tell her who I am, what kind of person I am, and I flinch, cursing the impulse that led me to this impossible situation. But she nestles lovingly in the hollow of my arm and mumbles contentedly how nice it'll be to have the whole night together. Finally a whole night. A whole night when I won't have a wink of sleep!

Until toward morning, after a brief, confused slumber full of jarring dreams, with sounds and smells and colors, I wake up with a murderous desire for her and pounce on her sleeping body as if wanting to take revenge for the long humiliating evening before. She wakes up with a smiling face and willing, wet heat and receives my saved-up rage of lust like an inert feather quilt of sensual complacency. It nearly drives me out of my mind to think that she can get something out of it even if she's never even close to a climax but just lies there like a melting snowdrift, majestic and unassailable in her defenseless, white contrast with the dusky masculine sheet, while I have to work in brief, hard fits of passion, rushing faster and faster in order not to lose the small wet spasms which everything is about, which contain all the love I know. And the strain and the work, the need and the aggression reach a point where you and the person who gives you "her all," become warped and turn into a writhing hostile mass of struggling limbs, of organs and senses subject to self-timing biological automatisms.

"How nice that you came," she whispers, absorbing my bombardment of contradictory feelings and intruding upon my loneliness.

The morning passes in a tangle of conversation whose threads and pattern are difficult to make out. It starts at the breakfast table—we bought food Friday afternoon, a lot of food ("crispbread bachelor breakfasts not permitted!"). She's eager to talk about her daughter and her relationship with her previous husband. This is a side of her I don't know and don't care to know, but I understand it means a great deal to her. And I also understand I'm somehow to blame that these thoughts are now coming back to her with such urgency, because we "are so happy together," as she says.

After we met she plucked up sufficient courage to visit her daughter during school hours at Ski, where she's in second grade. And a few days ago she contacted a lawyer in order to arrange the separation at last and prepare for the divorce. But she hasn't dared see her husband yet, and she anticipates that he'll move heaven and earth to keep his daughter. He's not without influence and won't yield an inch without a whopping battle. She knows him. ·

I ask how her daughter took it when she suddenly turned up at her school, although I understand this is a delicate matter. After being away for six months and living with a younger man, she'd changed so much that the child could barely recognize her. Furthermore, it was obvious that the daughter had adjusted to living with her father and had no desire to move. "Can't you be like before, Mommy, and come home to us again?"—this was about all she had to say. Bel Ami cries as she tells me about it; it had seemed so hopeless to try to establish contact with her again, regain her confidence. She had felt so poor.

She is due late on the job this Saturday, and we spend most of the morning talking about this. She asks me what I plan to do while she's at work, and I answer that I've thought of going to the movies. We arrange to meet outside the restaurant at eleven, when her shift is over.

But I don't go to the movies. Instead, I stay home till nearly nine o'clock, watching TV and trying to quiet down after the recent events. Trying to drive her memory from the apartment—as well as the expectation that in a few hours she'll be back in my place, with her openness, her emotional courage, and her enthusiasm: "How did I come to notice you? Why did you and you alone attract my attention?"—again and again she has asked these questions, speaking mostly to herself. I ask myself the same questions. What is there about me and the little I have to give that can satisfy a woman like her? Is it the fact that I try to be thoughtful and attentive, listening to what she says and asking questions that show I've understood? Is it the fact that I don't directly mistreat her physically or spiritually? Is that all it takes? The thought of how little is needed to touch a woman causes me to despise them a little—especially her.

At nine o'clock I find the time is ripe. I get dressed, walk down to the trolley stop, and take the Jar line to Ullern station.

Snow in the air. At Bekkelifaret hedges and fences and wrought-iron gates are on display with their hoarfrost trimmings. In the gardens the frost has laid down its untouched mat of prohibitions, of privilege. A cozy light is shining in the rooms of Ada Dahl. As I thought, a large car is parked in the middle of the driveway. A Mercedes. A managing director, perhaps a head of information, an undersecretary . . . ? A tête-à-tête is in full swing. Just as I thought.

But I've not come here to spy on her, to sniff around the walls like a dog, interpret the shadows on the curtains, and make myself cozy with my heated fantasy out here in the hoarfrost and the cold. I have a plan. In my pocket I have a little camera, with flashgun, which I stole long ago for no particular reason, disliking the thought of fixing something of my own, something that concerned me, irrevocably to a celluloid strip. But now I know something I can use it for. It's almost too easy. I squat behind the car, adjust the viewfinder so that I get the license plate number at the center of the picture and, besides, enough of the surroundings included to indicate quite clearly where the car is parked (the street number on the gatepost), and press the button. The brief blue flash could just as well have come from the trolley line farther down. And in case someone *were* to pass by and wonder, I have the press card, with such a blurry picture that it could represent anybody, but with a sufficient aura of authority to satisfy a casual curiosity. Here in the dark I feel doubly protected and anonymous.

The job is done and I ought to hurry home while I am in the elated mood that accompanies it, however difficult or easy the job is, however large or small the profit. But it is as if the illumination of Ada Dahl's warm living room, as reflected in the shiny car of the department head, exercised an irresistible attraction upon me. I try the door by the driver's seat; it's not locked. So that's how confident he is, her chosen mate for tonight! The coupe still holds a lingering warmth, along with the smell of gasoline and leather. Genuine leather upholstery. Dashboard of wood. The man must be at least a director. She'll get two or three thousand kroner for a single evening, as sure as gold!

I slide down into the soft, gently creaking driver's seat, take off my gloves and let my fingers glide along the steering wheel, the discreet molding on the dashboard, the short, chubby shift lever of the automatic transmission with its smooth knob, the smell of luxury . . . The subdued light from the living-room windows streams across the dashboard and gives a dim, glittering sheen to the car's interior, luxurious as the innermost bedchamber of the caliph's palace in Istanbul, the thieves' paradise, during the soundless hour of noon . . . I've never before masturbated in a limousine.

Afterwards I find the registration in the unlocked glove compartment: Christian Müller, administrative director. I take it just in case, along with a lighter, two packs of cigarettes, and the cassette player. So he'll think it was a regular theft when he discovers it.

13 At five to eleven she comes out; I've just arrived. She has finished her work quickly to save five minutes. Realizing this puts me in high spirits, it leaves me in charge and gives me excess energy for despising her in my benevolent, mildly patronizing manner. It gives me the exact distance I need, the distance I'm forced to maintain toward women in order to save myself.

It's too late to go anywhere, so we stroll down toward Majorstua to take the bus to Skøyen. She has taken my arm and asked if I liked the film, and I've told her what it was about (choosing one I saw last week, a spy film that was grotesque in its exaggeration and in its caricature of criminals, but refreshingly sensual in its sumptuous, relaxing setting of carefree luxury), and I notice during our walk that the distance between us shrinks as we huddle in the cold, her body sharing its heat even through her heavy clothes.

For a moment she's about to stop, as if something occurred to her, unless it is merely the presence of two males in a side street, looking at a display window in a way that seems neither peculiar nor unnatural. I take no notice of them and ask what's the matter. She shakes her head and pulls me along. In the bus she tells me she suddenly thought she recognized the two men; one resembled Payk, the other reminded her momentarily of her husband. But she must have imagined it. The two men don't know each other and certainly wouldn't have any business in town together so late in the evening. I add that Payk, after all, looks like most men between twenty and thirty of a certain type. She sees what I

mean, though she dislikes my saying it. But I can risk it now, conscious how I arouse her in the nearly empty bus, slowly and mercilessly, with the heavy sweetness left in my body by the half-hour in the limousine, forced up by the springy up-and-down movements of the bus: tonight I'll make it. Tonight she'll not find fault with my performance!

Sunday morning she says:

"I must go back there and pick up my things." With a smile:

"A toothbrush isn't enough. Not in the long run."

I start saying something to change her mind, but she hugs me tight and whispers:

"And I'm scared, I don't know why. Those men yesterday . . . If I don't go now something awful might happen." We agree she'll pick up a few things she needs, as much as she can carry, and pack the rest; we'll arrange for transportation here later in the week.

I've been afraid of this, because I know it won't work. She can't move in here, not for real. I'd really like to get out of the relationship now. I am beginning to know her too well; we've started doing the same things already, saying the same things. Since she came to my place I've had a clear advantage: she toadies, wants to please, repeats time and again how happy she is here, with me, as it is. But I feel monotony setting in already, I miss the suspense, the fear, and the thief's triumph—though this is what I've wanted, to reduce her to this state, make her "mine," as it said in those primitive short stories I used to read in the john at the magazine warehouse. In short, get it over with. Because once you get there, it's over; from the top the road can only go downhill. And I have other plans.

But when ready to leave she hugs me tight, and I know—and she knows—that she need only whisper a word or two to start me again; her robust directness smashes my flimsy defenses, strips me of my camouflage, deprives me of the necessary distance . . . So the upshot is that she leaves anyway. I notice she's uneasy and dreads meeting her faithful Payk, whom she now—for no reason, in my opinion—has begun to fear. When I offer to come with her she says no, as I'd expected; my presence would only make matters worse.

When she's gone I notice that her uneasiness has been contagious. The relief of being alone again is spoiled by my entirely new worry that she may run into something, an accident . . . What else? Anyway, scorned Per Kristian seems to be quite harmless. But the *situation* is not harmless, with relationships breaking up, concealments, the lack of clear lines in the game of power, of acquiring influence over people's feelings and actions, and with a disturbance in love's balance of terror. In the midst of my sense of well-being at being alone and rid of her, I'm suddenly gnawed by uneasiness, by impatience to have her with me again. I lie on the sofa trying to conjure up Ada Dahl, cool and luxurious. I admire her sure touch in managing her situation as a separated woman (I have no doubt that she chooses her "admirers" among those who can also pay physically and emotionally). She's the perfect embodiment of the thief as respectable, attractive citizen. My fascination with lovely Ada is more metaphysical than sensual, a gravitation toward an equal, toward perfection: that of a thief toward the queen of thieves.

Still I can't help being anxious about Bel Ami. I know enough to respect woman's intuition, even if her fantasy of imminent danger seems a bit hard to understand. The situation itself is an invitation to violence, I realize that. But her friend, Payk, seems as tame as a gelded goat. She has mentioned her husband on several occasions, spoken of him as a brute, a wife-beater. But one day when I pressed the point, asking if he'd really mistreated her, she admitted he'd used violence only once, after she'd provoked him. Besides, if he hasn't previously shown any interest in where she is and what she's doing, why should he pop up now?

So I try to concentrate on Ada Dahl again, on the sterling sense of quality that characterizes even the compromising mess in her villa after a night of love. She and I together: my dreams revived. My wildest ambitions realized! Madness! But my plan cannot fail, I reflect, cautiously checking if the scent of Tarzan's expensive aftershave lotion still clings to my fingers as I turn the LP with Henry Mancini from Hollywood Bowl, while the freezing-cold morning light on the hoarfrost-covered birches outside slowly merges into the softer tones of afternoon. And I detect beneath my comfort, despite my exciting plans and my optimism, a dread of some imminent act of violence, of something drastic. Irremediable.

64   She's late. So late that I'm quite beside myself with worry and restless-ness. Silly, like a schoolboy waiting for his girl friend. I'd planned it differently, figuring that from this point on indifference would set in: boredom, revulsion from the steady, nonbinding love relationship after all had been said and done. I'd looked forward to a quiet afternoon in my own place to establish the necessary distance. But no. The insipid Sunday morning TV program moves by almost without registering. The sports report doesn't even fill me with jaundiced envy of the flocks of shapely youths who get to be the center of attention for the whole nation simply by racing or skiing. The afternoon news report offers half a dozen concise lessons in the form of catchwords, incomprehensible and uninteresting. When the children's hour begins, I turn it off and start looking at my watch. I try to figure out what can be keeping her away for so long, wonder if she's had an accident, if something has happened to make her change her mind, about him or me, or if something has turned up that changes the situation once more. After all, she has lived in his place for several months; she has known me only a few weeks. Perhaps she's in bed with him at this very moment?

The last thought is hardest to bear and makes me really desperate: this is the very thing that was *not* supposed to happen. This is how the relationship was *not* supposed to be. What would happen if I threw myself at her feet (as they said in the short stories from last summer), begged her never again to leave me, impressed upon her how much I needed her, no, *loved* her? Even in my agitated state of mind I have to smile at the thought of such a scene. And yet I find myself again and again by the window, looking down the road. I'm constantly on the point of fleeing the house, but where should I go? Down to Dram-mensveien to be on the watch for her? Jump on the trolley to Grefsen? What if at this very moment she's on her way here by a trolley coming from the other direction, or has taken a taxi? My dilemma has no solution; the irony is painful: once completely unfettered and free to follow my fancy, with no job and no obligations except to myself, here I sit locked up in my own apartment waiting for a woman with whom I ought to have an uncomplicated affair but who is now about to become the to-be-or-not-to-be of my spiritual equilibrium! This is what is called "being in love," I realize that. It will pass, I know that too. But what can you do while it lasts? Anything at all can happen to me, I feel it! This is what I wanted to avoid at any price!

At half past seven she comes, out of breath and serious, with a suitcase full of clothes and two shopping bags with small articles. I can tell by the way she cuddles up to me that something has happened. And I have a notion what it is, but she doesn't say anything. Not yet. She says:

"It took so much longer than I'd expected." But she understands how I feel and embraces me, and this time she doesn't have to say or do anything at all to get me started. The mere thought of where she's been, the certainty that she's here again, the sense of her being close to me is enough.

But before we go to bed I notice something is holding her back. A few days ago this wouldn't have worried me in the least; rather, her absentmindedness and her passive compliance would have increased my desire to mount and conquer her. But tonight it's as if I'd suddenly acquired an extra sense besides the usual ones. I *understand* what torments her and *know* what must come and fear it, and the fear makes me hesitant and unsure, which makes her all the more remote and unapproachable, makes us strangers in the midst of an exchange of loving caresses. Until she's unable to hold back anymore as I become aggressive, squeeze and fumble, eager to get it over with and hoping, feebly and unrealistically, that the brief convulsive joy and the indolence and sense of physical well-being afterward will lead to clarification. Suddenly she fights me and wriggles away in tears. Then she blurts it out: she's been to bed with Payk, of course, without really meaning to, without feeling anything but indifference, not even disgust with him as he came at her, not even brutally, only imploringly, in whimpering self-abasement. She could have taken his anger, his scorn, his sense of being wronged, she says, but not this, his spineless begging. Yet he had an air about him she didn't recognize, watchful and expectant, which gave him power, which troubled and challenged her. Perhaps she'd acquiesced to demonstrate her independence? To regain her power over him? It was quickly done, like giving a hand to a passerby, throwing a coin to a beggar, like entering an old, empty house you once lived in and then exiting again. But now, afterward, she's repentant, feels dirty, feels she has failed. And only now does she understand how terribly much our affair has begun to mean to her. She wants to start afresh with me, she says; for us two there's hope! And then she has a stomachache too—and that makes her even more desperate. She cries and holds me tight. And regardless of the situation, I tremble with emotion, jealousy, and desire as I listen to what she's saying. I whisper back that, yes, she and I will start afresh, there's hope for us! And I mean it the moment I say it. I'm aware of that. And I notice that my cheeks turn wet from my own tears, my throat contracts and my body is shaken, for I'm crying too. And I know I'm lost as I lie there sobbing in her arms, fully dressed. This is the end. Now all hope is gone.

14 Monday I go to get the film developed and printed in a photo store downtown that guarantees delivery the following day. This is urgent. I feel my time is running out. Unable to form a clear idea of what will happen, I walk around with a sense of being in danger. What I have in mind is not primarily that the longer she stays with me, the likelier it is that she'll sooner or later come to suspect me and expose my activities. I'm thinking of the condition I find myself in when we spend time together. I think of last night, what I said, how I gave myself away, what expectations and hopes it must have filled her with, expectations that today, in full daylight and at a safe distance, I feel I have neither the ability nor the desire to fulfill. Still, I know I'm slipping, that the situation between us is slipping, and that this will lead to certain consequences. I have no idea which, but I fear the worst, whatever this "worst" should turn out to be. Of that too I have no clear idea. After all, I can't even say that I dislike having her stay with me, though I know how precarious it would be in the long run. I look forward to seeing her again, even though I tremble at the thought of last night, when everything was in a state of flux. Last night when anything could have happened, just as anything can happen to our relationship after this experience. The relationship between two people is always developing, and the way ours is developing scares me. It pushes me step by step away from what's safe, comprehensible, controllable. But until I find a way of intervening, I'm helplessly involved. Only death is static.

Up at Bryn, outside the apartment house on Jernbaneveien, I suddenly have second thoughts. Instead of acting the power station engineer, choosing an entrance, and authoritatively walking in and beginning to work on a door, I stop to watch people passing by on the road, women carrying shopping bags and with thin legs between the hems of their coats and their lined boots. Solitary elderly people shuffling carefully because of the hazardous condition of the road. Youths in groups of three or four playing hooky. It strikes me all of a sudden how much I know about them. I'm familiar with the apartments in the area, the standard is remarkably uniform, just as the level of income is approximately the same, not bad but not tops either. I can visualize the imitation ceramic tiles in innumerable kitchens, living rooms with sectionals and teakwood tables, showy wall units with stereo sets (usually with only about twenty records, chosen quite at random) and a color TV bought on the installment plan, bathrooms with plastic panels in mahogany finish and shaggy mats made from artificial fibers. The note on the kitchen table and the food in the oven, or on a plate in the refrigerator (I've tucked away many a helping from such!). I'm struck by the fact that I know these people passing by, so well that they seem like my own relatives. I know their lives and their habits. I know what they read and eat, how they dress. Their dreams and hopes are reflected in the details, in the exaggerations and lack of proportion of the woodwork, the decoration, and the furniture. Their perception of themselves and their situation is revealed by the doorplates, mirrors, ashtrays and lamps, personal objects, knickknacks, and jewelry. But their portraits still betray the reality behind the ideal image—if one has a mind for investigating such things. And an able thief does.

Today, however, I'm suddenly unable to use my knowledge, though it's absolutely necessary. The weekend with Bel Ami has severely drained my otherwise frugal budget. Nonetheless, instead of slipping into the entrance I selected (anyway, it might have aroused adverse attention now, after such long hesitation), I stroll onto the sidewalk and go with the crowd to the supermarket, among housewives, small children, and retired people. Instead of letting my knowledge strengthen my feeling of superiority toward these people, I give way to a moment's sympathy and understanding, even a kind of tenderness for the four or five I can see at this moment, and for all the others, in their cars and behind their kitchen curtains.

In the supermarket I help myself to the better sort of canned goods and various other provisions, taking care to fill the basket with the same kind of merchandise I stuff into my pockets. They've become more proficient at spotting thieves in large stores. For example, it's almost impossible now to walk out of a shoe store unobserved in a pair of shoes taken from the shelf. I'll have to be content with this today. It's a bit late anyway; the trip to the photo shop cost me almost an extra hour.

But at the cash register I'm again touched by an inexplicable tenderness. The cashier, with her colored hairdo and chewed nail polish, looks at me with a pair of deep brown eyes in her round face as she asks:

"Is that all?" Puts her hand in mine when she gives the change. She's young, barely twenty, and hasn't yet learned to be on her guard. An old-fashioned cardigan protrudes from under her uniform, a nylon frock buttoned in front. She sits in the draft from the door, and the heat fans point in the other direction.

Instead of eating in the restaurant I go home and begin to prepare dinner for her and me, as agreed. I have plenty of time; she quits at three, won't be here till almost half-past.

But shortly after two-thirty I already hear voices in the hall, just before the doorbell rings . . .

Voices?

While I wonder who it is (it could be her, of course, let off early—I haven't given her the key—but voices?), there's another ring and I rush to open, more bewildered than apprehensive, and there she stands on the doormat with a little girl, looking exultantly at me. The girl looks down.

"Hi!" She looks so expectant that I squirm.

"Say hello to Eli. Eli, say hello to the man. His name is Bel Ami. He's the one we'll stay with." The little girl looks like she wants to protest:

"But what about my things, Mommy?"

"We'll pick them up some other day," the mother says confidently, but with a quivering elation under her quiet tone of voice. The quivering elation of a thief.

"And in the meantime we can buy what you need."

"Come in, then!" My voice in the corridor sounds to my ears like the crack of a pistol shot. Never have I, in any way, attracted the attention of the neighbors!

They come in. The girl hesitantly. Bel Ami is immediately busy helping her off with her things (though she's big enough to manage herself), chatting and babbling around her. Now and then she brushes me with her glance, and I recognize in the luster of her eyes the thief's fanatic exaltation after a haul. I understand. I understand what she wants to invest in our relationship. She has turned herself into a thief to perfect our union! Mother, father, and child. A tragedy! She doesn't realize what she has done, not yet. She has only followed her instincts. The contentment she has felt when we've been together has created the expectation of an absolute harmony. Instead, she'll experience collapse. Soon it will be reported. And then the investigation. Police. Soon we'll have the police here! It's not only her own life she's spoiling this way, but mine as well!

My head seethes with thoughts and plans while we help each other set the table for three. Little Eli sits obediently reading the magazines she's been given. No homework today. No school tomorrow. Without wishing to provoke her in any way, I ask in a roundabout fashion (in order to avoid an open discussion in Eli's presence) if Bel Ami has considered the practical consequences. She smiles broadly and shrugs her shoulders:

"It'll be all right!"

The thief's presumption after a successful take, like throwing money around in an exclusive restaurant. The simplicity of an amateur.

"I just *had to,* you understand!" She whispers it to me in the kitchen while we're cutting up the chicken.

"Since the very moment we got together I've missed her so terribly! She belongs here, with us!" I nod and press her arm while I ponder, sick with anxiety about how to wriggle out of this without involving the authorities. The papers! I'm perspiring as I stand by the hot stove pouring the sauce into the sauce boat. My head is buzzing like a subway station. What am I going to do? How can I get rid of them both?

Putting little Eli to bed goes smoothly. She's a timid, obedient child, tired after the day's events. Bel Ami promises her they'll speak to her father in a couple of days. I wince when I hear how optimistic she is, how she believes wonders will come to pass simply because she feels she's found happiness with a man. I act friendly and helpful, but actually I'm disapproving and guarded. And I note my reaction with satisfaction: this morning everything was slipping. Up there in the Bryn supermarket I felt as if my entire life until then had been played in the wrong key. Something was about to change fundamentally and I resisted, though uncertain of the outcome. When I looked into the candid brown eyes of that heavyset young cashier and felt her hand with the change, I almost regretted my little bit of shoplifting.

But now everything is back to normal. I'm looking at Bel Ami, her angular hips, long legs and full breasts, and if it weren't for the fact that I have other, more important things to think about I would take her right this minute. I can even (not without a certain sensual delight!) imagine her feeble protests, her dislike of doing it here in the living room, on the sofa or the floor, with her daughter sleeping behind a half-open door just a few feet away.

She pours beer for us and talks nonstop about what has happened this afternoon, how last night made her really understand for the first time what our relationship meant to her. How she finally realizes what real human contact with a man is. And, with that, the thought of her missing daughter became unbearable, now that she feels "whole" in every other way, now that she feels a painful, obscure period of flux in her life is over (ironically enough, the very moment I've begun to feel that my own life is in a painful state of flux). When she refers to yesterday, as she does over and over again, I get uncomfortable. I remember her voice, which tempted me in my despair:

"Let go! Oh, do let go!"

And I squirm, because it wasn't aimed at the physical, it wasn't sexual performance she hoped to get; no, it was my total helplessness she was hungry for. My soul, my doubt and bewilderment, fear of being alone, of being tied down. Fear of losing whatever fixed point I have in existence, the apartment, the furniture, the décor, my things—which were of no help to me even though the light was on.

But now the situation has changed. Now I listen with half an ear, while my mind struggles with other matters: How can I get out of *this* quandary? My thoughts go back to an earlier episode when I was surprised in a row house (perhaps that's the reason I've had such respect for them since?) by the click of a key from the hallway. There I was with the drawers of the night table pulled out and their contents scattered all over the bedspread! I was saved by the door from the bedroom to the terrace. I slipped out like a cat, ran doubled-up under the windows along the shorter side of the row of houses, jumped across a hedge and down onto the road. Anyone could have seen me, figured it all out, and given the alarm. I still start sweating when I think of it. The only time I almost came to grief.

But now. This situation is a far more dangerous one: to be mixed up in something like that! To risk a search of the apartment, interrogation. I'm scared, but notice with satisfaction that my thief's instincts are awakening again: I will make it. I *must* make it! I've wriggled out of a scrape before!

Still, when she asks me to go and check on little Eli and I bend over my own bed and contemplate the soft profile on the pillow—the long, thin, semiblond hair; the broad lips and chubby cheeks of an otherwise thin, almost skinny little girl; the barely audible, deep, slow breathing—I waver, a prey to all sorts of fancies. I understand, no, I *feel* how a man can be caught by this: a woman, a child to be responsible for. A child who entrusts its helplessness to you. A woman who places a boundless, inexhaustible devotion at your disposal . . . I flee the bedroom.

When I'm back she asks why I act so quiet, what my reaction is to what she's done, how I size up the situation. I answer that she's acted rashly, no doubt, but that a great deal depends on what her husband will do (though *I* don't have a moment's doubt what he'll do, that is, exactly what I would do myself in such a situation, report the whole thing to the police and thus add an excellent card to my hand in the legal battle for custody).

But there is another complicating factor, I inform her. I'm expecting a visit from my separated wife one of these days, perhaps already tomorrow. And if *she* comes and finds her and Eli in the apartment, there will be trouble. Bel Ami understands instantly. Her fantasy has built up a drama in progress between my wife and me, with jealousy, espionage, threats of legal consequences. I've let her do so, because I understand that, to her, such a story automatically explains my somewhat irregular conduct. Nothing helps to excuse your unreasonable demands on others, and your injustice to them, as well as the nervousness you're struggling with, the pressure you're exposed to. The only thing that doesn't fit into the picture is that I drink only moderately. And that very fact makes me a bit of a hero in her eyes.

"I can take her with me," she says promptly. "She can wait for me in the restaurant. She can sit in the back room doing her homework. Before lunch there's little to do anyway, so I can be with her almost every minute."

A good idea, I reply, for I'd thought of proposing something similar myself. Then I'll call her at the restaurant and give my report. And if my wife were to appear, say, around dinner time, perhaps she and Eli could take a walk in town till the coast was clear? We agree on that.

She promises to get in touch with her lawyer to clarify her position after this last development. She's happy, optimistic, slightly intoxicated, wants to sit on my lap and make plans, has no objection at all to my wanting to undress her and pull her close. If she knew me she would be able to interpret my ardor, to understand it and realize that all's lost.

15 I'm reading the morning papers in the streetcar. Have intentionally taken one that leaves at ten past nine. Won't risk betraying myself and my plan, not even with a grimace or a movement of my hand.

Nothing in the papers about the kidnaping. Not very strange perhaps. Such cases don't appear automatically, even if reported to the police. Only if a police bulletin has to be sent out, and that may take another day or two. All the better, it gives me a day to take action. I get off downtown and walk straight to the photo store. The pictures are first-rate. The license plate number clearly legible, along with easily recognizable details from the driveway, and the gatepost with the street number. Perfect!

Then I call the police from a public telephone. I have no qualms, contrary to what one might expect, though the act I'm about to commit is called common squealing. "Honesty among thieves" is a romantic myth. Squealing is one of the thief's natural tools, betrayal a natural element of his psychology.

It's quickly done; the voice that answers when I've reached the correct department is calm and matter-of-fact, my message simple and concise: "Yesterday afternoon after school hours a little girl was picked up forcibly by her mother and taken to a place where the father won't find her. The parents are separated. If the matter hasn't been reported, you can check my information . . ." I give the name and address. I've done my homework, supplied facts. "I happen to know where they are at this moment . . ." The restaurant. The address. It's all over. What a relief! "Never mind my name, I don't want to get mixed up in anything . . ." One of hundreds of anonymous cases of informing handled by the police every single week.

At seven past the half-hour she comes. I spot her in the customary seat already before the trolley stops. There's no vacant seat in her proximity, so I stand in the middle of the car preparing my next move. We pass Thune, but the seats nearby are still occupied. I didn't intend to go home anyway—I have other plans. At Skøyen many people get off. The seat next to her is free. I sit down without attracting attention in any way, then wait till the trolley has started moving. Calmly and unhurriedly, I place my briefcase over my knees, open it, and as discreetly as possible take out the letter I stole from her hallway table, the auto registration, and the two photographs. Then I lightly touch her coat sleeve next to me.

"Excuse me, is your name Ada Dahl?"

"Yes . . ." A slight wrinkle at the root of her nose shows that she doesn't like to be accosted by strangers in the streetcar.

"I've got something here you ought to look at, I think . . ."

It may be the absolute self-assurance in my voice (the thief's self-assurance when he has secured his prey and his retreat is clear) that forces her to surrender her impregnable profile and take a look at the papers in my hand. A tiny twitch around her mouth and the corner of her eye tells me that she has seen—and understood—what it is: three small compromising pieces of evidence that may overturn her entire damage suit against her husband and perhaps create a scandal besides.

"That is, I have an offer that may interest you . . ." She understands. Among thieves it's immediately clear where the power lies at any moment. And she looks at me, smiles, makes her lips and eyes smile, and a faint flush breaks through her golden skin, the same as when she steps out of the caliph's airy bath chamber, where the tiles mirror the white stillness of noon while, in the galleries, blind musicians praise the everlasting fragrant night in the city of thieves, Istanbul.

And there are only three stops to Ullern.

Still three stops to Ullern!

THE DOG

1 The metamorphosis had already begun by the time she brought him home the first time. My glance, my expression, even my posture . . . I could see it in the mirror: things had gone that far, it had already become that obvious. I could hear it in my voice, or rather in my words, which came slowly, with difficulty, as if it got harder and harder to concentrate on anything except what was immediately at hand. When I wanted to tell her something, both the context and the details would suddenly escape me—anyway, she hadn't expressed the slightest interest lately in anything I said. When I tried to plan, think ahead, adjust to what I dimly perceived was imminent, every bit of reasoning was dissolved in a fog of vague pictures, and only an oppressive fear remained: the fear of the menace I sensed but couldn't logically pinpoint by rational deduction. The dog's fear when he sees his punishment is brewing and doesn't know what he has done wrong, just crawls into a corner and makes himself as small as possible.

Long before she brought him home the first time I'd already begun to avoid my own image in the mirror. I couldn't stand meeting that melancholy dog look, seeing the long hair parted in the middle and falling in soft waves on both sides of the narrow face, like the ears of a cocker spaniel. The sprouting beard, which gave the whole face a fluffy, puppylike character. In profile, I saw the stooped shoulders over the flat chest, like the back of a borzoi. This figure was me! This helpless, whipped mongrel who crawled up to his mistress on his belly after each round of beating, licked her hands and asked for more, was me!

Though there was no question of a beating at that time. Only indifference that gradually had become more noticeable. Irritation that showed up more and more often but could easily be due to other causes, any causes at all; irritation that could come from anywhere but must be taken out on the the nearest person, a mysterious part of the problem of cohabitation. But when I tried to talk with her about such things she showed an utter lack of interest. "You always talk too much," she complained. "You only want to talk and talk. Talk doesn't change anything. Your talking won't help anybody."

We who'd talked all summer long, talked and talked, discussed everything between heaven and earth, confided in each other for weeks, even months, from the very moment we got together, when she discharged all her pent-up need for expression upon me, her suddenly awakened zeal for an equal exchange of both verbal and physical communication, her need to take revenge on her husband, whom she'd spontaneously left after he "mistreated" her because she'd once been unfaithful to him, a long time ago, and had told him about it in order to hurt him. This was the way it began . . .

But it isn't easy to recall anymore what we talked about those long days and evenings last summer, when our attention hung on each other's lips and we slept together only when the urge grew so strong it distracted us from thinking, as if it were a matter of obtaining some peace and of gathering strength and concentration for long hours of fresh conversations, in outdoor restaurants, on park benches, in little cheap cafés, a "fancy" place once in a while when we thought we could afford it; I still had a bit of my student loan left, she the checkbook for the account her husband had generously supplied her with—"payment for services rendered in bed," as she called it, which agreed well with my own ideas at the time. I remember she'd often say I was the only one she'd met who "understood" her (that is, a man who didn't automatically take her frankness for a free ticket to her bed), and how fantastic she thought it was to be able to talk with a man about anything she liked, knowing that he understood what she meant, didn't think her stupid or uninteresting, and didn't sit counting the half-hours till it was time to go to bed. And I let her talk and talked myself, because I felt the same need to confide in a woman, to try out all the theoretical knowledge of life that several years of study and reading had provided me with, without the opportunity to test it due to a student environment where outward forms were everything and even abandon and sheer debauchery became stilted, a ritualistic act you could take part in without personal involvement.

She was the first woman I had met who was a *human being*. She was a good deal older than I. She spoke from experience of life, not theories in books, and therefore even the trivial things she talked about, banal fancies and confessions, had a character of near revelation for me. I trembled when she told me about her marriage. Intimate relations, which had slumbered in my head like neutral hypotheses or interesting speculations, took on validity and reality in her mouth. She sought to purge herself of the past, so to speak, by telling me as much as possible about her former life. Sometimes it became so overwhelming that I had to take refuge in romantic reverie, an exalted idyll that was the correct frame for my modest amorous art. While fear of, and fascination with, the real life she represented drove my adoration to the verge of hysteria.

She was the first woman in my life. Even though I wasn't completely inexperienced sexually when I met her, she became the first one. She made me realize that love is a state of mind, not a pattern of behavior. She taught me that sexuality is active between people all the time, not only in the rare, so-called intimate situations. With her, each piece of clothing, every movement, every tone of voice became an important sensual communication. And when I first discovered this, I became virtually obsessed by it. I tuned in completely to her signs, interpreted them, answered them. We became real experts in sexual communication; a glance, the hint of a grimace, a light touch would be enough. She received me untiringly, and told me how sweet and wonderful it was to find at last that deep sensitivity which women always miss in a man, that sense for what's unspoken, for subtlety. And I felt my emotions ripen like fragrant fruit in her warmth, noticed how I learned to pick up the delicate vibrations from her femininity, and developed an ability to achieve sexual contact at a distance. Our intimate long-distance communications in those early days would become so intense at times that we seemed able to give each other orgasms telepathically. We worked out a "conversation intercourse" that we used during visits to restaurants, at parties, on buses and in trolley cars, and in other "public" situations. We cultivated "telephone intercourse" when for some reason we had to stay away from each other for several hours in a row, "movie intercourse" when free play was hindered by lack of space and the presence of other people; during "museum intercourse" a simple shared visual experience (of one of the nudes in the Munch Museum, for example) would send us into a state of rapture. "Literary intercourse" overwhelmed us when we came across a lovely passage in a book we liked, or just a stanza from a poem . . .

I felt as if all the nerve strings in my body, dead to sensuousness till then, had been extended and lay like a floating fine-meshed net in the atmosphere, tuned solely to registering nuances in her sensual climate. It was an indescribable sensation and, needless to say, I already realized by then that it would bind me to her in an eternal and unbreakable relationship of dependency. Even if she were followed by other women, my experiences with them would always receive their resonance from the real revelation with her, the first person who'd managed to pry loose the barriers, release my locked-up loneliness and—for a short while— transform it into something that could have become independence, emotional courage, and the ability to love.

I understood already then that she was becoming my queen and that I would have to follow her humbly and faithfully, just as a well-trained dog follows his master in an established relationship of eternal loyalty that ends only at death.

And this state of affairs existed long before she invited him home and displayed my degradation, my dog status, as an object of ridicule. I recall earlier events only vaguely, without continuity. But the evenings when *he* came to our place stand engraved in my dog's brain with indelible clarity; I remember sounds, smells, the movements of feet, and the touch of hands (I seldom dared lift my eyes to their faces), and I still feel jealousy, the urge to raise my hackles, bare my teeth and snap! But it comes to nothing but a whimper, as so often, or perhaps a howl of grief over my loneliness and longing.

2 But other things too must have played a part in the metamorphosis I underwent. I mostly think of her, remember only
her, recalling how affectionate training was replaced by indifferent
dominance and finally by humiliating neglect, while I became her
dependent companion. But I have a hunch that other things, too, were
important. For the humiliation wasn't limited to situations between us,
or at home. I also remember episodes where I had to sit up before the
authorities, acknowledge the powerlessness of my humble situation,
await judgment, slink home with the tail between my legs.

It applied, for example, to getting a job.

I'd taken an M.A. degree the same spring I met her and was
uncertain what to do. Actually I was rather tired of studying, though I
understood that my student status made me especially "interesting" in
her eyes. She hadn't had any opportunities to meet intellectuals before,
since her husband was a businessman whose circle of acquaintance
consisted of people like him who ate and drank a lot, talked shop and
sports, and tried to make out with her when they'd had a few drinks too
many, while their wives were watching—empty, faceless women who
had no interests and didn't understand anything. She thought it must
be different among intellectuals. At least they must *know* something
about a great many things that she would just love to learn about. I tried
to live up to all this, while in reality breaking off my studies, that is,
giving up the one advantage that chance had given me over her and
setting out into the "real world," thoughtlessly and shortsightedly
inspired by my encounter with this "real" woman.

I remember showing up in the office of the manager of a publishing
house I'd made an appointment with, hot and flushed with her caresses,
which I carried on my skin like a diploma, tattooed on my body in the
school of life and worth more than the finest academic degree. I was
offered a position as proofreader, with the possibility of getting translation jobs after passing a language test. I shuffled out and sneaked home.
She consoled me: they didn't know how to value real merits. Even the
publishing business, liberal as it was, had been infected by the craze for
grades and GPAs . . . But I knew she was disappointed, knew from the
way she stroked me. This was not my first defeat; it was one of several
humiliating experiences with directors, personnel managers, and fore-
men. God knows I could have gotten a job, for there was plenty of
work, but I was particular, refused to take just anything; as a semiedu-

cated academic, I was at least semiqualified for something decent. But most important: I wanted a job that matched my new status as a living human being, as her lover! It was beneath my dignity to read proofs when she dubbed me king. In moments of rapture, emperor! When I was asked about my qualifications during interviews with those important men, I could barely restrain myself from shouting: Lover! For that's what I was, what I'd become during those summer weeks with her. Everything else seemed trivial. But these qualities, which I myself experienced as so transcendently important, were not in demand where I had to go to find employment. And the importance I attached to the sensitivity I'd built up, what to myself I called "my new human existence" (which pivoted on her, her, nothing but her), made me forget other attributes, more important in the others' eyes, which might have made a better impression on the bosses. I must have given them the impression of being a long-winded, irrational dreamer who could plunge into long monologues about abstract metaphysical problems, but sat dumb and uncommunicative when the conversation turned to practical work and concrete experience, to talents and personal qualities that would be useful to me in the job I was looking for.

We saw our first defeats as victories. The triumphs of purity over mediocrity. She repeated that *she* could work and support us. It agreed well with our attitudes: she yearned to get away from everything that reminded her of the oppressed housewife's role she'd fled from; I cultivated ideas of equality, the equivalency of roles. A man shouldn't feel degraded if he were to keep house and take care of a home or, if it turned out that way, were even to accept being supported financially. Through her awakening she'd extended my entire sensory apparatus. I'd been made to pay heed to so much that I'd hitherto ignored; the world was suddenly full of small details to respond to and take delight in. Forms and colors, light and fragrances, furniture and clothes, everything my senses came in close contact with (everything having to do with her, her, always her). And I thought: what if I could stay here at home in my own world of feeling, explore it and arrange it in such a way as to provide an even more satisfying background to our passion! I thought of food with aphrodisiac spices, incense and soft pillows, deep soul-colors, feeling-music. If I had the chance I'd transform my apartment (now ours) into a temple of sensuality, where I would be a servant and await her return from work every day. This is how I would think aloud to her, while enjoying her tender caresses and seeing her clear gaze wander . . .

Then the mood changed—everything had to be light, and the curtains were stripped from the windows of our ground-floor apartment, allowing the sunlight to stream freely through our dwelling, through our hearts! With our last money we bought an expensive glass table that let the light through and reflected it, making a pansy she'd left there look as though floating on a column of light. The fleshy fourfold flower head with its dull, soft colors around a central golden sun was like a picture of the passionate love we worshiped in this luminous space.

Then she was hired as a waitress and my spell as housekeeper began. But only temporarily, I consoled myself (a completely groundless consolation by the way); I'd applied for a job as substitute teacher to every school in the Oslo area, including Asker out west, Nittedal Valley, and the farmlands of Romerike farther north. Enjoy the summer fully and then in the fall . . .

We could still sleep late; she often worked a late shift. We still ate breakfast with open windows; it was still warm. I would show up outside the restaurant shortly after eleven, when she was through. But she was often tired and didn't have the strength to walk all the way to Grefsen as I'd hoped we would, as we'd done so many summer nights, walked home through streets where we still felt the summer heat coming at us from the walls of the houses . . . But now she was too tired. She liked the job; at least she never complained, said it was fun to learn the tricks, remember the orders, study the different types who would come there. Bel Ami was a superior place, a lunch and dinner spot, quite busy. Some days she'd get a tidy sum in tips. Some days, too, she managed to sneak home tidbits from leftovers in the kitchen. But the unfamiliar work drained her strength and she often fell asleep as soon as we went to bed, in the middle of a conversation.

Conversation continued to be our first priority. Having a good talk, opening up and discussing everything. Not least important to me, now that I was staying home, was the opportunity to tell her everything I'd been thinking about during the day, experiences, discoveries, questions I wanted to ask her. They might be trifles of a happy sort, but also little worries, things about her I suddenly felt I didn't know or wasn't sure of. I knew, for example, that she had a child, a daughter she never mentioned. That she'd left not only her husband but her daughter, too, had struck me as proof of how unique she was, how independent and liberated. To *her*, freedom was worth all that. Our life together meant so much that she never looked back, never had regrets . . . But was it possible? She didn't want to talk about it, not even when I tried to force her, uncertain as I felt walking around at home all day, waiting and thinking about her, checking the mailbox for answers from the municipal offices, playing records we liked, philosophizing on the weather and the few garden plants I could see from the window, the furniture, the posters on the walls—everything that was in danger of becoming flat and empty and meaningless to me when she wasn't there. Which it was costing me a greater and greater effort to keep alive in my voluntary captivity.

I began to imagine that people were looking askance at me, even in the store where I'd been shopping for three years now. Every one of them seemed to know about the empty mailbox. Even when greeted in a friendly way by people I knew, I read forbearance in their faces; I'd become a sort of pleasant mascot among all these shopping housewives. And when evening came and I beset her with all my accumulated uneasiness, my need to have her confirm that this was exactly what we'd wanted, that we'd consciously chosen to live this way, that nothing really could be finer or suit us better than precisely this life, then she would turn her head to the other side and fall asleep, whispering: "How you can talk. Be quiet a moment, won't you. I'm so tired . . ."

Or, when I brought up the subject of her daughter, virtually provoking her to tell me it was more important to live here, in our way, with me, than in the utterly false family idyll she'd run away from, in spite of the daughter she was bound to miss, she would parry with answers like, "This you can't understand, not having children of your own." But I refused to be put off by such answers, which only fed my self-contempt and uneasiness. I persisted, questioned and nagged, and we had endless discussions in bed—until one day she pulled back, as if wanting to take a closer look at me, fixed her eyes on mine, and said calmly: "What do you think the solution is then, Payk? To bring her here and let her live with us?"

It was the first time she used that idiotic nickname of mine, late one evening near the end of August. We'd known each other for barely three months: I'd loved her for eleven weeks with all the intensity and uninhibited enthusiasm the Norwegian summer can conjure up in our sort, the defenseless ones who see everything as though for the first time. I'd been a frisky and excessively cheerful puppy. Now I felt the metamorphosis beginning; I'd fought it and lost. She lay stroking my body, my hair, scratching me behind the ear: "Your hair is longer," she said.

I'd felt the metamorphosis, though it couldn't yet be seen. That night in August, through two open doors, my eyes could dimly make out the living room, with the glass table reflecting the street lamps, which were lighted earlier now, and an outline of the vase with the flowers in it, flowers I'd picked as usual, stolen from the beds of the landlord, as usual. Beds where nothing much was left anymore, except the pansies, which held their own: pinch off the heads as they fade and the blooms keep coming till late fall. I'd read about flowers. I'd stolen pansies for her, following an old habit. We had liked them best of all. We had felt as though the pansy's soft, dark petals illustrated the depth of our bright, happy lovemaking. But no longer. No more did we use flower similes for our love. Delicately fragrant plant tissue could no longer symbolize those deep, warm vaults of hers that I adored. Now it was herself I needed, her heavy closeness, her perfumed, sweaty heat, her hair and skin and membranes. How then could she ask if the solution was to bring her daughter here, to live with us! The very thought made me cling to her in blind terror: would I have to share her with a child? Would I have to fight for her care, her warmth and tenderness, her free moments, with a strange, empty-headed, selfish, demanding child? I barely managed to gasp that this was something we would have to consider carefully, until she took mercy on me and pulled me toward her, to the animal closeness I needed.

"Stop talking," she whispered. "Stop, Payk, will you. We'd better go on as before." But I was already sleeping the light, distrustful sleep of an animal in her arms.

3 Next day she complained for the first time that I'd begun to toss and groan so badly at night that she had trouble sleeping. A couple of weeks passed and it got worse. It affected her job, she said, acting out the way I whined and whimpered and squirmed, waking her up five or six times every single night. She was dead-tired all day, hardly knew what she was doing anymore; it couldn't go on like this much longer. But she'd worked out a solution. I could set up a bed in the adjoining room, the one we called the cubbyhole, a small unoccupied room half-filled with stuff we didn't use. I could sleep there till I got better. For she was convinced it was only something temporary, perhaps a symptom of stress because I was waiting for those damn answers from the school boards. Actually the outlook was quite bleak—of those who had answered, two wrote that they'd taken down my name and address in case a part-time teacher should be needed on short notice. That was all, with no more prospects, since it was mid-September already and way past the beginning of school. I was depressed.

"You mustn't give up," she said, giving me a quick pat in passing. "Something will turn up, you'll see. Besides, we're all right as it is. Don't worry about it, just throw that bed together like you promised."

And so she was out in the world leading a human existence, while I sat at home with my little pile of boards, making a bed for the cubbyhole. I'd already moved out of the bedroom and installed a foam rubber mat and bedding, only for the time being, till the bed was ready. I'd slept in there on the foam-rubber mattress, among cardboard boxes, discarded lamps, curtain rods, excursion gear, and boxes full of textbooks. I'd slept away from her for four nights and felt the loss of her, the closeness you're aware of even in sleep, pierce my body like a moan. She'd just wanted to sleep those four evenings, hadn't even let me come to her bed, had lain there quite remote and invulnerable, listening to my attempts at communication from the edge of the bed, later from the floor, my face as close to hers as possible. It was as if now, when the physical distance between us was greater, my very life depended on this communication. I needed to have every detail of our existence confirmed, every day. I had to know that she was contented. I had to know that I was the only one she wanted. I had to know that she was satisfied with the food I made, the way I took care of the apartment, the way our life together functioned. I needed to be reassured that she, too, looked forward to our evenings at home. I watched jealously for any hint that something she experienced "out there" might be more interesting and valuable than sitting in the apartment with me, because we were going out less and less often as time went on. I quizzed her about people she'd met, since I didn't meet any. I scrimped with the money she gave me for the housekeeping and bought things to make her happy. She said they did, but it wasn't enough. She had to repeat it. She had to show it in countless direct ways when she came home at night dead-tired.

Finally she asked me to shut up. The second evening I refused to go to my bunk in the cubbyhole, she broke down during my effusion and shouted at me: "Can't you stop talking, just for a moment? You know, you're killing me with your constant nagging! I'm here, aren't I? I'm living here with you. Isn't that enough?"

No, it wasn't enough. My eyes implored her to let me stay with her. I begged her from where I sat on the floor near her bed. I begged her from the doorway when I reluctantly dragged myself off to my room, to my dog's bunk. But she'd regained her composure and met my dog's eyes unflinchingly and without invitation, only whispered a brief good-night before she pulled the cover over her face and slept.

4 It was at this moment that our line of verbal communication was broken and my real dog's life began.

I knew she wanted me to talk as little as possible, and so I talked as little as possible. It was absolutely essential I try to satisfy her by any means still at my disposal. Though I had no concrete reasons to think so, I'd begun to doubt that she was completely contented. I'd gradually convinced myself, in fact, that she was really unhappy with me, and this made me desperate. To make her happy had become my paramount principle, a mission I staked more and more on as it became increasingly clear that my efforts weren't succeeding. I was no longer able to reason about our situation, analyze it and perhaps take action of some sort, make a move, *do something* that might start pulling us out of the dead calm we'd gotten into. I could only dwell, with vague longing, on the days (just a few weeks ago!) when the smallest ill-feeling was brought up, discussed, and dissolved in thin air almost greedily, as if solving our little problems was the proof how impregnable our love had become. In endless unanimous conversations we would praise fellowship, solidarity, love, the miracle that made words superfluous.

But now it was different. I was glued to her mouth, her eyes, trying to interpret her slightest hint, fulfill her least wish. But I wasn't terribly good even at this anymore, it seemed. Sometimes she'd be quite annoyed at my attentions: I misinterpreted, did things that left her cold, did too much, went too far. I even went too far in my tenderness and thoughtfulness. She often turned away, at least she seemed to. In the past we'd lived skin to skin, had measured the hours by our heartbeats, the days by the number of kisses and embraces, the months by her bodily cycle; now she often pushed me away when I fussed over

her, not knowing when to stop doing things for her: "Good God, I'm not a cripple!" In a matter of weeks I'd degraded myself from equal partner to being her servant. And now, when I couldn't even fulfill this task, there was nothing I could do except appeal to her care and sense of responsibility by transforming myself into her trustfully yearning lap-dog, who, sitting patiently at her chair or by her bed, begged her with moist brown eyes to be stroked, petted, or at least to be shown a little attention.

Besides the purely external signs of the metamorphosis from man into dog, which was becoming more and more apparent, I perceived other changes that contributed to my increasing bewilderment. During this time I was attacked by an anxiety I'd never felt before, which seemed to come from nowhere and would completely paralyze me as I walked around at home, longing and brooding in solitude. I would imagine she'd disappeared, that she quite simply didn't return after work, left me to sit there alone and starve . . . "Starve," I thought in my crazed fantasy, though all I had to do was open the door and go out, walk a couple of hundred yards to the store and buy some food . . . But I left the house more and more seldom, as if I were deprived of my freedom of movement when she was not around. It was as if I had to ask her permission to go anywhere, as if I needed somebody to accompany me, as if, once I got out, I'd lose my bearings and be unable to find my way back to safety again.

We'd started to go shopping together on afternoons when she was off. I let her make all the decisions, content with getting things down from the shelves and carrying the heavy shopping bag. I never asked for anything, never demanded anything for myself, was simply humble and grateful for what I got, grateful that she took me along, grateful that she accompanied me on the difficult way home, across two nasty intersections, past a treacherous place where we had to walk on boards to cross some deep ditches the road commission had dug in the road. But while I was delighted with these walks in the open air, I soon grew homesick for the sofa corner, the peace and safety I still felt within my own four walls, where nothing or nobody could break in from the outside and disturb the quiescence, the enclosed silence, which was all that remained of the solidarity we'd worshiped. And I felt all my dreams, hopes, and ambitions merge into a single vague desperate wish just to be allowed to stay at home with her, near her, be allowed to give her pleasure any way I could and watch over her well-being—her static shut-up well-being together with me, the faithful one, the only one she had . . .

Then one day a letter came from one of the schools where I'd applied for a job, a junior high school somewhere in the vicinity of Bestum, barely a quarter of an hour by bus from Storo. They needed a substitute for the two upper classes. English, Norwegian, and mathematics. Two weeks for the time being. Address. Telephone number. Please answer immediately.

What a break! Finally an offer to step out once more into human existence! To function! Make money!

I sank down on a chair completely overwhelmed by paralyzing, corrosive dread; I trembled, I laughed, I believe I cried . . . Bestum—a quarter of an hour by bus, a neighborhood I didn't know. A school full of screaming pupils, full of teachers happy to show me the vacant place of the one I would substitute for, chat pleasantly, be collegial so the new person wouldn't feel left out, all the while sharing their entire experience with one another, their sense of affinity, their friendship/enmity built up over the years. I had nothing!

"Please answer immediately."

It was obviously a splendid opportunity. I realized that. A chance, perhaps the last I would get (that's how I thought!), to break out of my ruinous stagnancy. An offer I *had to* accept. I realized that with the last remnant of my reason. And yet I sat there powerless, unhappy, indeed in a panic, as if nailed to the chair. I looked around the room like a condemned man before he's led to the scaffold. Whimpering sounds forced their way from my chest: *I didn't want to leave this place!* To leave this apartment had become, for me, to leave *her*. Every piece of furniture, every utensil, every ornament reminded me of her. Reminded me of the time I'd spent with her here, the *happy* times with her, the only happiness I knew I'd experienced in my adult life. To be in this apartment, go about the housekeeping, tidy up a bit or, as I did most of the time, just sit still, or lie motionless on the sofa and simply take in everything in the room, the memories that were connected with the things, recollections and associations from my earlier life with her— this was happiness itself for a dog. These moods seemed to wind me into a net of awe and dependency, of powerlessness to change anything, to interfere with our situation in some way and thus jeopardize the equilibrium on which my entire existence depended. Merely *being* here, in this atmosphere we'd created around us, had become almost a sacred act to me. I felt like a temple servant who faithfully guards his altar and his sanctuary unto death. This was all I had left. My life depended on its remaining untouched. Even dogs can go mad and perish when their life situation becomes unstable and threatening.

I got down from the chair, felt dizzy, dropped to my knees and crawled over to the sofa, laid my head on a pillow, sobbed, sniffed: the smell of her, of us, of our innumerable embraces on the sofa! Every single thing in the room made me divine familiar odors. After she banished me from her bed I'd become much more sensitive to her smell. I'd asked her to lend me her pillow for my bunk in the cubbyhole and went to sleep with the saturated, perfumed woman's smell tickling my nose. Dogs must comfort themselves as best they can when their masters are away, or are hindered from looking after them.

5 I was supposed to show up Monday, October 11.
Don't ask me how I plucked up the courage to call the principal for the necessary details. The conversation is quite vague in my mind; my heart pounded, my voice cracked. Afterwards I ran around the floor in circles, whimpering from joy and excitement.

I was terribly nervous when I told her about it, because I didn't know her well enough anymore to be sure how she'd react. Or more correctly, I knew her so well that I would be able to read her appraisal of me, and of our relationship, from her reaction. And her reaction turned out to be roughly as I'd feared: indifference. But, of course, she said, "Oh, is it really true, Payk, how fantastic!"—she used only my nick-name now—but I noticed her probing glance, as if she no longer believed I could possibly take advantage of an opportunity anymore, meet a challenge, and turn that merciless undertow which had, for weeks, drained me of all my strength, independence, and optimism. But the hug she gave me, and a wet maternal kiss at the corner of my mouth, told me I'd still be allowed to sleep with her tonight and, if it was successful—which it always used to be in an unexciting, repetitive way (mainly because I always came too soon, starved as I was from privation)—spend all night in her bed perhaps as a kind of special reward.

But that night I poured out all my dog's devotion on her, inflamed her with all my canine madness. Our long abstinence had given me a dog's sharp, indefatigable potency whose aggressiveness entranced her. The very distance that had arisen between us now became a stimulus, turning her into an alien creature with smells and lusts, a female to ride and to quench my bone-hard lust on. She stroked my hairy body, scratched the fur on my chest, whimpered and squealed and purred in animal fashion, deep in the throat, as if to let me know that she, too, realized we were committing sodomy, that this was something we'd be ashamed of in daylight and not repeat till her heat had built up again sufficiently to offset her aversion, the female's aversion for the male. But still—still I enjoyed it, perhaps more than when we'd been one soul, one body. It was simpler now, for this was all we had left; it added up to this: quenching our lust by riding each other.

For a dog sex is an uncomplicated matter. Everything else is subordinated to his need to ingratiate himself with the female, staying around till her smell and sounds give him a hunch that her chemistry is about to change. Then it's all set for the assault—a whining, begging rape. Afterwards a new wait till she's willing again. A dog can take many kicks and much abuse if only he's allowed to stay around, in her proximity, while he waits . . .

The following day the telephone rang the moment after she'd gone to work (after we'd eaten a silent breakfast, which I'd prepared, and she'd wandered about pretending to tidy up, though it was completely unnecessary, because I kept the apartment neat to please her, to demonstrate the success of our role reversals—she going to work, I staying at home—and to keep my own crazy feeling of not existing, *really* existing, at a distance for another afternoon. Her tidying-up was a ritual to conjure back the "normalcy" of our stagnated situation, to place a reassuring distance between us and the night's anomalous sexual encounter).

The telephone rang after she'd pecked me on the cheek in the entryway and talked about dinner; I was overcome by amazement—it seemed such a long time since we'd been in touch with anyone from the outside world: who would call us here, in this empty apartment where only the dog was at home? Then a suspicion dawned on me: it was for *her!* It was somebody she knew, someone she'd gotten in touch with, a man, one who knew her address, with whom she'd made a date perhaps! With suspicion tensing my muscles, making me walk on tiptoe and raise my hackles, I grabbed the receiver and barked, "Hello?"

And then it was only Arne, a fellow student from the spring semester, who wanted to know if I was interested in joining a newly started environmental group concerned with spreading information about the destructive effects that "industrial civilization," as he called it, was having on the quality of life.

Bewildered, I said yes, because offhand I couldn't find any good reason to refuse and because the sound of Arne's voice brought me back for a moment to a sort of normal state, back to Blindern, reading rooms, grilled dinners in the canteen, loose, noncommittal but enthusiastic conversations about big and complicated subjects, with faces you knew you'd never see again after this one contact. He asked what I was doing and I told him, evasively, how my plans for further study had collapsed during the summer, intimated I was living with someone and mentioned the substitute teaching job.

He laughed and said: "Good deal, old boy. I'd heard, sure enough, that you'd retired to the serenity of private life with a ripe, separated beauty."

"A separated what?!" I barked. "What do you mean?"

"No-no, I'm only joking. Some guy had seen you in the trolley and so I heard about it. You know, I'd wondered a bit what had become of you since you didn't come around after the holidays . . ."

"Yeah."

"I'll be seeing you on Thursday, then. Just bring her along. The more we get to join, the better."

"Okay, I'll ask her."

"I'm sure you can manage to persuade her . . ."

He hung up with an ambiguous laugh, and I laughed too. I'd said yes. He'd fooled me into believing in an existence outside the one I knew, one where people associated with other people in uncomplicated, friendly forms, where people were occupied with political issues and cared about what happened to others, even decided to *do* something . . . For a moment he'd made me believe that this life existed, long enough for me to say yes to his invitation anyway, to laugh with him and to believe it might be possible.

But as I stood there holding the dead receiver (which smelled of her perfume—how can people's smell stick so fast to bakelite?), my courage sank, because the illusion was broken and only the limitations of existence remained. I thought immediately, "I don't have to go, after all," but this thought somehow made me even more dejected. I tried to conjure up the mood that had come over me while talking to Arne, the moment when everything seemed possible, and I was struck by the thought that the telephone conversation had been a sign, a signal from the outside world that it was possible to escape from the impasse I'd gotten into. Assuming, of course, it was an impasse, instead of the very situation I wanted, one I'd chosen myself . . . I sank again but struggled to the surface once more: in any case a total change was imminent, due to the fact that I had a job—why not the environmental group as well? I tried with all my might to summon up optimism at the thought of the substitute teaching job, the money I was going to make, the people I'd meet. I made up my mind to let her decide about the group: if she was willing, so was I. But I was fairly certain she wouldn't be. Hoped so anyway.

But to my surprise she thought it was a good idea. "We never go anywhere," she said. "We never see a single person." Which had been one of the very proofs of how all-sufficing we were to each other, how unessential the entire outside world was, compared to us and what we had together. "And, after all, environmental protection is a tremendously important issue these days. If there isn't a change soon we'll all drop dead, chock-full of poison and metal oxides, and lie there like compass needles pointing north-south . . ."

Poisoning and pollution—what did she know about things like that? Where did she get her knowledge from? I hardly ever read a newspaper myself, certainly not features or long articles. And I used to turn off the radio debates. I preferred to listen to music on the radio, the dinner concert, even the morning "Nine O'clock Hour." Honest to God, I found the "Nine O'clock Hour" to be a great help during the difficult period of transition from sleep to waking, when the day was supposed to begin. The day that isn't a day for a dog but only a shut-up wait, yearning and blues: the same rounds about the apartment, a glass of water, a dry crust of bread if the refrigerator had nothing else to offer. With its friendly chatter and uncomplicated music, the "Nine O'clock Hour" made it easier to endure the daily awakening to nothing. When they played a tune I knew, a thoroughly nauseating, sentimental one that seemed to go with my mood of the moment, I even used to howl along with it . . .

While she walked around worrying about pollution and the fact that the politicians weren't doing enough!

Thursday night she put on a colorful smock, a batik scarf, and jeans. She found the way to the seminar room in Sophus Bugge's House at Blindern, which was our meeting place, with an ease that made *her* look like an experienced student, me a hesitant visitor. She immediately threw herself into the discussion, had viewpoints on what was talked about, earned complimentary glances from Arne and the other men present—and noticed it! Played up to it, basked in it! Sick with worry, I let her pin the environmental emblem to my sweater. She even agreed to cut a stencil on my typewriter (which didn't have a ribbon), an appeal to the students to support the action with money and volunteer efforts. On second thought I knew, of course, that she'd taken a secretarial course, but had forgotten about it. In a surprisingly short time I'd lost any sense that either of us had a past. The impossible, stagnant present was the only thing I could focus on. That's why I felt so uncomfortably misplaced in a situation like this, where what united people was historical insight, political understanding, and visionary imagination. My energy was spent keeping an eye on Arne, who in turn was gazing shamelessly at the bosom of my "ripe, separated beauty," while the room buzzed with conversation, and fresh perspectives and strategies became clear to everyone but me. And she had a great time, no doubt of that.

"They are a bit young, you know," she said when we were in the bus going home, "but still very nice. Fantastic how young people get involved these days. When I went to school we couldn't put two thoughts together, not on politics anyway. Almost a bit sad to recall now. But perhaps it's not too late to start?"

"Oh no—it looked like two or three of the 'idealists' were more than willing to cross the generation gap," I jibed in my wretched mood. She took it as a compliment, laughed, and gave my arm a loving squeeze. I understood that Arne's glances had aroused her, priming her for another coupling, in which I would have to redeem and discharge long-ings and unspoken needs aroused by the entire group of young, admir-ing, idealistic and sexually starved Blindern students.

But on Monday the eleventh I didn't even have this false, vicarious closeness to look forward to and console myself with as I stumbled down to the bus stop at daybreak, awkward in my unfamiliar clothes, not sure I was "correctly" dressed, unable to imagine how it would be to stand in front of a class (at the worst age at that!), let alone think of something to say to them. ("Well, good morning. I'm substituting for Mrs. . . . and this period we're supposed to have Norwegian. My name is Per Kristian, Payk for short, Tomter . . . Bow-wow, bow-wow-wow . . . yap, yap . . . bow-wow-wow-wow-wow!)

The bus was crammed with self-satisfied people who didn't seem interested in the fact that I was a dog, a low-level being, a dumb, unintelligent, dependent domestic animal who, according to laws and regulations, ought to be kept indoors or on a leash, here masquerading as a teacher on his way to a crazy misunderstanding, a parody of a teacher's mission for which the next generation would have to pay.

Bow-wow! I nodded curtly to a request to move my briefcase from the seat next to me. The sticky snow mixed with rain pasted my hair and beard into an unappetizing mat which gave off an odor of fur. I felt that my hands were moist and my toes clammy in the soaked shoes. But my body was warm and dry, as during an attack of fever. A dog sweats only on his tongue and between his paws.

In my nervousness I'd imagined lots of obstacles on the way, like delayed buses, changed stops, trouble finding my way to the right address, and so on. But, miraculously, everything went off without a hitch this gloomy October morning. Before I realized it—indeed, before I really wanted or was prepared to—I was standing before the squat, confused network of modern pavilions that made up the school. A steady stream of pupils, moving on foot and by bike, cut through the gates in the fence and disappeared between the buildings. A confusion of down jackets, lumpy boots, and jeans. Each face autumnally pale and expressionless.

No marker indicated in which building, or even in which direction, the teachers' lounge was located. What I took to be the teachers' parking lot lay some distance away. Cars were constantly pulling up before the many engine block heaters that, like rows of pygmy parking meters, assigned spaces to the employees. It would have been easy, of course, to pursue one of those hurrying figures across the school yard onto the unknown paths between the flat buildings, where most windows were already resplendent with light, but a dog is apprehensive about following people he doesn't know, afraid of being chased off with shouts, abuse, and threatening gestures. It would also have been easy to ask one of the many pupils passing by for directions to the teachers' lounge, but dogs are scared of children and have good reason to be. Who tortures dogs more than children do? Who throws stones at lost dogs? Even children who have a dog at home, and have been taught to respect him, can be incredibly cruel to strange dogs! There was no mercy to expect from those pale, buttoned-up young faces I saw hurrying past. Instead of being bold enough to speak to them, I began to fear attracting their attention as I stood wavering outside one of the gates, diffidently scouting the school area and looking up and down the street by turns to divert the attention of possible snoops, as if to indicate that my interest in the school buildings was only casual and temporary. Naturally I could have found the way on my own if only I'd been allowed to prowl about undisturbed between the buildings, sniffing my way to the place where the grown-ups—safety—were to be found in this storage bin for children. But now, with so many strangers swarming all around me, I didn't dare come near. I had to wait till the period started—and then it would be too late, because I'd agreed to be in the teachers' lounge at twenty after the hour . . . My dilemma seemed completely unsolvable. Worst of all, I needed to go to the john so badly I was about to burst. With dogs, agitation often affects the bladder. Now it had hit me like a bolt from the blue, making it impossible for me to stand still in one spot. With fear and indecision still tearing at me and forcing little whimpering moans from my chest, I wanted to pee so badly I could barely stand straight. Shifting quickly from one foot to the other and gnashing my teeth, I could see my salvation only fifty yards off, splendidly illuminated behind drifts of small rain mixed with sleet, school buildings with long corridors and doors marked "Toilet" and "WC" in every pavilion, not even necessary to ask directions, just make your way between the brats, get to the right door—and relief. But somehow my desperate situation made it absolutely impossible for me even to *think* of getting close to the buildings; it would be *too* embarrassing, *too* impossible to barge into a toilet deaf and blind with desperation and then, afterwards, have to go up and introduce yourself to people who might even have witnessed the wretched state in which the substitute, the new teacher . . . No! Tears sprang to the corners of my eyes, rolled down my cheeks, mingled with the rainwater in my mustache and dripped onto the sidewalk, where they merged with the water from the melted snow, ran into the gutter and trickled down into the sewer, a sound that made my situation seem unbearable. "At any rate it won't show on this wet sidewalk when I burst!" I thought with closed eyes and clenched teeth, one fist in my coat pocket pressed convulsively against my abdomen, while the other hand clasped the iron moulding of the lattice fence to help me stand straight as I battled the inevitable in a split-second race against time . . .

I was saved by the school bell.

As the last belated souls rushed past me through the gate, a couple of them sent puzzled glances to where I stood huddled over holding on to the fence (I hoped they thought I was having a coronary); then it was all empty around me. A car shot past, then nothing—except for the silhouettes I glimpsed in there behind the lighted windows.

I hobbled a few steps along the sidewalk, my eyes having found a place, instinctively. The dull pain in my abdomen was throbbing, making it necessary to hold my breath. With the blood pounding in my eyeballs and my eardrums, I reached a half-hidden pole in a corner between two work sheds evidently left by a team of road workers. Heedless of what the neighbors across the street might see, I opened my fly and let the steaming jet break against the woodwork. At least no school children around to see the dog pissing against the pole in the farthest corner of the school yard. No cruel children to shout and holler and throw stones at me as I slunk away, sick with regret and shame.

6 It couldn't have been more than a couple of weeks later that she told me she'd met some man, one of the steady customers at Bel Ami; she'd struck up a conversation with him by chance after work. I didn't understand till later why she mentioned it. I had other worries. The work in the environmental group was taking its course and I noticed how she amused herself by attracting the attention of Arne, for one, more and more openly as the initial ardor of working for a good cause began to cool off and cutting stencils and composing appeals and press reports (which were never printed anywhere) began to seem like a duty rather than a mission.

"It's fun to get out among people in any case," she used to say after our meetings. "And you have many nice fellow students, you know that?" Just to underline that our life together in the apartment had become increasingly boring to her and that I wasn't the only man around. I understood, of course, I'd dimly felt it for a long time—she could have saved herself the trouble of telling me; dogs are exceptionally sensitive to their masters' moods, adjust to them and reinforce them. A dog can never break out of the atmosphere his master surrounds him with; at most he can try to soften a threat by acting ingratiatingly and pleasing his master, trying to awaken his master's concern and sympathy.

But it doesn't always get him anywhere. After a thaw in the relationship just after we'd joined the environmental group, when she let me sleep in the bed several nights in a row and patted and stroked me more than she'd done for quite some time (a sort of signal that meant she felt stimulated and glad to have met some new people, rather than any new flaring-up of warm feelings for me—I understood that!), everything went on as before again. She'd made me buy more materials for the bed I'd constantly promised to put together, while I was actually waiting for a miracle—that she would change her mind, that everything would be as it had been at the start between us. In the cramped cubbyhole I struggled with heavy boards and poor tools. Ordinarily such work put me in a good mood, but this was like contriving my own failure and degradation and making them plainly visible. Needless to say, the job dragged on.

A small bright spot—from my point of view—at the last environmental meeting we went to together, or rather afterwards: four or five of us had agreed to go out for a glass of beer when the meeting was over. The Old Major at Majorstua was only a trolley ride away. Squeezed around a table, we picked up the threads of conversation at the meeting. We had nothing else to talk about, nothing else in common.

She was quieter than usual and said less and less, while the attentions of Arne, who was sitting next to her, became increasingly obvious as the beer settled. His thick fingers fluttered incessantly through the air, his lips talked, his teeth smiled. Time and again he'd touch her, her hand, her clothes, her hair, but it wasn't like the situation at the meeting, where passes were neutralized and any consequences made impossible by the presence of some twenty people. This was different, more serious, more insulting for a dog who worried about his master. And I noticed to my satisfaction that she seemed to shrink as she sat there under Arne's insensitive bombardment. We broke up early, and on the way back she snorted: "What kids you students are! Can you imagine, he tried to play footsie with me under the table. If he's that horny, why can't he come right out and ask, like a decent man!"

Joy—and new worry. She'd gotten tired of Arne's attentions, which had made no impression on her. But it made me uneasy to have her "decent man" drawn into the comparison. I was reminded that she had a husband, whom we had dismantled, shattered, obliterated all summer long. A husband we'd dissected, analyzed, and wiped out through our superior understanding of his faults and shortcomings and through our pointedly different, democratic sexual practice. He'd been the despised classic illustration of a "decent man," whom we'd mocked and annihilated and later forgotten. Had he come to life again?

Friday afternoon she told me coming home that a man had invited her out for the evening and she'd said yes. It was the same one she'd mentioned earlier, the steady customer at Bel Ami she'd happened to strike up a conversation with. A couple of days had passed since he asked her, but she'd forgotten to mention it, hadn't been sure she was interested, but now she'd like to go.

Forgotten to mention it! Hadn't been sure she was interested!

A dog scents a lie before it's uttered. A dog squirms the moment the lie is being formed on your lips—he has seen an ambiguous gleam in your eyes, perceived your hesitation, smelled the sweaty odor of uncertainty on the palms of your hands—and he squirms because he knows that he's the one who'll have to pay for this lie; the liar will want to take revenge for his clumsiness, for the distaste left by a lie; the liar exacts retribution for his squalor from the victim of his lie. A dog knows this, that's why he crawls off to hide when he notices his master is getting ready to lie. To the dog, who senses everything, the lie is the worst of all debasements, because the liar knows a dog senses everything and even so goes through with the lie. Next comes the inevitable: open breakdown, violence, a beating.

But what should I do? We had, of course, foreseen this possibility and discussed it, in hour-long conversations about freedom and fidelity and about owning and not owning each other, at an earlier stage of our friendship. We'd been in perfect agreement that the most beautiful thing in a relationship was one's ability to renounce ownership of the other, the ability *not* to succumb to the hideous feeling of jealousy in case the other should follow a completely natural desire to associate with and take an interest in other people as well. But we'd never discussed in any detail how the area of this interest ought to be defined, because at that time we couldn't possibly imagine we would ever have any time or interest left over for other people—beyond purely conventional human obligations. And thus we'd been able to debate a crucial question like this with extreme confidence and conviction. Such bold, hard and fast viewpoints can be held only by utterly starry-eyed idealists or by the totally disillusioned.

And now I was asked to discharge my obligations. What could I say? What else could I say but, "Okay, fine. Where do you plan to go? What will you do?"

"Oh, nothing special," she replied, "perhaps a movie, a drink someplace afterwards . . ."

Lies again! I could tell from her hands, already caressing the dress she was going to wear. I could tell from her feet, dancing from the living room to the bedroom and to the cramped, topsy-turvy bathroom. I sensed her excitement as she lovingly scrutinized her image in the mirror, visible to me through the open bathroom door. Her naked, autumnally pale skin framed by the straps of her underwear suddenly acquired a fascination for me far beyond what it usually had. Her excitement rubbed off on me—I suddenly found her irresistibly attractive as she concentrated on making herself pretty and alluring for someone else . . .

But a dog knows his place. Motionless, his muzzle on his front paws and a melancholy expression in his eyes, he follows his mistress's preparations in the bathroom, by the closet, in front of the mirror in the entry. He knows that his fate is to wait till his mistress returns, when she'll have a little time and care left over for him, perhaps. He knows that if he caused trouble, whined and howled or asked to come along, it would only be twice as bad. He'd catch a reprimand, perhaps even a beating. And if the improbable should occur, that it was possible to take the dog along and she was willing to, he'd still be excluded from the party, banished to a corner of the living room, a cold guest room or the entry, from which he would see and hear how his mistress enjoyed herself with the others—or the other—with no possibility of participating himself and every minute fully aware that his presence was completely unwanted.

The only thing a dog can do is exploit the leave-taking, during which his mistress takes pity on him with a little remorse in her heart for having—no, wanting!—to abandon him to himself, and with an extra bit of feeling produced by all the exciting, pleasant, and enjoyable things she expects will happen once she gets outside the dog's mournful horizon.

She was exceptionally sweet to me when she said good-bye, gave me a nice hug, stroked my hair, tugged my beard and wished me a pleasant evening. She probably wouldn't be late . . .

And the dog swallowed his tearful dog's sorrow and pressed his body against her legs, did the only thing dogs can do, stick his muzzle up between her thighs to capture the last fragrance of her, the faint, spicy odor of her expectancy—before she laughingly liberated herself and with a last, radiant "bye-bye!" slammed the door behind her.

7 At twenty past midnight I hear her key in the lock. I've been napping on the sofa, unable to set my mind at rest and settle down in my cubbyhole bunk before she's home. My dog's heart is pounding, my senses are tensed. What can the invisible and inaudible details of her behavior during these first seconds, her appearance the moment she enters—before the mask and the lie have been formed— tell me about what she *really* has been doing tonight?

Then I hear the voices. Of them both. First hers, then his: she's brought him along! They stand in the hallway, in *our* hallway, whispering and laughing!

"*Hi, here we are!*"

First a diffident relief: then she has nothing to hide, after all. Then it was a casual acquaintance just as she said, a human being you could talk to who'd invited her out for the evening—and why not? Here's the proof: bringing him home means he's not dangerous. You cannot take a lover, not even a would-be lover, home to a dog who sees and understands all. Therefore he's harmless. He's neutral. In mere seconds I've become prepared to like him—with a wag of the tail. He doesn't threaten me. He doesn't threaten *us*. Suddenly I feel an urge to meet him, I have to control my impulse to go to the door and meet them in the hall. For a dog knows his place. He knows that he'll be called when his presence is desired. Otherwise he has to stay where he is.

Are they taking a little more time than necessary out there in the hall, or is it only the dog's naive, enthusiastic impatience that makes him feel that way?

Then they come in, she first, then he. She in the doorway with her back to me, facing him as if to lure him in: "Come on in!" You'd hardly think it necessary, seeing him enter with mincing steps, eagerly, moving on his toes the way a boxer enters the ring, erect in well-fitting ready-made clothes, patterned shirt and striped suit, tie and handkerchief of the same design, swaggering in high-heeled demiboots, with the watchful, calculating glance that betrays a hunter in action and with an aggressive appetite for conquest that no pretense to modest manners can conceal. The same excited look in his eyes that she has, as if both were struggling to hold back their laughter. The same trouble in getting full control of their facial muscles and their gestures, all those subtle or crude signs of the emotions alcohol has released in them and which their bodies can no longer censor effectively. She has taken off her glasses! Her face unfolds like a flower when she looks at him, she can't help it:

"Come and say hello to Payk!" Here begin the insults and the degradation! His handshake and her smell on him! Cigarette smoke and the nauseating whiff of nightclub sticking to his clothes! "Places like that are damn noisy!" Her unnatural, bright gaiety (it's past twelve-thirty at night!), her offer of beer, perhaps food, as if it were a pleasant afternoon visit. Her shakiness in high heels (which must embarrass him, who's obviously bothered by being so short and tries to make up for it by being well-groomed, wearing fashionable clothes, and using studiedly masculine gestures: Lilliput-Tarzan!). His eyes squint even when he addresses me directly with some polite commonplaces. His appreciative laughter at my answer, which would have sounded exactly the same no matter what I answered, is in reality a declaration of war.

I begin wondering *why* even before my dog's anxiety grabs hold of me in earnest again. What can she see in *him*, in this stilted little caricature of a man? Granted, he isn't *that* short, but I must launch my

own attack, use anything I can think of to fight the fear and powerlessness that surged up in me the moment I sniffed her smell on him—
although this could be from perfectly natural causes: they've danced
together, she's held his arm on the sidewalk, he's helped her into the
taxi, they've been sitting close together—and which get a firmer hold
on me with every passing minute. What in the world has she brought
him home for? After a handshake and a few banalities ("Nice to live up
here, fine view . . ." "Bow-wow, bow-wow-wow . . ."), it's clear that he
and I won't ever have anything to say to each other, not anything *real*.
But why then? Because she certainly must know me well enough to
realize that there can never be any question of Mini-Tarzan and me
hitting it off. Is it a demonstration that she can find company on her
own, without having to fall back on *my* associates? Is it a demonstration
to *him* how happy she and I are together? Is it . . . ?

Of the dog's senses, hearing and smell are the best developed. For a
dog, human existence is a nightmare of smells and sounds, exaggerated
and overly distinct. I can sniff a sweaty hand before it touches me. I can
hear the race of a couple of fingers down the back of a long dress of
loose, flowered cotton. I can perceive which words are being spoken
under those that are spoken.

I smell the many drinks on her lips when she enters from the kitchen
with the beer and glasses. I hear her voice crack with concealed gaiety,
verging on malicious glee. I graze her hand as she passes by with bottles
and glasses and scent *his* stupefying aftershave lotion. There are plenty
of natural explanations, of course. Nothing *really* compromising. But
her voice rings with laughter in response to his. His breathing is
directly affected by her attention. He's perspiring under his wrinkle-
resistant shirt. She has caught him in her net, even if he holds back a
little, pretends to be calm and in full control of everything.

She pours the beer, first for him, then for me. He raises his glass to
say cheers and I catch sight of the tooth marks, fresh, fierce and red, on
the back of his hand. Left there by her. Of course! The love bite. The
ritual fusion of pain and pleasure. Imitation passion exchanged during
the charged intimacy of the dance floor, in a dark corner of the bar, in
the taxi on the way home—here: warm sticky saliva on the sensitive
skin smelling of aftershave lotion. Her tongue between his short,
strong fingers. (Is his prick as short, thick, and blunt?) Her teeth
cutting and chewing deep lines in the fat, hairy back of his hand: saliva,

sweat and *Brut* aftershave . . . She's made her confession, her open declaration. She has already taken him—symbolically. She wants to possess him—eat him!

Still I raise my glass, almost in time with him, while preparing to drink a toast and keep my countenance. But he says: "You're doing carpentry, are you?"

Or perhaps he said it earlier—the room is suddenly full of polite, well-meaning clichés, polite threats, polite condescension, polite scorn, the sequence doesn't matter. He asks if I'm doing carpentry, waving in the direction of the hallway where I've left some of my tools lying around, idiot that I am. Perhaps he asks out of politeness, out of sheer curiosity? Perhaps he has no idea . . . ? But her laughter makes it obvious that he's acquainted with my dog's life out there in the cubbyhole. He knows my dog's name and my humiliation. *She* has informed him of it in order to give him effective weapons in the contest between us, to secure the outcome. To egg him on to produce an erection on demand, when the opportunity is there. Erection as the primordial club to crush an opponent with. Erection as the primordial symbol of men's pleasure in destruction.

"Yes, as a matter of fact I'm putting together a bed . . ."

A rickety bunk where I can rest my misery and my longing. Where I can never hope that anybody will share my bed.

You see, for us dogs sex is different. We have to go out. We have to beg. Get up on our hind legs, raise our paws and plead, plead so fervently that a slim, bright-red tip appears at the end of the hairy sac we have between our hind legs, plead and hope that this humiliation—this demonstration of aching dog's rut, shameless yet self-effacing—will make an impression, melt a heart that craves a bit of tenderness, soften the indifferent will that ignores the most faithful of all faithful souls, flatter a melting female vanity. While every moment the sad adoration in the unfathomable dog's eyes softens the pointed, persistent offensiveness of the salmon-colored dog's prick.

So we drink a toast and laugh as I try to entrap her with my dog's glance, my dog's worship, steering the conversation to subjects that only concern her and me, tying the bonds of intimacy and dependency while her indifferent refusal, voluptuous gaiety, and open face (turned to him) oppress my furiously beating dog's heart with anxiety. I understand it now: she's brought him home to demonstrate how *little* I am, how insignificant a dog's love is when the lover enters the door, how little a dog's feelings matter to a human being, the dog's master, who has her free will, the ability to imagine something different and the strength to pursue her new goal. She treats him as if I didn't exist. She might as well have told me, "Go lie down! To your place!" She's completely taken up with him and his symbols of virility, his clothes from a men's boutique, his haircut, his expensive (too expensive!) cuff links, his elegant leather demiboots with high heels. She laps it all up as she sits there putting on airs for him. She doesn't even ignore me, she's simply forgotten me. And I understand all too well what it means: she's discovered that she prefers his short, thick club of a cock to my spare, slim dog's pizzle. It's that simple. That annihilating.

I force myself to sit on the sofa, observing them a moment longer, listening to them (to the guttural sounds beneath their polite speech), smelling them (the perspiration that breaks out when they are close to each other); then I can't take it any longer, stretch and yawn, showing my dangerous teeth (but who gets scared by a lapdog's teeth, however white and pointed they may be?), say I'm tired and want to turn in. No sooner said than regretted. Now they are in control of the battlefield.

"Already?" she says promptly, unable to prevent her joyous excitement and dark expectancy from coloring her voice.

I say good night but don't leave; delay the total withdrawal by lingering in the kitchen before sneaking off to my room, drinking a little milk from the carton in the refrigerator while I strain my ears to the utmost:

"Perhaps I ought to go—it's getting late," he says, mostly for my benefit, knowing I'm listening.

"It isn't that late," she interrupts, like a purring cat. "Only a moment—some more beer . . ."

Then, the door slamming, into the darkness of the cubbyhole.

Clammy, untidy bedclothes. The fragrance of summer sticking to the summer articles we've stored here, rucksacks, sneakers; her beach blanket, which is always enveloped by an aura of *Ambre Solaire*. Is it possible that just two months have passed since we were so happy? Is it possible that the woman I was lying around with barely three months ago, rolled up in this blanket in broad daylight at Katten Beach in front of everybody, can be the same one who's now sitting in our own living room with flushed face and shiny eyes opening the shirt buttons of this stuffed manikin she's brought home with her, who looks like a salesman in a men's store but has somehow caught her erotic fantasy? Can it be she who this moment is flicking her tongue around his ear, running it up toward his neat hairline? Can it really be she who's tickling his fly to test the "volcanic effect," as she likes to call it, hot and moist already? No doubt it puts an edge on her pleasure to do "our" things with this stranger, right here at home in our own living room, surrounded by our furniture and things. No doubt it increases the suspense for her while she succeeds in humiliating me, obliterating the memory of her faithful Payk, of the dog she's had such good times with before.

Can a poor dog really sink so low that he becomes horny and gets an erection at the thought that his mistress, sighing and laughing, allows a rival to get at her?

8 At the breakfast table the following morning she's friendlier than usual. Naturally. Both of us know that we both know. She's eager to find out if I'll make a scene but makes no obvious maneuver to avoid it. She's familiar with the dog—knows that he knows he'd better stay in his place and be grateful for the care and attention he gets.

So that the silence won't be oppressive, I ask:

"Did it get late last night?"

"Oh no!"

She answers with a liar's supreme naturalness. "We had another beer and talked for a while . . ."

"About what?" I can't stop myself.

"Oh, a little about his job; he works in publishing." One up on me, who had applied for a job at a publisher's without success. In early fall, incredibly long ago, when she kissed me good-bye, hugged me and wished me good luck, believing I would succeed, crying with me when I failed, consoling me by saying I was much too good for them, that the publishing business had been taken over by the technocrats, that it had nothing to do with culture or human values anymore . . .

And now she's started a relationship with someone in publishing who is the very image of our worst presentiments at that time. This makes it impossible for me to continue the conversation. But I continue my observation of her, openly, so she's bound to notice, unless she's prepared for it beforehand, has even looked forward to it perhaps! For in everything she does, in every single detail of her behavior and manner, she can't help betraying that she's slept with him, with Mini-Tarzan, that they copulated over there on the sofa last night just after I went to bed (they were that certain I wouldn't dare drop in on them after the door was closed!). Her contentment today seems like the imprint of his nocturnal erotic tricks on her, inside her, everywhere! It's reflected in all she does, an indolent, sort of rounded, mirthful, newly fucked well-being: in the way she lifts her slice of white bread; the way she changes her position on the chair, leisurely, relaxed, as if all joints consisted of ball bearings floating in thick, lukewarm oil, yet sensually awakened, as if secret lines of communication had been established between her and her surroundings in order to give her newly awakened sensuality the maximum stimulus and her drowsy, morning-ripe body the greatest possible well-being, absorbed from every detail in all she does, from everything she touches with her bed-warm attention; her tongue sucking a sugared strawberry off the jam spoon, her fingers playing with the handle of the smooth, ivorylike plastic butter knife. But not a word is directly stated—neither the accusation nor the confirmation clearly articulated . . .

"What's his name, really?" I ask when I can't stand seeing her like that any longer, resting in her fresh memories, her own self-satisfaction.

"His name . . . ?" She smacks her lips on yet another strawberry. "I call him Bel Ami."

"Bel Ami?"

"Yes, isn't that enough?"

"Enough? It's idiotic!"

I find it difficult to control myself; these ludicrous pet names make me see red. I show my teeth: "Bel Ami, what kind of silly name is that?"

"My, how you flare up today!"

Nothing I might say or do can break through the cocoon of sensual sweetness in which a successful night of love envelops a woman. "What does it really matter what his name is? Bel Ami is a joke between us, I never call him anything else. What does a name mean, really, when you feel you have contact with a person . . . ?"

Of course! Sorry! My fault! I ought to have understood by now. I ought by this time to be used to the fact that nothing *I* think or want is of any importance. What business is it of *mine* to interrogate her about his name? And so she's obliged to remind me how matters stand once more: ". . . when you feel you have contact with a person." Yes, indeed.

Contact. What kind? One kind of contact is obvious. The entire living room reeks of their nocturnal exploits. She hasn't even bothered to arrange the sofa pillows properly, has simply thrown them carelessly in a pile. The only things missing to complete the picture are crumpled handkerchiefs and wet spots. That kind of "contact" requires no name except the obvious! Though no word is said and everything is as before.

But once "contact" meant something else to her and me. When we met she longed for contact—close human, emotional, intellectual contact—so intensely that sex would sometimes recede into the background. It's this contact that has faded somehow, been lost more or less. More or less! Am I dreaming? It's dead, gone, wiped out. The garden where we roamed together has become a desert. The summer has turned into fall, the grass has withered, the leaves have fallen off the trees, and the frightened people have taken refuge between four walls, where their freedom of movement is inhibited, their imagination crippled, their courage to face life undermined. Only basic needs left to be satisfied: a bit of food, a bed to sleep in, and a little warmth. A dog can be content with so little. But *she* has to go out to get even this satisfaction, so simple and fundamental. I can't even give her that.

And this goes to prove that the blue-blue lake of summer in reality was like a puddle of water that froze over on the first night of frost. That the warmth belonged to the sun, the colors to the flowers, the song and the conversations to the wind and the insects; that the joy was that of cagelings as they were set free, she from her marriage, I from the tower of my virginity at the student factory. And that the infatuation belonged to the atoms and the electrons, the power of attraction that bodies of opposite charge exert upon each other.

9 A dog's psychology is strange: the more he's whipped, the more faithfully and devotedly he behaves toward his master.

Now that I knew for certain at last that she was betraying me, my servile concern for her became boundless. All my confused thoughts, all my restless dog's energy was centered on the problem of pleasing her. For in my innermost heart lurked an inexpressible fear: that she would disappear. That she'd simply leave me—for him—and abandon me to myself. Leave me to my fate.

We'd often talked about it, how one ought to conduct oneself when a relationship was over, when it no longer worked for one or the other, if "another person" were to turn up—how one ought at that point to seek one's freedom, because nobody owned another person and nobody had the right to demand from the other person anything that interfered with, or limited, his freedom. She and I had come together in freedom and practiced our self-centered, all-exclusive love in freedom . . . But that was last summer when light and sounds and smells united us, when it was quite unthinkable that one of us would ever get tired of the other, let alone prefer someone else . . .

But a dog is helpless without his master, degenerate as the race has become through decades, in some cases hundreds of years, of rearing, selective breeding and inbreeding. Very few dogs are capable of managing on their own without man's help. A common dog will perish if his master abandons him to his fate.

Dread of this happening filled me day and night. Since she so obviously preferred him, wouldn't she move in with him? Nothing I could think of bound her to our place if *I* didn't. She might not move right away but soon, when the time was ripe, when they'd tried each other out and become more sure of each other. But how long would she wait? And what would I do then? Terror made me doubly thoughtful, doubly humble. I seemed to be possessed by fear of hurting her even in the most trifling manner. Every time she got annoyed about something or other I went stiff with fright, expecting to hear: "No, I can't possibly stay here any longer—I'm moving in with him first thing in the morning!"

So I crawled and flattered, humbling myself, while using the last remnants of my common sense to try to map the situation, find out what the chances really were that she'd throw me over and move in with him. I tried cautiously to question her about him and his circumstances; a secret hope he might be married collapsed; he lived apart from his wife, but as far as I could tell the divorce wasn't settled yet, and so he probably had to be a bit careful about engaging a new partner too openly. A possible postponement, but for how long? I moped, suffering in silence as dogs do, fearful that my despondency would make her lose all patience with me. I agreed with her every time we discussed something. I offered to do several domestic chores to take work off her hands, small as her share was to begin with. Beside, her hours had been changed so that she didn't work so much in the evening, meaning that she was in a better mood during the hours she spent with me.

I sensed immediately that the change in working hours was connected with him. She'd been careless enough to tell me he was a steady lunch guest. (A dog remembers everything that has to do with the security of his existence.) So when she started quitting work after lunch four days a week, I understood immediately that this made it possible for her to meet him also away from the restaurant, quite naturally and as if by chance, without her having to keep me informed; she merely had to make sure they left the restaurant simultaneously . . . I would sketch these pictures of her intricate unfaithfulness in my mind, sulk, despair, and fume when I was utterly without hope, meanwhile trying to keep her in ignorance of what was going on, for fear it might give her yet another reason to be dissatisfied with me.

Still, judging by appearances, everything was the same as before. Indeed, better: we talked more, she was more often in a good mood and could afford to be friendlier to me than she'd been for a long time. An outsider would probably have called me hysterical and oversensitive, dismissing the story about her and him as my fantasy and seeing the whole affair as quite innocent, a casual encounter, just as she said, with a person she felt she had contact; perhaps she didn't have the slightest intention of keeping up the association . . . ? But I knew better, for a dog's senses are awake, and when his very existence is threatened they are sharpened to the utmost: I noticed changes no one else could have noticed. I could smell on her clothes that she'd been other places than the restaurant when she came home, saying she'd been delayed at two of her tables, that some people never got around to paying. I saw how she stood before the mirror and gradually, almost imperceptibly, changed her appearance, combed her hair differently, dropped the nonchalance she'd cultivated from the moment we met—one of the external signs of the newly won "freedom" from her tyrannical husband. Was this a coincidence? On account of the season? Or did she do it to please him? I had no doubt about the answer.

But she was very discreet, never mentioned him if I didn't directly ask; you'd have believed I, not she, was in love with him, judging by the way I plied her with questions, wanting to know all. For though I was almost morbidly afraid of the influence he'd acquired over her and of what I felt would be the unfailing consequence of their affair, I still seemed obsessed by the thought that I must know *all*, make an attempt to uncover all the hidden facts, get to the root of the reasons why she'd abandoned me—though only spiritually for the time being—find *the explanation* . . .

As if a dog could hope to find explanations!

In the beginning there was perhaps a hope of remedying the irremediable, if only the explanation could be found. But gradually this quizzing game of mine turned into sheer self-torture. It pained me in a way I eventually almost took pleasure in to watch her reactions to my questions, her efforts to keep her voice indifferent and control the play of her features when I steered the conversation to him, mentioning, as if by chance, something he'd said the other evening or things I'd noticed. In the midst of her hard-won neutrality she would suddenly betray herself, drop words and phrases that told me everything, and this gave me a strange satisfaction, though it also made me more scared and even more despairing than before.

"He has a strange form of self-esteem," she'd say. "He radiates strength without having to prove it by dominating others. He's so quiet on the surface, but you can somehow feel his real self glowing in there someplace, like a low flame. Don't you think so too?"

The dog's impression, obviously, was quite different. A dog perceives the vibrations of nervousness in a different way than people. During the brief hour I'd spent with them, I'd experienced how desperately he held back, how preoccupied he was with his immaculate, conventional appearance, as if this mask, and it alone, could give him the courage to associate with people. I'd noticed how afraid he was to open up even the tiniest crack in his armor and could tell by his eyes how quick-witted he was, how swiftly he'd fight back or find a safe retreat if he was attacked or pressed.

But it was pointless to try to explain this to her, let alone getting her to admit that he was a primitive, lonely warrior who fought his own battle in the macho jungle, the jungle she'd helped me out of by her sincerity and her courage to be herself, letting me be myself. Accepting yourself as you were; feeling gratitude for learning to see the small, invisible but essential things between people; the sweetness that had dripped down on us from the maple trees in the Palace Park—it had all started with her. And now I had a chance to reciprocate by telling her something, for though she'd known many men and, yes, liked and loved men, she knew nothing about men's secret trade in places on the social ladder, a sign language developed already in boyhood where everything goes by external markings, attire, facial expressions, gestures and diction, physical strength and stature; where men stand in line and must, for all eternity, go by the numbers they've been assigned and where all later attempts to sneak ahead a couple of places become nothing but pitiful gropings and dreams, regardless how much they pay in terms of possessions and camouflage, synthetic status and external facade.

Only a woman can rescue a man from men's tyranny, put him beyond the justice of the fist fight by ridiculing and nullifying it, as she'd done for me. As she now was prepared to do for him, though she would never succeed. That much I'd understood. I could tell from his face, his manners, and gestures as he stood in the living room those first few moments. I could tell by his clothes, by the things he attached importance to. Rather, he would use her as a stone in his own edifice, built around fear of defeat and a feeling of inferiority, and she would let him, the way women generally let themselves be used by men for whom they still glimpse some "hope." But I'd seen him and unmasked him, I recognized the gladiator in him, felt the suspense of the fist fight envelop us the moment we shook hands. For he knew, and I knew, that it really was *I* who had the advantage: I was taller than he and younger; I had education and culture; he was too short, with a tendency toward obesity that he buttoned up in a bulging striped vest. He was "self-made," a status seeker, a scaler of walls, crop-eared and polished, on the safe side; watch on a gold chain, gold-mounted cuff links, a heavy expensive tie: substitutes for winnings where it really counts! Even his prick was too short and with a tendency toward obesity from what I could see, crammed as it was into a bulging, striped pair of pants, too narrow and slightly too long in the legs.

Why then didn't I join battle with him, a battle I was bound to win? On account of the metamorphosis I had undergone, because I'd become a weak-willed dog with no power to govern my own life, without responsibility for my existence. It was only a matter of time before he too would realize it and take victory for granted.

But shouldn't I have warned her? I should have warned her!

No. A dog's opinions don't count on the same level as his master's. Once the master has made a decision, the dog can only wag his tail and lick the indifferently extended hand. If he pricks up his ears and anxiously whimpers in mild protest, he's ignored; if he insists, he's thrown out the door.

In the same vein, I interpreted her preoccupation with his "self-esteem" and the "low flame of his real self" as a euphemism for her sexual fascination with him. She'd fallen for the mythology that the neurotic so cleverly spins around himself. She interpreted silence as depth. Hesitancy as strength. Aloofness as unspoken promises. A complicated, introspective man (or a cunning man who knows how to manage his weaknesses with discretion and calculation) always becomes a "duty" for a woman, a mission and a challenge.

Naturally I didn't dare discuss my dog's insights and dog's perceptions with her. Criticizing him openly would merely confirm her conviction what an "exceptional" and "thrilling" person he was. Instead, I let my questions and my insinuations work on her as a stimulus. Without her noticing, I made her accept me as her confidant, and thereby as her co-conspirator. She was so much in love with him, she found it completely natural that I too was thrilled with him! By allowing her or, quite simply, forcing her to occupy her thoughts with him by my groveling, perverse, doglike curiosity, I noticed I could make her softer, milder, more forbearing also toward me and the small demands my hectic, whining dog's devotion placed upon her.

This shows how abjectly a dog must learn to grovel if he wants to get anything in a world governed by people's brutalized wills and obtuse longings!

10 I tried of course, in every way I could think of, to find out if she was still seeing him, or when she would see him next, but could never get any definite answer.

"You talk as if I were engaged to him," she'd say, with a laugh that made it quite clear that this was the goal, her wishful dream, perhaps come true already, in essence if not in any formal way. A laugh that sent me crawling into the corner, where I'd lie moping the rest of the evening, though I had no proof, except for my positive dog's instincts.

Countless tiny details told me she was constantly in touch with him. How could she avoid it if, as she said, he was a steady customer at the restaurant? Still she denied everything, or wriggled out of answering with a look, a laugh, or an accusation that I was an idiot to make so much of this; was I really that jealous? But her voice told me I had every reason to be. Three or four days after his late-night visit passed in this way. The floor was swaying under my existence, the joints creaking. Those days and nights filled with flirtation and masquerade—the rigid chess moves of jealousy against the cozenage of infidelity, the feverish spells of lie and counterlie—felt like weeks. Time stands still when an individual confronts his annihilation. The person sentenced to death sucks a lifetime of light and air into his body the minute before the hood is pulled over his head. The drowning person lives his life over again. The same is true for dogs.

Uncertainty that is due to certainty is unbearable. Those hours when I walked around the house during the day waiting for her to come home—I waited and yearned the way dogs do, from the very moment she walked out the door—had become unbearable. I couldn't take my mind off her—or him: at this very moment he might be entering that door with "Bel Ami" painted in elaborate, swirling white letters, looking around the room in order to catch sight of her and say hello—discreetly. Now he'd taken a seat and she rushed up to take his order (they'd naturally agreed beforehand which table he was to sit at, so she'd be able to serve him). Now she bent forward over the table to adjust the tablecloth or the centerpiece with flowers, while he, speaking softly and holding his head close to hers, said something intimate or witty that made her burst into laughter . . .

I couldn't take it! I couldn't stand being at home in the apartment hour after hour, while my fantasies about her and him assumed grotesque proportions. I was too distracted to tidy up the messy apartment, hardly even noticed the state it was in. She didn't seem to give much thought to it either, a sign, I gathered, that she'd already moved out, just came and went for a while yet, to eat and sleep. My dog's yearning to be near her, to make sure that nothing untoward happened to her—to *us* and our life!—even if it were nothing but a hindrance, a disturbing element between them that might delay the inevitable development for a while even now, a few days at least, assumed the intensity of paranoia: I simply had to! Had to keep a watch on her! Look out for us!

I broke loose. I opened the door and ran out—down the sidewalk. Rambled on, shaky and lost, blinking against the unfamiliar frosty light, though the sky was overcast. It must have been days, perhaps a week, since I'd stepped outside the door. The cold air nipped my sensitive nose, my breathing grew heavy. I slowed down. I would never get there if I wore myself out up here, in Grefsenveien. A dog reaches his goal by modest stubbornness. He doesn't rush ahead only to give up later; he waits, struggles, and endures.

I'd simply planned to run to town, unable by instinct to think of any other means of transportation; a dog slinking along at the edge of the sidewalk would hardly create a stir. But when I approached Storo I changed my mind: it was too far. I'd be late if I went all the way to Majorstua on foot. The No. 11 trolley would take me almost all the way. I knew when I stopped to think, of course, that people would never be able to detect the metamorphosis I'd undergone, unless they made a very careful inspection. The dog's face still looked like a human face with mournful, hairy features. Surely nobody would refuse a human-looking dog like me permission to ride the streetcar by himself.

I got off at Majorstua and sneaked onto the sidewalk in the stream of pedestrians. I imagined that at every contact with others, every chance nudge, a hateful glance was shot in my direction: Get away, you damn cur! I leveled my eyes at their feet, shoes, men's and women's coat skirts: boots and shoes tell a great deal about people—I keep at a safe distance from pointed and polished ones. And from boots with hard toes. But there's also soft footwear, boots with upward-curving tips, felt mukluks, shoes with thick soles and slack, flapping laces . . . Some people in high heels trip along regardless of the weather and the condition of the street, in a way that makes it almost irresistible to follow them, at least a short distance . . .

I took up a position in an entranceway diagonally across from the restaurant. Nobody finds it strange when a dog sneaks into a backyard to nose and scurry about, then hesitates briefly at the gate while sniffing in the direction of the noise and the bustle in the street . . .

I didn't have to stand there very long. *He* emerged first from the restaurant, smartly dressed in coat and hat today. Thick suede demi-boots. Neatly pressed trousers. A dressed-up doll who avoided looking at passersby, with an expression that was a mixture of arrogance and fear.

Then *she* came, good-humored, hurrying along while still buttoning her coat: that's how scared she was he might have to wait a moment! I'd been right: changing her work shift was obviously a trick to give her the opportunity she wanted to leave the restaurant with him. This was how she'd become acquainted with him, of course, running into him "by chance" in the doorway and smiling, then dropping a remark—as she did when we met. So friendly, so inviting, so searching, and still so nice: all possibilities open, with an appetite for new adventure, a new acquaintance, a new man; the old dog had grown too sluggish, life demands life, people demand vitality, dynamism, and change. A human being can change his place of residence, profession, and appearance. A human being can chase a dog away and get a new one. But a dog cannot replace his master, regardless of what happens. A dog's entire life depends upon his master's care and kindness.

She'd taken his arm as they walked close together down the sidewalk. I followed at a safe distance, hardly needed to keep an eye on them. My sharpened senses, indeed my *instinct,* told me where they were. They entered The Old Major, as I thought. A quick rendezvous before she felt she must get home to look after the old dog, who'd sat at home alone all morning, poor thing. I was in a fix, couldn't very well follow them in there, no way. Still I craved to be with them, close to her, to destroy their intimacy, delay the debacle, avert the catastrophe . . . The catastrophe that had already occurred, of course. That I knew. Everything indicated that. But like the dog I was I needed to have things repeated. Dogs are slow on the uptake—although I *knew* for certain, and almost enjoyed tormenting myself with this certainty, it looked as if I'd never get enough.

I could tell from the way she held his arm, the way her thigh swung against his, from their feet keeping time on the muddy sidewalk. When I ventured to raise my eyes, their heads told me all that the feet alone couldn't tell: the distance between his head and hers was much too small for their relationship to be merely friendly. The way she leaned her head toward his was a revelation in itself, a symbol, a way of putting her cheek against his shoulder without actually being close to him. And even he, that constipated dry stick, had thawed in those places where she got close to him, accepting her body and movements to permit a synchronism that betrayed to all, at least to a dog, how intimate they were, skin to skin, even with their clothes in between.

But a dog doesn't dare raise his eyes for very long at a time. Rather, a dog must concentrate on trouser legs and shoes, skirt hems, and legs.

They walked down the street like fast friends, thigh against thigh, leg against leg and in time, her worn and discolored winter boots beside his newly brushed suede ones, he in his highest heels, she in her lowest. How considerate! How obliging she could be to someone she was stuck on! A short time ago that same all-encompassing concern had benefited me. Hadn't she even said that my very inexperience with women made it so much more beautiful for her?

But a dog doesn't reminisce, or recall the past in detail. To a dog it's today that counts: two pairs of boots in time on the sidewalk, one of which makes a false step into the gutter, wobbles as if about to trip. Playacting! A pretext! An opportunity to take a firmer hold of the confident arm that likes to let its muscles play under the coat—balance restored thanks to . . . Dependency. Subservience. How *can* she? We who used to ridicule Man's Unenlightened Despotism together! We who made our bedroom into the most advanced foxhole of the war for equality. A glance at his face: a thank-you, a smile as of a thousand suns in the November afternoon. The same suns that thawed the ice within me last summer. My only summer! God! Oh God!

And now inside The Major, face to face in the semidarkness over one of those small rectangular formica tables, where only a couple of weeks ago she'd resented Arne's helpless pressure with elbows and knees. Was she twining her fingers and toes with *his* now?

I knew I must be careful, yet couldn't help myself: I sneaked past both windows, peered inside in passing, saw nothing—well, perhaps over there, a silhouette that could easily be her, a silhouette without glasses. I could almost hear her deep, slightly halting voice explain how a pair of glasses get misty when you come in from the cold: a pretext to undress her face for him!

My fear and despondency drove me on. A dog is not permitted to stop and look in on the cozy intimacy where people have their private lives. A dog must stay outside in the cold until he's most graciously let in. I slunk, dejected, along the curb, wet and disheveled, my tail drooping, so crushed, so down-and-out that nobody noticed me, not even to fling a word of abuse, an unkind grimace, or the hard toe of a boot in my direction.

11 Nobody can endure for long the certainty of his own imminent destruction, the annihilation of his existence. Nor can a

dog. Even a dog takes refuge in wishful thinking, in arguments that will prove, with the help of desperate, inflamed logic, that the dreaded event will not come to pass, *never can* come to pass; that at worst it's something temporary, that everything will turn out all right . . .

One of the dog's most characteristic traits is his "fidelity," his monogamy, which is of course nothing other than his lack of imagination, his being bound by habit. A dog's life is determined by his own biological clock and by the vital rhythms of his master. The first factor can't be regulated, and too great irregularities in the second induce nervousness and depression in a dog. When both elements are in harmony, the relationship between master and dog is at its best. Then it's easy for the dog to imagine that his master is just as dependent on monotony as he is himself. And when this stability, which the dog believes both depend on, is tampered with or quite simply threatened with dissolution, the dog begins to fool himself into thinking that his master also longs to get back to an "orderly state of affairs," to the equilibrium that existed before the threatening, unforeseeable thing happened, just as he does himself. He forgets that people are differently constituted.

I knew, of course, that she was fond of me, of me *too*. She had to be; everything we'd done and experienced together all summer couldn't simply be erased, given over to indifferent oblivion. It just wasn't possible! I managed to convince myself that this affair with *him* was an episode, a digression—honest to goodness, I knew such things could happen to the very best of us. When I stopped to think I saw clear signs that their association was of a fugitive nature. First, they were so poorly suited to each other. He was no man for her—this hurt my dog's pride the most—he must have "tricked" her into it somehow, found a weak spot in her and made his frontal attack there. That was the explanation.

But sooner or later she would realize this herself—she simply *had to* realize it, since it was so obvious to all! It *couldn't* take long before she'd unmask that dressed-up publishing cheat. God knows if he was telling the truth anyway; his personal data were perhaps just as false and puffed up as his decked-out facade. And *when* she discovered it, then she would understand everything, realize how thoughtless she'd been, how ruthless toward the faithful dog who sat at home waiting for her, and feeling sorry, she would manifest a love ten times as strong . . .

But what if she didn't succeed in seeing through him? What if she were so trapped by her fantasies about him as an ideal male project that she'd permanently disconnected her reason and dismissed her intuition regarding him? What if she never saw her tragic error? Then the dog could only rely on *his* attitude and actions, but these, by contrast, could never be in doubt: just as he'd managed to trick her into playing his lewd game, he would slyly maneuver his way out of the relationship again the moment he got tired of it, that is, when he'd had his fill of her and of the entire adventure, the very moment when she would begin to make demands on him—which she was bound to do, which it was part of her nature to do, in her proud awareness of her newly won self-respect. Accordingly, when he failed her on this point, where it would hurt the most, she would have to understand at last and return to her dog, who had understood all along and sat at home waiting, yearning for her and wagging his tail, ready to forgive everything . . .

During the couple of days after I followed them to The Major he again seemed to be absent. This pause in my torments enabled me to perfect my chain of thought, which brought me to the conclusion that everything would be all right again. In the end I managed to convince myself quite firmly that she, too, had only a single wish, namely, that everything would be as before. She acted friendly and forbearing; she took pity on me and let me come to her bed, and I lay there solemnly enjoying her nearness with bated breath and self-effacing chastity, somewhat like a person sentenced to death who doesn't dare go near the table where his last meal has been set out. Even though my rough dog's logic told me that this was the beginning of something new— perhaps things were going poorly between them already? Perhaps this was the first phase of the rebuilding of our relationship? A poor dog can fool himself this way when he doesn't have pictures or circumstantial evidence freshly imprinted on his retina.

She was kind but evasive, smiling and in good humor. One evening she helped me tidy the cubbyhole, patted me, said she was sorry for me but that it had greatly helped her sleep to have my snoring and groaning, my howls and moans, behind a closed door. Then she looked at the watch and said in a light and completely natural tone of voice: "Gosh, it's already half past seven, he could be here any moment now."

"Is anyone *coming*"? My voice barked as if I couldn't believe my own ears, though I knew the same moment that I'd only been waiting for this without daring to think the thought, without bringing myself to imagine the continuation:

"Who then?"

As if I didn't know!

"Bel Ami, of course, who else? I told him he could drop by if he wanted to. It doesn't matter, does it? You know each other, after all!"

Her voice was completely neutral, her tone undramatic, as if it didn't cost her anything to tell me about it this way.

"But today is *Thursday*!"

"Sure it's Thursday."

"The group . . ."

"Ugh, yes, that group—I don't think I can make it tonight . . ."

During the last couple of weeks the environmental group and nothing else has been holding us within the framework of a "normal" existence. In any case we have been going there every Thursday and every other Tuesday. Together with Arne and the others our existence would be the way it used to for a couple of hours. This in spite of the fact that she has seemed capricious and uninspired recently and has cast some critical remarks my way, no sooner uttered, however, than regretted and taken back. "They're too young for me, you see," she'd often say. "You know, they're so nice and idealistic and well-informed, well, quite simply impressive, and yet they seem to know so little. Besides I get so tired of having little boys trailing after me . . ."

A speech to me of course, indirectly. Arne and the others are more or less my own age. We're all "little boys" compared to *him,* the king of the jungle, dressed in a striped ready-made suit and high cork heels. Doesn't he comb his hair over the crown of his head, too? Now it's suddenly a handicap to be young, ten years younger than she. A mere couple of months ago it gave her a "totally new and fantastic feeling of freedom . . . Like holding hands walking through the grass . . . For the first time to want a man and be able to tell him without fear of being misunderstood or abused . . . To have a lover who can also be a friend . . ."

I treasure these words fanatically, along with the sound of her voice when she uttered them, as if my very reason depended upon my not forgetting them. I take them out and listen to them as I lie in my dog's bunk in the cubbyhole at night unable to sleep. When I feel her eyes give my body the once-over now, it's almost with distaste, as if I knew, without anything being said, that she must find me too thin, too neglected, my fur too unkempt, an abortive puppy, unfinished, untrained, not quite presentable. But I console myself with evoking her voice in my memory: "You're so handsome—the very fact that you're so thin makes me feel like arousing you, you know? When we're with the group and I see you together with the others, I get so hot for you . . ."

But now she wants to cut out the group because of his visit. I can't just sit there and say okay, I must fight for this last remnant of stability in our relationship, these last fragile threads of a system, of a predictable arrangement that gives a dog faith and a sense of peace. But before I've gathered my wits about me, before I can get my well-disciplined, humiliated brain to work in a reasonably efficient manner, I hear the doorbell. He's here already! What am I going to do?

"There he is!" she says in the same natural tone of voice, as if I and my fear, my revolt and my worst presentiments didn't exist.

She goes to open the door. I clear my throat, regain the use of my voice. I've lost, but at least I don't intend to make it easy for her:

"Who is it?" My voice barks at them as they stand in the hallway; I won't let him imagine himself announced and expected. I won't let him think the situation is perfectly clear, that the dog can simply be kicked out into the hallway when he comes . . .

"Oh, its Bel Ami—I asked him to drop by . . ."

Naturally she doesn't let on that she knows I know—that she understands I'm being difficult to spoil the mood between them. But I refuse to give in, having nothing to lose at this point: "Today?" (Yap, yap?) I've taken up a position in the kitchen doorway and hope I look thoroughly unfriendly and inhospitable. Our working clothes should tell him clearly enough that we're doing something we'd like to finish, that he's butting in and disturbing us. But she's turned her attention to him now, doesn't deign even to glance at the dog, let alone answer his ill-bred nagging. But I refuse to give in—a dog can't be expected to apprehend and react to people's demands for politeness, for the elements of good form, in every situation. I go on yelping:

"But we are going to a *meeting!*" (Yap, yap, bow-wow!)

I can see this is news to him. My dog's sensitivity spots an insecurity that expresses itself through extreme politeness, courteous considerateness. He says he's sorry, that he didn't know we were going out, that he'll go right away, of course, if he's intruding. But then she intervenes. She too has noticed his discomfort, sees her plan being threatened and the evening ruined, and meets my barking insistence head on:

"You can go to your meeting, I'm not up to it tonight!"

So much for that. She's got me. This was both an order to get out and a trap: after all, by my unrestrained barking a moment ago, I myself have shown that this meeting is important, at least to me. Now it will look more than strange if I don't go.

"I'm getting a beer, Bel Ami," she says, turning her back to the havoc she's made—a crestfallen dog crawling diffidently onto the unoccupied armchair, certain of being chased out of it at any moment. She doesn't include me in her beer invitation but dutifully pours a glass for me, too. I know I've lost. I know I have no right to sit here with them, I spoil the mood: the slightly strained friendly tone hints that there's one too many present, that they wish the old dog to go to blazes, that I ought to get out of here, the sooner the better. But something like spite, almost anger, makes me linger a while. I feel the humiliation gnawing at me and wonder if an obedient, housebroken mongrel might still become unpredictably, furiously dangerous. A dog, too, can have his moods. A dog, too, can be stubborn, though usually it blows over before it gets serious enough not to be corrected by a sharp tone of voice or a clenched fist.

In any case I experience a certain satisfaction from noticing that I've pierced his complacency—or haven't I, after all? Is it perhaps only consideration for her (and for me!) that makes him appear so apologetic, so reserved and amenable? At any rate, the mood that's come over me is such that I'll make dead sure to exploit the situation to the utmost—since the battle is lost anyway, since everyone realizes by now that I'll have to go and they're just waiting for me to get up.

"And what do *you* think about environmental protection?" My voice snarls a provocative question as though it contained a direct threat. A dog's strategy is to intimidate his adversary, to bark and snarl and show his teeth, raise his hackles and make as much noise as possible. But he rarely goes as far as making an attack. You seldom see dogs fighting, a dog is content with advertising his strength and his anger. His powerlessness. As a rule he assumes he's lost before it starts. Most dogs are cowardly, miserable, afraid of getting whipped; they give up and slink away after a brief demonstration of barking and growling. As if I didn't already know what he thinks about environmental protection or, more correctly, what he *doesn't* think about environmental protection. Oil extraction. Nuclear power stations. PVC-production. As if I didn't know that he can demolish my attack with a couple of clever phrases full of conventional commitment to environmental issues: *everybody* is concerned about environmental issues! Or he can make a counterattack, of course, trivialize the problems, ridicule my commitment with a few facile remarks about "student revolt" and "red-wine radicalism," the economic situation and the need for power development, and so forth. Which will it be? I tremble already at the outcome, the counterattack, and prepare my retreat.

But she's the one who makes the counterattack, ridiculing my commitment by asking me to "stop recruiting . . ." Adding for his benefit by way of explanation, "He's so committed to 'causes'." Poor fellow. She might just as well have added it: Poor fellow!

How patronizing they both are. A dog doesn't mind being patronized by her, for as long as she's patronizing she can't be angry with me at least, or find me disgusting. But when they're both patronizing at the same time it's intolerable! The gleam in his eyes betrays him when he asks politely:

"So you're doing a bit of refurnishing?" Referring to our working clothes. Referring to my misery! And she—she simply explodes in laughter at his remark, at the thought of the old dog in his cubbyhole, lying there night after night with moist eyes and his hairy sac tight with pressure, but recognizing his position and knowing that he must keep his place and wait, wait until it pleases his mistress to pat him, rub him behind the ear or across the small of the back, perhaps in a happy moment across the chest or the belly, enough to make the pointed, pink dog's prick rise and stand erect till it becomes noticeable even to her, who naturally doesn't have to feel that the poor old dog's comic, panting excitement puts her under any obligation, who doesn't have to feel bound by anything, she who has both man and dog and who at best reveals her awareness of the dog's anguished predicament by bursting into laughter, giving him a slap and sending him away with an ironic remark. Only when she is in a special mood, downcast or unpredictable—times when I believe she's thinking of *him* and doubting, when she may even have a vague notion of the sort of guy he really is—do I get a chance. Then even a dog's wordless, primitive devotion can give consolation and support. Unless she's beside herself with desire and can't wait till the next rendezvous but must quench her impatience by riding the one who is closest at hand, even if it's only the dog . . . How long is it since she last let me do it? A week? Two weeks? A dog doesn't remember very clearly; I only feel it's a long time ago, *too* long, so long that I've started feeling diffident also in this area, the last refuge of an intimacy that, in rare moments, has reminded me of what used to be . . .

I know I've lost. I know I must get out. I feel the moment approach, hear the make-believe conversation between them come to a dead stop, and see the glances they exchange, even though I'm hanging my head and staring at the floor. I look at my watch:

"*It's ten of!*"

Like a yowl, a futile prayer to her to come along anyway, to restore the little that's left of normalcy around us, a helpless howl into the empty space of loneliness created by their impatient, even hostile indifference—a dog's grievance against the mocking light of the frosty moon, the light that's no light but makes the darkness deeper, the isolation more bitter, and turns the fear into a devouring, unalterable presence that cannot be pushed aside.

"I've told you I'm not up to it! You go ahead!"

My marching orders at last, clear and unequivocal. I've expected them, have received them before, though not in so many words. It takes time before they sink in properly—a dog's inertia before he obeys an unwelcome command. Moist glances and reluctant movements, a little wag of the tail against his better judgment while he looks forward to an unlikely change of mood, that his master will yet change her mind and let him stay and enjoy indoor warmth and good cheer together with people, a little wag which shows that a dog never gives up his vain, foolish hope, never can be so humiliated that he stops trying to ingratiate himself, to attain the unattainable. It's this total lack of pride that makes most people love dogs, believing they're faithful and kind-hearted. Accordingly, a smart dog knows how to display his cowardice, his shortsightedness and his inconsistency, because he understands that only in this way can he get anything from his master. For pity and patronizing sympathy is something. Perhaps not as attractive as love and respect but something—most of us cannot hope for more.

As I get up from the sofa I notice that her foot, naked between the sandal straps, is already brushing against his soft, polished leather.

12 I'm afraid of Arne's obvious curiosity, afraid that his interest will be one more voice in the chorus of mockery and condescension that has driven me out onto the most desolate paths. But I'm even more afraid of arriving home too early, perhaps to surprise them in the midst of it, to have to put up with their breathless sense of guilt, see traces of their intimacy everywhere, listen to their stammering loose talk improvised to divert my attention. So I come along reluctantly when he proposes we take a glass at The Major; we're the only ones left in the seminar room, busy packing stencils and display material. He tells me bluntly I look like I need a drink. It shows how observant but also how stupid he is: a dog never needs a drink, can't stand alcohol, in fact. A drink is a stimulant for human beings, a means of forgetting, of self-assertion, false optimism, stupor. A dog's problems aren't localized in such a way that alcohol can solve or diminish them. A dog must carry his problems along with him, an inflammation in every fiber of his body; they can't be forgotten. When a dog experiences conflict he becomes ill, and alcohol aggravates the symptoms of illness.

Therefore it's a disastrously bad idea to go and "take a glass" with Arne, but my fear of unmasking them, perhaps seeing and hearing them in the act, is stronger than all my doubts, more frightening than all my misgivings . . .

"So she's put you in a tough spot?" he mumbled thoughtfully over his half liter. "You mean she's picked up with another guy and got the hots for him?"

I've talked too much, naturally. He has asked questions and I've answered; I've let out the situation little by little. Arne, nodding and sucking on his cigarette, has considered it soberly and manfully. Now I tremble both before his erroneous conclusions and before the fact that in half an hour it's closing time. What should I do? Where can I go till it's safe to return home?

"Frankly, I think you should teach her a lesson," Arne goes on, acting too wise for his years. "I mean, a fellow just can't take everything lying down! Such behavior . . . I mean, drop the chick on the spot. Leave your boot mark on her, if you know . . ."

How little he knows! The two half-liters have turned my torments into open wounds that merely get irritated by his manly heartiness, as fake as it is mistaken. But then he's a peripheral party to the case; isn't there a malicious joy under his affected, sympathetic concern? For according to her, he's tried to make out with her himself, played kneesies and footsie with her in his childish way and been brushed off. So doesn't he have a reason to try and get even with her? Get even with me, who took the last trick that time?

He continues:

"She's married, isn't she? She's run away from her hubby, kids too maybe. Does she keep in touch with them? No? Perhaps it might be an idea to tip off that hubby of hers where she's hanging out and how she's carrying on? Perhaps he'd turn up, get her into line again so she'd stop running around and leading people a dog's life . . . Do you have his number? No-no . . . As you like. Well, there's time for another half liter . . ."

Just before we leave he starts again:

"Honest, don't you think we ought to call up, eh? A short little peep to that hubby of hers. Just the right smack for her. You've said you're through with the chick, so—how about putting a hanky over your kisser: 'If you'd like to know where your wife is . . .' Eh?" Arne doubles up with high-spirited mirth. We walk out of the place laughing.

We part. He slaps me on the shoulder: "Be firm, turn them in. And just give me a call if you need help. Old Arne at your service: the good Samaritan on the battlefield of passion. The Red Cross of the war of the sexes. Trust me!"

When I finally dare go home she's just taken a shower. A smell of soap all over the house, wet tracks from the bathroom to the bedroom. The bathroom door open, the mirror steamed up. Half an hour after midnight and she's taken a shower!

She sits at the kitchen table eating bread with jam and drinking tea. Eating and drinking wrapped in her robe, with wet hair and shiny nose, wide-eyed, a smile on her lips: "Hi. You're late. Did you meet someone?"

Couldn't care less about my answer. Doesn't really want to hear it. Can't think of anything but her own newly bathed comfort and her sensual appetite. Nothing could more blatantly announce what's been going on here. Even if she'd shouted it out in so many words, pointed at the jumbled sofa pillows that she hasn't bothered to straighten out this evening either, and the beer glasses standing side by side on the floor at the headboard where her eyeglasses are also lying. And she always gets such a yen for "something to nibble on." Afterwards. I remember those nocturnal food orgies from last summer when we hauled the entire contents of the refrigerator into our bed, regaled ourselves with sardines, cheese, leftovers from dinner, splashes of wine, beer, smacking our lips, eating and licking our fingers . . .

My recognition is so clear and so painful that I don't catch what she's saying, casual words and sentences between her mouthfuls, perhaps intended as a kind of tactful camouflage of the lurking disaster. But it doesn't get to the dog, who's already living *his* disaster. My attention is riveted on the tuft of hair that appears in the opening of her robe (what indifference! what lack of consideration!), newly washed and rubbed down, a bristling cloud of blond fuzz, a corona of bubble-bathed, newly curried wool: this is what has possessed my thoughts all evening—the limelight of my worries, the focal point of my desire, the center of gravity of my doggie life. All my dog's hunger for a bit of tenderness and love, all my longing for solidarity and harmony with her has been reduced to an animal fixation upon this quite unsensational wisp of hair and the wrinkled slit that's hidden underneath. And the perpetual question: What can I do to entice it into coming alive, make it swell and open, let me have a crack at it? For a dog's yearning doesn't diminish if his mistress pushes him away, it just grows stronger and more intractable, until the poor beast is at his wits' end! So I sidle up wagging my tail, with drooping ears and an imploring look, and fall to my knees before her, possessed by a single impulse: to put my muzzle up between her thighs, inhale the smell of soap, feel her salty taste on my tongue. She used to like it, it would start her up even on evenings when she was too tired and asked for mercy—if only I stuck my muzzle up there and found her salt with my dog's tongue, then she'd melt, swell up, clasp my head, gently tug my hair, pull my ears gently, oh so gently, and whisper: "My sweet! Oh, my sweet!"

But tonight she just pushes me away indifferently, impatiently:

Here at the table? Good Lord, not tonight. Don't I know what time it is? Hey, stop! Oh, cut it out!

Then my nature can no longer contain itself, the dog shows his teeth and snaps at her—blurting out his accusation, disappointment, bitterness, and fear. It had to come out sometime, and it must be now when the sofa pillows still reek of his sickening men's perfume and she sits there with straddling legs under her robe, licking jam from her fingers with a pointed red tongue, her head crammed with thoughts of the assorted adulteries she's committed with him, and will go on committing, while she pushes the dog away with her foot. I yell at her face, telling her all I know, all I've seen, understood and felt, what I think of him, what I think of her and her behavior. My barking echoes back from the walls. At first I get almost frightened at myself, then grow even more excited by the intensity of the dog's attack: I pull no punches, I show my teeth, arch my back, feel my hackles stand up and hatred burn in my eyes, which I screw up to narrow cracks. This should make an impression on her! This should make her manageable so she'll understand, repent, realize what her behavior jeopardizes . . . I go on snapping, let myself be intoxicated by the echo from the kitchen walls, the way a dog lets himself be impressed and excited by his own noise, until he imagines he's powerful and dangerous.

But in the midst of my exhibition of wounded pride, unrequited feelings and righteous indignation, I can't help noticing that she's not the least disturbed, neither wincing nor repenting as I'd expected she would. She barely changes her expression, merely revealing by a gleam in her eyes perhaps that she's *interested*, really interested, in something I'm saying for the first time in weeks and months. She leans forward and looks at me as if she hadn't seen me in a long time, but I can only read a hint of mistrustful surprise in her beloved features, which I'd expected and hoped would swell up, get baggy and dissolve in bitter tears and a plea for forgiveness at this point. Then, calm and considered, comes her rebuke:

"For God's sake, get hold of yourself, will you!" A cold and clear command that easily cuts through the baying of the old dog. "Trying to accuse me of being unfaithful, eh?" My answer, all my answers, suddenly dissolve in confusion, my obedient dog's brain is in a crazy whirl. Sure! Sure I am! But her reproachful tone has already branded my outburst as improper for a dog. My courage sinks. My tail creeps between my legs. My glance becomes furtive and flutters from side to side. I've made a mistake of course—a dog has no business to demand, a dog has no right to be jealous. I ought to have realized that too.

"So this is the 'freedom' and the 'mutual respect for the other's personality and integrity' we've talked about so grandly?" I know we've talked about this and agreed in theory. But this is reality! I must try to say something about ruined loyalty, trust and solidarity between us (Grrrrr, bow-wow! Bow-wow-wow-wow . . . Bow-wow!), but it sounds so pitiful and meek, nothing but woofs and yelps and finally a whipped dog's cowed whimper, insufferably apologetic and despondent.

"Here you walk around thinking you're entitled to 'know what's going on' when I am with others, right? And 'seeing the writing on the wall.' And imagining one thing or another based on all sorts of strange reasons?"

Nothing to answer. Nothing to say. After all, we've been through this. We know that "nothing lasts for life." She has her alibi all set. (Bow-wow-wow-wow! Wow! Woof. Woof.)

"And what if the terrible thing *has* happened, Payk, eh? While you were out? What about that mentality of ownership we refused to accept? Our contempt for jealousy? What if he *is* my lover? Do you find it impossible to imagine I might live here with you and have a lover at the same time? What do you imagine anyway? That I go stark raving mad if I get interested in somebody else? That we fuck all over the place, morning and night, because we like each other's company? That he and I are doing all sorts of nasty things together? What do you think is going on, really? (Here she seems to suppress a smile!) Do you think, perhaps, he asks me to sit on your glass table while he lies under it to get a really good peek at my treasures before he comes at me, for example? I've heard there are men who go in for such things, too. Is that the sort of stuff you're picturing to yourself?"

Her voice quivers. Laughter? Tears? Has she really straddled above him and let him take a peek at her through the glass slab? She would never have thought of saying it, otherwise. She would have thought of something else to hurt me with, something less odd. My dog's instinct sees through her: she *likes* to repeat their sexual excesses in my presence. It titillates her sexually to confide in me this way, to relive the flirtation in her mind, plant ideas about activities in my head whose subtlety and perversion my uncertainty blows up tenfold. I can't bear it. The dog's whimpers and whines become bitter howls.

"Tell me, what did you hope to achieve with this supervision of yours?"

Nothing! Nothing! (Yip, yi-i-i-p! Yap . . .)

"You know, if I thought I needed a lord and master I could've stayed where I was. No lack of discipline and jealousy there. I really thought you'd understood one thing, Payk, that the great thing about our relationship was that it was free and voluntary. We found each other, we needed each other, we loved each other, and it was right and beautiful because that's how it happened, without either of us feeling a need to own the other. But nobody can guarantee what's going to happen. I'd never thought either . . . All right, let's get it out: I *have* become quite interested in Bel Ami, and I have permitted myself to feel exactly what I do feel for him. And I won't take orders from anybody as far as this is concerned. It's that simple, Payk. It's that easy. And stop sitting there looking like a whipped dog!"

But even during this tirade she doesn't bother to pull her robe properly around her, and her look, which ought to have sharpened to make a fitting accompaniment to her clear and matter-of-fact words, turns inward to where her well-being still remains after *his* ingratiating presence and its fragrance of aftershave lotion earlier this evening. And even in his crushed position the dog ponders if his whining and begging might possibly get him a little of the warmth she has left, that excess of sensuality which an evening of good human lovemaking can give a woman.

13 A dog's devotion is inexhaustible. A dog's fidelity has been inculcated through a long and laborious process of learning in which his whole apparatus of feeling has become keyed to his master, limited to meeting the master's needs and expectations. But though a dog is incomparably loyal and capable of adaptation, his emotional equilibrium depends upon a certain minimum of stability. A pattern must be established that the dog can learn to master and feel secure with. Even if the pattern is liberal and permits certain deviations, it must recur and be recognizable, so that the dog can feel secure within the framework of repetition of something he knows. As long as events take place within this pattern, a dog will be loyal till his dying day. If the pattern is radically broken, the whole fine net of acquired responses and reactions will also be destroyed. The whole laboriously established system of communication between a dog and his master gets broken. Chaos follows.

A master can behave so deviantly and capriciously toward his dog that he becomes ill. A dog whose trust has received a death blow, whose equilibrium has been deeply shaken by the master's eccentric conduct, grows agitated, nervous, and capricious. When something similar happens to people we say they are neurotic. When a dog is involved we say he becomes treacherous. Dogs have sometimes suddenly, without warning, attacked a master to whom they had shown obedient devotion for years.

It hits me as I walk around the apartment the following morning in order to tidy up (she's made *me* tidy up after them!): a rage so overwhelming and so hateful that I almost feel dizzy—a childish, blind rage full of wild fancies nearly impossible to control or suppress, full of hatred for her, who thinks she's entitled to make me so miserable, hatred for him who has broken into our life and destroyed it, but mostly for her who lives here with me, walks unceremoniously in and out of the bathroom when I'm around, toasts bread in the morning and asks if I want any, calls sweetly "So long!" as she leaves and, "Perhaps you could tidy up a bit while I'm gone?" as if nothing had happened, as if it were still she and I as we dreamt it would be forever, at any rate for a long, long time yet—a relationship that was to go on and on . . . While in reality everything is quite different, the cat's out of the bag, and she makes no bones about having an affair with this fellow who comes tiptoeing around here, stiff as a poker, his ready-made pants tight with pressure, while he looks with contempt at my jeans and my T-shirt full of holes. Indeed, it's much worse, for she fucks him here on our own sofa and then sits down in the kitchen to eat and stuff herself, obviously delighted to be able to relate their carryings-on, which naturally makes the whole thing even more unbearable! Meanwhile she walks around me every day, talks to me in a bright, friendly tone of voice, gives me a little pat on the head every now and then, scratches me behind the ear, then gently pushes me away when my hope is kindled and I become aggressive, with a "Come, come . . ." It's this duplicity that drives me wild, this having it both ways. It would have been easier if she'd made a clean break, packed and left . . . No! What am I saying? What would become of me if she left? What becomes of a dog when his master disappears? In whimpering despair I bury my face in the pillow I'm holding, full of his and her smells, scented soap, and men's lotion. A dog's sense of smell is forty times sharper than that of a human—their odors in this room are more than I can stand! And the rage surges up in me again—I hurl the pillow across the room, grab a ceramic ashtray and smack it into the tabletop, the glass slab where they perform their most loathsome exercises. The earthenware piece is smashed and leaves behind a wound, a rose in the tempered glass. I run panting back and forth in the room, mad with lust for destruction, paralyzed by contradictory impulses; two or three knickknacks get swept down from the bookcase, awakening my bloodthirstiness by the sound of shattering porcelain. I want to raze, tear down, destroy everything, *everything* that can remind me of her! Her clothes . . . With a groan I break open the closet door—out with it all! I throw myself to my knees on the heap, want to tear up every garment, rip everything to shreds with my teeth and claws . . .

I actually manage to rip off some buttons, slash a blouse, and make the seam on a skirt come slightly undone; it's harder than I thought to destroy clothes. I break a nail, it hurts, but not as painfully as I want to make her suffer just then: I want to injure, harm, annihilate her! But I cannot bear the thought of losing her . . .

Sobbing, I sink down upon the heap of clothing, torn apart by my contradictory moods, knowing that at this very moment I'm barely sane. What's going to happen? How will it all end? What will become of me? Yes, what does happen to a dog who's abandoned to himself? I lie there in a seeming stupor of tears and hopelessness for a while, yet underneath my sorrow an inextinguishable anger is smoldering, for she destroyed something in me when she destroyed our relationship. I know I'm unreasonable now, perhaps crazy! While I bawl with grief over losing her, my limited, inflamed brain simultaneously struggles with plans for revenge! Dogs sometimes go so mad that they turn their weapons against their masters . . .

It takes quite a while before I calm down. A crystal-clear, frosty peace envelops me. I straighten out the clothes while fragments of incoherent fancies sail through my head, memories of long ago and recent ones, pictures and sentences, which turn into a discontinuous cavalcade I hardly notice anymore. Apart from a tiny thing, a sentence that's got stuck, a remark from The Major yesterday: "Why don't you just call her old man, tell him where she is and how she's carrying on. Then you'll be rid of the jade and she'll get a smack . . ."

Not for a moment have I thought of going through with it, but I can't get rid of Arne's voice; the more I listen to it, the more convincing I find his brutal argument. My despair tells me it can't go on like this. My dog's hatred demands revenge. But if I were to attack her physically she'd simply run away to *him*. This way I'd be able to get even with them both.

Without yet having completed my thought, I find my hands on the telephone book. I know his name after all, the name of his business—it would be the simplest thing in the world: a quick anonymous phone call . . .

I dial the number, still without having made up my mind, not by an act of volition or conviction. My teeth chattering, I am trembling all over at the thought that I won't be able to make myself properly understood anymore, not in human language anyhow. Apparently he isn't there, and the whole thing will pass like the crazy whim it is . . .

A voice answers and it's him. I have no doubt. A dog senses such things at once. It's a calm, firm voice, the voice of someone who's been able to go on living without her, who's perhaps consoled himself, forgotten her, what do I know.

To make sure, I stutter his name.

"Yes, that's me . . ."

Hang up! Forget the whole thing! Don't go any further with your nasty squealing!

But a dog's hatred demands revenge. I press the receiver to my ear as if wanting to keep him there, while I search for the right human words. At first I can think of only one thing, giving him the address of the restaurant and asking him to go and look for her there. But what if he takes her away with him? It occurs to me that I might never see her again that way. This is a thought I can't stand, however vindictive I may be.

"Hello, are you there?"

The voice again. The voice of someone who must have gone through roughly the same thing I have. Suddenly I'm filled with sympathy for him, so strong I can feel the tears surge up behind my tightly screwed eyelids when I whisper: "If you want to know where you can find her, she's here, here with me . . ."

Then I blurt out the address and slam down the receiver before he has time to answer.

Most likely he won't understand anything, will think a child or some nut was playing with the phone. Forget the whole thing. But the rest of the morning I seem to walk around in a quivering field of electrical tension, continually looking out the window and down the garden path.

My secret makes me elated. My treason makes me bubble over with high spirits. The thought that I've exposed her to her husband, that I'll get my revenge, makes me alert and happy. Light-headed. I must get out!

It's still only about midday. I feel an irresistible urge to look for her, though I wouldn't know what to do if we met, what to say. Even the usual dog's role will present problems now; squealing has stamped out my training, my mechanical dog's devotion—a distance has arisen between us, a desert, a burnt-out lot where nothing grows but where the last act of the drama can freely take place, the last act in the love drama between woman and dog that the dog himself has staged! I feel powerful, unbeatable! I've made myself a stray. I'm a wild dog, a wolf, roaming around and left to his own devices, his own cunning, his own strength. It feels fabulous! Intoxicating! It can't last.

I understand, of course, that I can't show up outside the restaurant. To run into them as they come out together would be both odd and embarrassing. So I post myself in the entranceway. And I don't have to wait long: He appears first on the sidewalk, takes a couple of steps and waits with his back to the entrance. Then she comes, puts her arm in his and says something so that he has to tilt his head closer to hers. Their postures, gaits, the distance between their heads are details that tell a dog an infinite number of things . . .

But it doesn't matter today, not with the high spirits that have taken hold of me now. I have the advantage. I know something they don't know; I've prepared a little surprise for them. Ha ha! Bow-wow! I feel an urge to raise my muzzle and send a shrill echo along the gray walls of the apartment houses, a cocky fanfare of fragile, short-lived insolence, but I check myself. Don't attract attention! Don't ruin it now!

I steal after them along the opposite walk, slinking close to the house walls, slipping in and out between the passersby like a shadow. Like a dog. But today there is none of a dog's cowed, weak-willed jogging after his master, rather a pursuit, the sly trot of a wolf when he has picked up the scent of his prey.

They cut across Jac. Aallsgate and enter The Major. Of course! As if I didn't know this is what they do every day. But I know something they don't! Bow-wow! From the opposite sidewalk I can see them vaguely taking a table not far from the window. Now they're sitting in open view. If they look out they'll catch sight of me. Let them! Let them see that the old dog has broken loose, and wonder a moment. Just let me spoil the mood between them for a couple of minutes—it's only a small foretaste of what lies in wait for them.

14

At home again, exhausted.

After the agitation comes the reaction. Suppose he doesn't pay any attention to an anonymous phone call? He's probably the kind of guy who takes such things in his stride. His voice betrayed a balanced, self-assured person—suppose he quite simply has written her off, is no longer interested in where she is or what she does?

I notice I'm about to start an intense communication with that unknown husband of hers: he's scorned like me, he has lived through the same thing; he must be an ally in the battle I'm fighting—not a battle directly against *her* but against the chaos and the confusion she's plunged me into. Which she also must have plunged him into, a little more than half a year ago. Unless he's made quite differently than I am. Unless it's the height of pretension for a dog to compare his feelings and reactions with those of the Husband. Has *he* experienced that condition of nameless panic when the very ground you stand on begins to tremble, when no truths can be trusted anymore, and causes cease to have effects? Can the Husband experience, the way a dog can, how treacherous gaps suddenly open up in existence itself, though until then everything seemed safe and secure, because his lord and master suddenly can't be trusted anymore? He was married to her after all—he's still married to her . . . If he still cared for her, wouldn't he have moved heaven and earth to find her again? Alerted the police? Brought her back home by force? If he felt the same about her as I do?

The more I think about it the more despondent I get, the more certain that he has just let her go, that he has consoled himself elsewhere and found a new balance in his life, perhaps even forgotten her. Anyway, not attached the slightest importance to my silly phone call this morning—how could I be stupid enough to imagine that such a crazy idea would succeed? With all my misery I'm tempted to laugh at myself: here I sit regretting his absence as if he were a dear friend who's forgotten a date. In fact, I'm already establishing a whimpering, servile relationship with her husband, in reality my foremost rival!

But as the hours go by, other thoughts arise too. It becomes clear to me how impossible this situation could have become if he'd *really* taken my shabby squealing seriously: what if he *had* popped up here? When she was at home maybe? Had referred to the telephone conversation? How would I have tackled *that* situation? What would she've said? What would she've done? What would I've become an accessory to? As evening approaches I feel more and more relieved that I haven't heard anything from him and probably never will (when I haven't heard anything *now* . . .). While growing more and more restless because *she* hasn't returned home yet. She usually isn't that late, even when she allows herself a tête-à-tête at The Major after work. And even if, say, he'd talked her into going to a movie with him, she ought to have been home by this time.

Restless and beside myself, I pace around the apartment, waiting. Even try tidying up a bit to make it cheerful before she comes (not that she's noticed how the apartment looks lately . . .); glance down the garden path toward the gate every other minute.

The November evening closes in so abruptly, so totally, so somberly that not even the beaming lights from Ringveien down there can do more than outline a number of blurry spots in the darkness. A dog doesn't like to be home alone when it's dark, even if the lamps are lighted inside.

I've just put on the kettle when I hear her on the stairs outside. My senses are so tuned to her steps that I can hear her soles scrape against the frozen gravel. No steps beside hers: thank God, she's alone!

Then the doorbell rings . . .

Outside is a man I've never seen before, tall, strong, dressed in a sporty down jacket, cord trousers, and trim jogging shoes in the cold. He's bareheaded, a touch of gray in his thick dark hair. His whole figure aspires to physical vitality, a youthful athletic dynamism that his age has obviously begun to outdistance. His waistline is a bit too heavy. His chin a shade too massive. His eyes, light and blue, smile coldly into my imploring brown ones—charming, masterful:

"Hey, was it you who called this morning?"

And when I can't utter a sound resembling a human answer right away:

"So it's you she makes hell hot for now?"

He really has dog appeal!

Alarmed as I am about this sudden visit, he soon manages to soothe me and talk me into letting him in. With a couple of friendly words and a pat (on the shoulder as he crosses the threshold into the living room), he transforms an anxious, suspicious dog into an obedient and trusting comrade. Some people have this natural ability to radiate a compassionate authority, an ability that immediately makes an impression on dogs. He speaks to me as if we had known each other for a long time. He openly sympathizes with my situation, which he seems to understand without my having to degrade myself by telling him everything in detail. Through tiny nuances he intimates that he virtually knows *more* about my own situation than I do, though his self-confident personality doesn't give the impression that he has ever experienced a dog's life himself.

Still, when he talks about her he seems to be discussing a common experience. That's comforting. It makes me feel secure. And, strangely enough, it doesn't make me the least bit jealous. It creates a sense of mutuality between us, though it's a different kind of mutuality from what I imagined in my excited daydreams after the telephone conversation. It's a mutuality in which he dominates and I confirm. But I've grown used to being dominated in my dog's life; here I've finally found a human being who can dominate me without depriving me of my self-respect. Who succeeds in being authoritarian, in using his power and working his will, without being brutal.

"So she's been living with you?" he declares. "And I suppose it was fun while it lasted?"

I eagerly yelp yes.

The role assignments are built into the situation. After all it's *he* who's married to her. *He* would have every possible reason to be jealous, to abuse me, even beat me, since I've had an affair with *his* wife.

That, on the contrary, he treats me with forbearance, addresses me as a comrade, a sort of obscure colleague, makes him irresistible in my eyes and gives him an undeniable advantage over me. Actually I find him quite attractive, though he and I are extremely different types. He's tall but not as tall as I, squarely built and muscular. His face is regular and sharp, with no secrets, shaven, with a long straight nose and thin lips. Healthy tanned complexion despite the season.

She has told me he is a businessman and has been active in athletics, in the same tone of voice she might have told me he suffered from venereal disease. As I sit face to face with him I suddenly gather comfort and strength from his reassuring conventional figure and his obvious physical vitality. "Don't trust physical fitness buffs!" we'd joked, she and I, as we lay entwined on the grass in Frogner Park, where the sweat suits were jogging around bathed in perspiration and gasping for breath. I thirst for his sympathy and understanding, the sympathy and understanding of *a decent person*. For the first time the feeling of contact with a person has engraved itself in my dog's brain, ousting the constant painful speculations on my relationship with her.

"But now she's run away, leaving you with that day-after feeling, is that it?"

He looks about him as if to locate traces of her, and of her injuries to an innocent fellow creature. Though I'd like to agree with him in everything, I try to tell him she hasn't exactly run away but that complications have arisen in our relationship; actually I'm expecting her home any moment . . .

"Don't be too sure she'll come, with a new man on the scene!"

The indifferent self-assurance with which these terrible words are spoken fortifies and soothes me. Here with him I can feel, at least momentarily, that whether the world stands or falls doesn't depend on her remaining, or not remaining, with me. Though I've *known* all along of course—with my last remnant of common sense—that disappointment in love wears off, that no partner is irreplaceable, this has not been a reality to me, and the thought of losing her has not been easy to bear; for a dog the chances of finding another mistress to take the place of the old one seem infinitely small. But the sound of his confident voice and the sight of his powerful hands, which alternately rest on his thighs, clench themselves and fold over his knee, make me feel secure: there's comfort in a common fate, women can't be trusted, luckily there's more than one fish in the sea . . .

"You know, don't you, that she just up and left me and the little girl—without a word, simply ran away one day. Not even a note on the kitchen counter. Well, there was a phone call the day after, first calm and matter-of-fact, chilled tones to confirm what had happened, so to speak, that she 'couldn't stand it any longer'" (he clenches his strong fists), "then tears and accusations when I tried to tell her straight out what she'd gotten herself into, then the slamming of the receiver in the middle of a sentence—you know the style. After that I didn't hear a word till summer, when a letter came. I assume it was after she'd met you, for she wrote some highfalutin stuff about having found a friend, a 'male human being' and so on—obviously just a piece of nastiness to say that I was a 'male brute'" (he clenches his hands again, I wag my tail in agreement—such things won't do, even if I must admit being a bit flattered by the designation 'male human being'). "Then another letter came, around mid-September. She'd started to work, she wrote, but not a word about where. Needless to say, she asked me not to try and track her down, meet her, or try to persuade her to come back again, for that could never be, and so on . . . As if I were interested in taking *her* back into my house again! No sirree! I'd put the hook on the door a long time ago. But I would have liked to meet her to arrange the formalities. I've had the papers prepared by a lawyer. She requests divorce because she's entered into a relationship with another man and waives custody of the little girl, the whole thing rounded off with a certain monthly sum. Damn it, by rights she shouldn't even get that much. But to settle this I have to talk to her and get her to sign, you know—explain to her that this is the best for all of us, the child especially. To begin with, you know, I had an awful job trying to explain that Mommy had only gone away for a little while, that she was staying with someone we didn't know—what can you tell a kid? Now I think she's begun to understand, but I'll be damned if it was much fun while it went on; she cried for Mommy every night. That slut should've heard her!"

A dangerous strength and aggressiveness lurk under his balanced, well-proportioned exterior. Though I know I ought to feel an in- stinctive need to protect her against such accusations, especially from him—after all, I have her version of the story, too, I know how tyrannically, indeed brutally, he behaved toward her, how intolerable her marital situation gradually became—my reaction to what he says is almost one of malicious glee. By my fawning agreement I confirm his

side of the case every inch of the way. I need his bitterness, his self-righteousness, his wounded pride—it helps to restore the self-respect of a neglected dog. I feast on his masculine vanity, which rests with obvious weight in his broad shoulders, his powerful thighs with the tight-fitting trouser legs, his alternately open and clenched hands with their long, strong fingers tipped by broad, self-assured nails. Oh yes, there's a dangerous strength and an explosive temperament lurking in his well-coordinated movements, a cold rage with a slow flame that can flare up any moment and release a detonation of vindictiveness, of raw male force—exactly such vindictiveness and force, exactly such signs of a man's natural, self-evident authority that impress a dog, make him prick up his ears and be attentive. "You don't know where she is right now?" he then asks. "No, of course not, or you'd have been out there throwing monkey wrenches into this new romance, wouldn't you?" (He actually credits me with the initiative and courage to do such things!) "If you let me know where she works, perhaps I could . . . No, it would be awkward if she decided to make trouble—we'd better take her by surprise here. So perhaps you'll tip me off when there's a chance she'll be home. If she does come home—like I said, you can't be too sure . . ."

He winks and smiles as if this were a good joke between the two of us and not the to-be-or-not-to-be of my life. But his intimate dumb show makes us pals of sorts, almost equals, spirits of an exclusive brotherhood who're struggling with the same problem but know how to unravel the difficulties. Though how can a man like him know a dog's problems?

"Well, I guess I'd better be going. My little girl is visiting with a school friend. Can't be late . . ."

He gets up. I follow him to the door, excited, tail up.

"So long now. Perhaps you could give me a call when you know what her plans are? As I said, it's only a mere formality that has to be taken care of, I don't intend to stage any crime of passion—God forbid! What happens between you two is no business of mine, but if you want a piece of good advice, get rid of her and find yourself a decent woman. 'Bye. Nice talking to you!"

He disappears down the garden path with springy steps. I bark contentedly after him before I have to close the door against the cold. His strength and optimism still burn for a while within me. I can feel that, with his help, I'm about to undo that loyalty unto death which I imagined bound me to her in an inviolable union. I'm about to tune in to other signals, bind myself to another master: He and I, Man and dog, an invincible team!

But alone in my apartment, it doesn't take long before the panic of loneliness starts once more to oppress my dog's heart: Why doesn't she come? What in the world is she doing? (As if I didn't know! If I had the strength and the courage, I could evoke the picture of them to the last horrible detail!) With her husband for company it was possible to keep the terror at bay for a moment, warm myself in his strong, healthy, masculine reactions, but now, alone, a feeling of impotence steals upon me from all sides. It's not easy for a dog to free himself from dependency on his master. All the lapdog's pent-up emotional life is tied to his mistress with innumerable threads of strict training and loving remembrance. It's different with him, the husband: *his* memory transforms recollections into experience, logical patterns he can analyze and judge, while colors and emotional contents can be turned on and off according to his own convenience. But my memory-pictures, the dog's chaotic longings, pop up with no guidance from the will and attack me—without a plan or inner coherence and before I can defend myself—with sounds and smells stupefying by their excessive sensory vividness, engulfing in their depth and sharpness, unbearably beautiful in their wistful emotionalism. Faced with these pictures, I'm powerless.

Several half-hours pass. I give up. I'm lying prone on the sofa, with my muzzle on my forepaws and my eyes fixed on the door. Waiting. Waiting as only a dog can wait. The wait torments my whole body, wrenches my chest, gnaws my bowels. Now and then a hopeless sigh forces its way across my lips. I think vaguely I haven't yet eaten today— a dog doesn't have the sense to help himself to food. It occurs to me I should try to eat something. On the way to the kitchen I pass the mirror, where I catch a depressing glimpse of the dog in all his abjectness. His hair unwashed and repulsive, falling in long waves on both sides of a face that seems unnaturally long and narrow, like the face of an Irish setter, with a pointed, drooping nose, untrimmed reddish beard, and melancholy, bloodshot cocker spaniel eyes. A stooped neck, bent back and slinking gait. The bones sticking out everywhere on the lean body. Tail squeezed between the hind legs. I'm on the point of letting out a howl of pain and discouragement as I stand there looking at what's left of myself. *Her* work of destruction. I know I ought to feel anger and insult, be filled with thoughts of revenge, as *he* is. But all I manage to recall of our meeting is a couple of remarks, the sound of his ironic, confident voice: ". . . *If,* that is, she does come home . . ."

If she comes home!

If she has run away again, as she did from him, what will I do then? What if she doesn't come!

What if she doesn't come!

15 Saturday. Where did Saturday go?

I wake up late in the morning, frozen stiff on the sofa and sore from dozing on my stomach.

The first thing that occurs to me is that she hasn't come home. I haven't heard her all night—after my metamorphosis to dog became an ineluctable fact I've awakened at the slightest sound. It will soon be eleven o'clock. She's been with him the whole night. She's still with him! She hasn't even bothered to call and say she's been held up, that she was detained last night and unable to come home. She doesn't even take the trouble to find a tolerably plausible excuse for her absence, something that stands to reason, that at least *could* be true, a gift of mercy to a worn-out dog who thirsts for a little consolation, for a little encouragement to enable him to face still another day of waiting and longing . . .

Longing? Well, not anymore. Slowly and painfully, I realize there's nothing to long for anymore. The only prospect I have is the confirmation of my worst anticipations, something I've been aware of from the beginning but that my dog's brain has managed to distort and repress as long as possible: that she'll move in with Tarzan and leave me here alone. What I've feared most of all, like death itself, is now a fact!

A dog's sluggish brain needs many repetitions; a dog's hope can withstand many disappointments, and his body needs many kicks before the signal sticks, before the meaning becomes clear, before the dog's trust—his stupid optimism without a sense of perspective, his sentimental gamble on anybody who shows a little tolerance and concern for him—is undermined. But no evasion is possible anymore. Now even a dog's slow understanding must realize the facts. Now all you can look forward to is to see her scurrying around the apartment collecting her things, hear a brief good-bye, perhaps feel an absent-minded, friendly pat before the door slams.

And all the same I wait, groaning on the sofa, whimpering with pricked-up ears by the living-room window, by the door to the entry, endlessly whining from one room to another. For the worst of all is to lose her this way, without even a word, without a name, an address, without a place where my fantasy can place her when it wants to torment itself with thinking about her. Worst of all is this *nothingness* I'm now experiencing. Even *he* received a telephone call, a letter or two . . . Anyway, I didn't know she'd written him while we were living together. Perhaps there are many things I don't know about her when all's said and done?

Every single thought I have on this slushy-wet, oppressively gray Saturday in November pushes me deeper into loneliness and despair. I want to get out, away from these depressing rooms, but I have nowhere to go. A dog has only his home; he's dependent on his territory, on a center. He can roam for a while, but he must always know he has a home to return to and a master there to receive him. Quite simply, I don't dare go out. I know that out there I'll meet my wretchedness face to face without even the false memories and broken hopes of known surroundings to protect me from it. Out there I don't even have the last visit to look forward to. Out there, alone, I would cease to be.

I try to think of yesterday, of her husband's visit, try in vain to recall the strange, elated mood I suddenly found myself in with him, at the thought of sharing the same fate as this strong, self-assured competent man. Should I give him a call now? He asked me to contact him—in case she should come back, that is, to agree on a time when he could come here and meet her. It will look pretty ridiculous, won't it, to call him just to say she's *not* come back? Of course it will look ridiculous— *plus* it will give him a pretext to show his hindsight: What did I tell you?

You can't at all be sure that slut will ever be back! Words that keep thundering incessantly in my inner ear. Words that drive me out of my mind with fear.

Nevertheless, I am dialing his business number. A strange voice answers—sorry, but the boss isn't there today, he doesn't usually come in on Saturdays.

Sure, that makes sense. On Saturdays he has to take care of his daughter, his female acquaintances, or both. The voice suggests I try reaching him at home, and I mumble thanks but feel my courage sink: to interrupt him in a tête-à-tête or in the midst of his paternal duties with my disturbed, whining worries, with problems he has already foreseen, a sorrow that he himself has been through, gotten over, and now considers a trifle—no, I'm not up to that.

All that's left is to wait. Waiting. A dog's wretched waiting alone in a closed room, where the stuffy air increasingly betrays the fact that the only occupant is a dog who's been locked up too long. A dog's ever hopeful waiting. For the dog's soul is incomplete, it exists only in concert with his dominant half; and therefore he can't really understand that the impossible separation must soon come to pass. Therefore, faithfully, hopefully, he waits for annihilation itself.

In my dream she whispered: "It's so good with you. You make me feel free, I'm not afraid of you at all. Not of anything about you! I'm so active sexually with you because you allow me to be!"

In my fragrant dog's dream, glowing with colors, she slipped down from our bench in the Palace Park and crept in between the bushes, where she simply squatted and peed in the grass. Birds and squirrels in the trees all around! People strolling along the paths, ecstatic with summer! Long beams of golden light streaming through to her, the sun hanging low above Uranienborg! And my smiling face as she came crawling out again, drying her fingers on some leaves: my human face, not a single canine feature yet!

When I woke up, worn out after another hysterical night of waking, waiting and dozing, painful spells of troubled, anxious slumber, she was standing beside the sofa, not quite near enough for me to touch her leg or knee or hip by stretching out my hand, and watching me with a look of strained friendliness, saying: "I've just come to pick up my things. You go on sleeping—you seem to need it. You look too awful for words . . ."

So it was happening now, at this very moment, in this untidy room where we'd spent so many lazy Sunday mornings intertwined on the sofa. The words were spoken. The nightmare became reality: You go on sleeping . . .

She's already in the cubbyhole, gets out the suitcase, a carton, a few shopping bags. Then into the bedroom, the cabinet doors thrown wide open, drawers pulled out. Into the bathroom, rapid, firm steps across the floor. The kitchen full of things we've bought together (the joys of the table were always a prelude to the pleasures of the bed)—would she really take it all? Could she claim it was hers? But what good would it be to me when she was gone? Quickly out of the kitchen and into the entry. A couple of hurried words to the old dog on the sofa en route: "I'm only taking what I can carry, the rest will have to wait till we pick it up."

We.

Four or five garments off the hangers, her shoes collected, two trips, boots, extra gloves, crocheted caps and scarves. Something forgotten in the bathroom. The whole thing happens so incredibly fast, the dog can barely keep up: half a year's cohabitation is wound up as if it were simply a matter of going on a fall holiday or tidying up before the big cleaning, effectively, impatiently. The dog's slow understanding cannot quite grasp the full scope of what's happening. In reality, he's still soothed by her presence, by the fact that she's come back, even if she did come like this, just as he feared. In some obscure spot, of course, the sluggish dog's consciousness *knows* what this trotting around the apartment really means, but he still finds it comforting to see her, to observe the known movements as she bends to put something in the suitcase or a box, and her impatience, which makes her clumsy and causes her to explode in oaths of irritation, oaths that aren't oaths in her mouth, not to the dog. The dog is glad and relieved by the mere fact that she isn't changed beyond recognition or hasn't had any serious mishap, that she's here with him again and gets so close every now and then as she passes back and forth that he could touch her if he wanted to. For the dog the *apparent* is always the decisive thing. Although his intuition perceives conflicts and can sense a breakdown with unassailable precision, a dog's actions can never be directed by anything but the present;

his famous "fidelity" is in reality sluggish apprehension, deficient intelligence and imagination, and, above all, lack of courage to intervene in events that concern his own existence, to intuit consequences and take appropriate measures.

There he sits, his body full of torment and his breast full of sorrow, following his mistress with trusting eyes while she packs. And he understands with increasing despair as he sits there what's about to happen (what he has *known* all along!), but it doesn't even occur to him to make a final attempt at discussing the problem with her, getting her to see his point of view, appealing to her loyalty or sense of responsibility, trying to change her mind about moving out, perhaps proposing that they look for another solution together, even if only a temporary one, a last resort for saving their relationship. No, such things don't occur to a dog. Instead he sits there stooped, with drooping ears and his eyes on the verge of tears, speculating in dull, melancholy panic how he can manage to prolong the farewell, delay the moment—the unthinkable, irretrievable moment when the door will slam behind her and he'll be left here, in this apartment, utterly alone to die . . .

So it's only when he realizes she'll be through packing in a matter of minutes and she's bustling about on her last rounds, only when the dog's slowness at last takes him from motionless despair to naked deadly fear, that he finally manages to give out a sound, react sufficiently to catch her fluttering attention—not in order to argue or make a plea, but to postpone the worst, the unthinkable, for another few brief moments, get her to sit down beside him a minute here on the sofa, so he can cuddle up and let her feel how his dog's heart beats for her in spite of everything, put his face close to hers so she can see the sparkle of dog-like devotion in the depth of those brown eyes, place a paw on her thigh, heavy and imploring, so she can remember how his skinny dog's body has become expert at humoring her slightest hint and satisfying her tiniest wish . . . This is how the dog exploits, helplessly and with no perspective, her last bit of friendliness, of tact, her feeling that she can't simply go, calling a brief good-bye from the doorway—perhaps she thinks she owes an old dog *something* after all, for the sake of the good old days, a thank-you for a good partnership. So she pats his back a little, scratches him behind the ears, lets him put his muzzle up to her face and lick her, wetly and humbly—the old doggie deserves that much. After all, the breakup is imminent, and when the hour of parting arrives the many pleasant moments come back so much more clearly . . . And a dog knows how to exploit the slightest hesitation of his mistress, her smallest compliance, with his fawning humility and hunger for love. Long training as a lapdog has made him adept at searching out his mistress's soft, sentimental points; the long humiliating period as self-demeaning asshound has made him into an expert at awakening her dormant sensuality and luring her to indulge in the claustrophobic rituals of dogmaster intercourse.

"My sweet . . . My sweet . . . ," she whispers during my panting attentions. "What do you imagine you can do with me . . . ? Stop it, Payk!"

But a dog can distinguish between a plea and an order. My dog sorrow has brought out feelings in her that have been hidden: "We were happy together, weren't we, Payk? For a while anyway . . . ?" And she cries with me over the fact that everything must finally come to an end, and between her sobs and my devoted-dog caresses she sputters: "But damn it, don't ask me again how I'd like it. Do you hear?!"

"Oh God, what's this!"

Blood on the sofa cover, blood on our clothes: she's gotten her period while we were making love. She buries her face deep in my hide, groaning: "Oh! And I knew I might get it any moment. I should've been careful!"

She who would always shock me with her frankness about such physical intimacies: "Look at the mess I've made on you!"

But a dog isn't upset by a little blood, sniffs the air absentmindedly, and looks away as if to hide his tactful interest. Dogs are pedantically interested in everything that people turn away from. They like to inhale the odors of excrement and vomit, as if they sought a confirmation of their degrading position in the very repulsiveness that in people's eyes surrounds the bodily functions. It's as if his loving tolerance of the wet spots on the sofa could bring the dog closer to his mistress.

I soothe her: I can remove the spots. It's nothing to make a fuss about. But she's suddenly inconsolable, everything becomes so enormously complicated for her; it's late already, she really shouldn't have lingered here, she should have been with him, she'd promised . . . What was the matter with her? What was the matter with us both? And now,

now she has messed herself up—and me . . . She who should have been on her way a long time ago, on her way to *him,* her new man!

I wag my tail and cheer her up as best I can, but she's turned her attention inward to her physical functions, the anticlimax after the pleasure of being with her lapdog. Her weakness now appears sinful and perverse, a betrayal of her single-mindedness, her ability to govern her life, which is the quality in herself she values the most, a betrayal of the new relationship she stakes so much on. And now the pale drops of blood seem like the deluge itself.

She's gotten up and stands beside me, naked from her sweater down, motionless, awkward and unattractive for one doubtful, indecisive moment: "I must get washed—can I use your towel? Mine is packed, I think . . ."

I wag yes. I enjoy seeing her exactly like that, humiliated, exposed, abandoned to the dog's friendliness and help: I'd gladly lick the blood that trickles in a rust-colored drop down her white thigh, to underline my devotion, my tolerance, my feeling of being at one with her right now, especially in view of the embarrassing, shameful situation.

She seems to grasp my communication and stands so close for still another moment that I could stretch out my hand and touch her, her legs, her narrow square hips, her hand that she presses between her soft thighs in order to stop the flood—a moment when the tensions ease off and she mumbles, while bending her head and studying her body intensely:

"What a muddle, Payk. Me with you here today, in the middle of the morning, when I was supposed to be moving. And then this mess! Damn it . . . That's woman in a nutshell: a mess and a muddle! Look here . . ." She slowly extends her hand, fingers stained with brown blood, toward me: "Isn't that true—that's women for you, nothing but a mess and a muddle?" She smiles and shakes her head, while a tear trickles down her cheek and another drop of rust-colored blood traces a streak on her winter-pale skin: "But I'll show you I'm serious. Just wait!"

16 He comes fairly late Monday evening, rings the bell, and knocks hard and violently when I don't open fast enough. His face is pale, his eyes blue, his jaw clenched. His fists open and close. His thighs swell. His voice has none of the jovial, friendly character by which the dog was so charmed the first time they met:

"Is she here?"

When I don't open the door quickly enough, he pushes forward and enters, filling the hallway: "Have you seen her? Has she been here?"

In whimpers and little barks I try to explain that she was here on Sunday to pick up her things and say good-bye, then left, presumably to go to *him*. But I don't know where he lives, not even who he is, have only heard the ridiculous pet name she uses for him. She says he's working at a publisher's . . .

"Damn little help, I'd say!"

We're standing in the living room, he in his street clothes. I don't dare ask him to slip them off and sit down. He seems volatile, almost insane—a dog must learn to read a person's state of mind, predict the actions it may touch off, and choose his distance accordingly. He puts his hand over his eyes and rubs them as if he had stared long and intensely at something hard to bring into focus:

"She's taken the child, you see. Little Eli. I've called the school. I've talked to her girl friends, who tell me a woman picked her up after school today. It must've been her. What the hell does she plan to do now? For all I know she may be far away . . ."

"But the police . . . ," I remark, needing to say something. It's disconcerting but not really surprising that she's carried off her daughter. The few times she was willing to talk about her she was always full of self-reproaches ("I who left her in the lurch with that man . . ."). What shocks me is that she has now evidently staked *everything* on her relationship with that charlatan, Bel Ami, to the point of losing her head and kidnaping her daughter.

"The police!" The man snorts, still in his down jacket, a sporty, well-fitting affair with red, white, and blue patches for trimmings. "I won't mix up the police in this until I have to!" He rams his clenched fist into the open palm of his other hand with a smack that makes the worried dog jump back several steps. "I want to straighten this out myself. If only I had her here . . ."

"She's probably with *him* . . . ," I think out loud.

"Bravo, I'd certainly not have thought of that without your help!"

His voice lashes the dog, making him squirm. At this moment he'd prefer to withdraw, hide, and have him—the intruder—go away, leaving the poor dog alone with his afflictions. Yet, the commanding, almost brutal element in the man's manner seems to have a hypnotizing effect on the dog. Against his will he feels an awakening urge to please, be obedient, to sit up and play along with the expectations directed at him:

"But the restaurant . . . Bel Ami . . . Perhaps they know something there . . . ?" Eager barks and tail-wagging. He can hardly keep from placing his paw on the man's knee, the dog's perpetual plea for recognition and praise: "She's not working tonight, but . . ."

The man's accumulated energy explodes into activity at the telephone; I'm afraid he'll tear the phone book apart simply to demonstrate his muscular prowess to me. He dials the number, curses feverishly when he gets a busy signal. Circles the floor gritting his teeth: "If only she hasn't run away from her job as well. She was here and packed her suitcase, you say? Did she take everything?"

I explain that there is a carton in the cubbyhole, which she said they'd pick up later.

"Well, I'll be damned, but it doesn't have to mean very much. She can still take it into her head to skip out, regardless. She won't be able to cross the border, though, not having a passport, and if she's gotten a passport she still can't take the girl with her. To hell with the crazy woman!"

He tries to get in touch with the restaurant for the third time. She hasn't given notice, nor has she given any new address. They expect her for the early shift tomorrow morning.

"Fine, then we'll catch her there. In case she isn't too scared to turn up. She can't possibly *know* I won't tip off the cops—though she knows perfectly well what I think about those boys. You see, I was almost caught for drunk driving once. Luckily for me, one of the men at inspection recognized me from the time I'd been an active athlete, so he steered me through. Can't say I've been very fond of them since that episode . . . No, she'll probably count on my not getting the cops involved. She'll turn up all right. After all, she hasn't the faintest idea I'm on her trail—you didn't tell her I'd been here, did you?"

"Bow-wow, bow-wow-wow!" (No, are you out of your mind . . . !)

And so the mood turns, imperceptibly at first, then more and more noticeably. The man's dangerous, panic-stricken aggression gives way to the hunter's confident swagger at the thought of the game he'll kill tomorrow. And the hunter's zeal, his controlled hatred, his ritualized urge to kill, rubs off on the dog, who so easily makes his master's motives his own, which he must do if he's to become an able and useful hunting dog. And, for his part, the hunter is careful to include the dog in his plans for the hunt, to work up his temper and promise him his share of the quarry:

"It came sooner than expected, didn't it? Her skipping out, I mean, simply packing and leaving. Is that the way to treat a decent person? No, that woman ought to get a smack once and for all, don't you agree? I mean, just look at the way she treated me and the child first, and now you. There's no rhyme or reason in it. But revenge is sweet, my boy. We can't just sit there and let women walk all over us, can we?"

And thus the hours pass in the cozy campfire light from the fireplace, with camp-fire talk and coarse stories. With his dog the hunter can let himself go, forget his inhibitions, brag and tell tall stories about other hunting expeditions and other game, about conquests of women and feats of sport—simple, banal ideas, ravings and dreams . . . The mutually respectful relationship between a hunter and his dog demands an admixture of vulgarity and vanity. Everything outside their circle of light, whether people or things, is sacrificed to their camaraderie this night before the hunt, the night before the quarry will be slain and the hunter's mastery, his indisputable dominion, confirmed. And the dog lies at his feet with pointed ears and moist muzzle, listening to the hunter's made-up stories and letting himself be lured into the slow, stealthy intoxication of the blood a good hound should be filled with the night before the hunt.

A quick cup of coffee before daybreak. Dawn comes late in November, it's past eight; both hunter and dog quake and shiver after the night by the fire—the sticks of wood in the fireplace burned down early. In the gray morning light you feel the cold in the walls, the draft from the windows. But that's the way it ought to be on a hunting expedition.

Hunter and dog have little to say to each other at this moment, just before they break up. The strategy has been agreed upon and the procedure established according to a pattern handed down from times immemorial: the dog leads the hunter to the game and waits while the hunter kills his prey. When the time comes he, too, receives his share, his reward. The division of labor is the most logical and reasonable. The final triumph belongs to both.

The restaurant opens at eleven. She comes to work at ten. At nine o'clock the gray November day breaks outside the window, and it's time to make the last preparations, dress, get ready (hunter fashion, we've eaten half-dressed and unwashed). The last few minutes' nervous hesitation. The last lukewarm drop of coffee—the rest is emptied into the dirty sink. Breaking camp. The kitchen's hutlike atmosphere suddenly becomes unbearably claustrophobic for both hunter and dog, whose bodies begin to feel restless, impatient to get out and start the hunt. The excitement is discharged in exaggerated physical reactions— the chair overturns when the hunter gets up from the table, the coffee cup bangs against the counter. Street clothes are put on with a sullen air and a show of muscular force. The door slams behind us. We both raise our faces toward the drift of raw November wind rushing down from Grefsen Hill; the cold air stimulates the skin and awakens senses dulled indoors. Hunter and dog breathe deeply and stretch their legs to get rid of morning stiffness: they're on their way.

They have plenty of time. A hunt must be well planned, with an ample time frame. A hunt will never be successful if hunter and dog are in too great a hurry. They must get to their post, evaluate all the details of the terrain, choose the best spot—a hiding place where one has a full view without being seen, the place where the quarry will be forced to break cover, step unsuspectingly into open terrain, leave its flank uncovered and walk into the trap . . . Even the rail song of the No. 11 trolley is like the murmur of deep forests to the ears of hunter and dog, like the wailing of tall spruces during an autumn storm as the quarry fearfully takes cover in the underbrush.

From the entranceway we have the street in full view, both up and down. I don't know where he lives and from what direction she can be expected to come, but my dog's instinct tells me she'll be coming from Majorstua. Valkyriegaten has been like a fixed axis in their movements every time I've spied on them. It's five of, we've been at our post ten minutes, and we both sense the instinctual restlessness that tells the hunter and his dog the quarry is approaching.

I catch sight of her first—I know her colors, clothes, and gait better than he does and can easily tell her apart from the other people on the sidewalk, hurrying from one store to another in the morning shopping rush. The moment I see her I feel my body turn rigid, and when I try to say something my words disappear in a low growl far down my throat and become a wordless communication from dog to hunter, who realizes that I see her, peers out himself, catches sight of her a moment later, breathes heavily and curses in an undertone: "I'll be damned, she's got the girl with her!"

I too have seen that she's with a little girl, a schoolbag on her back. They walk in the direction of the restaurant, a good half-block away. No problem for hunter or dog: let them go in, let the hunter steal after them, and then . . . But the dog notices that the hunter is agitated, and that's a bad sign—a good hunter must never lose control the moment he catches sight of the game. He must not, as my companion is doing now, get the woodland tremors, start breathing heavily and stamp his legs; if he doesn't control himself he'll betray us and frighten the prey!

We're standing in the entranceway across from the restaurant. They're approaching on the opposite sidewalk. There are so many pedestrians, and we're standing in such a deep shadow, that her chances of seeing us are small, if only he doesn't do anything stupid. They have sixty feet left. Behind me I can hear the hunter mutter softly to himself, an exorcism under his heavy breath sounding like: "Hands off the child, you slut! Damn it, won't you leave the child alone!" But my attention is glued to her now, to her and her daughter. They've paused for a moment—she must help the girl with something, a shoelace: mother and daughter bent over a shoelace on the sidewalk in the morning bustle. The sight moves me with a strange power, even though I don't know her in her maternal role and feel miles away from her right now. But though I look at them like two strangers, the way a dog looks at the quarry he knows so well but still must keep his distance from, it moves me to see them like that—the little girl with her hand on her mother's shoulder, the mother tense, with some loose wisps of hair straggling from under the edge of her scarf as she bends uncomfortably to tie the rebellious shoelace. Suddenly I hope, quite illogically, in defiance of my hunting-dog instinct, that they may be spared, that the hunter will make a mistake and miss, that they will escape and go on living together, living and running around as they wish in the wide forest!

But then the hunter rushes out. He too has been moved by seeing them, but differently than the dog, being frantic with rage, with self-righteous agitation: he dashes out recklessly, wants to kill his prey on the open sidewalk! In the middle of the street he must wait to let a car pass. She's tied the shoelace and straightened up, but they haven't noticed him yet. He stands in the middle of the street, a knotted bundle of muscles: I can see the nape of his neck swell above the collar of his hunting jacket with its red, white and blue stripes, I can see his jaws work, I understand that he's insane with murderous lust—what was supposed to be a clean, wholesome hunt, a controlled sports contest of man and dog, is about to turn into a disaster. And nobody perceives disaster the moment before it occurs as keenly as a dog!

Three cars pass and his path is clear. I can't control it, can't hinder it, must simply follow my dog's instinct, lift my muzzle and howl, a drawn-out wail of disappointment, remorse, and fear: this is partly my work, I'm taking part in the hunt, I've led him to the quarry, I can't pull out now! I've sworn fidelity and partnership to the hunter, I've realized that my own interests coincide with his: she has treated us both badly, I want revenge and reparation for myself, as he does for himself. I want to punish her for leaving me in a fix I don't think I've deserved. He has a direct breach of the law to avenge. He's a man, I'm a dog. Men and dogs have lived in a mutual relationship of fidelity since time immemorial; men have exploited the dog's stupid unselfishness in order to exercise and consolidate their power and have in return given their canine servants a few morsels from their spoils. I have realized that I'm tied to the hunter by a common fate, stronger than what I thought tied me to her. He and I are two sides of the same purpose, of the same motivation, men and dogs are made to hunt together—and still, still I let out a loud howl to warn her and prevent disaster!

He has crossed the street in three long bounds. Looking up and seeing him, she grasps the situation, seizes the girl's arm and runs toward the door of the restaurant. He rushes after. It turns into a race that nobody can win. She manages to grab the doorknob with one hand, pulls open the door and pushes her daughter inside—then the hunter is upon her, grabbing her from behind by the hair with one hand while the other jerks the door free of her convulsive grip on the handle, flings it wide open so that its return movement with cruel precision must hit her in the head, which he holds as in a vise as the heavy edge of the door does the job of twenty fists in her face. One-two-three times he flings the entrance door in her face, smashes her screams of terror to a helpless gurgling, and in the end keeps her limp body upright by holding her under one arm, the way you hold a rebellious child, while he uses his right hand to make the door continue its work of destruction, implacably and effectively. Our clean, sportsmanlike hunt has been transformed into a blood bath.

When he finally lets her go and straightens up, without taking notice of the many people who've stopped on the sidewalk, flocking together in gaping passivity, there's blood on his red, white, and blue sports jacket, blood on his dark-blue cord trousers, blood on his red, white and blue striped jogging shoes, streaks of blood on the shiny brass kickplate on the entrance door to the restaurant Bel Ami.

The dog writhes in spasms of agitation, fear, and horror. Whimpering and shifting from one foot to the other, he scents the smell of blood and feels how warmly and intoxicatingly the spicy odor stimulates his animal instincts, while he feels sick to his stomach at the sight of this brutal incident and paralyzed by fear at the thought of what state she's in, whether she'll come through, suffer permanent injuries . . . At the same time the sight of the Man fighting animates him in a consuming, uncontrollable way! His display of energy during the brief fight, his calm physical control in the very midst of his atrocities, the self-evident authority of his rage, his brutal explosion, so commanding, so obvious that it doesn't occur to a single bystander to do something to stop him, even though a fellow human being is destroyed. For a dog, power and dominance are the only things; an incident like this *must* appeal to the self-tormenting, cowardly element of a dog's psychology.

But when a car drives up to the sidewalk and stops, and a couple of men jump out, make their way brusquely through the flock of spectators, pounce on the man, grab him by one shoulder each and in an instant hustle him between them, his arms pinioned behind his back, as they give brief instructions to the spectators, the dog finds it almost unbearable. With his dog's brain he understands it must be the police— but why did they turn up? Who has summoned them? The incident at the door to the restaurant lasted only two or three minutes; if someone inside gave the alarm it would still take time before anyone could get here from the nearest police station. This mystery utterly baffles the dog's dim power of comprehension. This, and the metamorphosis he is witnessing, the Man's disintegration: docile, sniffling like an unresisting graybeard, he lets the men convey him into the waiting vehicle.

Gone is his strength, gone his authority and temper, that dangerous tension beneath the violent disposition whose ticking was barely audible, like the delayed action of an explosive. The hunter, full of self-confidence and belief in his right to kill his prey, is obliterated.

156   This is such a shock to the lonely, terror-stricken dog that he loses the power to control both himself and the reactions that have so carefully been ingrained in him: he whines and whimpers, agitated to the point of frenzy as he circles around with tripping steps, then can't contain himself anymore and empties his bladder in the open street right in front of everybody. In front of everybody?—well, who takes notice of a wretched old dog whining in an entranceway and piddling in his pants as he watches a police car turn into the traffic and slowly disappear down Valkyriegaten with the Man, his lord and master?

THE PRISONER

1 The crack-up usually comes on the fourth day. This is true at least for those who're locked up when drunk. The fourth day the roof comes tumbling down on their heads and snakes crawl out of the cracks in the wall. You soon get used to the screams and moans, the chorus of laments, tears, and prayers that is the constant background noise inside the walls of this collection site for the dangerous, callous, most hardened members of society.

In my case the crack-up is a slow process, no drama with screams and fear or sudden claustrophobia. It comes with my gradual adjustment, the acceptance of my situation as a detainee, the slow loss of perspective on my existence, fading recollections from my life outside that grow increasingly meaningless. I feel my hatred of those who've locked me up slowly wearing off, together with my superior attitude toward them; I can chat with the guards, I've begun to cooperate with the psychiatrist who'll be observing me. I've stopped insisting on my privileges as a prisoner awaiting trial. I don't use much money to get supplies from the outside anymore, a bit of luxury, tobacco pipes, magazines, expensive cigarettes, advantages that the other inmates can't afford on their fifteen kroner per day. I've begun to eat the food here with a hearty appetite.

For me the crack-up means the slow disintegration of my personality, my attitudes, my sense of what's right and wrong, in short, what the psychiatrist calls my "identity."

I said that this destruction occurs slowly, but in reality it happens very rapidly. In two short weeks I've changed so much that I can't recognize myself. Well, of course I can; it's just that prison causes traits you thought you had to crumble and disappear, to be replaced by others you didn't previously know you had, or don't care to know about.

Take the guards, for example. Prison guards, in my opinion, must of necessity belong to the scum of the earth; I've always held this opinion and still do. For someone to enter, without compulsion, a profession as watchmen over people society has deprived of freedom can only mean, as I see it, that he is a sadist and feels a morbid need for authority. The day I came, when I was searched, undressed, and washed by two guards while the policeman who'd brought me to the prison sat watching indifferently, I could barely control myself when attacked by their quick, brutal, intolerably offensive itchy fingers. For a while I was afraid one of them would stick a long finger up my rectum to see if I'd hidden something there, and with tears rolling down my face I swore I'd never speak a word to anyone who treated me like that, looking at me like something that smelled bad as I stood undressed waiting for my prison uniform. Detainees are entitled to wear their own clothes, but the clothes I had on were covered with blood and had to be dry-cleaned. Not that I'm particularly embarrassed in the presence of men, by no means! And I'm proud of my body. In my days as an active athlete I spent more time with naked men than with naked women, but out there in the "Reception," as the inmates call it, with a bench, a table and a chair where the grain shows through the worn coat of paint, with yellowish gray walls full of streaks and stains and high uncurtained windows with frosted glass—as I stood naked in there with two guards and a policeman in uniform, I felt my skin break out in goose pimples, and I wanted to clench my asshole and howl with shame and ignominy. And I swore never, never to utter a word to the two gorillas who took turns sticking their heads into the shower to see if I was washing myself properly, not to look in their direction even. And if I met them in civvies when someday I got out of here, then . . . ! It would be my revenge on them personally and on the whole system.

A bit later I found that their names were Bassen and Ludo. Bassen, 161 the older, is actually named Benjamin Lassen and Ludo's name is Ludvig; he's gotten his name from the game he wastes his free time on (and a good portion of his working time as well). I've discovered that Bassen is really a pleasant and jovial character, helpful and kind, fond of his family and his bit of a garden, where he grows vegetables for the winter with diligence and care. And Ludo, a fellow in his thirties, unmarried and helpless, gladly gives you an extra quarter of an hour in the prison yard for a pack of cigarettes. "Special service for deluxe inmates," as he calls it. From sentenced prisoners, who only have their fifteen kroner a day to spend, he obviously can't demand such rates for his services.

It was only a matter of days before all my indignation and hatred of these fellows seemed to have been swept away, and I chatted cheerfully with Bassen and looked forward to my turn in the prison yard with Ludo. My dislike of them had vanished without a trace, though I felt ashamed of this weakness when alone in my cell, collecting myself and trying to review all the disgrace and indignities I'd experienced in the prison the first couple of weeks. To keep my hatred warm. To hold on to the last remnants of myself, the person I knew.

2 I'd really expected it to be worse. For everybody "outside," after all, prison is the very symbol of how badly things may turn out, both in a social sense—what with the humiliation, the shame, the ruined trust and reputation—and in concrete terms, as punishment: to be deprived of *liberty*. Can anything worse be imagined?

No wonder claustrophobia is one of the most common afflictions among first-time inmates: suddenly the cell walls close in on the prisoner, the ceiling drops, the bunk bed rolls like a barge in rough weather. Nothing of the sort happened to me. After the drama that Monday morning, the arrest, the commotion at the police station, preliminary interrogations, the first nights in the cell at 19 Møllergata wall to wall with bawling drunks—before being remanded in custody and transferred to a "peaceful small institution in a neighboring town" as my attorney so daintily put it—it was almost a relief to come out here. Naturally I cried a bit when I was left alone, and my anger and sense of insult at the fact that these inhuman louts—who treated me like an animal—should have managed to break down my resistance in only half an hour's time, made my crying even more violent. But after a brief visit from the doctor and a tranquilizer tablet, I could sleep, and I slept with only brief interruptions the entire first twenty-four hours of my stay here in the "Manor," as the inmates call the institution. It has gotten this name because it stands near the edge of town, on a property that once belonged to a landed estate. From a row of windows on the third floor of the North Wing you can see, behind the tall prison-yard fence, the now tumbledown, abandoned farmhouses and the barn, whose wide roof may cave in any moment. Farther back, where rich fields once opened out, now stands the newest housing development in town, with row houses and single-family houses in tightly packed, uneven symmetry within the framework of the drawn-up street system. At first glance it gives an impression of being equally confined and claustrophobic out there as here. But the "repeaters" in this institution, habitual criminals who can take only three to four months of liberty at a time before they let themselves be nabbed for pilfering or disorderly conduct, who've walked in and out of this prison for a number of years, can tell you about the days when the view from the North Wing was a real panorama, with fields, meadows, and woodlots in light and dark patterns against the distant line of hills to the north and east, a sight so beautiful as to make the wretched inmates wish they were dead, especially when spring came around.

It's surprising how little time it actually takes to adjust to prison life. Once you've been through the purely transitional phenomena, your unfamiliarity with the dismal cell and the furniture there, your insomnia on the hard mattress with the strange bedclothes, the jungle sounds, the animal smells, you easily fall in with the institutional routine: up at seven, half an hour for coffee and breakfast and tidying up the cell, after which the convicts go to the shop, where they begin work at eight. Those awaiting trial don't have work duty. Instead, we're taken one by one to the prison yard on the north side. Then dinner from twelve to one and an hour's group exercise in the yard for the sentenced prisoners, who go back to work again at three-thirty. At five back to the cell for the evening meal, coffee, bread and butter, and milk. The choice of activities in the evening is, of course, limited. Card games are popular, but it's the guards who decide who will play with whom and for how long. An old TV in a naked room with two or three rows of steel-tube chairs provides the opportunity of watching the news and the enter- tainment programs the majority want, but they must be over by nine-thirty, when all prisoners are locked in their cells again. Before, the lights went out at ten o'clock sharp, but now the prisoners turn out the light when they want. There's also a small workout room, with two or three pieces of apparatus and some weights, ironically called "The Gymnasium." It's extremely popular and must be used by turns, be-cause no more than two are allowed to exercise at the same time for "security reasons." Detainees must apply for special permission to use the "Gymnasium," but for me there was no problem since I could refer to my period as an active athlete. The head guard even remembered the Nordic championship where I won a silver medal.

To keep the body in good shape is a popular activity in the prison, just as the TV sports programs are the prisoners' favorite entertain-ment. It was exhilarating to discover this, as if it presented me with the possibility of overcoming my isolation from my coprisoners in the long run. For as a violent criminal I'm not exactly one of the most popular card partners on my row. I understand now that this is something I ought to have been prepared for. The pecking order among prisoners in institutions is universally established. At the top of the ladder are the thieves, those who commit crimes for gain—gangsters, smugglers, grand larcenists, with the corps of experts, the safecrackers, as an unassailable elite at the summit. Traffic offenders, tax dodgers, and embezzlers hardly count as prisoners; they're simply fools who've had a bit of bad luck. They also usually take their stay in prison lightly, read and write, take courses, and prepare for their comeback. At the bottom are the violent criminals and the dope addicts, with sex offenders at point zero, an absolute deep-freeze, socially speaking. A sex offender can literally walk around for weeks without a single word being ad-dressed to him.

As a violent criminal I'll therefore have to lead a rather chilly existence, though the threat of a trial in superior court ought to inspire some respect for me. As a detainee my possibilities for normal contact and association with the other inmates are also reduced. I'm told this is done to "protect" the detainees, who according to the law must be regarded as innocent until proven guilty, but in reality such well-meant isolation feels like extra punishment. Even the privileges granted prisoners awaiting trial increase the distance between them and the others, and the little material bonuses you can allow yourself while you are in custody, such as good food bought on the outside, your own clothes, furniture, books, pictures, merely serve to make the true situation even more obvious, the deprivation of liberty even more depressing. These privileges confer a ludicrous touch of caricature both to the stay in prison and to the liberty outside, as if the distance between prisoner and free man weren't so very great, after all. My own things in the cell, an armchair, a reading lamp, dressing gown and slippers, books and magazines can make the evening hours quite homey . . . And the prison routine makes few demands—with its sleepy, wearisome repetitions it isn't unlike the pattern a man must stick with out there, in "life."

If an inmate wants to preserve an idea of something other and better than life in prison, he must give up his privileges. If he doesn't, he'll resign himself.

There are days filled with sense impressions that consciousness is loath to register or interpret.

The first period in prison is an intensive learning process for the inmate. For the first, perhaps the only, time in his adult life he experiences what the expression "a new world" may mean concretely.

The new world of the prison is a world of new smells and sounds, a smell of noise and sweat, of bodies and chlorine, of people who live at too close quarters, of lime and cabbage and toilets. And the prison's buzzing, sighing, moaning, laughing, yelling chorus of distorted human sounds echoes back from the walls like a mutter, trembles in the woodwork, vibrates in the iron bars and reverberates under the tall ceiling with the skylight, which casts its sallow light along the corridor.

It all tells a story about forms of life that the inmate is not acquainted with. About tones of voice that betray states of mind he hasn't even read about. About depravity and squalor, sentimentality and self-hatred, lechery and suffering. And most of all about dire need.

The first few times when a prisoner is led down the corridor by a guard to a meeting, an examination, or a walk in the prison yard, he feels gaped at and attacked by everybody. Later he understands that nobody cares, and learns to appreciate every opportunity for a little change. Even a walk down the straight, narrow twenty-yard corridor is better than the cell's six by twelve feet, with a window high up the wall. Even the rough humor of the guards is preferable to aimlessly jogging around in your own worn-out tracks of thought.

A new and abnormal world, and what's really frightening is that this world has always been only a short distance from the prisoner's own, except that he hasn't wanted to see or hear it. But now he recognizes it, and it's this recognition, rather than the strangeness, that strikes him with an obscure fear, oppresses his heart, and makes him toss in his bunk.

3 The first days the prisoner thinks only of himself. He lies groaning on his bunk with his arms clenched around his body and his knees pulled up to his diaphragm, as though it were up to his physical endurance, his own panic-stricken power of concentration, to hold body and limbs together in one piece. His breathing is heavy, as if the tidal waves of unbelievable upheaval, the brutal and irrevocable change that sweeps over him, literally threatened to drown him. His eyes are fixed in a wide stare upon unknown, inhospitable localities, as if wanting to engrave every single detail for ever and ever. He listens terror-stricken to the song of eternity in the corridors and starts at the slightest sound. He weeps from fear and helplessness, and from the certainty that it's precisely this—his terror, panic, pain, and nothing else—which prevents him from disappearing, disintegrating, vanishing into thin air under the avalanche of metamorphosis that shatters his existence.

His first few days go by like this, until he understands that he's still alive. Life—some sort of life—continues: he opens his eyes every morning one minute before the guard opens the peephole with a clatter and shouts into it. He opens his eyes every morning, and for a lovely fleeting second he has no recollection of where he is. But when the first week is over he knows even in his sleep what his eyes will see, and he shuts his eyelids tight and doesn't open them till after the guard has rattled the peephole and yelled his rough morning greeting and his footsteps are receding down the corridor, at the same moment that the ward-boy's pushcart with breakfast and morning coffee can be heard approaching from the opposite direction.

After the first week the coffee doesn't taste so bitter anymore, and the bread chunks with margarine don't swell up in your mouth. After the first week the prisoner's insecurity and fear shift from his own suffering self to the vacuum he's left behind in the real world. His concern begins to focus on his family, his home and job, the practical consequences of his absence, everything that has to be taken care of, all the things he didn't have time to put in order (naturally!), things he can't bring himself to take hold of now, everything he won't have a chance to straighten out as an inmate. A new inmate can break down in despair at the mere thought of his next-of-kin's safety, their finances, the social situation he's left them in by conducting himself in such a way that he ended up in prison. The prisoner may torture himself with such thoughts for long periods; his self-reproaches can threaten his health, his depression become pathological. But you seldom hear real anger vented in prison.

A prisoner seems incapable of repenting the act that has brought him inside the walls. This is especially true for us violent criminals. The crime of a violent criminal is determined by the situation. If mentally healthy, he never plans his misdeed in detail beforehand. But if he's unlucky, the act of violence occurs just as naturally as setting one foot in front of the other, as inevitably as night follows day, as impossible to stop as a tempest. Being sorry afterwards strikes him as superficial, showing no sense of circumstance or proportion: is the shipwrecked person who clings to a raft *sorry* that the ship sank? No, repentance and a seemly humility are only absurdities in relation to disaster. The tears of self-reproach never concern the act itself but its consequences. Assurances of mending one's ways belong to the courtroom, where a controlled demonstration of self-despising grief is in fact expected from the accused, by the presiding judge, his associates on the bench, and the spectators, as if to fortify them in their belief that the criminal has already seen the light of reason and is now set on the path of virtue. A successful demonstration can actually receive its reward at the setting of the sentence. And if the accused drops a tear at the sight of his next-of-kin or the one he committed the crime against seated on the front bench of the courtroom, it's hardly because he repents or wishes his outrage undone—that would be as useless as to conjure the rain back to the sky—but perhaps because he knows he'll never be able to have his case presented, that no process of examination with question and answer and verbal explanations, no courtroom terminology, no words in any language can explain a catastrophe rationally and thereby throw a bridge across the gulf between his life before it happened and his present existence. If he sheds tears, it is because he hears he's absent at his own trial, and if he sends imploring glances in the direction of family and friends, it's a plea to them to forget him, since he no longer has any contact with their world anyway. The criminal's isolation is due to the incomprehensibility of the crime and only secondarily to its psychological and social consequences. And a crime is most incomprehensible if it is so obvious as to seem natural, a deed anybody could see himself doing, even may have wanted to do, but that only the one unfortunate person actually *does*. Then especially a strong reaction is called for. Then especially the condemnation becomes unrestrained and the psychological shock crippling.

I have plenty of time right now for thinking such thoughts, I who never before felt I had time for, or cared much about, reflecting deeply about my life and what happened to me. Previously, I saw my life as a series of chance occurrences bound together in an unbreakable pattern, and personal initiative and free will, so called, have very little to put up against chance occurrences and fixed patterns. It has always been a hustling to and fro, always expediency before pleasure, always the uncomfortable longing to be *some other place*. I realize now that I've never felt free, not "out there" either. If I ever did, it must have been on some rare afternoons in the boat shortly after a competition, when the pressure of training was less and I made an outing with the single scull for the sheer fun of the thing—blue hours of calm sea and a slight breeze that made the temperature just right and carried smells from the land, increasingly strong as the shadows onshore deepened, while the fjord mirrored the sunny sky and struck sparks in the oarsman's face for a good couple of hours more. When the breeze is nice and the hour gives the light the right slant, the scull seems to glide forward weightlessly and the sea splashing against the hull is echoed in the oarsman's regular breathing, while the body labors and the strength of arms and back feels inexhaustible, as if it could last forever . . .

I think a great deal about little Eli, worry and reproach myself. She lives at my mother's temporarily, until *she* will be well enough to take her in.

When I think about the child—only then—it occurs to me that I've committed a crime, acted rashly, destroyed something. What kind of life will she have after this? What will it mean for a young girl's development that she knows she has a mother who abandoned her and a father who sits in prison for an act of violence? I can't endure the thought that something I did will destroy her chances for happiness. Yet, that's precisely what has happened.

I know I really tried with Eli. I may not have been the most attentive father the first few years, but when *she* disappeared and the responsibility suddenly rested on me, my attitude changed in a way I wouldn't have believed possible. All at once the child became the center of my existence. Something happened to me those first nights when she cried for Mommy and I had to take her into my own bed. I couldn't think of anybody with a better claim to deal with the situation. There was nobody but her and me. Little Eli and I were alone in the world—alone against all. This discovery filled me with a panic-stricken concern for her. It suddenly became all-important that the child shouldn't suffer any privation. I realized how little I knew about children, how little I really knew Eli, her desires and wants. I made mistakes, was insensitive, impatient; I scolded her, we argued, she cried. I was close to tears myself for falling short where it really mattered, because a human being's start in life was at stake. It wasn't easy. It meant a rearrangement of my existence, a total overhauling of what I'd hitherto seen as very essential. Previously a great deal of time and effort had gone into working up the business; I had to strike while the iron was hot, while I still had a name as an active athlete—fortunately, I had sufficient foresight to understand that sports quickly devours its stars. It turned out well, I got publicity, success pursued me from the regatta course into business, a new arena of competition that made equally high demands on a man mentally and physically. *She* never understood that what she called my "activities" had to cost so much time and energy. That is, she did understand—she wasn't stupid—but she didn't accept it. So perhaps she was a little stupid anyway. She often said she felt so alone. But she never felt as lonely as I did those first weeks with little Eli, that I can vouch for!

It's the thought of the child that I find unbearable. At the moment she's safe as far as that goes, installed with my mother, that poor well-

meaning person. But when *she* gets on her feet again, what then . . . ?
Oh Lord! After this I suppose I'll barely receive visitation rights—
when I get out of here someday. If I do get out . . . And everything is
her fault. And mine. We could have continued, Eli and I. We'd found a
kind of solution to the situation. We'd started getting to know each
other. It may sound ridiculous that a father starts getting to know his
daughter only when she's going on ten, but that's the way things are: an
ordinary man trapped in an ordinary trade has very few possibilities for
making really close contact with his children. But most of them never
discover that. I often think of Eli. When I cry, I cry for her future, which
I have destroyed.

4 *Her* I think about very seldom except in connection with the
child. And except when I have to—that is to say, during the visits
of the psychiatrist.

He's appointed by the court to keep me under observation, a bit
younger than I but already balding, of slight build and with a tendency
to develop a potbelly, and he smokes too much. Despite his intelligent
vocabulary and sarcastic humor, he can't disguise how nervous he is.
He looks more like a couple of drug addicts here in the prison than a
specialist in legal psychiatry—he's probably just as nutty as they are,
too, only he's learned to hide it better. His name is Knut Klaumann,
married and divorced, now living with a friend and her two teenage
sons. He sees his own children, a boy and a girl of eight and three, every
other weekend and during the summer vacations. He told me this
during our first talk. A judicial observation takes a long time, and it's
important for the physician to establish a confidential relationship with
the subject under observation, gain his confidence if possible. Much
depends on the outcome of our meetings. Is the indictment to be
"attempted murder" or only "criminal assault"? Will we succeed in
turning the "exceptionally aggravating circumstances" into something
more attenuating? Is it even possible, perhaps, that the accused was
temporarily insane at the moment of the crime?

I handle these expressions with the greatest naturalness, as if they
designated merchandise in a catalog. I'm emotionally incapable of
associating such concepts with *me*. Rationally, yes—I know, after all,
why I'm here. But "attempted murder"? I've come to understand that

legal formulations are very important. After just a few weeks in prison I've become wise to a great many legal gimmicks, picked up from those clever enough to exploit obscure points in the verbal magic of the apparatus of justice. The repeaters know exactly where to draw the line to avoid too severe sentences in case they should get into trouble. A theft must be "simple," never "gross." You can fight with your bare fists but never with weapons. Never resist arrest, never use violence against an official, and if worst comes to worst, drinking can be used to cover up many things . . .

An indictment for attempted murder is serious; to be found guilty can mean three or four years in the lockup. "Exceptionally aggravating circumstances and risk of repetition" can mean an additional year, plus preventive detention. So, much depends on my conversations with psychiatrist Knut Klaumann. All the same, I can't make myself like him. His attempts to inspire confidence are lost on me, I know his type too well: dried-up windbags who've spent a lifetime behind a school desk and then are let loose on those who are the most helpless. Hothouse plants without meat on their bones, with no initiative or talent for anything but talking, talking and writing. In an emergency, with no municipal salary or municipal residence, they couldn't manage a week. But I hide my antipathy. I play the game, of course, have no choice but to cooperate—it's for me everything is at stake, not him. Though I sensed from the very beginning I could never trust such a guy, and when I answer questions I just tell him what I assume he wants to hear, what I think will make a trustworthy impression. Every now and then I go so far in my efforts to please him that I despise myself, seeing this whole degrading game as yet another demonstration of how life in an institution devours what I used to call my "personality." And it will all be to no avail in the end. For how can *he* grasp anything of my situation, he who tells me he's still friends with his divorced wife and, yes, that they even take a quick fuck on the sofa when he drops off the children, "because they like each other well enough, only discovered they couldn't stand living together"?

He tells me such things as if he thought he had to pay me back for the information he wants me to give him. This, of course, means everything having to do with my marriage and with the relationship between me and her, including all the technical details. That doesn't present any particular problems. In bed it was plain sailing. I had the impression we were very compatible sexually, that she too was satisfied, that I didn't have to resort to "violence" in bed at least—on the contrary, the dry spells would sometimes be too long during periods when I had a tough training schedule, as well as later when building the business demanded so much time. But I came back with a vengeance in between and we were doing all right—I've never had any problems with my potency. That, incidentally, is a point good Dr. Klaumann has paid much attention to: impotence. He believes there must be some connection between what he calls a "sexual conflict" and my "irrational conduct" that fateful morning at Majorstua; can I say for sure that fear of impotence isn't lurking somewhere in my subconscious? Isn't there some forgotten episode I'd prefer not to bring back again? Was it perhaps an attack of sexual jealousy that made me lose my head? The situation did, after all, involve a confrontation between me, my wife and her lover . . .

Lord, how little that guy understands! Though I'm willing to strain a point to confirm his theories, I can't bring myself to agree with anything so ridiculous. Our sexual life had long ago settled down to an even matrimonial level, with no great efforts or great dislocations. I assume most married people live like that; their sexual life runs a middle course, neither sensationally good nor especially bad. That a person should feel a need for a little change after a few years in the marital bed should be no cause for surprise, but the majority want to go back once the element of novelty has rubbed off "the great experience." I know it was like that with me, and it wouldn't have surprised me if she too felt an urge for a little fling every now and then. In fact, I know it happened once, without turning into a drama of very great dimensions . . .

But I can well understand that a fellow like Knut Klaumann is preoccupied with impotence: *he* certainly doesn't seem to be any great shakes in bed! Like so many young men these days he looks physically defective, underdeveloped and unhealthy, with poor skin, narrow shoulders, and incipient beer-belly. True, I've put on weight myself since I ceased being active in sports, but I take care to keep in tolerable shape and I'll keep up my physique till sixty, that I've set my mind on.

No, he doesn't get anywhere by trying to sink our quite ordinary marriage with riddles and clever questions. We got along well, no better and no worse than most others, and if she hadn't turned and left we would still be living the same way today. That's the simple truth.

"The Gymnasium" is a little smaller than an ordinary schoolroom and the equipment is beneath criticism—but what can you expect? At least there's a ribbed wall and a horse, weights and bull-workers, various dumbbells, and jump ropes. I've been given an hour a week with Ludo. He's also training, enthusiastic and sweaty, trying to get his formless body into shape in the belief it will improve his luck with the girls. The first time I showed him what I could do with the weights, his eyes nearly popped out of his head. Since then he's treated me with a certain chummy respect, in any case with more friendliness than a violent criminal can usually expect. Ludo is obsessed by the idea that running is the best exercise. "When you run you train all your muscles at once," he gasps as he dashes along the walls of the all too narrow room, looking like a hamster in a cage: "Nothing beats running!" I've tried to make him jump rope, but he insists on his theory and plods on, panting and puffing on stockinged feet and in uniform shirt and trousers—after all, he's supposed to keep me under surveillance, not work out himself! Except for Ludo I have this hour all to myself, as none of the others apparently feel the urge to exercise with a roughneck. I bet they wouldn't be so shy if I were small and thin, then I'd have to take both knocks and kicks. But inmates know how to appraise a man's physical strength, and in a small institution like this they don't dare go as far as making an organized assault on a man.

I myself do some strengthening exercises, mostly out of old habit, and then limbering-up exercises to compensate for all the sitting around, for not being able to move. For me the physical deprivation of liberty is much worse than the mental. Though here, in "The Gymnasium," with a couple of dumbbells in my hands, six-kilo ones as when I trained for the Nordic championship, I almost become what I was in my best days. When I close my eyes and just feel my muscles work, feel how I must win back what's been lost after my lazy years, how my head eases up and my thoughts get clearer after a long, pointless conversation with the psychiatrist, it's almost the same as before, as out there before a regatta. And the contentment afterwards is just as great, the physical heaviness as pleasant, even if you're accompanied down the corridor by the guard afterwards and locked up in your cell, if it's that late.

A prisoner is also permitted a certain minimum of direct contact with the outside world, if there are no special considerations to prevent it: he can receive visitors once a week, for an hour. Convicts are allowed to be alone with their visitors, their wives or their fiancées, in the visiting room, furnished with a table and two chairs. The young and fearless ones come sailing along with a rug, plaid, or perhaps a foam-rubber mattress they can lie on; they don't mind the peephole in the door. The older ones are more sedate, talk, and perhaps content themselves with touching each other through their clothes.

A detainee doesn't have problems of this sort. If a detainee receives a visit, a guard must be present. It's a situation that encourages nothing but brief messages. Eilert has been here, nervous and flustered, wondering what's going to happen to the business. I asked him to run it all as usual, said I'd try to keep an eye on things from here as best I could, but saw his glance flicker. He probably wondered if he could trust me—a jailbird who'd mauled his wife in the street. To tell the truth, I wonder a bit myself. When I try to think about practical matters in connection with the business, it's difficult to collect my thoughts for more than a couple of minutes at a time. My ability to concentrate fails me, things close at hand intrude and disturb the picture: the thought of dinner, an ice hockey match that is to be televised, the constipation that's beginning to get better . . . Trivial stuff that slowly poisons the brain and erases the sharp contours of things out there.

5 "You probably feel I'm ungrateful to leave you like that. You probably don't understand how being married to you gradually became a prison I had to get out of, at any price. (I'm expressing myself like an idiot—as you always took care to point out—but now it's serious, isn't it?) You probably think you did everything in your power to make our marriage work, and perhaps you're right. In that case it's even *worse*, because then the possibility of something better never really existed. Then you and I never should have gotten together, because the trouble wasn't that our marriage got worse and worse, the trouble was it didn't get better and better. The worst thing was that it was neither good nor bad, it was simply *nothing!* It went on and on without growing. *Nothing* grew out of our life together, did you ever think of that? We grew ten years older side by side, that's all. I can hear you protest that we had a good sex life—and you're right, we did, when you had the time or felt like it or weren't too tired. But that also wore off, became a habit like everything else that's simply repeated. You were good enough as far as that goes, but I sought the man, not the stud— and that is a difference you've never learned to see. I had Eli and was saved for a while. When pregnant or nursing, you feel you have a duty to perform, almost a mission. That you're doing something creative, something *real*. But after she began school, this role too seemed to become less important. That's why I could do it. Not that I'm giving up little Eli—you won't get her, that's not what I mean. But I can't become a good mother to her till I find a way of living my life that will turn me into a better and more complete human being. You probably think I'm living it up now, you who were always so jealous (so typical of you to think I was having affairs just because you were having affairs yourself). I can tell you I have a friend, no professional seducer of runaway housewives, no show-off like you, but a male human being I can talk to and who understands what I say. Perhaps he and I can accomplish something together. It's too early to tell, but I can tell you at least that I'm happy, happier than I've been with you for many, many years. The tragic thing about you—and men like you—is that none of you are capable of imagining that other people might be different from your- selves. In reality you've never been interested in anyone except *yourself;* when you said you loved me—and perhaps you believed you did?—it was only because you wanted to see yourself and your muscles in still another mirror. I was your little hand mirror for many years—thank God I fell out of the frame at last!

"Am I ungrateful then? Am I selfish, thinking only of myself and my own comfort and leaving you stuck in a difficult situation? Where's the affection a person is supposed to feel for someone she has shared her life with for so many years? Affection—if not love. I'll tell you: that affection was spent while I sat alone those evenings you were out training for one of your rowing meets, or the evenings we sat alone together at home. My affection was used up during those endless hours you sat at meetings and dinners, those afternoons you had to go out and look at merchandise, those weekends you were on a 'business trip' with your plump little champion swimmer! That's where my affection went, and it has left nothing behind except emptiness and regret for ten years of my life.

"I suppose one can never altogether justify oneself in a letter. I'm writing this because I want you to understand that leaving you wasn't something I thought up in great haste and rushed into headfirst. On the contrary, it was the only rational conclusion to our marriage. If you'd been more understanding, less violent, we might have talked the matter over, come to an agreement, and said good-bye as friends. As it is, I think I did the right thing.

"I hope you won't try to find out where I am, because it won't be any use. When the time comes I'll get in touch to take care of the formalities. At the moment I can't bear to think about such things.

"Oh yes, I certainly miss you now and then, the house with our things, and poor little Eli, whom I feel I've failed, but never badly enough to make me waver for a moment—can you believe it? Never enough to make me wish it undone for a single moment. And that to me is proof that I did the right thing . . ."

It goes on for another couple of pages, the first letter she wrote me after her vanishing act. The closely written pages are crumpled from my initial reaction, which was to throw the whole mess in the trash can. All the same, when my anger subsided I got the sheets out again, straightened them out and read them again, and yet again, with an eagerness that resembled an obsession, as if her slightly too solemn formulations, or perhaps something about her open, somewhat careless handwriting, would be able to tell me something important, something about myself, something I ran the risk of never discovering . . . But what this letter in the final analysis told a great deal about was, of course, her—her self-centeredness and selfishness, her lack of imagination and understanding: *she* was the one who failed to understand another person's situation, not I! *I* could have fired that broadside against *her!* Still, a couple of expressions have stuck with me and, for some mysterious reason, make bitter twinges of pain shoot through my heart when I think of them: "Sitting at home alone together and growing ten years older side by side . . ." That she could bring herself to write something like that! Those ten years with her that were so full and meant so much to both of us! When so much happened! It was when we got married that I started to scale down my athletics. Of course, not immediately or sharply; I continued for the sake of amusement, participated in minor regattas, did my part of the club work, but that was like nothing compared to the effort I'd put in when I was participating in the big meets. Even so, she complained that I trained too much. And then the business I started right after we married. It's no joke to begin from scratch in that particular line. Luckily, I got a fine start because of the good will from the time I'd spent as an active athlete. But such an enterprise doesn't happen by itself, no matter what. I even had to take evening courses to get a business school diploma. The first year I kept the accounts myself. I'd hoped she would understand that when I worked so hard from morning till night it was for both of us, because we had to have something to live on and wanted to be comfortably off. I've never yet seen it fall into someone's lap.

And when she got pregnant we planned to build. By that time the business had just gotten off to a start. Although competition is tough in the sporting goods market and an explosive expansion is taking place in the number of products, with a consequent demand for large investments, the business turnover also increases nicely . . . Good Lord, I talk as if I were discussing a sales presentation with colleagues—it will probably take years before I'm worth anything as a dealer in sports articles again, if the time will ever come. True, I have Eilert, who can take care of the store and the employees from day to day just as well as I, but what will happen when big decisions have to be made? When orders have to be placed? When the market must be evaluated? That's where I made the right investments during the early years—a run of luck combined with the knowledge of the business I'd acquired incidentally by being an active athlete. I saw the potential of the new materials: fiberglass skis, carbon fiber poles, boots, training suits. As an active athlete I knew how new equipment can push an entire branch of athletics forward and, not least, force the public to become aware of it. As an active athlete I have myself known the joy of using good equipment and colorful, well-fitting clothes. Television was a factor in creating the new market: fifty thousand amateurs wanted the same equipment used by active athletes. I saw it and made my gamble a season or two before most others got going. And it paid off. My credit rating improved. I could expand. I bought a really nice building lot near Ski. I planned a new house, 50 by 35 feet plus half a lower floor: we'd have everything. Part of the expense for materials was absorbed by the business. I did most of the woodwork myself. Everything would be the way I wanted it; besides, it's expensive to hire craftsmen and they don't always do good work. I've always liked using my hands, that's how I do things. I'm a very physical person, my body makes demands. I'd hoped she'd understand I had to exercise a bit, considering the work load I carried—otherwise I couldn't have managed!

"Ten years older side by side . . ."

I built a house for her. She had everything she wanted. The baby was born. It was strange and moving, but unfortunately I couldn't be home very much during that period. Besides, she was so engrossed in the baby that we got a bit cramped for space somehow. It was as if she constantly had to demonstrate how much better she was at taking care of the baby and its needs, which made me feel more bumbling than I really was; I can see it now. That great mother love of hers, what would she do with it when she was no longer obliged to putter around the little bundle all day? It looked as if the baby was to serve as security for what she'd lost physically through giving birth—because she had lost something. The baby was to compensate her for the ugly marks on her abdomen, marks of stretching that refused to go away, for her breasts going slack when there was no milk in them anymore, for the varicose veins on her legs that made her reluctant to take off her stockings. She asked me if I thought they were ugly. Sure I thought they were ugly but said it didn't matter. Still, it seems, I was to be punished: little Eli was the compensation, I the scapegoat. She didn't let me sleep with her after the normal period of abstinence had passed; she complained of little aches and pains and cried when I tried to get near her.

I planted roses in the bed at the edge of the terrace the summer Eli was born. But she said: "They'll never make it—that variety needs a milder climate, I've read about it . . ." True, some of them withered from frost, but most came through and are now thriving, even if I could never find the time to look after them as I ought to . . .

I wanted to build a carport by the garage, but she said: "You know very well I'll never get a license." But the carport became a useful shelter for our bikes and the garden tools. I wanted to build a sauna as an addition to the downstairs room, but she said: "I can't stand saunas—to sit around sweating with other people . . ." So instead we got a bar, an expensive affair in brass and maroon veneer that was used only at the Midsummer Eve celebration and the traditional Christmas party. I used to bring home a load of toys when I'd been out traveling, but she said: "Don't you realize she's still too little to be interested in such things . . ."

I could go on, but why torment myself with such things now? Now when it's all over? Still, that letter makes me angry. For some reason or other it had been left among the personal papers I asked to be brought here. Though I suppose I knew it had been put there . . .

She constantly insisted I was unfaithful. In the letter she mentions the "plump little champion swimmer," as if Unni were a stranger to her and she didn't know we never had a regular affair. Needless to say, I did yield to temptation occasionally in the course of those ten years, but never in the deliberate, calculating fashion she suspected. For she suspected me constantly after that ill-fated episode with Unni, which was a coincidence, neither planned nor important in any way, starting from the simple fact that the women swimmers' get-together in Arendal coincided with a large business conference, and naturally we socialized, since some of us knew a few of the girls from before. And so it was Unni and me for a couple of days, until the conference was over and I returned home to her, who was pregnant. That is, she was in the hospital already when I got back—there had been signs of irregularity and her time was approaching. And when I hurried to the hospital without realizing what was up, saw her lying there pale and thin-faced under a majestic quilt and was told there was nothing seriously wrong with her—they'd admitted her that very week just in case—I was so happy and relieved and yet so weighed down with guilt for abandoning her for nearly a week at this critical time that I felt a closeness and devotion to her I'd hardly ever felt before. And the touch of those pale hospital lips against my skin made me remember Unni's salty kisses, a swimmer's kisses, and I was deeply ashamed and wished it undone, though I've always regarded absolute marital fidelity as an impossibility and a myth; and this sudden feeling of tenderness for her in the hospital bed, anxious, immobile and shapeless, drove me to do the one fatal thing I never should have: I confessed! Though I didn't exactly kneel at her bed, I told her everything, with a stammering voice husky with remorse and emotion; I think I even cried, put my head on her quilt and begged forgiveness!

She never forgave me. It was as if this casual, completely unimportant little sidestep gave the deathblow to her trust in me. The only words she could utter were: "And it had to be *now!*" as though the moment suddenly played a decisive role. Later, of course, I understood, after we'd had a good talk and settled the matter (though this particular conflict, it seems, could never be "entirely settled"), that the period of pregnancy is a vulnerable time in every woman's life, that she feels big and heavy and disgusting, and that unfaithfulness then feels exceptionally painful. Of course. I should have understood that. Still, to be called to account for it again and again years afterwards? Besides, I've understood since then that it's very common for husbands to be unfaithful to their wives, perhaps for the first and last time, precisely when they are pregnant. Nor is that very strange: to many, after all, pregnancy means weeks or months of abstinence, during which the wife's refusal can easily acquire a tinge of something more and deeper than regard for hygiene and safety. On the other hand, this is a time when the husband can feel most absolutely certain of her; the fact that she belongs to and depends on him is demonstrated physically and indisputably. Perhaps it is his position as absolute ruler with unlimited power during this brief period that makes it so tempting for him to abuse it, to cut loose for the first and last time, before the bonds and obligations grow even more insurmountable now that the child is on its way and before the strength of his manhood and his will become even more of an illusion . . .

At any rate she took her revenge quite literally when we gave a garden party late that summer. She was in fine shape again and looked well, with fabulous tits from all the breast-feeding, but she still didn't want to have anything to do with me in bed. We were only twelve to fourteen people, made a barbecue, drank wine and, later, highballs. Feeling somewhere in between a proud, happy father and a scorned, pushed-around husband, I had too much to drink, of course, and passed out. When I woke up on the sofa of the ground-floor parlor next morning, she told me in an amiable tone of voice that she'd used the occasion to sleep with Eilert, my closest associate in the business: "He was drunk too and not much good," was the laconic conclusion to her report. When I managed to stand up and, furious, hurt and still befuddled by drink, gave her a smack, she laughed as if she had won a personal victory! "Yes, go on and hit me, you brute! I knew that's what you were like! I knew it! I knew it!"

I don't know to this day if her story was true. Perhaps she just made
it up to make her revenge taste even sweeter. Actually, such behavior doesn't seem like her, and I know she cared no more for Eilert than for the rest of my friends. But how can I ask *him* . . . !

6 "What did you really expect from your marriage?"

All impartial interest, Knut Klaumann leafs through his papers while asking the question, as he always does when he knows it's one I'll have difficulty answering.

What *I* expected from the marriage? I don't think I've ever thought about that before, and I can't find anything to answer.

"If you feel it's difficult to answer offhand, perhaps you could tell me what made you marry her, if you've thought about it?"

How it came to be her specifically? Oh, well. I guess it was the right moment. I'd turned thirty and realized my time as an active athlete was coming to an end, thought more and more often that I'd probably been pursuing it long enough—I couldn't make a living from rowing, after all, and it was only thanks to the director of the shipping firm where I worked, a rowing enthusiast who gave me all the time I needed for training, that I was able to keep it up as I did. But I hadn't thought of ending my days as a shipping agent. And besides, thirty marks a magic limit to athletic performance in most fields.

But why did I choose her of all people?

I remember she often came with a woman friend to the place where we used to go after training. I remember she laughed a lot and kept putting away half-liters of beer; she was a fledgling secretary, made fun of her boss, and seemed eager to have an adventure. She went along on a trip to Copenhagen that four of us had planned. After that trip she became my steady, so to speak. We were often together on weekends, unless there were special training projects going on. She also came to several regattas with me. We laughed and drank beer together. She didn't care for the boys who cracked jokes. I tried to get her interested in rowing, but couldn't, though she had the right attitude. My little apartment on the Josefinegate seemed empty the weekends she didn't stay overnight. On my training excursions life in the single scull suddenly seemed lonely to me, who previously had taken so much pleasure in measuring training distances on the map, finding landmarks and testing myself against the clock, taking my pulse, feeling in control of my body as if it were an obedient machine, constantly keeping my performance close to the absolute limit where an oarsman breaks down and vomits.

On a weekend excursion to a cottage I'd rented we agreed to get married. For me it felt like a confirmation of something that had been decided long ago. Nor did she seem very surprised; she was calm and happy, convinced like me that this was the right thing, and said she looked forward to quitting her job and beginning to "play house." It was in late August, so we had the rocky beach all to ourselves, bathed in the nude, and sunned ourselves as long as the slanting beams of August gave any warmth. She picked flowers that faded the moment they were put in water. It was the coming of fall.

At the next club meeting I announced that I'd decided to quit as an active athlete. At New Year's we got married.

But what did I expect? Love, fidelity, and eternal happiness? Nonsense. As an adult I'd seen enough of my acquaintances' marriages, which worked poorly or not at all, to know that nothing turned into a bed of roses quite by itself. But she was good-natured, seemed uncomplicated, and made few demands. We were in love like any other newlyweds. She devoted herself to "playing house" with great enthusiasm and ardor. I had quit my job in the shipping firm and had already started to look for housing for my business. I pretty much expected we would go on much the same: she busy with her own things, satisfied enough to give me the stimulus to go on with my things. And a bit of cheer when we were together. Perhaps cooperation is the word for it? A little patience and a little kindness? That she would understand a man isn't always free to do exactly what he wants, even though it might seem to be the most important thing at the moment. Perhaps that a man is almost *never* free to do what he would like to do most of all . . .

I know in any case what I *didn't* expect our marriage to be: a prison. A prison within the walls of a newly built private house in a good neighborhood at Ski, where two convicts for life, she and I—kept under surveillance by economic pressures and obligations, the panicky feeling of responsibility characteristic of parents with kids, the conventions of affluent Norwegian society, the demands for performance that weigh upon everybody, especially someone who wants to be independent, and the monotony of our own daily habits—in the end had nothing else to bring to fruition together than personal differences, divergent views, disagreements about what was most important, feelings of estrangement, disappointed hopes, dead expectations, a lack of the most elementary contact, folly, antipathy and hatred.

When he handed me the sheets with the Rorschach inkblots and asked me to tell him what came first to my mind, in order to uncover the most obscure, most impenetrable aspects of my psyche with a view to presentation in the courtroom, I saw only cunts and explosions.

My lawyer has also been here a couple of times. We don't have much to talk about so long before the trial. He tells me I shouldn't hesitate to send for him if I can think of something that may be important to my case, and I say, yes of course I will. But I know I'll never send for him, for though the thought of the trial stimulates me—at least it scares me, in a way that helps to keep me mentally alert—the thought of my "*crime*" remains unacceptable: the minutes out there in the street, on the sidewalk, and on the stairs outside the restaurant are encapsulated in a nightmarish panic, though I'm still capable of placing myself *on the outside* and reviewing the complete course of events in detail, as in a slow-motion film. But it's as if none of these versions really concerned me; I cannot acknowledge the "*crime*"; I hardly ever think of it, though this is exactly what interests everybody else and what makes me such an interesting person here in "The Manor"; Knut Klaumann and my lawyer, the guards, even prisoners who keep up with things, seem to be more preoccupied with it than I am.

We're almost in mid-December, the darkest, saddest month, with the threat of the Christmas celebration weighing heavily upon the darkest abyss of the year. The doctor's office that Knut Klaumann uses when we have our consultations is in the North Wing. From there I can see the lamps being lighted early in the afternoon on the short little streets running straight as an arrow through the residential neighborhood of single-family houses. A little later, lights are turned on here and there inside the houses. Gray, buttoned-up figures appear, seeming to hurry from street lamp to street lamp. More lamps are lighted in the residences. The cars are returning home with a sweeping amber beam, and I reflect: "Poor devils, poor, poor devils!" These are the slaves of economic conditions and of mortgage payments, the coronary patients with gray faces from the strain of their convict existence, with its tedium and monotony and joylessness, from worries over how the budget will bear up under the compulsory extravagances of Christmas.

In December it's just as good to be a prisoner here as a prisoner at large out there. In December, life outside is just as nasty as life within the walls, perhaps even worse. Though I'm told that Christmas Eve can be rough alone in your cell, I find it hard to believe it can be much worse here than in a private house at Ski. And remembering the faces of those hurrying home from work to their prefab dwellings on Spruce Road, Bluebell Road, or Siskin Road, I recognize the same troubled, introspective expression I see in my fellow inmates when we're moved to and fro, past one another, in the corridors of this institution. And their mouths have the same tense lines, as if a constant effort were needed to keep their lips closed and block the scream—their despair at life and what they have made of it, at how impossible it seems to be to change anything, alter even the slightest thing for the better.

7 Christmas Eve. Porridge at twelve o'clock noon. A joker down the hall calls through the peephole: "Hey, maybe I'll find a real almond among all the lumps, eh? Maybe I'll get a Christmas present from the management?"

"You bet," Bassen replies amiably. He's the one in charge of rations on this darkest day of prison life. "Of course you'll get a present—the key to the main gate! Just come and get it!" The peephole bangs shut, cutting off the resigned groans of the inmate. Then a boring wait for dinner, like any other holiday, with the difference that today every man knows beforehand what he'll get, namely, spareribs and sausage, a bit of sauerkraut, and four potatoes.

Except for the menu, Christmas Eve in jail resembles any other holiday, dull and boring, and idle even for prison. But for most inmates it's worse than ordinary holidays, without work and without evening activities; few can imagine how feelings, sentimentality, and a sense of bereavement hold sway here among these hardened, dangerous, morally obtuse, and unprincipled men on a day like today.

What I myself miss the most is my weekly conversation with the psychiatrist. It gets canceled this week, because Christmas Eve happens to be a Thursday, which has been our regular day for consultations. So I'll be sitting here next Thursday too, New Year's Eve, and not get an appointment till Thursday, January 7. Not that I've suddenly begun to like Knut Klaumann, or decided to cooperate with him. But I've discovered that our conversations, his camouflaged interrogations, and my evasive maneuvers keep me mentally alert and concentrated in a way it would otherwise be difficult to sustain in prison. Our conferences have become a challenge to my mental ability, my resourcefulness, and my intellect. When I talk to him, it's as if the prison walls around us didn't exist; we are two equal opponents fighting a slow battle, though officially, of course, we're supposed to cooperate and arrive at a conclusion that will make it easier for the court to understand my case. The only difficulty is that Klaumann must work on the basis of the theory that I'm somehow sick and that my action must have been a manifestation of my lack of balance. While I'm convinced I'm just as healthy and normal as any other male at large out there, any other husband and father who struggles home Christmas Eve with the last, hurriedly purchased merchandise, to a family whose expectations have become so inflated that no purchases whatsoever could fulfill them and thus redeem him from his guilt feelings, from the certainty of not being adequate as a father and provider.

The psychiatrist has become my last gamble on the real world here in jail, and while the remaining days of the week tend more and more to crumble away in apathy and futility as time goes on, the days of consultation turn into a veritable horse cure for the "jail sickness." I'd like to believe so anyway, for I notice that life in prison has begun to make its impact: it's becoming more difficult to follow a chain of thought without somehow being forced to end up with my own person or my own situation. Gradually a prisoner's thoughts become as isolated and self-centered as his physical existence has become. My preoccupation with what is directly in front of my eyes erases both memory and perspective. My mentality is adapting perfectly to prison existence: my thoughts move less and less often beyond the rectangle of 12 by 9 feet, with a height under the ceiling of ca. 7 feet. In other words, all I have left is an intellectual capacity of 750 cubic feet.

But when Knut Klaumann leans his stooped body forward, lets his birdlike head sink down between his peaked shoulders, gives his body a perceptible physical momentum with his feet under the table and asks, looking penetratingly at a point a bit to the right of my nose, if I've ever been conscious of hating my wife and, through her, all women, it's like being plunged into cold water—my memories surge up, the arguments against his conjecture tumble through my brain like an avalanche, my skepticism about him and everything he represents makes my temperature rise two or three degrees, and it takes an extra effort to keep my tone neutral and friendly: he isn't supposed to know that I'm working against him, after all. It's almost like being out there again, like fighting for your hopes and your rights, for yourself and what is yours, in real life, against all those who're out to ruin you when they see their chance!

In a small way, they're out to get you here, inside the walls, too. You notice it especially if you're a violent criminal. If a guard doesn't like your mug, your rations grow smaller, hours get shifted around to your disadvantage, messages may take an eternity to arrive and a reply just as long. Though the law says that detainees shall be considered innocent until the sentence has been handed down, they are actually sentenced here in jail. I've received two years plus preventive detention for brutal assault under exceptionally aggravating circumstances. Both guards and inmates are experts in such matters. To my amazement I discovered that the majority here knew my case; they'd read newspaper accounts of the incident outside the restaurant Bel Ami, had discussed and evaluated it. Due to a peculiar sense of discretion, nobody directly mentions the crime to the inmate who has committed it, unless he expressly invites it. But among all the others such things are regular subjects of conversation, and almost as interesting as the TV sports broadcasts. It's a way of being interested in your fellowman that I've gradually learned to regard as not a purely negative one. Here, inside the prison, locked up within the same institution, we're bound to be concerned with one another in a different way than out there in the great society, the point of departure for most of us. The closest comparison is with small, isolated village environments where, similarly, the individual's surveillance of his fellowmen is sharp and the sentence hard, not because people are especially intolerant or critical but because they realize that what the individual does concerns everybody: the individual becomes the responsibility of all, and is responsible *for* all. In jail it's the same. Ludo, who is an inexhaustible source of information and gossip about everybody, explains it this way when we take our exercise in the prison yard: "A troublesome prisoner can hurt the entire institution. You notice right away if a guy is a troublemaker. Troublemakers think about nothing but the mischief they can do once they get out, and they boast about it to all the others. They can stir up an entire unit. Sometimes the boys take care of such types on their own. If they don't, we have to try to isolate them as best we can. If we let two of them get together, you can bet an attempted escape will take place fairly soon. Often they even get two or three of the all-right boys to go with them. It's too damn bad."

The first days after I was locked up, I did all I could to wipe out the incident outside the restaurant. But shortly this fear of the concrete aspect of the "crime" disappeared. In fact, I jumped at newspaper reports and other superficial information that might give a hint how my case appeared from the *outside*. Inside the walls I received the institutional version, directly and indirectly, more or less reliable facts with a dry matter-of-fact commentary. My assault on my wife had become common property, slowly digested and distorted in the verbal metabolism of the prison, where facts grow into fairy tales and deeds into myths. And my sudden interest in newspaper reports of the incident was probably due to the fact that I felt I must try to save as much as possible of what was "mine," keep it outside the walls of the institution. Like my contest with Knut Klaumann, my preoccupation with society's interest in me and in what I'd done became a strategy in my fight against the jail sickness. But no newspaper had very much to say about it.

Though I think a lot about this, I seldom think of *her*. I don't have a clear image of her, though I know from the clippings that she's in the hospital "with skull fracture and major superficial injuries."

Just as the prison environment allows a man his crime—except the morals cases who live in a deep-freeze from the day they're locked up—it also shows tolerance for his self-deception. All prisoners are pathological liars. Those who're proud of their criminal status dream up fantastic coups. Those who want to forget, justify themselves. A man who has soundly beaten his wife can always blame *her*—any male will understand—but I've abstained from this as long as possible: to play the game is a symptom of the jail sickness, which I've tried to defend myself from . . .

But today, Christmas Eve, I'd be glad to play any game whatever, to relate the fight on the stairs outside the restaurant, in detail if necessary, to lay it on thick, hold forth about her behavior—how she left the child and me in a tight spot when she ran off to live with that drooping student of hers. I would start off with the disgrace of it all, my wounded pride, my righteous indignation. My stock would rise with my fellow inmates. I'd probably be invited to the card party in Cell 8, with Dynamo, already a veteran at just over thirty, now doing time for vagrancy and for stealing a cassette player from a car.

Tonight, Christmas Eve itself, the most depressing day of the year, longings surface in your cell, too—the childish wish to be close to people and feel solidarity with them, to be fond of somebody in a simple, uncomplicated way and feel that someone is fond of you: Christmas Eve, a huckster's market for all the most tender human sentiments. On Christmas Eve you feel just as lonely and unhappy sitting in the favorite chair of your private prison, buried under Christmas paper and trying in vain to light your cigar, as you do sitting on the bunk bed of a prison cell, clasping your chin and staring at the heap of two-day-old newspapers on the floor, a few cards on the table, Christmas greetings from those who thought they ought to send a word despite everything, the letter from Mother—I wrote to ask her not to visit me out here—the card from Eli, a bunch of half-read books, an easy chair and a lamp brought from home to make the cell as "homey" as possible. I've succeeded—I feel just as miserable here as in my private house at Ski, where we used to go to bed early on Christmas Eve the last few years, as soon as the TV program was over and we'd gotten little Eli to bed, excited and unmanageable as children tend to be with all the uproar and the many presents. Just as lonely and dejected here as there, even with my little pile of girlie magazines on the toilet cover.

This prison has four double cells and one cell for four persons. They almost always remain empty. The large majority want to be by themselves. But tonight it might have been possible to fill them. I hear a gentle noise drifting in from the corridor, sounds from the other cells. There's no card party going on tonight, as far as I know. They're sitting there alone, each by himself, brooding and mumbling. Some are groaning or crying. I can hear it clearly. Those are the homesick ones, who go around thinking that Christmas Eve "out there" is better than Christmas Eve here. And then there are those who've been in and out so many times they don't have anything to yearn for anymore. And those who know that in the end it doesn't make much difference whether you're here or there, the sense of loss is the same wherever you are.

8 New Year's and a new man in the ward, a mere boy, barely nineteen; he's going to the school for prison guards and will be a trainee here. The first few days he walks around with the ward-boy to learn the routine. He's fair-haired, good-natured and friendly, seemed a bit shy to begin with. His name is Reidar, but he was immediately baptized Radish because he blushes so easily. He's seeing a girl in town. Everybody knows all about him.

When I go to the prison yard, he comes along with me and Ludo. Ludo explains about the detainees, special treatment and privileges, something he's obviously familiar with beforehand. He walks with his hands in his pockets, constantly glancing up at the tall board fence topped by barbed wire, almost as if *he* were locked up here, not *I*. "How tall is it?" he asks Ludo. Ludo shrugs his shoulders: "Fourteen to sixteen feet . . . ?"

"Fifteen," I correct him. If there's something every inmate does know, it's the height of this fence, the thickness of the brick walls, the size of the squares between the window bars, and the trademark of the locks, all those inessential details that spring from the great common daydream: to escape sometime!

He smiles for thanks—he has brought his smile to the prison. Then he seems to notice something and stops dead, scrutinizing my face. Slowly it comes, "Aren't . . . Aren't you . . . ?" He can recall having seen me before. Red as a beet, he tries to recall my name: "Nordic single scull champion. Quite a few years ago now . . . Right?"

I nod, then come to the aid of his recollection: "Silver medal."

"Gee whiz!" is all he can say for some time. Then, "You know, I had the picture of that crew above my bed for many years. And you were one of them!" Now it's Ludo's turn to gape: "Gee, you hear that, Ali? You've got a helluva guy here!"

He calls me Ali after the boxing champion, a discreet hint at the treatment I dished out to *her*.

"Perhaps you've done a bit of rowing yourself," I say, trying to make my voice as friendly as possible. The gruff, sarcastic, snapping prison tone is not exactly suitable for ingratiating yourself with somebody. Again he turns scarlet. "A little. I was cox for the rowing club here when I was younger. Then I got too big and heavy and had a go at it by myself . . ." Abashed, he smiles, rocking his shoulders. He does have a gorgeous physique, as far as his uniform and his outdoor jacket enable me to judge. He moves well. No lack of talent there!

"But nothing much came of it. They only had an old in-rigger for training, and it's too heavy. Then a couple of the most enthusiastic boys moved, and both the club and the training got pretty mediocre . . ."

He comes to the gym Wednesday evening when I have my training period. It's been arranged with Ludo, who is quite happy to dispense with me as spectator of his perspiring exertions—he's supposed to have a steady girl now anyway, a secretary in a wholesale business, and can switch his charm strategy from the purely external to the more intimate . . .

I work with the weights, can feel that some of my strength has come back, after only a few weeks. He looks at me admiringly: "Gee whiz! I could never do that many!"

"Try."

I put away the weight. He takes off his jacket, which he has to wear on duty. He's really very well built, with broad shoulders and strong arms, his torso perhaps slightly too large for the lower body; many think this is the way oarsmen should be, large and broad with short little legs, but in reality long legs for a powerful kick are just as important as strength of arms and torso if you want to achieve really good results. He positively hurls himself upon the weight, jerking it up and pressing it above his head, stands trembling like that for a moment with quivering arms and neck muscles hard as rope under his skin, till he drops the weight on the mat with a bang. "Gee, that was heavy. How big was it?" He's too eager to impress. I say, "It doesn't matter how big it was, the most important thing is you'll ruin your back if you throw yourself around like that." He's embarrassed but defends himself:

"I've worked with weights before . . ."

"But you'd like to be an oarsman, wouldn't you?"

"Yes, more than anything—that is, if it isn't too late."

"Nonsense, with your background it isn't too late, but you must work sensibly. Sheer strengthening exercises won't be important till later."

"What should I start with then?"

Our relationship has already been established: one of teacher and pupil. Trainer and talented young athlete. I feel strangely exhilarated at the thought; he's so timid and shy, yet at the same time so handsome and strong and full of promise as he stands there. His handling of the weight shows that he has plenty of strength; what he needs is a plan and the correct, purposeful mentality. That I can give him.

"Well . . . ," I say, trying to sound professional, as if I were a real trainer with schedules and programs in his head.

"General physical training to start with, running, swimming, general gym and jump rope, to strengthen coordination . . ."

"Aha . . ." He nods, taking in everything: he's in my power, not the other way around. "The swimming pool is open late three days a week, so I can go there . . ."

He's delightfully willing to cooperate—with him I could go far, if only . . . I astonish myself: on the verge of forgetting my actual situation after a few minutes in the gym with this boy! His quick and willing response is stirring new thoughts, and I discover how I must have missed the contact, trust, and companionship that sports offers, though I never fully realized it.

"But we can work a little extra with the back—the back is important for someone who wants to row, the stomach muscles are used mostly for stabilization, but the back is in there pulling . . ."

I take him over to our ramshackle horse, place him double across it, then hold his ankles and tell him to clasp his hands behind his head while raising the upper part of his body as high as he can. It's an unfamiliar exercise for him, and he works himself into a sweat, then collapses with a laugh after a few tries. "Gee, that was a tough one, you'll have to give me some time on it."

He has brought laughter into the prison.

The perspiration forms beads on his smooth, fresh skin as we jog around a bit and shake loose.

"Let's try some push-ups instead—the first to fifty!" He throws himself down and begins. I can't very well refuse, stick with him till about thirty but notice he has more reserves than I. At fifty I'm five or six behind. He grins triumphantly and rolls over on his back. "You fell behind there!"

"Behind and behind—anyway, there's nothing wrong with your arms. It's probably the back we'll have to concentrate on to begin with. And physical fitness, as I said. Do you ski?"

"A little. There isn't very much snow here, usually. And now, with this job, I probably won't have much time."

"Try to ski as much as possible. If there's no snow you can run. When spring comes we can begin to practice technique in the boat. I bet you can't even square away properly!" I have to secure the advantage again, draw on my reputation and my long experience. It makes an impression. He becomes humble again and begins to apologize: "You can't learn properly in an old in-rigger."

"Sure you can, if you work it right. Just wait and you'll see . . ." Again I forget where I am, who I am.

"All right, wave at me from your cell when I row past then, okay?" There is a mirthful, boyish sarcasm in his voice, cocky but not at all malicious. Now he's on top.

"If you become good enough, they'll have to give me leave so I can train you, just wait!"

We're not lying side by side on the floor talking at the ceiling anymore. We've gotten up. We stand beside the horse again. I'm about to propose that he do the back exercise once more, but he interrupts me: "No, no, no. No more of that today . . ." Suddenly his hand grabs mine: "Let me see if you're any good at arm wrestling instead!"

We wrestle with the leather horse as a base. He's strong, but arm wrestling isn't simply a question of strength. Endurance, strategy, and shrewdness determine the outcome. And here an older man has the advantage. After a couple of minutes I feel I've got him, can even relax a little and then work myself up again. Another moment and I can easily put him down.

"Gosh, you're tough!" he pants, "but I almost had you . . ." I let him believe it. He's pleased at wrestling the sports hero he's had a picture of over his bed, and "almost winning."

It's nearly time. We jog a bit in the cramped room. I show him some relaxation exercises—he has a tendency to get a bit tight when he's running.

"Sure nice to train with a pro," he smiles as he bends down to tie his shoelace. The sight of him resting on one knee, his head bent as he busies himself with his shoelaces, stirs me to a strange excitement, and I cannot restrain my desire to stretch out my hand and rumple his blond hair as, seemingly by chance, I take a step in his direction. His hairline is sweaty and the nape of his neck is broad and hot.

Then it's time. Ludo rattles his keys as he lets us out. He's the one in charge, after all; Reidar is only a trainee, not crafty enough, not morally obtuse enough to be able to handle us hard-boiled criminals on his own. But it's easy to play the prison game with Ludo. He's glad to cut out for an hour in return for a pack of cigarettes.

"Well, sporty boys, did you manage to work out a bit?" Ludo is brimming over with sarcastic geniality—he probably won the card game this evening in Cell 9, where four of them hold tournaments with chocolate and cigarettes for prizes. "I guess you can use it"—he nudges Reidar—"the way you wear yourself out in that rooming house evening after evening . . ." The Radish blushes. His girl goes to business school and lives in the municipal students' residence hall. "And remember, if you have any trouble opening her treasure chest, we have several boys here who're real experts at that sort of thing." He laughs heartily at his own dirty joke. Reidar gives a crooked grin, seems to think he's too young and green to respond in kind, tries to come up with a flippant answer and blushes an even deeper red. "Just don't worry, boy," Ludo comforts him, catching my eye. "Don't mind what those shitheads say. In this place, you know, the men think only of one thing—getting the key into the lock!"

9 "In spite of the feelings of aggression you were obviously accumulating against your wife . . . ," Knut Klaumann lectures cockily, his head sunk low between his pointed shoulders, even though I've never hinted anything of the kind but rather held back any hostility that might pop into my mind while sitting here answering his questions—"in spite of all this aggression . . . , didn't it ever occur to you that she too might be undergoing a development during those years when you lived together? That she came to realize she had needs which married life with you just couldn't satisfy? That she was *a woman on her way*, so to speak, on her way to a new understanding of herself, and that you weren't able to stimulate this process or even to understand it properly, so that you interpreted her "selfish" conduct, as you call it, negatively, as an attack on you, whereas in reality it was . . ."

Phew, how he can talk, good old Klaumann! "A woman on her way . . ." Kiss my ass! A woman on her way to making life impossible for everybody around her, sure. A woman on her way to destroying everything that had been built up during ten years of marriage. A woman on her way to transforming every good and positive feeling between us to hatred. For it was from *her* the hatred came, not from me. It was with *her* that the hatred started: sudden sallies, accusations, charges. After that affair with Unni she accused me on the slightest provocation of being "brutal," though I never laid hands on her after the argument we had following the garden party. She complained I was never home, never paid attention when she talked, or cared what she said. I had married my business, she said, using one of her favorite expressions, but when I asked her how the hell I could meet my mortgage payments if I didn't work, she had nothing to say, and she was obviously very pleased to be able to move into a private house and settle down comfortably—until that too became something negative in due course: now it was suddenly so far from the city. At Ski she knew so few people and had no real friends, and she felt very lonely to be puttering around in the house all day. It was when the kid turned four or five that this refrain started. While Eli was little she'd been completely occupied with care, nursing and upbringing, both in theory and practice, for a certain period. Then it was I who could have said, rightfully: "You don't even listen when I'm talking, or attach importance to anything I say." But I didn't say it, often as I felt that way, simply because I took it for granted that women were in closer touch with small children than men. It was only later, when I was left alone with Eli, that I understood how mistaken I'd been.

Anyway, I did suggest a few things that might help keep boredom at bay while she was staying home, such as courses she could take and hobbies she could pick up; or she could continue her education by correspondence if she felt like it. But she didn't. "Drops in the ocean," she'd say. "Band-aid on the wound—I don't need first aid." But what she really needed she was unable to say, at any rate so I could understand it. Nor did she feel like going to work again. "I don't know anything but secretarial work, and that's the pits!"

Though Eli, up to the age of three, was everything to her, the goal of her life, she positively refused to consider having more children. Even when her dissatisfaction with staying home "without anything to keep her busy" had become apparent, after the child was a little older and didn't need attention around the clock anymore. It would make her feel tied hand and foot, she said. "Imprisoned for life." Yeah. And so she broke out of her prison at Ski, cast off her chains, abandoning Eli and me. Mamma went off to have fun, screwing around with pimply student punks, while Papa and the kid had to manage as best they could. And then, when this free-spirited fun had lost some of its glitter perhaps, Mamma suddenly wanted to be Mamma again and just went and kidnaped the girl, out of mother love and caring no doubt . . . Oh, to hell with it!

It's this picture I can't get rid of: her body bent, halfway squatting on the dirty sidewalk outside the restaurant as she helps the child tie her shoelace—the loving, caring mother with her daughter. And little Eli's pale, confused, gaping face, white among all the dark winter coats flashing by, with small, tired eyes from lack of sleep, with the schoolbag on her back, though it was way past the time when she should be in school; *her* hand on little Eli's crocheted hat that I myself had found for her: Mother and daughter, the epitome of love, harmony, and tranquility even on a filthy sidewalk that damp morning in November; a thief with her stolen goods, and yet what a charming scene! What a tender picture! What harmony between mother and daughter! What a total erasure of the father, who worked for ten years to lay the foundations for a carefree family life (I swear I did!) and then toiled for six months as a single provider to keep body and soul together, both my own and the child's, while steering the business past the most perilous rocks—the competition in my line of goods is keener now, the necessity of investing greater than ever, at a time when credit has tightened . . . Mother and daughter in a tender and natural communion, a loose shoelace, a hand on her hat, a pat on her cheek; the father forgotten, irrelevant, superfluous—at worst a threat to their intimacy there on the sidewalk . . . The sight of them overwhelms me when I try to think of other things; its falseness, disproportion, and injustice drive me mad!

"You must have confidence in me if you want me to help you," says Knut Klaumann, fixing his gaze on a point to the right of my nose. "You must tell me frankly what you think; it's important you should answer spontaneously, from the guts, if you see what I mean. All of us have things we keep hidden from our consciousness, things we're reluctant to let out, which get suppressed by our reason, censored so to speak. But if we want to get to the bottom of a psychological problem, it's particularly important that these very things be brought to light. Therefore you must have confidence in me and tell me everything that occurs to you, even if it seems trivial and unimportant. Especially then perhaps . . ."

Good old Klaumann has understood that I hold back with him. Easy for him to talk about "confidence." An ordinary doctor has to maintain professional secrecy; Klaumann has to provide information to the Norwegian judicial system and the Norwegian public. All intimate details will receive front-page coverage in tabloid dailies like VG as sure as death. The "closed doors" of the courtroom are always ajar for a legal-psychiatric tidbit. How can I have "confidence" then? And what kind of mental problems is he talking about? My history is clear as daylight; what happened to me could have happened (and does happen) to dozens of other Norwegian males: I got damn angry and lost control for a moment. It could have happened two or three years ago. It might have happened in a year or so. In any case, it would most likely have happened sooner or later—the crown on the work of matrimony, the discharge of all the hatred that had accumulated between us.

"So you think the aggression really came from *her,* that *she* was more hostile to you than you to her?" How do you explain to Knut Klaumann about the hatred that arises when the purposes, wishes, and hopes of two human beings never agree, can't even be expressed in such a way that the other person understands what drives you to act as you do? How do you explain to Knut Klaumann the hatred that must spring up between two convicts locked up each in his cell with a glass wall in between, where both feel that the other's prison must represent freedom, along with everything that each must find missing in his, or her, prison existence? How do you tell Knut Klaumann about the mass of misunderstandings, stillborn good intentions and ingratitude that builds up till it forms a dam which finally bursts, carrying everything away in torrents of bitterness, self-righteousness, and disappointment? How can I explain to Knut Klaumann that I'm really a peace-loving man, not at all brutal, that I wouldn't have treated a chance acquaintance the way I treated my wife out there on the restaurant steps, but that I still think I was within my rights, that even now, when I can bear to think about it, I gnash my teeth in aggressive fury and feel she deserved it?

. What does Knut Klaumann know about such things, someone who claims he and his ex-wife are just as good friends now, even better, and screw on the sofa whenever opportunity offers? What can *he* understand of my situation, living as he does with a friend and her children, no doubt a flat-chested feminist who teaches him expressions like "woman on her way" and the like? How can I feel "confidence" in a man who's charged with proving in court and to all the world that there's something wrong with *me*, not with her or with marriage or with the divorce law, let alone with the building or credit policy, with the banks' mortgage terms, the rise in prices, commuting to and from work, pressure for achievement or the race for success, or with any one of all those things *outside* that build prison walls around a man and make a lifelong prison out of his life?

How is a type like Klaumann to understand how monotonous and boring married life can be, with his comfy setup both in bed and on the sofa, without any papers or obligations whatsoever, a sheik of psychiatry with a learned formula and a quick theoretical explanation for every crossroads of human existence? What does he know about not being able to express the good intention behind an action so it won't be misunderstood, misinterpreted, or used against you at the next confrontation? How can he with his eternal chatter understand that a few years of being married deprives men and women of the basic language they shared?

Through the window behind Klaumann's head, nodding slowly in time with the ball-point pen racing across the scratch pad, I can see the fine, dry January snow falling across Angels Slope (as I've begun to call the building site out there). Lovely. Reidar will have a chance for a quick turn on his skis this afternoon. He's really paying heed to my trainer's advice with great energy and enthusiasm, catches on quickly, and puts all his youthful drive into the execution. As far as I can see, he's a great sports talent, and in addition to his fine physical prerequisites he has what's most important of all: the will to win. I've noticed that he wants to match himself with me in all the exercises we do together; sometimes I actually lose despite my background and my experience. Where I still have the edge on him I notice he's catching up, strenuously, pulse beat by pulse beat, and when he sees that he's reached my level he rolls over on his back and laughs with his white teeth up at the spotted ceiling of the gym. His aggressiveness is purely instinctive, professional, determined by gender. It has nothing to do with him and me or with our personal friendship. That's why I can regard his zeal forbearingly, even joyfully, the way a father regards his son's efforts to be just as big and strong as he. The difference in age between us makes real competition impossible and our friendship possible: he understands what I tell him. He sucks it in with his wide-awake senses. To him I am the authority, fame, the champion, *the one who has done it,* everything he has dreamed of doing himself. Here he has a sports expert, one who's interested only in him, all to himself!

Still I'm afraid now and then that he'll lose his respect for me. I don't know, after all, what kind of stories he may be hearing about me around the prison, from the guards or the other prisoners. A violent criminal doesn't have a high rating, unless he's outright dangerous and, preferably, has enriched himself by his violence. A desperate bandit is much to be preferred to a wife-beater, judging by prison prestige. And the real enemies of society give rise to tales and legends: mail and visiting bans, constant searches, change of cell, discovery of secret communication lines to the outside, dismissal of guards involved—the worse the better. Then he'd respect me, sure—but now? A fellow who beats up his wife in the street, who doesn't even have enough common sense to do it at home where nobody can catch him and drag him to court for it?

I know the boys are talking. I notice their eyes. The fact that I was once a top sportsman makes their malicious glee even more sincere. But to try something—no, they don't dare. An oarsman's chest muscles are too well developed!

But fine snow is quietly falling outside, turning the residential neighborhood into a slumbering landscape of cottages; the straight asphalt roads narrow down to paths, and the people hurrying home loaded with shopping bags and financial worries limp and stumble on like old, doubled-up brownies and brownie wives after visiting the cow barn, where they've managed to filch a drop of milk and a spot of butter.

"That's all for today," Klaumann says, squinting down at his notes. "That is, if you have nothing more to add . . ." His irony is all that's left of the contact he's tried to establish. He's failed in this, and he knows it. I'm the one who'll suffer for it, I'm aware of that.

"There are only three consultations left; then I must write the report and the preliminary legal investigation can begin. But I guess you aren't

particularly interested in that either . . . ?"

No, that's just it. I'm not at all interested anymore, either in Klaumann or in the contact he represents with the "outside." I'm thinking of Reidar, of the surprise I have for him, and I look forward like a boy to the next hour of training in the gym.

10 He sees it the moment he gets there, and his face, red and fresh from the cold outside, lights up.

"Wow! Where did you get hold of *that?*"

In reality, it was quite simple to get the rowing apparatus installed here in the gym. I explained to the head guard that I had a used apparatus standing around in my store which I was quite willing to lend to the prison free of charge. I emphasized the great value of the contraption as an exercise tool, and he had no objections. I omitted mentioning that the rowing apparatus would be of great importance to Reidar in developing his boating coordination; for intense fraternization between a prisoner and a guard isn't taken lightly here, though it often happens that inmates make special friends among the guards— after all, guards and prisoners are somehow in the same boat here inside the walls, united in a form of shared life that must affect both parties. Besides, it's supposed to be part of a guard's task to help provide human contact; that's what the regulations say in any case, as far as I know.

"Gee, how elegant!"

He's right beside it at once and, true to form, wants to try it immediately, but I restrain him a bit, explain all the fine points, how the different loads function, how they can be regulated.

"Thanks!" he exclaims radiantly as he plops down on the sliding seat. "Real nice of you, wow!"

He hasn't the slightest doubt that I've gotten the apparatus for his sake. He and I understand each other perfectly.

"Careful now, don't spoil the kid for us," Bassen mumbles. He's the one who lets us out today. "You see, he gets so swellheaded from all the attention you give him that he'll soon be impossible to have around!"

Reidar blinks his eyes and turns red, pulls himself together to answer:

"It doesn't happen every day, you know, that a guy gets a job with a built-in trainer. You've got to grab the opportunity!"

"I guess you could use some training in more than one thing," Bassen teases him. It's an open secret that things aren't going too well between Reidar and his girl friend. Ludo is our chief informant, full of exaggerations and nasty cracks, for his own feathers are unruffled at the moment. And the Radish turns red and acts as if the whole thing were of no importance.

And it certainly isn't during the hours we can be together in the gym, where we try, with the modest means at our disposal, to plan a fairly systematic training program: running, coordination exercises, and some of the strengthening exercises he loves so much—there the results can be quickly *seen*. We must also work on the back, his weak point, where the rowing apparatus will help. In the gym with me he can work off his sexual frustrations and his vexation at being twitted by his colleagues. With me he's in good hands, with someone who wishes him nothing but the best.

"You're really great!" he'll say, laughing the way he doesn't dare when he can be seen by the guards, laughing the way he can laugh only with me, with whom he shares something. "Taking care of me like I was an infant prodigy or something . . ."

"Well, it helps keep me busy," I reply. "You know, time drags a bit now and then in my room . . ."

He reflects a moment, risks a direct question:

"When is your case actually coming up?"

"Don't know—I imagine in late March or early April. I got four months custody . . ."

"Why did you beat her up like that anyway?"

"Hm, that's hard to say . . . Well, first she kidnaped the child, just picked her up and vanished without a word; that got me both scared and angry, you know: imagine, first giving us the slip like that and then suddenly sneaking back months later to grab her rights, so to speak . . . Ugh! But it had been pretty rough going long before that, you know— it seemed like we couldn't talk, not about anything at all, and each time we tried we'd just start arguing, about God knows what. It was ridiculous. We weren't any good in bed either anymore, even if there, at least, we'd been doing fine all along . . . And so something snapped the moment I saw her there on the sidewalk with the child . . . It's not so easy for you to understand perhaps, but I just couldn't control myself. Too much pressure had built up, it had to come out. I'd been holding in too many things for much too long, hadn't been able somehow to express how miserable I felt *I* was, had only been listening to her complaints, right up to the moment she ran off . . . And so I blew my top . . . You see?"

He nods agreement, biting his lips and pushing his chin forward:
"Women are a damn nuisance!"

"After the twentieth we can start training twice a week," I tell him after a brief pause. "I convinced them that I need two hours a week for the sake of my physical fitness. The doctor who drops by here isn't at all bad. He backed me up."

"Fine, then we can run a tighter program!"

"We can try at least."

I place a comradely hand around his neck as we hear keys rattling—the signal from Ludo, who's back at his old place after a week of early duty.

"Jeez, what a hot friendship!" he grins. "Just look out or he'll get so fond of you he'll start treating you the way he treats his wife. Then some weird things could happen to that sweet puss of yours."

His laughter reverberates between the walls of the narrow corridor.

"Do you yourself have any explanation of how you suddenly could lose your head like that—I mean, since my models of explanation don't seem to meet with much favor . . . ?"

Knut Klaumann tries sarcasm today. I suppose he's beginning to grow rather tired both of me and of this job, which will soon be over. I feel I've told him as much as I can. Well, no, not really, but his way of asking questions, making it perfectly obvious what answer he expects and how *he* would prefer to understand the problem, sets up a situation where many things simply can't be said, both because I have such trouble finding the right words and because the reality behind what has taken place lies beyond what Knut Klaumann's clever clichés can reach.

"I understand that you must have begun to feel betrayed by her in some way and that this became clear to you quite concretely when she left home, but still I'd like to know . . ." I've tried to explain our language problems to him. I've told him about the bad feelings, the misunderstandings, the monotony. Should I tell him about the only picture that I still remember? Of her and Eli on the sidewalk, the mother kneeling, the daughter pressed against her with one hand on her shoulder, the mother tying the loose shoelace quickly and ably, then giving the little girl a friendly pat on the cheek, letting her hand rest on her head for a moment? A small scene, yet this succession of actions and facial expressions makes the harmony between them complete, totally annihilating the father and anybody else who might think they had a stake, a part, in the two of them . . . That *love* of theirs which they invoke with every expression and movement! That intuitive connection with all and everything, a sort of deeper and more fundamental understanding of all things, against all reason and logic. "What a horrible evening," she would say when we'd been out with friends having a good time, without a single dull moment, "don't you think so?" Then their demand that everybody else should be tuned in to the same wavelength: a mystical insight, like a dark, viscous stream of sensuality that connects them with the nightside of things. Take flowers. She always had a special relationship with flowers, was disappointed and insisted I didn't love her if I didn't notice she'd put flowers on the table. Or if I noticed them too late. Flowers! Out on those rocky beaches that first summer during a brief holiday week in August, after all the regattas when we really had a little time for each other for the first time and decided to join our lives, she used to pick fall flowers and put them in jars and glasses. One day when we lay sunbathing she suddenly ran over to an uninhabited cottage and picked a large bouquet of pansies that she began to decorate her hair and lap with. In the end the whole barque was full of pansies!

"Isn't it pretty," she laughed. "Isn't it terribly pretty?" And I said yes, though I've never liked pansies; they always remind me of darkness and death. They're flowers of mourning with their fleshy petals, their nocturnally dark color with a small melancholy glimpse of gold in the center. I'd have decorated her in that particular spot with something different than pansies if I'd been asked to. I'd have planted a maypole in her with laughter and song! A vigorous spring in August! But I said yes, how beautiful! How pretty! How pretty they are! And how pretty you are!

It was already starting then.

11 "It'll be coming up soon now," Reidar says. He means the trial. "I hear they're beginning the preliminary legal investigation next week."

"Yes, I had a visit from my attorney today, and he says the same thing." We're loosening up after some hard rounds of jogging with knees raised high. I've gotten him a new sweat suit. He looks gorgeous. In my mind's eye I can see him already at the regatta course, skipping along the dock on his toes before the competition starts.

"Too bad." He jumps into a handstand, an exercise he masters as naturally as walking on two legs. "What will happen with the training then? I mean, you'll be moved afterwards—it'll be Ullersmo prison for you, no doubt of that. Dangerous man and all!"

"Come on, let's do some push-ups," I command. "The first to fifty!"

He wins, of course. I have other things to think about. What he said hit me in my most vulnerable spot: I don't have much time left here in "The Manor." I can expect a sentence of at least two years, preventive detention to boot, perhaps. Prisoners with sentences of over nine months must do their time in a bigger institution, one of the national prisons. That is the rule, which nobody can get around. What about the training then? What about the conversations and our times together, which I've begun to appreciate so much? Can I stand the thought of sitting in prison for years without contact with this boy, this open, trusting kid with such a first-class talent for athletics?

"Perhaps I'll apply for a transfer to Ullersmo in a year and a half, when I'm finished," he laughs as we lie side by side on the mat catching our breaths. The sweat pearls on his smooth neck. His fresh fragrance suppresses the sour, stuffy institutional stench for a moment. "The training will be interrupted of course, but . . ." Under his flippant tone I can tell he's just as sorry as I am that this is coming to an end.

"God, imagine . . ." He even triggers my own dreams now: "Spring will be here soon and there sits the fjord . . . Imagine a fine new boat, not some old, warped in-rigger, light, not more than twenty kilos, fiberglass perhaps or carbon fiber, the very latest! Then you can do

2,000 meters in less than 6 . . ." The way he can daydream: "Have you ever rowed a double scull, you who are such an expert on single?"

"No, but it would be fun to try . . ."

I go on fantasizing at his invitation: he and I in a spanking new double scull, I in the stroke seat as the stronger and more experienced, he in the bow seat, adjusting his rowing to my instruction, the contact and understanding between us put to the test—for the rhythm can be spoiled by even trivial irregularities. And the fjord beneath and around us is a mirror broken only by the gentle, barely perceptible breeze, just right, which gives a good, steady thud to the hull, so helpful to row by . . . I see the preparations for the trip in my mind's eye, him and me bent over the map to measure off training laps and working to put up landmarks, until we are steady enough to row long distances by the clock. The preparation of the boat, the slim hull that has to be enameled and rubbed with silk rags . . . I spent ten years in a single scull, drove myself as far as I could and reached my limit, satisfied my ambition to be the best; it sufficed for a silver medal in Nordic and bronze twice in a row. Good enough for me, I'd made it, I was in the elite; I was at one with my boat, I functioned in the boat as if I were inside my own skin and liked it; nobody made decisions for me or directed me, everything depended on *my* concentration and *my* strength. Even on exercising trips after I was married and no longer active, I could get drunk, so to speak, on my sense of independence there in the boat; the boat and I were one and the same, we were and remained tops. In some strange way nothing else mattered when I was rowing . . . It took me twenty years to discover that life in a single scull can be lonely. Now I know I'm ready for a double scull together with Reidar.

"Do you know anything about these new boats? Carbon fiber, for example? They're supposed to be weightless . . ."

"No, I haven't rowed them, but I've read a bit about them in the journals. I'll be glad to get you some literature if you want. But the exact type of boat may not be the most important thing at the stage we're at now . . ."

You could have any boat you wanted, Reidar, if only we could go on training together!

"Shucks, I'd like to drop school and everything and just train; this is what I *know*, damn it, and what I want! Wish I could get out of here, away from the whole mess. Then I could do it right, get to be real good!"

You certainly could, Reidar, believe me!

The thought that we'll soon be forced to part obviously makes him, too, a little desperate. Before we leave he says, teasingly: "But you'd better sharpen up a bit on those push-ups; today you were trailing by ten!"

For thanks I thump his shoulders hard with my fist. From the adjacent room the clatter of the ping-pong table can be heard, a pastime for drifters or drug addicts who can't bring themselves to do anything else.

Prison is the ideal place for self-deception. One day is so like the next that you can imagine time standing still; you can manipulate your perception that the days are passing. I try to push away the thought of the approaching trial. Just two months ago I clung—without illusions but desperately—to the thought of this trial, my last contact with the real world before being buried in an institution for years. The preparation of my defense was to be the last and most effective cure against the prison sickness, that sneaking preoccupation with only what's near, with the mundane, your own person and the inmates and personnel in your proximity; loss of interest in everything outside, which I regarded as my degeneration and death. Now the center of gravity has changed. Now I have my life here in the prison, in the gym Monday and Wednesday—due to his companionship, the suspense I feel at the thought how he'll manage the programs I've put together for him, his progress, his trust in me and his gratitude. The feeling of being useful, of doing things for somebody the first time in my life perhaps and receiving so much in return. I think I felt something similar once in a while when I was alone with Eli, helping her with what she needed help with, doing the laundry, preparing some sort of dinner. But Eli had nothing to give in return except her helplessness, which increased my fear of falling short. With him it's just the opposite—every round that he runs, every springboard jump he does, is a confirmation that I too am worth something, and important at least to one person . . . I've ordered books through the library and am busy reading—quite a few years have passed since I trained systematically, and much has happened in the meantime. I do some exercises here in my cell, in order to keep up with him. I barely keep track of time passing and put off the thought of the trial, refusing to think of it between the visits—increasingly more frequent—of my attorney, who wants me to collaborate on a line of defense with him: he proposes emphasizing her irresponsible traits, her obvious dissatisfaction with the marriage, her inexplainable flight into a casual relationship, and later yet another one, and finally her reckless kidnapping of Eli, a step that would have been the last straw for any man, whether the marriage had worked previously or not—and since ours had worked only indifferently and she had, so to speak, systematically undermined my self-confidence, my identity, my loyalty to her, and had sorely tried my patience . . .

I say yes and agree. It's the truth when you come right down to it, even though it's difficult to recognize it in these words, in these surroundings. He says he believes we'll win the court's sympathy for the view that a man can be pushed only so far, that the case may, in fact, be one of diminished consciousness at the moment of the crime. Am I certain I wasn't under the influence of alcohol?

Even if I fight it, I realize more and more with what common sense I have left that the day is imminent; that means the door will be barred for Reidar and me, and it upsets me in a way I can't control. More and more often, I mingle suppressed sobs with the chorus of tears that always sends a sigh along the prison corridors in the evening. I break down in the middle of my last round of push-ups and lie writhing on the floor in my cell, completely overcome. I have problems sleeping, have had to ask for tablets, though I swore I wouldn't contribute to drug abuse in the prison—I despise the pill poppers in Cells 2 and 3 who get the DTs if they have to wait a paltry half-hour for their degressive rations. When Reidar isn't on duty I sometimes detain Bassen in my cell one half-hour after another, talking aimlessly about nothing at all from sheer restlessness. I listen as he tells me all about his family and his bit of a garden. He lives close enough to bike to work. He was offered one of the finest lots on Angels Slope but didn't want to live within view of the prison, understandably.

The consultations with Knut Klaumann have come to an end. I couldn't care less. The last thing he said to me was: "All right, then, we'll see how pleased you are when you hear it all in court . . ."

I'd even tried to tell him about this picture of her and Eli on the sidewalk, how it revolted me and still revolts me—that tenderness in her movements, her monopoly on delight in physical closeness, that damned *ability to love* that women claim to have, which makes them vague, impregnable, impenetrable, which covers up their subtle brutality, their selfishness . . . A hand on Reidar's perspiring neck means only what it means: it's honest, pretending neither to stop the revolution of the earth on its axis nor to eclipse the sun or still a storm on the ocean in the name of *love*.

He has told me he'll be posted in the carpentry shop for two weeks. I apply for a work permit right away. A detainee isn't required to work but may be granted a work permit if he wants to and can justify his wish. On the other hand, it means he must renounce his privileges as a detainee—no purchases with his own money, no personal belongings in the cell except for those allowed by regulations. I gladly renounce my privileges, if only I can be close to him a few hours extra every day. Every day!

I get the permit. They probably believe it might have a positive, stabilizing effect on me now that the trial is approaching. It's set for April 3. Just over two weeks away. Things are turning out well in the carpentry shop. I'm capable, with a knack for doing things with my hands. The garden furniture we put together is simple in construction. I work mostly with one of the "veterans" called the Bag. He's a cheerful, dry little fellow, an alcoholic grateful for these periods on the wagon inside. Outside, he cracks up after two days. He talks incessantly, is deft and quick. He makes frames for my tabletops.

Reidar is with the guards, wanders around, talks a little with everybody. Almost painful to see him like that, with a smile and a cheerful remark for everyone who troubles him about something. He has a gentle, obliging disposition that everybody finds charming. I realize with anguished gaiety that I'm suffering the torments of jealousy. But when he stops at my place as if to inspect my work, whispering, "Ten hard ones now!" while I'm planing, my uneasiness dissolves and I understand he puts just as much into the training program as I do. And back in my cell, alone, the long evening seems endless, yet passes too quickly, for tomorrow the separation has drawn closer by one more day . . .

12 The preliminary judicial examination has started. The days are suddenly filled with meetings, conversations, speculations. The assistant commissioner in charge of the investigation into my case has been here to interrogate me. It lasted two hours the first day, and he'll be back. They must get all the facts on the table, appraise and elucidate everything from all angles, before drawing up the indictment. For the prosecution the main question is whether the "assault" was planned. I reply no. Then they drag in the testimony of the student, how I went to see him the evening before the "assault," how we planned to show up outside the restaurant when she came to work, stationed ourselves in an entranceway across the street, made sure she couldn't see us from afar, and so on . . . That damn student! When I was interrogated after the arrest I gave his address in the feeble hope he'd be able to support my side of the story. Now it looks as if he has actually stacked the cards against me. I try to maintain that what I wanted most of all was to speak to her, get her to abandon her insane plan of carrying off Eli, and agree finally to the practical arrangements of the divorce. But I hear how thin and unconvincing my words sound between the naked walls of the visiting room; "skull fracture, a cracked jaw, knocked-out teeth and severe superficial injuries" seem to carry another kind of conviction and authority.

And then my attorney the same afternoon: "One point has remained unclear to me. Could you tell me, in strict confidence, whether you really feel *guilty*? Now and then as we talk about what happened, it's as if it didn't concern you at all, as if it happened to someone else . . ."

What can I answer to that? Of course I'm "guilty" in the sense that I know I've done something I shouldn't have done, inflicted serious injury upon another person, and I acknowledge that I must be punished for it. On the other hand, I don't see how I could have acted any differently. From the moment I jumped out of the entranceway into the street, my head filled with nothing but those two on the opposite sidewalk, my actions were subject to a logic I could neither resist then nor explain now. I was at war. I fought the battle of the sexes with my bare fists, a battle I'd fought evasively, fruitlessly, beset with counterarguments and guilt feelings, during ten years of marriage. Can my worthy elderly attorney understand that? Can the prosecution accept such an explanation? Can *anyone at all* understand what feelings the helpless, pale face of a nine-year-old girl can bring out in a father—feelings of bereavement and insult, grief over the loss of an entire dimension of existence, rage against the person who tries to block the attempt to save even the pieces? Between her and me everything was over, erased, burned out. But I'd begun to develop a friendship with Eli, after the pain of losing her mother had subsided. We'd begun to understand each other, tacitly and respectfully, and find our way toward a shared pattern of life. And while I was experiencing this strange joy of commitment that the responsibility for a child gives a man, this illogical pleasure at every extra load you'll never receive any compensation for and which, further, sets the chemistry going that imperceptibly, little by little, will change your life in a decisive and irrevocable way—while I was learning to experience this new way of being human, *she* came and . . .

"Perhaps you find it difficult to answer this question," my attorney says, accommodatingly; he's well-meaning enough, though only routinely interested. To him, the legal task is to convince the court that I didn't act on purpose and "with premeditation," regardless of what I did and what reasons I may have had for doing it. "In my time I've met many people charged with serious crimes who've been unable to connect what they did with their own persons. It's as if their shock at the consequences and their dismay at the deed itself created a sort of barrier that reason was unable to surmount . . ."

He stops when he sees that I put my head on the table, giving free rein to my tears.

The easy chair, the reading lamp, and most of my books have been removed from my cell now. The same applies to the two or three pictures I'd hung, and that's good. What's the point of trying to transform a prison cell at "The Manor" into the living room of a prefab private house at Ski? The parallels are conspicuous enough as they are. I'm extremely indifferent to my surroundings—in fact, aesthetic qualities have never meant a great deal to me. A bare room with a bed and washbasin, chair, table, and a toilet in the corner is, after all, all I need. Everything else reminds me of *her* pleasure in decorating, refurnishing, refurnishing again, buying new things for the kitchen and living room. The expense of it all and the boredom of having to take a stand, always choose this color and style or that, *this* high or a shade lower, or a bit more to the left . . .

In the cell I try to calm down a little, but it's not easy; I didn't see him either today or yesterday. Interrogations and conferences. My attorney was here for over two hours. Then it was dinner. Soup, pork and beans. I couldn't eat. Then Eilert came. I'd asked him to get ready to sell the house. Naturally I can't undertake any transactions at this point, until all the legalities have been cleared up, until the financial situation between her and me is clear, but I ask Eilert to explore the market for buyers. When the time comes, I assume she won't object to selling the house. She can't possibly live out there with Eli alone. She'll probably have to find a place in the city, near to where she can get a job, and to do that she'll need cash. But when Eilert came, my mind refused to concentrate on the practical aspects of selling a house; I stammered, got lost, finally asked him to inquire at the bank and in the real-estate market as best he could. He looked gravely at me and said: "Everything will be all right, you'll see. And now you've got to take it easy. You look just awful!"

And I who had the impression I was well-preserved! Reidar, in any case, has been anything but stingy with his compliments:

"You sure have a dandy pair of shoulders!"

His spontaneous admiration as he sat watching me lifting weights the last time we trained together. "It'll be a long time before I catch up with you there!" Then downcast: "Damn it, to have to quit now that we're well on our way—we should just run away from the whole mess and start by ourselves!"

Reidar, Reidar! Shall we escape together? Shall we get away from here to a place where we can have the peace and the right circumstances for doing a decent job?

It's only two days since I saw him, only pure chance that I haven't run into him somewhere, like the corridor, considering how much I've been on the move, but two days have passed and I can barely stand it!

I lie in my bunk trying to sleep. My heartbeat is so fast that my whole head echoes with it, faster, faster, faster. Should I call the guard and ask for a tranquilizer? Like those wretched creatures in No. 2 and 3 who blubber and cry and beg for valium and whatever it's called as soon as they feel a bit low? I must be able to pull myself together . . . When I close my eyes I see the commissioner's face blending into that of my attorney, I can hear their voices repeat the same empty, trite phrases over again.

". . . *must* surely have been haunted by the thought of taking the matter into your own hands, since you didn't report the kidnaping to the police—you can't deny that? . . . Clearly, you were pushed as far as a husband and father can ever be pushed, and that'll certainly get the court to accept . . ."

No!

With clenched teeth I try to suppress the dispute going on in my mind:

"Good night, good night, crawl under your coverlet stitched with carnations, trimmed with roses, with silver-white leaves from the raspberry hedge . . ." Little Eli's favorite jingle that I had to recite over and over again when she was lying exhausted, tear-stained and yearning for Mommy.

The peephole rattles: "My, you've turned in already? I've been put on evening duty instead of Ludo. Thought I might drop by . . ." He has never been in my cell before. Now and then he'd give me my coffee in the morning, during the early days when he walked around with the ward-boys in order to get acquainted. But he never came into my cell. Now I jump up and make room for him on the bunk, flustered like an old aunt, hoping he won't see I've been crying.

"I was just wondering if they've been riding you hard, I mean during the interrogations . . ."

"No, I guess it was no worse than usual. They just can't make up their minds whether I'm a psychopath or a cold-blooded murderer . . ."

"A helluva system," he mumbles. "Putting people into pigeonholes that way . . . Do you believe true justice really exists?"

"Well, among animals it's the right of the stronger—perhaps just as good. They don't kill each other within the species, at any rate. They arrange things practically and logically, according to the nature they've been given. When will people learn to do that?" I try to strike a more cheerful note: "Speaking of nature, how's the training coming along in the rooming house?"

"Just lousy . . ."

I knew, I'd heard it was over between him and his girl friend. But I want to hear it from him, over and over again.

"I wish I could get the hell out of this damn town, far away!"

You can, Reidar, with me . . .

"To Germany, for example! That's where they have the best boating clubs, the best equipment, with courses on every river and lake. Bet the two of us could make out real well in Germany!"

We still sit jabbering and daydreaming on the bunk for a little while before he has to go. He gets up, having to let out the card party in Cell 11. In his guard's uniform he looks younger than his age, a bit helpless and unfinished. In the gym he's full-grown, powerful, a big high-spirited blond boy with muscles that any professional athlete would envy. He appears dejected—I punch his back a bit:

"Tomorrow we train as usual."

"You bet . . ."

"Go skiing tomorrow. It snowed again today."

"I'm so bad at waxing my skis, they slip so easily on fresh snow . . ."

"Meaning a bigger load for your arms, think of that."

"My arms will be all right, but my back is a problem."

"Nonsense, it went nicely last time."

Finally he smiles: "If you say so, then . . ."

"Of course. I keep well posted, even if I am a psychopath . . ."

He becomes serious again: "How many times do we have left, do you think?"

Many, Reidar. As many as we want, if only I can put my plan into effect!

13 There are many ways of hurting yourself, going on sick leave, and getting into a hospital. But I have to be careful and choose the right one. In the workshop they look after the tools, and a guard always runs the band saw. The Bag explains: "It's because so many inmates try to disable themselves. A couple of weeks in the infirmary is better than this silo when spring comes . . ."

But chopped-off fingers isn't for me. They can't be repaired afterwards—I don't intend to make myself an invalid to get out of here.

It's madness, of course, to think like this, but it's also madness just to sit here listening as attorney and prosecutor turn your life into mincemeat, humbly waiting for your quota of forfeited liberty to be handed down: two years? three years plus preventive detention? At any rate, more than those magic nine months, which means transfer . . .

Out of despair and disgust at having to stand outside my own fate without the means or authority to intervene, a fanatical spite has sprung up in me: I'll show them, damn it! I won't allow them to break me! I won't allow them to crush a man who's still in his right mind! I still have strength! They haven't succeeded in transforming me into an animal, an obedient old dog who puts up with everything its master commands!

I've decided to escape. Not in a dramatic way with sawed-off prison bars and ropes made from knotted sheets. No, I've decided to escape by guile, fool them, outfox them. And I'll take Reidar with me.

The plan has ripened recently, in between weeping spells and attacks of the blackest despair. Needless to say, off and on I've abandoned the whole idea, laughed at it—it's just not feasible, I've read about escapes and attempts to escape; they never work . . . But something inside me continues this crazy train of thought. Considering an escape with Reidar, starting a new life with him, has become my only definite contact with something real, my only defense against the prison sickness, which has paralyzed everything that makes me an individual during the last few months. The bright points have been the hours of training with Reidar, but back in my cell the circle has become narrower, my thoughts emptier, my body lazier when I didn't make an extra effort—which was happening less and less often . . . And after several years behind the walls without Reidar, I can hardly imagine myself as an active, dynamic person anymore; then a helpless amoeba, an aged, reduced and self-centered specter will be all that's left of what once was a man.

And so for the last couple of weeks I've been wavering between a grimly humorous optimism and deep depression. But my plan has taken shape—in bright moments I've felt some of the same excitement, suspense, and desire to win as before a regatta in my days as an active athlete.

I haven't discussed my plan with Reidar, naturally. He's so young, so inexperienced, his face is like a book. If he found out something now, beforehand, he'd ruin it all. So I'll have to start the preparations myself and trust that he'll show up when the time comes to strike. And he will, without the shadow of a doubt!

I'm eating soap. Have been doing so for some time already, in order to test the result, and it's exactly what I hoped for: nausea, dizziness, lack of appetite. In the cell, of course, you don't have a great many possibilities for making yourself sick if you must decide yourself *how* sick you want to be; sick enough to be admitted, and then . . . First I thought for a while about paint from the walls or plaster from the cracks in the floor, but it was too unpractical, too easy to detect. Soap is the perfect substance in every way: easy to get down—a bit of shrinkage passes unnoticed—and with such a disgusting taste that nobody would seriously think a person could make himself swallow it. But I have. I've eaten soap. It works.

Smaller institutions like this don't have their own infirmary, and the prison hospital is far away. A sudden case of illness is often treated in the town hospital, in any case where "light" prisoners are concerned. The surveillance of such prisoners is also taken more lightly. To escape from the hospital is as easy as a polka.

"You seem a bit weak today—is it tiring to go around waiting like this?" Reidar is bouncing around like a rubber ball. We're training for suppleness to compensate what he lacks in leg length, though on the rowing apparatus I notice that he has plenty of strength there too. The boy is simply unique.

"Guess I'm not in the best of shape. Been feeling a bit off lately. A trip to Germany would help, I think . . ."

He grins. I feel the sweat pouring off me. No wonder I'm weak, having escalated the soap dosage so I'm barely able to swallow food anymore. The spells of nausea are nearly defeating me. Bassen saw me standing doubled-up over the toilet this morning, giving back my morning coffee, and kindly asked if I was ill. I replied I'd felt a bit poorly for some time.

The way I've planned it I'll have a minor breakdown just before the trial, recover sufficiently to squeak by the first day—so there's less of a chance that someone will think I'm faking it out of fear of the trial itself—and then go down for the full count. The case will have to be postponed and I'll have time to recover a bit before the escape. My escape, and his. I feel I'll be able to plot its course quite precisely. As an athlete I have an intimate sense of my body, and I think I already know the degrees of the soap's different effects. Though I haven't taken much yet, it has thrown me off balance, and I feel sick and miserable. What if I doubled the dosage?

"Do you need a doctor?" Bassen is sheer benevolence.

"No, thanks, I think it'll go away . . ."

Better not overdo it. Not yet.

214   The trial is set for Thursday, April 3. That suits me perfectly. I can have my collapse on the weekend.

Saturday, exactly one week before D-day, I begin to increase the dosage, nibbling long shavings of hand soap, washing my hands well afterwards to erase the tooth marks while I try to breathe deeply and evenly with my mouth shut tight, concentrating on keeping the poison down. My aversion for the taste and smell has gradually built up so as almost to overcome me, but as an athlete I know how you can overcome even the impossible. I nibble soap, slurp it up and swallow it with water, trying as best I can to control my revulsion, the vomiting.

I've noticed a touch of diarrhea all week, but after increasing the soap dosage I'm running all day while my stomach cramps keep me doubled up in a knot: I throw up my dinner, throw up my supper. The guard, one of the mean boys—a fat, close-cropped fellow named Olsen and nicknamed Ass-Olsen—peeks in and grins broadly: "Christ, you'd better pull yourself together, Ali, or I'll blab to the cook about this!"

Sunday I lie in my bunk with fever and stomach pains. Monday I ask Bassen, who is on guard, to send for a doctor.

"None too early," Bassen mumbles warmheartedly. "You've been looking like a ghost all week!" The doctor has his office hours in the prison Monday morning. I've figured out everything.

After the examination he asks the usual questions: How long has the condition lasted? Have I had anything similar before? Have I eaten or done anything out of the ordinary lately? He thinks it looks like poisoning but can't say for sure till he's taken some tests. We have to wait and see if the condition takes a turn for the worse. If that happens I must let him know. I promise to do that. I know, after all, that my condition will improve, little by little . . .

I lie dozing between attacks of vomiting all afternoon. There's been a change in the weather outside, a spring day in March suddenly. I can tell from the light that falls obliquely across the ceiling through the window, which is tilted in such a way that you can only glimpse a narrow strip of sky. The low sunbeams gild the flaky yellowish-white paint on the ceiling and walls. Time for an oarsman to start thinking about his equipment, enameling the boat and the oars, silk rags up and down the slim, golden laminated body . . . Soon the fjord will be lying clear as a mirror beneath us and around us, broken only by an almost impercepti-ble breeze that flicks little waves against the delicate hull with small, plopping rhythmical thumps . . . He and I in the double scull—he in the bow, I in the stroke seat—the words between us a murmur above the level water between the rhythmical, rippling heave of the oars: ten hard ones every other minute, twenty hard ones . . . a spurt to do 2000 meters in less than 6 minutes . . . Spring already out here on the fjord, while the frost of winter grips the shoreline, holding on tightly . . . He and I in the elegant boat, no thicker than skin, the two of us with one resolve, motivation, and motion; words are superfluous, the boat, our technique, and the clock decide, along with our strength and rhythm: a unity that surpasses all other intercourse.

Spring on the fjord, the boat with its oarsmen, and the ice still lingering along the shore . . .

Wednesday I'm on my feet again and swallow a little food, though my stomach doesn't quite work as it should. But the vomiting and the headaches have subsided.

In the late morning he drops in:

"Hear you're sick in bed?!"

"I'm up again now . . ."

"But are you . . . Will you be well enough to train tonight?"

"I'll give it a try, anyhow."

"It'll be our last time, won't it . . . ?"

Oh no, Reidar. Not the last! Quite the opposite. My plan is working perfectly!

It turns out to be a strange training period, Ludo being with us most of the time, as if he sensed that something special was afoot: "I have to make sure our patient here doesn't have a collapse suddenly. After all, he'll be in court tomorrow and Saturday in the newspapers, in VG . . ."

And so we don't get to talk much, even less than usual. From my viewpoint it's just as well, knowing what's going to happen and that I can't give myself away. But he clearly suffers from being under sur-veillance, is stiffer than usual, finds it hard to do many of the exercises he's never had any trouble with. Ludo watches skeptically: "Actually a nice little service on the part of this institution, letting you two run a regular workout institute by yourselves . . ."

What if he knew that this "service" has given me a new life!

He sees to it that we quit on the dot: "Have to make sure the patient

gets the rest he needs—he'll be taking a ride tomorrow, you know . . . Actually he shouldn't even have left his cell today, the way he carried on yesterday. But some get special treatment . . ."

"Oh shut your trap a moment, Ludo. Ali is okay again, can't you tell!"

Thanks, Reidar, for trying to stick up for me. If you only knew how my knees are trembling!

We have to part at the guardroom as usual.

"Take care, I'll drop by this weekend to see how things are going. Good luck!"

"They'll probably go to wrack and ruin—'bye!"

There isn't time or space for more, with Ludo between us. I feel very sorry for him as he slinks into the guardroom, thinking that this is the end. Not knowing that it is only the beginning!

14 The first day of the trial is spent in an attempt to arrange my sense impressions. First, the automobile ride to the court building, with street noise, people's voices, the bustle of the city through the barred windows of Black Maria, the paddy wagon. I myself spruced up in my best suit, which has grown a bit tight; I guess I've put on weight in prison, after all.

From "a peaceful small institution" in a neighboring town to the commotion of the capital. Then the throng in the courtroom, which breaks up the monotonous somnambulism of prison life and produces a vacuum of fear and bewilderment in the soul. Besides, I'm still indisposed and feeble after the soap cure. The curiosity and suspense that this event made me feel, in spite of everything, have gone. My only desire is to get away from this place and begin the second and decisive act of my escape.

But I'm stuck here and they swarm at me, my attorney, the psychiatrist—unrecognizable in suit and tie—and the assistant commissioner who interrogated me. And then *she*—at the last moment she sneaks onto the bench beside the prosecutor and the commissioner, taking good care not to look my way. She still has an inflamed blue mark diagonally across her nose and discolored patches around her right eye. She's pale and has let her hair grow. I have the impression that a stranger is sitting there and can't understand how she was able to kindle such a rage in me, small and insignificant as she is. For some reason I think about Reidar's fresh face and strong, athletic figure.

The first couple of hours are filled with wearisome formalities that I, in my condition, can follow only with difficulty. I understand that the indictment alleges willfulness but that the section of the charge concerning attempted murder has been dropped.

Then a pause, in which my attorney leans back and speaks encouragingly to me in a low voice. That they've dropped the attempted murder charge means, in his opinion, that the battle is already half won.

The rest of the day is spent listening to statements by the prosecutor and defense attorney in favor of and against the indictment. According to the prosecutor's view, the assault, whose "repulsive brutality" he emphasizes at every opportunity, was premeditated and took place in exceptionally aggravating circumstances, the expression of a mentality of violence for which he hopes the court will mete out the deserved punishment. The defense attorney, on the other hand, considers me a good, law-abiding citizen, hard-working and conscientious, one whose sense of decency and proportion—if not quite simply my entire identity as a husband and a human being—was gradually so sorely provoked in the course of a long, unhappy marriage that an explosion eventually had to come. And that it came in connection with the dramatic circumstances surrounding my wife's flagrant kidnaping of our daughter, shouldn't surprise anyone . . .

Then it's Knut Klaumann's turn. He rattles out his report from a bundle of typewritten sheets. He's found the defendant to be well equipped intellectually, but inarticulate, inhibited, and reluctant to collaborate when under observation, which, together with a number of other symptoms, such as an exaggerated need for self-assertion, arrogance, and general emotional deficiency, points toward psychotic traits in the defendant's personality. The defendant's sex life must be characterized as normal, though the observation has brought to light a strong latent aggressiveness toward his wife, an aggressiveness that the defendant tends to transfer to all women. On the whole, the defendant seems to feel most comfortable in the company of men, in an existence structured by masculine principles and standards of value, though there's no question of any homosexual tendency in the usual sense. Despite the defendant's explosive temperament, poor emotional endowments, and a paranoid unwillingness to cooperate under test conditions, the observation has brought to light nothing that suggests the defendant wasn't fully conscious and aware of his actions when he attacked his wife outside the restaurant Bel Ami on the morning of November 21."

"That one's worse . . . ," my attorney mutters, more to himself than to me, as he gathers up his papers after the first day's proceedings. I have my own thoughts as I stand with trembling knees beside the police officer in my somewhat tight trousers: "So that's what you got out of it, Knut Klaumann—but we'll see if it will help you any. We'll see who comes out on top!"

"Psychotic traits, a paranoid personality and emotional deficiency—doesn't sound very good . . ." The policeman who's supposed to look after me lectures expertly in my ear. "You'll probably get preventive detention."

I've spent a sleepless night at "Number 19." Fortunately, tonight I'm going back home to "The Manor." Even if the effects of eating soap have subsided by now, I feel miserable. I'm not even curious about the witnesses, not about anything anymore, only wish I were back in my cell where I can prepare everything for the escape. But the second day's proceedings are in progress, starting with the examination of the witnesses. My wife, behind dark glasses today, listens intently: the headwaiter at Bel Ami is relating how she conducted herself on the job, that she was quick and accurate. Then he relates his own version of what took place on the morning of November 21. There's nothing particularly new to me in his account, apart from one detail: that during the scuffle I'm supposed to have "growled and snapped like an animal." Indeed, I may have.

The defense attorney gets his round of questions. What were her relations with the clients like, especially with one particular steady lunch guest? Wasn't it a fact that her acquaintance with this special client gradually assumed more regular forms? Was there, in the opinion of the witness, anything conspicuous in the way this relationship developed?

The prosecutor objects to the question as irrelevant. The defense attorney replies that the wife's moral character can in no way be said to be irrelevant in this case.

Then it's the student's turn. He looks even more wretched and browbeaten than I remember. With nervous gestures and in a hesitant, barely audible voice he relates how they met, that an affair developed and they decided to live together, how they gradually drifted apart from each other when a new man entered the picture, and that she finally packed her things and moved out. Yes, he has often heard her refer to the defendant as "brutal," though he cannot recall her mentioning specifically in what way he was brutal. He had the impression that she was scared to meet the defendant. His own impression of the defendant: friendly and straightforward, as far as that goes—he didn't have the feeling that the defendant was planning a direct assault, he didn't seem exceptionally agitated or unbalanced in any way. But they *had* planned to surprise her, place themselves in ambush so to speak, that was true. What was the point of that unless the defendant intended to use force? Hm, well, he had the impression the defendant was afraid she'd refuse to meet him, refuse to talk to him—considering the situation that had arisen after the kidnaping of the child, that wasn't so strange perhaps . . . But he wants to emphasize that he himself tried to prevent what happened when he understood they were headed for trouble: he'd called out to her, tried to warn her when the defendant ran across the street in an obviously agitated state . . . He sends apprehensive glances in my direction.

The defense attorney asks him if he hadn't felt she made a fool of him when she suddenly started a new relationship, if she had been sincere with him, put all her cards on the table and made him wise to the situation, or if she'd simply been unfaithful to him but fooled him into thinking they were still lovers while already having an affair with her new friend . . . These questions are clearly very painful to the student; he stammers and has trouble finding words. In the end it becomes apparent that he did feel betrayed by her and has at times been extremely bitter. The crisis he went through after their relationship was dissolved made it difficult for him to resume his studies.

The prosecutor objects: it's the assault we're here to throw light on, not the sexual conflicts of the witnesses. Moreover, he finds it dubious, to put it mildly, that his opponent is endeavoring to undermine the court's confidence in the wife's conduct. One ought to bear in mind her difficult situation at this time, as she's starting to build a new life for herself and her daughter after her long illness.

I've already heard: she has applied to nursing school.

The third witness is the lunch guest. That mysterious new friend who outmaneuvered the poor student. He's well-dressed and looks good but is very nervous, declares he's been unemployed during the last year because of psychological problems. A couple of attempts at holding down a permanent job have led to a relapse. He's seeing a doctor regularly and they have discussed hospitalization. He describes his relationship with her as a casual acquaintance in which she always took the initiative and, as the active party, in effect forced the acquaintance into a sexual relationship. When she moved into his apartment, it was completely on her initiative. Yes, he too has heard her speak of the defendant as "brutal," and she also hinted he'd laid hands on her, without going into detail. He assumes that such episodes are not uncommon between married people. He's divorced himself. He describes her as an unusual woman, whose behavior toward the student she lived with he finds especially astonishing. He would characterize it as rather ruthless. He relates how they once had intercourse on the living-room sofa while the student was sleeping in another room. He says he knew she had a child from her marriage but was horrified when she turned up with her daughter one day, and realized she'd simply carried her off without the defendant's consent and intended to keep her. His attempt to make her listen to reason failed, and he could see no alternative but to tip off the police where she and her daughter were to be found. It was that very morning, November 21. He wanted to remain anonymous, didn't want to get mixed up in anything, was only relieved to put an end to this affair, which had developed into something far more binding and problematic than he had originally intended . . .

It's interesting to see her reactions during this last testimony. The moment he gives his name, her tears begin to flow. She has to take off her sunglasses and dry her eyes continually while he speaks. When he steps down from the witness stand, she hurriedly leaves the room. It strikes me that these witnesses, these men, the prosecutor's witnesses, have in reality strengthened my case, not hers.

"Anyway, it is anything but a lily-white ingénue we're dealing with, judging by the facts of the case. We'll have to go on that. Have a pleasant weekend!"

My attorney snaps his folder shut. The policeman signals to me that we too will be leaving. "Perhaps you'll be spared preventive detention, after all," he muses nonchalantly as we make our way toward the side exit. "Really, such a woman could bring a poor devil to the point where he might do anything, no matter what . . ."

I ask for permission to go to the john.

"All right, but leave the door open."

I take a leak and stealthily nibble a few soap shavings while washing my hands.

On the way back to "The Manor" in Black Maria I go into vomiting fits, and by the time we get there I feel really sick. It's Friday night and Ass-Olsen is on duty. He grins: "A little green around the gills after facing the machinery of justice, eh? That's the sort of thing you risk, you know, by trying to use strong-arm tactics."

Saturday I eat soap as often and as much as I can stand. Vomit and eat. My stomach pains make me writhe and groan in my bunk. Vomit and excrement everywhere. The head guard and the doctor drop in to see me. I get some medication and am placed under observation, but I manage to swallow a little more soap during the evening and night. Sunday my condition is just as bad and, besides, my fever has risen. It's decided that I'll be hospitalized, so the necessary tests can be taken. When they want to summon the ambulance I protest: I'm not so sick I can't be transported in a regular car. The reason is that I have to take along my own clothes—you can't escape anywhere in prison pajamas!

15 I share my room with an elderly man who's just been operated on for stomach cancer. That means, as far as I understand, that he has been opened and sewed up again and that they've done all within their power to make his last few weeks as free of pain as possible. He usually lies in a motionless coma, and only faint clucks from his glucose bottle reach me now and then. He's the ideal fellow patient, leaving me free to do what I want.

They've taken their tests. God knows what they do with them, but I'm careful to eat enough soap to maintain my high temperature. At the same time I make an effort to hold down some of the food they give me, for fear I might otherwise be put on intravenous feeding, which would be a snag, to put it mildly.

The nurse who takes care of us is young and friendly. The badge on her breast says her name is E. Holme. "Eva . . . ?" I try, "Evy," she corrects me. She wears glasses and has about the same build as my poor disfigured wife, but she's fifteen years younger. Between attacks of nausea I lie here contemplating the wonders a nurse's uniform can work on the female figure and feel more strongly than ever before during my prison stay how long it has been since the last time.

It's Monday and I try to rest up and relax. Tuesday is D-day.

On his rounds, the doctor comes in together with the head guard.

"It isn't so easy to figure out what's really wrong with you," he says. "Meanwhile the trial has been postponed for a week, and by then we'll have you on your legs again."

"Just ask them to go on without me," I jibe. "Nobody listens to a paranoid psychopath anyway . . ."

Before they leave I ask the guard if he could send up the folder with the private papers I left behind in my cell. I explain I've been arranging the sale of the house through my business manager and need some pertinent documents; he's been notified. My attorney has been in contact with my wife, who has agreed to this solution. He has also arranged for the transfer of some money to her account for the present. Until all the formalities have been taken care of. The guard promises to have the papers sent up tomorrow.

"Let Reidar drop by with them," I propose. "Anyway, I'd be glad to talk with him about his training—now that I can no longer be there and look after him."

"All right." The head guard is somewhat of a sports enthusiast himself. He understands.

After supper E. Holme comes in with a tablet and a glass of water: something to sleep on. I say thank you but don't touch it. I must have a clear head tomorrow, can't risk a pill hangover. Besides, I think I'll sleep well here in the hospital. The prison stench has been replaced by the antiseptic ether of the ward. The bedclothes are white, smooth and comfortable. I haven't eaten soap since the last time my temperature was taken and feel better. And E. Holme whispers sweetly good night and wriggles her round bottom through the doorway as she leaves. My God! In prison, women are the perennial topic of conversation, the erection every man's pastime, and masturbation a team sport in which everyone is encouraged to participate. It's been part of my struggle against the prison sickness to try and stay away from this form of companionship too, and though I have obviously not succeeded in being consistent, I have at least held back a bit, tried to steer my own course. But here . . . I can't recall the last time I grabbed hold of it in my bunk.

Improvement Tuesday. The fever's down. No vomiting. The condition satisfactory both for me and the doctor: "Tomorrow we'll transport you back to the luxury hotel again if you continue to recover at this rate . . ."

But I have other plans. I'm expecting Eilert any moment. I called—by permission of the head guard—asking him to come up as soon as possible to discuss the details of the house sale. I asked him to take my car, which has been used by the business since I was locked up. The trip by car up here takes an hour and a half. I've gotten up, slipped into a robe, and sit waiting for him in the visiting room. We can't receive anybody in the ward, except during the visiting hour from one to two.

He shows up at twenty past eleven, even more flustered and con-fused than usual: "Goodness, what are you doing in the *hospital*? I didn't know what to think when you called, I . . ." He perches ner-vously on the extreme edge of the chair I point to and follows everyone walking by with his eyes.

"I guess I've caught something . . ."—I try to make light of it. "But I'm better now . . ." I don't want to give him the impression that I'm perfectly healthy.

"I've read about the case. They're coming down just as hard on her as on you, aren't they?"

"Well, that's what we're hoping, my attorney and I . . ."

"And what will be the verdict, you think?"

"No idea—if I escape preventive detention I'll be back in the store selling in a year's time. Perhaps . . ."

"Goodness—that would be great!"

"Meanwhile we have to try and take care of some practical matters . . ."

I talk and act as confidently as if I were sitting outside my body and running it like a machine. Way at the back of my head somewhere I realize how insane my enterprise is, how infinitely small the possibility that everything will work out right, how much I stand to lose by taking a chance like that, the business, the income from the house sale—which will go mainly to her anyway, regardless—my homeland and friends, just about all I've got. But the picture of Reidar and me in a double scull on the Rhine, on the Elbe, on the Lahn, has got stuck on my retina, and everything else has become gray and unimportant. I've read somewhere that suicides also feel this way: once the decision has been made, they can behave quite normally, even cheerfully and vivaciously, while all the time preparing, in calculated detail, their last and ultimate coup . . .

I tell Eilert I've received a tip that the real estate department of the local bank has good contacts, suggest he bring the necessary papers and set up a conference with them: "It's right up the street. You can just leave the car in the parking lot down here for a while. And you'll drop by again and tell me how it went, won't you?"

He has always done everything I tell him.

It's a quarter past twelve. Reidar may be here any minute now. If I'm not mistaken, the head guard will send him up during dinner break. There's nothing of importance for the house sale in the folder he's bringing, but nobody knows that.

Evy comes mincing by: "Well, well, so you're *that* spry today?"

"Not bad," I smile, "but perhaps I've been a bit too optimistic. I think I'll stretch out on my bunk again for a while . . ."

In the corridors the ambulatory cases tramp around with crutches, canes, and walkers.

My roommate snores quietly. I start dressing in a hurry. The time is drawing near. Just wait, Reidar. I have a surprise for you. A big surprise!

I notice that the uphill work has taken its toll; my hands are trembling and I can feel beads of sweat breaking out. But my stomach pains and the fever are gone, and I'm only a few minutes from my goal . . .

When he knocks and enters I'm perched on the edge of my bunk, fighting dizziness while trying to tie my shoelaces.

"Hi! They said it was all right to walk in, since I was bringing a message from the Big Boss." He comes up to me, bright-faced and fair-haired, throws the folder on the bed as if he, too, understood it was just a pretext to allow us to meet: "I read everything I can find about your case. The boys think you might get off easier . . . Why, you're up, dressed and all? And I thought you were lying here at death's door . . ." After taking a closer look at me he notices the perspiration on my face. "Are you having a hard time tying your shoelaces? Look here, let me help you." Kneeling before me he ties my laces, quickly and deftly. I place a hand on the nape of his neck as I get up from the bed and let my hand rest there in this crucial moment:

"Listen," I tell him, and my voice seems to come from far away, though it's still controlled: "We don't have much time . . . We're going to cut out, Reidar! We'll get away from prison and trial and the whole caboodle here, go to Germany where we can find the time we need to train properly, just like we've talked about!"

I can see by his face, close to mine, that he finds it difficult to grasp the substance of what I'm saying, so I continue, talking at breakneck speed as if it were urgent to get it all said before he has a chance to voice his reaction: "I've planned everything! Listen to me: there's a car down in the hospital parking lot, a blue Audi. It's mine. You go down and get it, and drive it up in front of the entrance. Meanwhile I'll simply walk down the stairs and stroll out. It'll soon be visiting hour, lots of people. It can't fail! Nobody will recognize me in these clothes anyway, they'll think I am a visitor. With the folder and all! Won't they?"

He hasn't said anything yet, but a big sneer of distrust begins to pinch his open features. "Listen, will you . . ."—I'm getting desperate. I've figured out we have roughly an hour before it will be discovered. By that time we have to be well on our way to the Swedish border. "Reidar! I've figured out everything. You'll find the car key inside the duct directly underneath the door on the driver's side, a magnetized reserve key. It shouldn't present any problems. Then I'll come out and we drive off! I have money too—you don't have to worry about that, I've thought of everything. My own bank account is frozen, but not hers. It's a joint account, and only a couple of days ago 35,000 kroner were transferred to it. We can use those! They should last two or three months at least. I have a checkbook in the glove compartment . . . Do you understand? It's completely safe, watertight! Before they find out, we'll be out of the woods and on our way to Sweden! And from Göteborg there are boats to Denmark and Kiel all day! What do you say, Reidar? Come on—let's not waste any more precious time!"

His face, which blushes so easily, is now quite pale:

"You really plan to *escape?*" He pronounces it as if it were the most disgusting word in the language. "And you think I should run away with you?"

"*Yes!* And we don't have time to stand here jawing much longer!"

"But damn it, Ali, what made you think I would take part in anything so absurd?!"

"*Think?* You haven't talked about anything else. How you longed to go to Germany, to train on the big rivers. How lovely it would be if we two . . ." My voice suddenly gives out. I know I've lost, but it is impossible to follow that thought through to its conclusion. I *must* get him to go with me. With trembling knees and sweat pouring down my temples, I feel like I have to clutch his shoulder to keep from falling:

"Reidar—don't you see what an opportunity this is for you, for both of us? You have talent, I'm telling you. You have the stuff to become one of the very best! And I could get you up among the best if only you'd let me! But two or three years in the can will ruin everything, can't you see that?"

He, too, is excited now:

"And helping a violent criminal escape and joining him in the escape, that won't ruin anything, right?"

"You're thinking too narrowly—we'll start over again in Germany! I have good business connections there. In a year we'll be partners both in business and in the boat!"

"Bullshit!" He pushes my hand away from his shoulder. His movement is so abrupt I almost lose my balance, have to cling to him with both hands:

"Reidar—you can't let me down! Do you hear?"

Feeling him tense his body to free himself, I throw both my arms around his gorgeous neck, cling close to him, bury my face in the hollow of his throat, hear his pulse beating and my own voice begging and whimpering: "Reidar! You've got to! *You've got to!*"

"Damn it all, man, pull yourself together!" He grabs both my upper arms, tears himself away from my grip—he's strong!—and pushes me backward against the bed. "Are you one of those sneaky old fags, or . . . ?"

It's over. Everything is over. I can only lie on my back on the bed watching him go. Hearing him go. Hearing the last breathless words over his shoulder:

". . . And if you hatch any other stupid plans, you can be damn sure I'll report this. Every single word!"

Then he slams the door, making the glucose bottle of the cancer patient produce a gurgle.

The end. Nausea. Misery. A sneaky old fag who can look forward to three years plus preventive detention. Exhaustion. Impossible to register the magnitude of the disaster.

Gentle Evy Holme appears in the doorway: "Why, you're already dressed? Don't you think it's a bit early? You were still running a fever this morning. And you really look quite fagged out. Look here, let me at least help you take off your shoes . . ."

She comes up close.

"Feel here, sister . . ."

I take her hand and place it on my fly, so she can feel the fine erection I have from the incident a moment ago; not bad for an old fag!

"What kind of a cure do you have for that one?"

I assume this is a situation that every nurse encounters several times in the course of her career and that a kind of professional ethics requires them to treat such cases as discreetly as possible, without any kind of fuss. I want to take advantage of this; I can remember making out well with similar shock maneuvers before in my life. I slip my hand under her uniform skirt and up her tights, until I feel the edge of her panties. She stands quite still, as if she were holding her breath: it's working! I grab a good chunk of her round bottom with my hand, whispering: "Don't be scared, it won't bite you if you stroke it a little . . ."

Then she reacts at last, trying to step back from the bed, but I have such a firm hold on her that she can barely move: "No, please. And you aren't even well!" With a sad gravity in her voice that I find hard to take seriously and in any case can't interpret as an absolute refusal.

"Oh, you know, certain parts of me don't have much wrong with them . . . !"

"Listen—don't be childish! I understand you're having a difficult time right now, but things like this will only get you into more trouble . . ." Her voice is professional and cool, but she still attempts a smile, extends her hand to stroke my forehead and pats my hair with tenderness and love, the way a mother pats her sleeping child. A woman has so much love and patience that she can stroke the man who molests her and smile at him through her glasses! It's insufferable! I think of Reidar who stamped out of here in a temper: "Women are a nuisance!" and now this smile!

With the hold I have on her behind I jerk her close to me while directing a blow at her diffidently smiling face with my right fist: Away with that suffering smile! Away with that self-sacrificing tenderness! Away with that sickly-sweet, unselfish love, so-called, on which women have a monopoly and which all fucked-out poor devils think they need more than anything else in the world! This "love" which makes them invulnerable, impregnable, impenetrable to a man's reason, to his will and innermost desire!

I put all my hatred, all my self-righteousness and lust for revenge, into this blow, which hits her with terrific force below the ear—her head is flung sideways. She loses consciousness with a sigh and falls forward, over me, and lies motionless with her head dangling over the edge of the bed as if her neck were unhooked from its joint.

There is a gurgle from the glucose bottle of my fellow patient.

I lie here thinking about Reidar. Whether he'll ever apply for a transfer to Ullersmo. Oh, yes—he and I somehow belong together now. Sure he'll come to Ullersmo. When nobody remembers anymore an insane oarsman who killed a young nurse because she wore glasses that resembled his wife's. Then we'll again be able to train together, though perhaps not with the idea of competing among the elite, but I can still turn him into a fairly good oarsman. It will keep me occupied during a long prison life, and help him avoid the worst prison sicknesses, obesity and indifference toward himself, poor posture and bad manners. A sportsman always carries himself well. We'll keep company throughout the years, the way the inmate and his keeper somehow must share their fates, become one in a strange way: I'll grow old and he'll grow up. I'll die early, because something in me is dying already. But I'll still take great pleasure in his gorgeous body for many years—you don't often find a physique like that in an ordinary youth! In our many years together at Ullersmo we'll develop habits, good and bad, more or less like any other married couple. He'll marry and have children—I couldn't save him from the Tampax world—but it's with me, in the prison with me, he'll spend most of his active hours, and we'll still be able to joke together and say that women are a damn nuisance. And when the time draws near for me, some evening after the TV program is over and all the inmates have been locked up in their cells again, he may still take a few minutes of his evening watch to sit on the edge of my bunk and talk a bit about this and that with an old convict, perhaps the oldest on the row. And if sleep should overcome me while he sits there, freezing my glance and silencing my breath, just as the breeze would suddenly drop while you were in the middle of the fjord some day in July, he'll close my eyelids and wrap the blanket around my shoulders before he goes to call the doctor and write his report. Surely he would, he'd wrap the blanket well around my shoulders and breathe a few soothing words, as if to comfort me: "Good night, good night, crawl under your coverlet . . ."—words that aren't needed anymore, because there's nobody there to hear them. Yes, he'll place a hand on my forehead and close my eyelids, tuck me in nicely and whisper good night. Like a friend. Like a son. Like a brother. It's a comfort.

Sverre Lyngstad

AFTERWORD

Knut Faldbakken (b. 1941) began his writing career in the mid-1960s, a moment of change in Norwegian literature. In 1966, a group of young writers associated with the magazine *Profil* (*Profile*)—Dag Solstad (b. 1941), Espen Haavardsholm (b. 1945), Tor Obrestad (b. 1938), and others—initiated a belated wave of European modernism in Norway, where, with some notable exceptions, literature had remained relatively untouched by formal experimentation. But the modernist experiment was to be short-lived; by 1970, the above-mentioned writers, now a left-wing splinter group of Marxist-Leninists, had abandoned programmatic modernism in favor of a politically committed literature. For an entire decade, a phalanx of ideologues dominated the Norwegian literary scene, using their influence to promote a local variant of socialist realism.

Faldbakken, who spent ten years abroad during this period (1965–75), was not involved with the ideological movement. Most of his fiction, from his first novel, *Den grå regnbuen* (1967; *The Gray Rainbow*), to *Glahn* (1985), follows a realistic aesthetic. Norwegian realism, which emerged in the 1870s and 1880s with the bourgeois dramas of Bjørnson and Ibsen and the family and social novels of Kielland and Lie, is characterized by a tendency toward social criticism, but usually without an ideological underpinning. Faldbakken deepened the realistic perspective through psychoanalysis, as Sigurd Hoel and others had done before him, thus transforming social criticism into cultural critique, and he diversified it through formal devices assimilated during his European travels.

In its origin, Faldbakken's seventh novel, *Adam's Diary (Adams dagbok,* 1978), was no doubt, in part, a response to a decade of ideological writing in Norway, especially the literature of militant feminism. But it does not contain an ideology. Along with its literary excellence, the absence of ideology may have been one of the reasons for its success: most critics hailed it as the author's best. It was awarded the Riksmål Prize and, like most of Faldbakken's books, has been widely translated.

The novel's title intrigued the reviewers, many of whom played with it, more or less wittily, in their headings (see Bibliography). The title seems to suggest that, while adhering to realism ("Diary"), the author wants at the same time to go beyond it ("Adam's"). One critic's question was clearly predicated on realistic assumptions: confronted with the work's composite Adam—Thief, "Dog," and Prisoner—he commented that, surely, there must be more versions of the male, a fourth, fifth, etc. (*Morgenbladet,* 12 Dec. 1978). Faldbakken would probably agree: *Adam's Diary* is not an allegory. The quasi-biblical title is obviously intended to be provocative.

Still, while falling short of allegory, the book probes deeper than most realistic works. It is far more than a story of three men and the woman they all love. As in the twin novel *Time of Troubles (Uår)*—*Evening Land (Aftenlandet,* 1974) and *Sweetwater* (1976)—the surface realism is informed by an underlying vision. The everyday scenes from the Norwegian capital and environs, however vivid, are important chiefly for what they reveal about the cultural matrix of Norwegian society. Under the surface of increasing affluence and egalitarianism, with liberalized gender roles and behavior codes, Faldbakken finds a besetting sexual malaise and tragic human failure. His deep-probing artistry produces a style that combines an almost hallucinatory rendering of surface experience with image motifs of deep psychosocial import.

A pivotal stylistic device in the book is the metaphorization of character, which largely determines both the substance and the language of the narrators. The Thief, the first narrator, is more than a petty criminal; his thief's persona invades the entire psyche: all his relationships are based on stealing. The Prisoner, the woman's husband, sits in a real jail but is also a "prisoner" socially and psychologically, trapped by the sexual stereotypes of middle-class society. Though the student's cognomen, Dog, can only be metaphorical, the double exposure of man/dog is skillfully and consistently maintained.

Faldbakken's bifocal vision, juxtaposing the social scene with reified metaphors of male roles, invites an ambivalent response. Because his characters are so readily recognizable, we understand them, at times even identify with them, despite their marginal status. Yet, the eccentric narrative perspectives—of thief, "dog," and prisoner—defamiliarize what is represented. Though we are drawn in, we simultaneously stand apart from a world made strange.

This dual effect is enhanced by the narrative point of view. Purportedly a diary, the novel consists, in fact, of three consecutive narratives, with long stretches of exposition and cutbacks, especially in Parts II and III, and only occasional reminders of the diary form. Thus, no act of writing is documented and, contrary to diary style, the present tense predominates. Still, the resulting simultaneity between event and telling, reminiscent of the moment-by-moment registration of consciousness in the internal monologue, produces a good semblance of diary discourse. It should be noted, however, that Faldbakken's narrators are "performing selves," with an eye on the public, a reader, and behind their postures we perceive an implied author whose attitude is a mixture of compassion and ironic distance.

The presence of the implied author is clearly evidenced by the playful use of traditional forms and by recurrent motifs and devices. Each narrative recalls a well-known genre, the picaresque tale, the initiation story, and the prison autobiography, but these genres are treated parodistically. The Thief is a modern *picaro,* going from place to place and living by his wits. The substance of his diary, however, is incongruous with the picaresque model, his adventures being constantly undercut by private emotion, nostalgia, doubt, even panic. The

Dog's story relates an apocalyptic erotic experience that ends up as a reenactment of childhood traumas. Eventually he regresses to a pre-Oedipal stage, one of total identification with the mother/mistress: the narrative presents a mock-initiation. Initiation or development proper, curiously enough, is found chiefly in the third segment of Faldbakken's triptych, the prison tale. Through reflection and recollection, the Prisoner comes to see his past life in a new light and to find contentment in jail. While the planned escape follows another well-known form, the thriller, the murderous resolution exceeds the demands of the genre, casting an ironic light on the entire undertaking and its would-be perpetrator.

Among the recurrent motifs and devices, five are noteworthy: the hunt, metamorphosis, "squealing," flowers, and mirroring. The first three have primitive, catastrophic, or morally degrading connotations. The Thief is a "hunter" in the city jungle, the Dog and the Husband (the "Prisoner") stage a ritual hunt at the end of Part II. The effect of this image, with its hint of a primordial dynamics in civilized life, is enforced by the ubiquitous Kafkaesque motif: the student changes from human being to domesticated "dog," lone "wolf," and "hound"; the Thief from married man and humble wage-earner to sexual adventurer and petty criminal; and the Husband finds his existence shattered by an "avalanche of metamorphosis," with "fag" eventually superseding the macho image. The third motif, squealing, gives a moral dimension to the growing primitivism and bestiality. Its insidious energy produces a sense of moral nihilism, betrayal of the very image of man. All these motifs have a significance that exceeds the bounds of the separate stories, indicating the steady eye of an authorial presence.

The symbolic use of flowers and mirrors enriches the aesthetic texture and strengthens the thematic coherence of *Adam's Diary*. In the order of chronology, the Prisoner's fiancée (later wife) gathers pansies on the beach, decorating her naked body, her hair and pudenda with these flowers, described as having "fleshy petals, . . . with a small melancholy glimpse of gold in the center." To the student (Dog), a pansy shimmering on a glass table, the "fleshy fourfold flower head with its . . . central golden sun," becomes a picture (*avtrykk*, literally "imprint") of a shared "passionate love." Sitting on this table momentarily in "The Thief," the woman, naked and steaming, traces a "large juicy flower" on it, "with the outline of her bottom and her broad thighs as four petals around a big, messy scar." Her comment, "An imprint [*avtrykk*] of my hot love," will resonate ironically against the above-quoted passage in "The Dog," with its worshipful aura of summer romance. Finally, almost a hundred pages later, the Dog in his jealous fury smashes an ashtray against the table top, leaving a "wound, a rose in the tempered glass." The flowery emblem of love is transmogrified into a metonymic representation of the female as sheer cunt. In addition to stereotyping the woman as a sexual object, the last two images (the pudendum as "scar," "wound") function as threatening castration symbols.

As these instances show, the woman in the novel serves principally to "mirror" the attitudes and feelings of the male narrators. When criticized for his allegedly unflattering portrayal of her, Faldbakken replied: "To me, part of the success of the book's composition is that the woman is seen and described by the men she knows. She becomes important because the way they see her reveals *them*" (Larsen, p. 22).[1] This is borne out in the novel by the woman's letter to her husband, in which she attributes his love to the desire of seeing himself and his "muscles in still another mirror. I was your little hand mirror for many years—thank God I fell out of the frame at last!" Since the narrators are all narcissists, in one sense or another,[2] this mirroring technique is very apt: depiction of the woman is unconscious self-portrayal. Such narcissistic self-reflection is shown in other ways as well. The Thief contemplates his own image in the mirror as he masturbates in a strange apartment, the Dog begins his narrative with a description of his face in the mirror, and the Prisoner envisions the fjord "clear as a mirror" in his dreams of sculling, turning a common cliché into an ego-inflating image of cosmic proportions.

Faldbakken's method prevents him from directly expressing the value norm that underlies the character portrayal and the plot of *Adam's Diary*. His depiction of the woman, however, may provide a clue as to its nature. Though the novel is a male triptych, the woman's voice is heard in the letter just quoted, as well as in reported dialogue. While she is sensual and somewhat vulgar, she also seems open, courageous, and spontaneous. The letter suggests that the exit from her marriage was not motivated simply by a chase for sexual pleasure. Her search seems to spring from an uncompromising ideal vision: more demanding than Ibsen's Nora, a prototype of feminist revolt in Norwegian literature, she wants everything—the traditional satisfactions of family and motherhood as well as the independence of a liberated woman. Characterized by the Thief as an "unusual" woman, she can be dismissed as a fool who caused her own ruin, or seen as a near-tragic victim of the men she loved. One thing is certain: *she,* if anyone, is the character who embodies an ideal norm in *Adam's Diary,* one that the society represented in the book cannot satisfy.

Contrary to the woman, the male characters do not enact a personal quest; in whatever they do, they conform to roles determined from without, even when they are deviant ones. The deepest conflict in the novel may be defined, in the words of a reviewer, as one between "role and individual" (*Ny Tid,* 13 Dec. 1978). The author elucidates various aspects of this theme—sexual, moral and social—from three divergent perspectives. Sexually, the three diarists represent the exploitative thrill-seeker, the romantic dreamer, and the conventional husband; morally, cynic, idealist, and pharisee; socially, criminal outsider, dropout, and bourgeois. Faldbakken interrelates the characters' private and public experience, showing how personal relations are conditioned by public roles and by socially imposed paradigms of behavior. Thus, the anonymity of the Thief's sexual posture, with its attendant secrecy, deception, and fear of involvement, expresses his role as social outcast. The sexual degradation of the student is a direct result of his status within the minisociety of the home: by assuming the wife's role, thus reversing the age-old stereotype, he suffers the same ills as previous generations of women—insecurity, anxiety, loss of identity. And the moral bankruptcy of the Husband is ultimately due to the socially sanctioned ideas of love, marriage, and family that he uncritically accepts. In *Adam's Diary* social determinism acts like a force of fate, producing existential anguish and individual tragedy.[3]

The dominance of the public sphere is strikingly evidenced by the fact that all relationships in the novel, except those that remain utopian fantasies, are based on the exercise of power. The narrators are veritable studies in overcompensation, a fact that would argue the influence of Alfred Adler; but Faldbakken claims he is not familiar with his work (interview, 24 May 1986). The Dog reveals the relevant dynamics when he reflects that the Thief, to whom even a phrase like "love's balance of terror" comes naturally, will use the woman "as a stone in his own edifice, built around fear of defeat and a feeling of inferiority." The Thief's behavior is a repertoire of ego defenses: denigration of the Dog, a mild contempt for the woman, general condescension toward his victims. When the Thief appears on the scene, the Dog treats him the same way, building himself up by running his rival down. Similarly, the Dog is treated contemptuously by the Husband, who assumes the same attitude toward the court-appointed psychiatrist. By contrast, the woman is capable of giving credit even to the men she has stopped loving. She is less obsessive than the Thief, less insecure than the Dog, less repressed than her husband. Is it a mere coincidence that, once a provider with a "masculine" role, she too is caught up in the power game?

The invasion of the intimate, existential sphere by the performance-oriented attitudes involved in jockeying for place and position in society leads to emotional desiccation and inauthenticity. The accompanying lack of communication, especially between men and women, is evident everywhere in the novel. Whereas the woman, "Bel Ami," believes in the possibility of genuine communion, the Thief does not; the Prisoner, on the other hand, subconsciously yearns for it. The Dog becomes the woman's willing disciple, but his new "language" is useless when they are no longer attuned to each other.

Despite being an outsider, the Thief is the character most firmly trapped within the "sign language" of male society, one valorizing "physical strength and stature . . . , synthetic status and external façade." Waging a relentless battle for advantage behind his respectable mask, he refuses direct communication with people; words and gestures mask rather than reveal his thoughts. He prefers one-way communication through the mediation of objects; the "contact with people" he obtains through things, he claims, is a "better, truer contact" than he would have "meeting them face to face." His fetishism is one example of such mediation, a sexual fetish being a metonym for woman and, according to Freud, a "token of triumph over the threat of castration."[4] Another kind of mediation, by way of the "injured third party," is a decided sexual stimulus in his affair with Bel Ami.[5] When the latter threatens to break through his defenses and make contact with his "soul," he reverts once more to Ada, his female double.

The Prisoner's language predicament takes on a paradoxical aspect in the course of the novel. No less constricted by the "sign language" of male society than the Thief and obsessed with career and status—to the extent, in fact, of making even amateur sports subservient to business success—he soon develops "language problems" in his marriage. He mocks his wife's attempts at using symbolic language, such as flowers, and ridicules women's reputed flair for an "intuitive connection with . . . all things, against all reason and logic . . . : a mystical insight, like a dark, viscous stream of sensuality that connects them with the nightside of things." In prison, however, he finds the language of "reason and logic" to be of little help: he fails to recognize the "truth" of his crime in his attorney's brief and finds the psychiatrist's specialized logic to be irrelevant; the subjective meaning of his crime, he feels, escapes rational explanation. At the same time, the memory of his interrupted relationship with Eli, his daughter, causes him, sub-consciously, to change his attitude to women's deeper "insight" into things, though overtly he continues to vilify them. The obsessive image of "love" and "harmony" between mother and daughter that he con-nects with the sidewalk tableau of his wife tying Eli's shoelace becomes the symbol of an incapacitating lack in himself that he would like to remedy.

But the Prisoner's repeated violence demonstrates his inability to learn a new language. He stubbornly holds on to his naive attitude toward his own sportsman's "language," refusing to consider the pos-sibility that it could have a hidden, emotional, import not covered by sports usage. He insists, for example, that his hand on Reidar's neck "means only what it means," presumably male camaraderie, but to the reader it becomes more and more apparent that it signifies a homo-erotic attachment. (Sculling in general has unacknowledged sexual connotations for the Prisoner; thus, he lovingly refers to rubbing the "slim, golden laminated body" of the boat with silk rags, and so forth.) When, after Reidar's horrified reaction to his escape plan, the maternal manner of the nurse, Evy, reminds him once more of his wife, and of women's reputed aptitude for intuitive communion as symbolized by the sidewalk scene, the nurse must take the brunt of his accumulated envy and hatred, as well as of his inadmissible sexual feelings for Reidar. In this perspective, the tragic denouement of *Adam's Diary* is brought about by the Prisoner's lack of an adequate, culturally accepted code of emotional communication.

Among the welter of languages available in contemporary society, none, if I read Faldbakken correctly, will enable us to communicate in a meaningful way. The Prisoner, trapped in his role, cannot learn enough of "woman's language" to understand either his wife's world or his own. Instead, he throws "reason and logic" overboard as he abandons himself to a utopian fantasy about a wordless communion between Reidar and himself in the boat, "no thicker than skin." He lulls himself into a mystical state of total fusion with the other, a "unity that surpasses all other intercourse" and makes words "superfluous." The woman is equally unable or unwilling to learn the "sign language" of men, specifically the Thief. She has accepted the anonymity behind their shared nickname (Bel Ami) and the consequent mediation by means of fantasy images, thereby agreeing to play the game according to his rules, yet she employs her own intuitive-sensuous code to interpret his actions. Not surprisingly, she mistakes mere physical closeness for mutual understanding. The Dog, on the other hand, learns the woman's code with a vengeance. "With her," he writes, "each piece of clothing, every moment, every tone of voice became an important sensual communication." But his expertise in the "unspoken," such as the description of an entire repertoire of "intimate long-distance communications," produces mere absurdities, a parody of the very idea of human communication.

These themes—the dominance of role over self, of power over eros, lack of communication and inauthenticity—testify to a critical dimension in Faldbakken's character portrayal. His critical attitude, decidedly ironic in view of the narrators' positive self-appraisals, is further evidenced by their internal contradictions. The Thief, believing himself free, slavishly conforms to respectability; the Dog, radically rejecting the conventional male-female role distribution, confirms the pattern through a grotesque negative; and the Prisoner, though a believer in free enterprise and competition, comes to see society as a prison. The implicit conflict between subjectivity and social role is resolved in favor of the latter. Those who break out get caught in an equally oppressive role.

In more specific terms, the deviant thief acts the same as anyone else, even more so: in his fascination with the "goods," and with objects in general, he is a perfect example of the power of advertising, its appeal to the average person's insecurities and anxieties. More than most, the

Thief tries to solve his problems with the help of merchandise. And despite his mask of total self-control and isolation, associated with hard images like stone, statue, and a "castle with its drawbridge up," he is "soft" inside, desires contact, and cries in his beloved's arms. Finally, his freedom and control are a mockery, since he can retrieve them only through a dastardly act, squealing to the police, the enemy. Under the bourgeois mask, the Thief remains predatory *and* soft; he is so different from himself as to suggest a split personality.

The Dog's and the Prisoner's stories are riddled with similar contradictions. The Dog's "free" relationship soon becomes a "net of awe and dependency," and the new equality a grotesque mirror image of the old stereotype. A parody of the "soft," sensuous man he dreams of being, he becomes a "hard" avenger: instigator and stooge in a brutal skirmish in the "battle of the sexes." As with the Thief, a freely chosen, deviant persona turns into its opposite, to be superseded only by a vicious mask of male chauvinism and neofascism, while his ego remains undeveloped or in a state of disintegration. Similarly, the Prisoner's hard persona of businessman, athlete, and macho husband collapses into its opposite, that of a soft utopian dreamer full of sentimentality and self-pity. Even worse, the male camaraderie in which he seeks refuge from the prison of society is predicated on the glorification of sports, a blown-up fragment of the system he has rejected. These patterns of contradiction, with opposite roles collapsing into one another, inform *Adam's Diary* with an almost fatalistic ethos, turning the narrators into the butts of an inescapable, near-cosmic irony.

And yet we feel sorry for these characters. Granted, they are insecure, even paranoid, but they may not be entirely to blame. Something must be wrong with society at large for human lives to go awry in such a radical way. This suspicion is confirmed by our sense of complicity, which tells us that the narrators voice some of our own discontents and disenchantments.

The Thief's knack of viewing society from the underside, so to speak, exposes—at times disturbingly—the deep structures linking the individual to his culture. To such an expert semiologist, the objects people surround themselves with become a clue to their innermost selves, their dreams and desires. Besides, he knows the value of things and can distinguish the fake from the authentic. Through the Thief's discerning eye, Faldbakken casts a dubious eye on contemporary mass culture. More importantly, perhaps, the Thief deconstructs the very concept of identity: just as his apartment is furnished by stolen items from the strange homes he has burglarized, so the Thief acquires his identity through what he steals. But, allegedly, he is just like everybody else: we all steal, perhaps—gestures, habits, opinions, and ideas. The Thief's story confronts us, in impressive detail, with the societal genesis of identity.

The Prisoner's and the Dog's perspectives are almost equally disturbing. The Prisoner sees all policies and institutions, including marriage, as bricks in the "prison walls" that make a "lifelong prison" out of a man's life. No discounting, however radical, can entirely remove the sting from this admittedly paranoid view. Whatever the Prisoner's faults, his story is a terrifying demonstration of the stultifying emotional effects of the struggle for wealth, power, and status in society. The diary of the Dog, who sacrifices success on the altar of love, implicitly condemns repressive ideologies and cultural stereotypes. While the male-dominated ethos is suspect, its opposite seems equally so. And the grand illusion of sentimental-romantic love fares no better. The Dog's story represents a bathetic fall from sublime romance to grotesque "sodomy." With his animal optics and his knack for the semiology of the body, of gesture, touch and smell, the Dog evokes the physicality of love, and of people's behavior in general, with uncanny force. His sexual phenomenology, while crude and morbid, renders sexual frustration, pain, and humiliation so intensely as to suggest the spiritual anguish of the damned.

In general, *Adam's Diary* describes a society where mass culture is on the rise, threatening to destroy age-old traditional ways of life. Consumer society values are invading the private sphere, causing the cash nexus to become the only link between people. Describing the newly constructed suburban towns, the Thief comments on the "buying mania" characteristic of such places, since "things" alone signify a "connection" between people. Kinship-based links are conspicuous by their absence. None of the characters is given a past transcending his own individual life, and even the nuclear family seems on the verge of disappearing. With traditional values and institutions on the wane, no wonder that primordial images and rituals return, at times in sinister forms.

Why should anyone read a book that offers such a bleak image of contemporary society? Perhaps in part for that very reason: by telling the worst, refusing to gloss over the lurking dangers under the surface of affluence and sophistication, it proves honest and courageous. We may feel saddened and shocked by the cruel way civilized people treat each other, but cannot help experiencing pleasure as we recognize its truth. The characters are skillfully individualized, each having his distinctive voice and style. The Thief, with his seductive narrator's persona and his magnetic personality, is a masterpiece of portrayal. Each embodies a specific way of dealing with an important contemporary issue, the so-called "male question"; at the same time they are all mythomaniacs, providing an ironic lesson in self-deception, a classic theme that will still be of interest after the topical surface theme has lost its urgency. While Faldbakken eschews a strong, externally suspenseful plot, he arouses our curiosity even when the narrative is unsensational. And those who must have a bit of suspense reap their reward if they read to the end. Parts II and III, in particular, have a resounding denouement, like an explosion. The Prisoner hints at the rationale for Faldbakken's delayed climaxes when he speaks of "the mass of misunderstandings, stillborn good intentions and ingratitude that builds up till it forms a dam which finally bursts, carrying everything away in torrents of bitterness, self-righteousness, and disappointment." The form of the plot is an aesthetic analogue of psychological repression.

It is also delightful to read an author who knows the tradition to which he belongs, not only in Norway but in Europe as well. *Adam's Diary* is a rich source for literary comparison and intertextual exploration. The section "The Thief" invites comparison with Jean Genet's *Journal du voleur* (1949, trans. as *The Thief's Journal*, 1964), "The Prisoner" with Camus's treatment of crime in *The Stranger;* and Faldbakken's characteristic technique of description, the use of massive blocks of concrete, exactly observed details, has much in common with the *chosisme* of the French New Novel. The explicit relationship of Faldbakken's text to Kafka's story "The Metamorphosis" has already been mentioned. More subtly, the Prisoner's final monologue contains an echo of "Åse's Death" ("talk a bit about this and that"), reminding us that *Adam's Diary* shares the theme of male self-deception with Ibsen's *Peer Gynt*. More amusingly, is it too farfetched to perceive a mocking echo of Kierkegaard's "three stages" in the attitudes of the main characters: the aesthete and seducer (the Thief), the ethical upholder of the family (the Prisoner), and the religious believer (the Dog, with his "religion of love")? Taking our cue from the Prisoner, who hears the imagined voice of Reidar soothing his last moments of life with Eli's nursery rhyme, we may discover that the chief comfort to be culled from *Adam's Diary* is a purely literary one. We shall have to be content with that.

Port Jefferson, New York, September 1986

NOTES

1. In Jungian terms, she is a projection of the men's anima, the mother imago being transferred to the wife or the lover. See C. G. Jung, *Two Essays on Analytical Psychology,* trans. R. F. C. Hull (Cleveland & New York: Meridian Books, 1961), p. 208.

2. For discussion of narcissism in *Adam's Diary* from a Freudian viewpoint, see Øystein Rottem, "Sprekker i mannsbildet," *Vardøger,* 16 (1985): 96–103. Rottem has treated the subject more extensively in an unpublished manuscript, of which he kindly sent me a copy. An interesting general study is Christopher Lasch, *The Culture of Narcissism* (New York: W. W. Norton, 1978).

3. Jung writes: "These identifications with a social role [the persona] are a very fruitful source of neuroses" (*Two Essays,* p. 204). More to the point, they leave the self undeveloped, as a "shadow-side" that is largely projected. A Jungian analysis of *Adam's Diary* could be very fruitful, helping to elucidate not only the character relationships in the novel but also the interaction between role and self.

4. Sigmund Freud, "Fetishism," *Standard Edition,* 21, 154.

5. Sigmund Freud, "A Special Type of Object Choice Made by Man," *Standard Edition,* 11, 166. René Girard has analyzed a similar phenomenon as it appears in literature in *Deceit, Desire, and the Novel: Self and Other in Literary Structure,* trans. Yvonne Freccero (Baltimore: Johns Hopkins, 1965).

Askeland, Elsa. "Et skritt videre" ("One Step Forward"). *Verdens Gang*, 2 Nov.
1978.

Bache-Wiig, Harald. "Adams tre ansikter" ("The Three Faces of Adam").
Vinduet, vol. 33, no. 1 (1979): 75–76.

Bore, Marie Rein. "Adam på et fat" ("Adam on a Platter"). *Vårt Land*, 30 Nov.
1978.

Engelstad, Irene. Review of *Adam's Diary*. *Ny Tid*, 13 Dec. 1978.

Eriksen, Ove André. "Knut Faldbakken på sitt beste" ("K. F. at His Best").
Aftenposten, 30 Nov. 1978.

Kittang, Atle. "Romanforfattaren som mytograf. Formproblem i Knut
Faldbakkens *Uår*-romanar" ("The Novelist as Mythographer: Problems of
Form in Knut Faldbakken's Novel Sequence *Time of Troubles*"). *Vinduet*,
vol. 35, no. 2 (June 1981): 17–27.

Larsen, Ida Lou. "Det mest reale er vennskap mellom menn" ("The Most
Forthright Thing Is Friendship between Men"). Faldbakken interviewed by
Ida Lou Larsen. *Sirene*, no. 3 (1979): 20–23.

Nordrå, Olav. "Dagbok for syndebukker" ("Diary for Scapegoats"). *Morgenbladet*, 12 Dec. 1978.

Norseng, Mary Kay. "The Crippled Children: A Study of the Underlying Myth in Knut Faldbakken's Fiction." *Scandinavica*, vol. 22, no. 2 (Nov. 1983): 195–209.

Paus, Arnfinn. "Personforhold og samfunnskrefter i Knut Faldbakkens roman *Adams dagbok*" ("Character Relationships and Social Forces in Knut Faldbakken's Novel *Adam's Diary*"). Thesis, University of Oslo, Fall 1980.

Peterson, Ronald E. "Knut Faldbakken: A Norwegian Contemporary." *Scandinavian Review*, vol. 73, no. 3 (Autumn 1985): 80–85.

Ramberg, Mona Lyche. "Fanget av natur og samfunn. Knut Faldbakkens diktning med hovedvekt på dobbeltromanen *Uår, Aftenlandet* og *Sweetwater*" ("Trapped by Nature and Society: Knut Faldbakken's Literary Work, with Emphasis on the Twin Novel *Time of Troubles: Evening Land* and *Sweetwater*"). In *I diktningens brennpunkt. Studier i norsk romankunst 1945–1980*. Ed. Rolf Nyboe Nettum. Oslo: Aschehoug, 1982. Pp. 254–71.

Rottem, Øystein. "Sprekker i mannsbildet. Om Knut Faldbakkens *Adams dagbok* og Erling Gjelsviks *Dødt løp*" ("Cracks in the Male Image: Knut Faldbakken's *Adam's Diary* and Erling Gjelsvik's *Dead Heat*"). *Vardøger*, 16 (Nov. 1985): 86–112.

———. "Stakkars Adam" ("Poor Adam"). *Kontrast*, no. 2 (1979): 61–64.

Solumsmoen, Odd. "Adam og Eva—de nye mennesker" ("Adam and Eve—The New Humans"). *Arbeiderbladet*, 8 Nov. 1978.

Ødegaard, Bent. "Psykologi og samfunnskritikk. Linjer i Knut Faldbakkens forfatterskap" ("Psychology and Social Criticism: Lines of Development in Knut Faldbakken's Writing"). In *Norsk litterær årbok*, ed. Leif Mæhle. Oslo: Det Norske Samlaget, 1982. Pp. 89–108.

Øverland, Janneken. "Fins det et Adam etter døden?" ("Is There Something called Adam after Death?"). *Dagbladet*, 21 Oct. 1978.